# FORBIDDEN DESIRE

They made their way down the hall with Lena leaning against him. Mark fumbled the door open, then helped her to the bed. "Are you all right now, Lena? Do you want to me to...?" He motioned, indicating her clothes.

"Yes, please," she whispered. "If you would be so kind."

She lay back on the bed, and he removed her stockings with trembling fingers. Lena turned on her side while he unbuttoned the row of buttons running down the back of her dress. Feeling almost boneless, she sat up while he removed her dress.

He stood up and became a hulking shadow with the light behind him. "There, can you sleep now."

"The rest? Please, Mark?" A part of her was appalled at the brazenness of her behavior.

A gusty sigh came from him. "Lena! Do you know what you're asking of me? I'm flesh and blood..."

# The Redeemers

**Clayton Matthews**

BANTAM BOOKS
TORONTO · NEW YORK · LONDON · SYDNEY · AUCKLAND

THE REDEEMERS
*A Bantam Book / October 1984*

ISBN 0-553-24051-X

*Published simultaneously in the United States and Canada*

*Bantam Books are published by Bantam Books, Inc. Its trade-*
*mark, consisting of the words ''Bantam Books'' and the por-*
*trayal of a rooster, is Registered in U.S. Patent and Trademark*
*Office and in other countries. Marca Registrada. Bantam*
*Books, Inc., 666 Fifth Avenue, New York, New York 10103.*

# The Redeemers

# 1

At the age of seventy-five, Nora Moraghan was dying. The year was 1885. Nora had often joked of living into the next century, but it was not to be.

Holding tightly to Stonewall's hand, Debra Lieberman stared down at the wasted woman sunk deep into the feather bed. Dr. Jed Potter, Grandmother's doctor for as long as Debra could remember, stood by the side of the bed. He was ancient, afflicted with arthritis, and Debra thought that he was almost as old as her grandmother. He had retired from active practice some years ago, but he still had time for those remaining few who had been his patients over the long years.

Debra said tensely, "How long do you think, Dr. Potter?"

Dr. Potter looked at her, his rheumy eyes vague behind thick-lensed spectacles. "Can't predict, young Debra. Her heart is old and plumb wore out, don't know what's kept it beating this long. But she has a strong will to live, does Nora Moraghan. Could be anytime. Tonight, tomorrow, next week. Maybe God in His wisdom could tell you, girl, I can't."

Debra tightened her grip on her husband's hand. "Stony, I must stay here with Grandmother Nora, but will you ride in to town and send a Western Union to Daddy and Mother?"

"Of course, dear. I'll leave at once." He lowered his voice. "How about the children, shall I bring them back with me?"

Debra hesitated. "No, not yet. Something like this is always tough on children, no use exposing them to it any longer than absolutely necessary. What you might do,

Stony, on your way in to town, is ride by Brian's place and
tell Anna to get herself over here.''

"But I thought word had been sent to her?''

"So it has, but you know how stubborn she is. She
hasn't set foot in this house since Uncle Brian was killed.''
She smiled wanly. "Use your lawyer ways on hers. Use
your persuasive powers on her, that golden voice that's
gotten you elected circuit judge for three consecutive
terms.''

Stony said dryly, "I hardly think Anna Moraghan voted
for me.'' He sobered. "But I'll do my damnedest. Try not
to fret too much, Debra.'' He leaned down from his great
height to kiss her. "I'll be back as soon as I can.''

Debra nodded absently, her gaze on her grandmother.
The doctor and Stony went out of the room together.
Debra moved around close to the head of the bed, and was
astounded to see Nora's eyes not only open but clear and
aware. Nora's lips moved.

"What, Grandmother?'' She put her ear to Nora's
mouth.

With a touch of that bawdy humor that had delighted
Debra for so many years, Nora whispered, "You see to
what lengths a crotchety old crone like me will go to to get
her loved ones by her side once again?''

Debra had to laugh. She touched her grandmother's
cheek with gentle fingers. "I don't think you should be
talking, Grandmother. Dr. Potter said—''

"Hellfire and spit! What's talking going to hurt me?''
Nora's voice gathered strength. "I heard every word that
old quack said. Tonight, tomorrow, next week, indeed!
What does he know! I know one thing, I'll live to see my
Kevin one last time. Debra Lee . . .'' The faded eyes
pleaded. "He will come, won't he?''

"Of course he will, Grandmother,'' Debra said soothingly.
"He'll be on the next train as soon as he gets Stony's
wire . . .''

She broke off as she noticed that Nora's eyes had
closed. Debra's heart almost stopped—Nora looked so
white and still. Then she noticed the almost imperceptible

rise and fall of the frail chest, and she breathed a sigh of relief.

She tiptoed out of the room and down the hall, lit by one oil lamp in a wall bracket. She stepped out onto the long porch. It was late spring in East Texas, and the humid night was alive with the strumming of insects. There was a quarter moon, and she could see the silvery glitter of the river down at the bottom of the slope.

Debra stood, unconsciously resting one hand on Nora's old rocker, gazing to the south and west, as though she could see across the long miles to that adobe house some distance outside of Brownsville. *Would* her father answer the summons? Kevin Moraghan had not been on Moraghan for twenty years, and he had sworn he would never return.

But certainly the news that his mother was dying would bring him back?

Debra just didn't know. Kevin Moraghan was a proud, stubborn man, stubborn to a fault . . .

She gave a gasp as she realized that, without thinking, she had set Nora's chair to rocking.

It was almost a sacrilege. She snorted at the fancy, yet she gently stopped the chair from rocking, then took her hand away.

Actually Kevin Moraghan and family—wife, Kate; daughter, Lena; son, Michael—no longer lived in the adobe house. Oh, the house was still there. It had been occupied briefly, by Michael and his bride for a year, until she died suddenly of smallpox. Now the house stood empty, used as a storage place for alfalfa for winter food for the stock.

Three years ago, Kevin had built a larger, grander house, still a Spanish-style adobe, but a fine hacienda. Kevin had prospered of late years. Those dreams he'd had when coming here over twenty years ago had finally been realized. Water was plentiful now, and the land, nourished by sweet water from deep artesian wells, was fruitful—citrus fruit in abundance, melons, and garden vegetables of almost every kind. Where once he could look across his acreage and see only brown, blowing dirt, there now was rich greenery the year round. Prosperity had allowed him to buy more land, and he now farmed double the original acreage Sean Moraghan had left him in the will.

But the relative prosperity of these last few years had done little to assuage his bitterness at being disinherited—at least so he had viewed it. When Sean Moraghan died, he had owned Moraghan Acres in East Texas, a few acres of swampland near Beaumont, and this section of sand down in the Rio Grande Valley. Sean's will had left all but ten acres of Moraghan to Brian, the eldest son, and Kevin had been left this section. Kevin had stormed away from Moraghan with his family, despite Nora's pleas, vowing that he would never set foot on Moraghan again, and so far he had kept that vow.

Brian was dead now. But not even the news that Brian, in his arrogance and greed, had depleted Moraghan Acres, and that his family was now practically destitute, while he, the disinherited, had prospered, alleviated Kevin's rancor.

But the telegram changed everything: "Nora dying. Please come quickly. Debra Lee."

Kate, graying now, a little thicker around the waist but still a damned attractive woman, looked up from the telegram. "We *are* going, aren't we, darling?"

Kevin said without hesitation, "We'll be on the first train out. We have to go, Kate. Momma . . ." He choked up suddenly.

"I know, Kevin, I know," she said softly.

Kevin began to smile. "You reckon our Debra Lee has mellowed since she got married? I noticed that she signed the telegram Debra Lee, not plain Debra."

"I wouldn't wager too much on that, Kevin," she said in a dry voice. "I'm sure that Stony sent off this wire, not Debra Lee."

"Then why didn't he have the gumption to put his name to it?" he grumbled. "What kind of a man is he, putting his wife's name to a telegram?"

"Stony Lieberman is quite a man, Kevin, as you very well know. If not for his brains and gumption, our Debra Lee might very well have hung for a murder she didn't commit!"

"All right, Kate, I know."

He limped to the parlor door and called down the hall, "Lena? Michael? Can you two hear me? Pack your duds, we're going to Moraghan. Your grandmother is dying."

Despite Stony Lieberman's urgings, Anna Moraghan refused to set foot in that house, and nothing any Hebrew lawyer had to say was going to change her mind!

Mark, her eldest, had been present when Stony made his plea. After Stony left, Mark said, "Judge Lieberman is right, Ma. You should go, it's the right thing to do. She's your mother-in-law and my grandmother."

Always a big woman, Anna had let herself go after Brian's death, and she was grossly overweight nowadays. Puffing, she made her way across the parlor and lowered her bulk into the big chair before the fireplace. This winter and spring had been mild by East Texas standards, but Anna, contrary to the popular belief that fat people suffered from the cold less than others, was always cold. She had been cold since Brian's murder. Once, Mark, in a moment of exasperation, had snapped, "Since Daddy died, Ma, I think you've had an icicle for a heart. There's no warmth, no affection, in you. And you're always carrying on about me going off from home so much. Why shouldn't I? This isn't a home anymore. It's just a house."

"And why shouldn't I be coldhearted? My heart broke when Brian was killed—"

"That's bull, Ma, and you damned well know it. There was nothing between you for years before he died. You think that I don't know he tomcatted around, or that he spent as much time in whorehouses as he did at home?"

She slapped him across the mouth with her big hand. "You watch your mouth, snotnose! Don't think because you're a grown man now that I can't still take a switch to you. I'm your mother and I'll have respect!"

He glared at her out of eyes so much like Brian's. Tears had come to those eyes from the force of the slap. "I'll give you respect, Ma, when you earn it."

And now, after Stonewall Lieberman's visit, Anna said to Mark, "Nora Moraghan is no kin to me. She gave up that right when that slut of a granddaughter of hers killed my husband.''

Mark said wearily, ''She didn't kill Daddy, Ma. Tod Danker killed him—''

''That was just a cover-up, to get her off. They never fooled me for a minute. And she ran a whorehouse down in Corpus Christi, now can you give the lie to that?''

''No, that part's true enough. But it's not all that terrible. Debra Lee had to make a living some way.''

Anna snorted. ''She wasn't suffering any, not with her daddy making it rich down there in the Rio Grande.''

''Ma, you're getting it wrong again.'' Mark sighed. ''That was eleven years ago and they were poor then. *We* were the ones well off, until Daddy ruined all our land. Now things are reversed. Maybe that's why you're so bitter, Ma. But you shouldn't blame Debra Lee or Grandmother. Daddy was the one ruined the land, so it won't grow anything but weeds.''

''I won't listen to you bad-mouthing your daddy!''

She heaved herself up, hand upraised to slap him, but she wasn't nearly quick enough. He caught her hand in an iron grip.

''I'm going over to Moraghan, Ma, to pay my respects to Grandmother and Debra Lee. And Uncle Kevin, when he comes. You stay here and make yourself sick with your own bile, if that's the way you want it.''

Releasing her hand, Mark turned on his heel and left the house. Anna sank back into the chair, dry-eyed. A few minutes later she heard the hoofbeats of Mark's horse as he rode off.

It had been Kevin's fear all the way from Brownsville that Nora would expire before they could make it.

When Debra opened the door to his knock, he looked his question. She smiled palely. ''She's still hanging on, Daddy. She told me she refused to go before you all made it.''

Then she was in his arms, sobbing on his shoulder. ''Oh, Daddy! It's been so long since I've seen you all.''

Kevin patted her shoulder. "Four years ago last Christmas, Debra Lee."

She raised a reproachful face. "Yes, and we had to come all the way down there. Trains and stages run both ways, you know."

"I know, girl, but we have been busy and we ain't as young as you and Stony, your mother and I."

Kate spoke behind his shoulder. "Your father's getting set in his ways, Debra. I swear it's a chore to get him in to Brownsville once a week for the mail and supplies, much less somewhere this far."

Debra disengaged herself from Kevin. "Hello, Mother. I'm glad to see you." Mother and daughter embraced briefly, then Debra looked at her brother and sister.

"Michael, I was sorry to hear about May Beth dying," she said solemnly. "I wanted to come down but I just couldn't. One of my own was down sick."

"It's all right, sis, I understand."

Michael was twenty-eight now. He was a handsome man, with dark blond hair and brown eyes. Always on the thin side, he had lost weight since his wife's untimely death, and he laughed rarely nowadays.

Debra's glance went to her sister. "You're full grown, Lena, and pretty as a picture."

Lena blushed prettily, her gaze dropping to the porch floor. She had Kate's rich auburn hair and Kevin's gray eyes, and something of Kevin's lean build, but she had filled out considerably since Debra had last seen her, and there was certainly nothing masculine about her full breasts and rounded hips.

Debra said, "Let's see, you're what, Lena? Nineteen? I would expect to have heard you'd be married to one of those old boys down there."

Lena said scornfully, "I wouldn't have any of them. They're all dull as dishwater."

Debra laughed, throwing back her head. "Does that sound familiar, Mother?"

"It's a familiar refrain, yes, Debra," Kate said dryly. "I heard it often before you up and left us."

"But it turned out all right, didn't it, Mother?"

"It did. I couldn't ask for a better son-in-law than Stony. Is he here?"

"No, he's in Nacogdoches. He's presiding over a trial this week, but he'll be out for the weekend, and of course I'll let him know immediately if anything happens to Grandmother. And that reminds me, Daddy. She wanted to see you the instant you arrived."

Debra led the way down the long hallway toward the back, and Nora's bedroom. At the door she paused to say hesitantly, "She asked to see you alone first, Daddy, before the others."

Kevin nodded, squared his shoulders, and went into the darkened bedroom. It had the odors of all sick rooms—stale air, vile-smelling medicine, urine. Kevin had always had a horror of sickrooms, and this was his mother, not only sick but dying, a woman he'd only seen once in twenty years.

Laden with guilt, he approached the bed with dread. His vision adjusting to the dimness, he could make out the form of his mother under the sheet. His breath caught in his throat. She seemed so frail, and he detected no movement, no rise and fall of her chest.

To his surprise the veined, almost transparent eyelids lifted, and to his further astonishment, her eyes were clear.

In a voice like the rustle of dry leaves, Nora Moraghan said, "Kevin? Is that you, boy?"

"Yes, Momma, it's me."

He leaned down to kiss her dry lips. Nora's hands came up, framing his face with a touch as light as a feather. "I told Debra Lee that I'd survive until you got here." Her voice gathered a little strength. "Pull up a chair, son. Are Kate and the little ones here?"

"Yes, Momma." He pulled up a chair by the bed and sat down, taking her hand in his with a chuckle. "Only they're not so little anymore. Michael is twenty-eight and Lena is nineteen."

"Michael was little when I last saw him, and the girl, Lena, was not even born." Her voice was matter-of-fact, without reproach.

"I know, Momma, but you know I swore that I'd never

set foot on Moraghan again. And I did see you when I came here with Stony to charge Tod Danker with killing Brian.''

"And *I* had to come in to Nacogdoches even to get to see you.''

"I swore an oath to myself, Momma, and I couldn't break that oath.''

"Your *oath*! Men and their blasted honor. Hellfire and spit!'' Her voice burned with scorn. "Why did you come here now, then?''

"Momma, please!'' Kevin said miserably. "It's been over twenty years and you're—'' He broke off, appalled.

"Dying. Go on, say it. I had to be on my deathbed to drag you back to Moraghan.'' She laughed harshly, then was seized by a paroxysm of coughing.

She motioned frantically, and Kevin put his hands under her back and raised her slightly. As she continued to cough wrackingly, he looked about wildly, thinking of summoning help.

Divining his intention, Nora shook her head. Then the coughing stopped, and he eased her back down.

"I'm sorry, son,'' she said in a raw, panting voice. "Forgive an old woman. Living alone all these years, I've grown crotchety, a regular hell cat, in my old age.''

"There's nothing to forgive, Momma,'' he said gently. "I'm the one to ask for forgiveness.''

"Now that you're here, you're forgiven, Kevin.'' Her hand crawled across the coverlet until it touched his. "Now, I want to see Kate, and my grandchildren.''

"Momma, don't you think you'd better rest a little first?''

"In a short time I'll rest for eternity, son.'' At his expression she smiled wanly. "Don't look so down at the mouth. I've lived a long and full life, long past the years most folks spend on this earth. At my age what doesn't hurt, doesn't work. But I'll make a bargain with you... Send them in one at a time, not altogether. Kate first.''

"All right, Momma.''

As he turned away, she spoke again, "Kevin?''

"Yes, Momma?''

"I want you to promise me something. All I have left is Moraghan, this house, and ten acres. Plus a few fine horses. It's all I have to leave, and I'm leaving it to you. No, Kevin, hear me out. I don't expect you to move back up here, since you're doing so well down there, but I want you to see that it's kept up. I don't want it sold off to some stranger. I'll be lying out there alongside Sean, and I don't want strangers around. Promise me that you'll always hold title to Moraghan, and that you'll keep it up."

He nodded. "I promise, Momma. But I won't be around forever, you know."

"Then leave it to your children." Her voice was considerably weaker now, little more than a whisper. "I thought of asking Debra Lee to look after it, but she and Stonewall have their own house, and she has her own life to live . . ."

Lena had looked forward eagerly to the trip to Moraghan. She had heard about it all her life but had never been there, had never been farther from home than to the King Ranch once for a barbecue and square dance. Most of all, it offered a chance to escape the heat and boredom of the Valley. All anyone there seemed to be interested in was produce, citrus fruit, or anything else they could grow. And the boys, dear God, the boys! What dull, boring clods!

But now that she was finally here, Lena wasn't sure that she was happy about the visit. She had never met Grandmother Nora, and eventually she was expected to go into that room and meet a dying woman she had never seen. Having grown up on a farm, she was familiar with the life-and-death cycle, but a dying *person* was different.

Her father came into the room, pale and shaken. He said, "Momma wants to see you all, one at a time. She asked for you first, Kate."

As her mother left the room, Lena experienced a lurch of dismay. It might not be so bad, in there with all the family present, but *alone*?

At the first opportunity, she slipped out the side door and into the yard. In the Valley when they had left, it had been blazing hot. But here, the night was pleasantly warm, scented with late spring flowers, and alive with the songs of crickets and the croaking of frogs along the river bottom.

She walked to the edge of the grass and stopped under a tall pecan tree. A pecan crunched under her foot. She squatted down and felt along the ground with her hands. There were several nuts scattered about, left over from last autumn. She gathered a handful and stood up, leaning against the tree trunk. She cracked the pecans between her teeth and ate the meat. It was somewhat dried out from having fallen so long ago, but the rich, full taste was still there. Eating, she stared down at the river, silvery in the moonlight.

Cracking the nuts had disguised the sound of footfalls, and she started violently when a voice spoke at her elbow. "Hello there."

She took a step away, poised for flight. A hand caught her arm, held her gently.

A male voice said, "I *am* sorry. I didn't mean to frighten you."

"I was cracking pecans . . ." She could make out the form of a man, his features indistinguishable in the dark. Then the glow of a cigarette lit his face, and she saw that he was older than her by several years, but he was leanly handsome. And as he grinned, a crooked, charming grin, she thought for a moment that she recognized him.

"I'm Mark Moraghan," he said. "And I expect you'd be one of Uncle Kevin's?"

She knew then why she'd felt the nudge of familiarity. His father had to be her uncle, Brian Moraghan, and although she had never seen Brian in the flesh, she'd seen pictures. And her mother often talked of Brian, and she had mentioned his dark good looks, his charming grin. She said somewhat breathlessly, "Yes, I'm Lena."

"Welcome to Moraghan, cousin. What's left of it." His voice had a bitter twist. He drew on the cigarette, then ground it out under his toe. "This your first time here, isn't it? You were born down in the Rio Grande Valley and never been up here, right?"

"Yes, I—"

She was interrupted by her mother's voice, "Lena? Are you out here?"

"Yes, Mother. Over here."

Kate's tall figure came toward them, head down, shoulders slumped. She looked startled when she saw Mark. "I didn't realize anyone else was out here."

"Hello, Aunt Kate. I'm Mark."

"Oh. How are you, Mark?" Kate's glance went to Lena, and her breath caught in a sob. "Your grandmother is dead, Lena. Nora is gone, she passed away quietly a few minutes ago."

# 2

The day they buried Nora Moraghan was a brilliant spring day, cloudless, with a warm breeze scented with flowers. She was buried in a small grove of oaks at the edge of her ten acres, buried beside Sean Moraghan.

Standing alongside her mother, as the preacher droned over the pine casket, Lena was astonished at the size of the crowd. All morning, buggies, wagons, and horses had pulled up before the house, and many had arrived on foot. At a fast count there were close to two hundred mourners present.

As the casket was lowered into the ground, Lena whispered to her mother, "Where do all these people come from? I didn't know that many people lived around here."

"Nora has been here a long time, and knew people all over. I wouldn't be surprised if some people here didn't come from as far away as Fort Worth and Houston. Now hush, darling."

Lena turned her head back just as Kevin, on the edge of the grave, head bowed, dropped a single flower, a yellow rose, into the grave, then stepped back.

Two men moved forward with shovels, and that was

taken as a signal. People coughed, shuffled their feet, cleared their throats, began to whisper, and there was a general exodus toward the house, where food and drink awaited the mourners. Kevin moved to stand beside Kate, and they stood side by side as a few people, those not staying for the food and drink, came up to offer their condolences.

Lena stole a furtive glance at Mark Moraghan, wondering if he would stay. He had appeared, solemn in black, just as the services began, standing off to himself the whole time. Now, as Lena looked, he was turning away. Clapping the black hat on his head, he strode off without looking back.

One person who came up to take Kevin's hand was a tiny, dried-up little woman of sixty some years. "You probably don't recollect me, Kevin Moraghan," she said in a high voice. "But I knew your mother many years. I live down the road a piece, alone now since my Sam died. I'm Marsha Johnson. Well do I remember the shows Nora used to put on in that little schoolhouse down the way. Shocked the drawers off'n some people, I can tell you." She cackled laughter, then sobered. "I'll miss Nora, may the good Lord take her to His bosom. I'm poorly these last years and couldn't come pass the time with her as much as I used to."

"I'm sure Momma understood, Mrs. Johnson," Kevin murmured. "Thank you for coming."

As the next one in line engaged Kevin's attention, Lena whispered in her mother's ear, "Shows? What did she mean, Mother?"

"Oh, your grandmother used to stage plays in that schoolhouse Grandfather Sean built on Moraghan." Kate smiled slightly. "People came from miles around to be entertained. Of course they weren't *always* entertained. I will never forget the uproar Nora caused when she put on a production of *Uncle Tom's Cabin*. And that was during the war, you understand. Many folks never spoke to any of the Moraghans again."

Kate broke off, turning to accept a weeping woman's embrace. Lena looked off to the right. Standing under an oak tree some fifty yards away from the little graveyard were two people, male and female. Lena had noticed them there after the services began, but they had never approached nearer than they were now. She had wondered about them, and wondered anew at their still being there, as if purposely waiting to be noticed.

And now, as the last hand was shaken, Kevin seemed to notice the couple for the first time. Staring at them, he said in a low voice, "Kate, who are those two?"

"I have no idea, dear. I noticed them arrive, together, just as the services began. But then there's no reason I should know them, I haven't been back here in years, remember?"

Kevin glanced about. "Maybe Debra Lee knows them."

"She's already gone up to the house."

Kevin squared his shoulders. "Well, I'm going to find out who they are. There's something odd about them standing off to themselves like that."

"Kevin, why bother? Let's go on up to the house."

But Kevin was already limping toward the pair, who stood unmoving, waiting for him.

"Damned, stubborn man!" Kate muttered angrily and hurried after him.

After a moment's hesitation, Lena tagged after them, but not too close, just close enough to hear as her father planted himself before the pair, and said, "I don't believe I know you. I'm Kevin—"

"We know who you are, Kevin Moraghan," said the young man, who was at least a half-dozen years older than the girl, who, Lena judged, was about her own age.

Kevin spread his hands. "I'm afraid you have the advantage of me, young fellow. It's been years since I've been back up here."

"Yes, Moraghan, I very well know the last time you were in East Texas. You killed my daddy."

Kevin went rigid. "Your daddy? You're a Danker?"

The young man nodded. "Yes, I'm Bud Danker. This is my sister, Cassie. Tod Danker was my daddy, and Sonny Danker was my grandpa. You murdered them both and your daddy killed my—"

Kevin made a move toward the pair, and Kate restrained him with a hand on his arm. In a low, furious voice Kevin said, "What are you doing here, on Moraghan property, and at my momma's funeral? It's a sacrilege!"

Bud Danker smiled slightly, but his dark eyes remained still and cold with hate. "We came to see her put into the ground. She was the cause of your daddy killing my two great-uncles."

This time Kevin struck Kate's hand off his arm, and limped forward, fists clenched. "Get off, get off Moraghan! Or by the Lord Almighty, I'll kill you with my bare hands!"

"Oh, I ain't afraid of that." Bud sneered.. "You're an old man, and a crip to boot. But I wouldn't want Cassie a witness to my killing you, so we're going. But take heed of me, Kevin Moraghan." His eyes began to burn. "There will be other Moraghans put into the ground before the debt is paid."

The young man gave his sister his arm, and they strode away, heads held high. Although Lena had felt the threat of pure violence in the air a moment ago, and had been frightened by it, she had to admire the tattered pride of their posture as they entered the grove of live oaks and disappeared from view.

Kevin stood glaring after them, his breath coming hard. "The gall, the unbelievable gall!"

Kate gave a heavy sigh. "Does this mean that that old feud is still alive?"

"What does it look like?" Kevin said in a growling voice. "Tha Danker clan is like a snake—cut off one portion and there's still enough left to strike and kill. As long as a Danker lives, I reckon they'll hate us. Well, this is no day to think about the Dankers, the very thought of them poisons everything. The mourners will be wondering what happened to us."

He linked arms with Kate, and they started toward the house, three hundred yards distant. Lena followed behind, more slowly.

She had of course heard about the feud since she was a child. The details were vague in her mind, since she'd been so removed from its inception. But now, the chilling scene she had just witnessed made Lena realize that it was not fanciful, not just a legend, but brutally real, however unbelievable such a thing seemed today, almost at the beginning of the new century.

She pulled at her mother's arm, holding her back, while Kevin limped on. "Mother, do you think Daddy's in any danger from that man?"

Kate shrugged. "I wouldn't think so, dear, although the Dankers have always been a brawling clan, starting with Ma Danker. But back when your grandfather was killed, the country was more lawless than it is today. I think it's mostly bluff, just the young man venting his spleen. But just the same, I'm thankful that we're going back to the Valley within a few days, out of harm's way."

Lena felt a pull of disappointment. "We're not going to stay a while?"

"Your daddy stay up here? Stony'll be lucky to get him to stay around long enough to get the legal matters settled."

"But I've never been here before, I'd like to get to know Moraghan, and get acquainted with Debra Lee and her family."

Kate gave her a keen glance. "And get away from the Valley a while? I don't know why all our children hate the Valley so. Even Michael . . . Still, it took me a number of years *not* to hate it. But it's my home now."

"Does that mean that I can stay a while?"

"I didn't say that, Lena." She took her daughter's hand and gave it a pat. "But we'll see. Today's hardly the time to discuss it."

Bud Danker strode along with rapid, angry strides, and Cassie had to hurry to keep up with him. Finally, almost out of breath, she gasped out, "Slow down, Bud, I can't keep up!"

"You know how long a way it is out here. By the time we get to those broken-down old mules and ride all the way back to Nacogdoches, it'll be long after dark."

"I don't know why we came, anyway."

"I didn't ask you to come." He turned those muddy Danker eyes on her, his expression hard as flint.

"I thought we were coming out to pay our respects to Nora Moraghan."

"Respects!" He gave a bark of laughter. "I have about as much respect for a Moraghan, *any* Moraghan, as I would a rattlesnake. No, a cottonmouth. At least a rattlesnake gives warning before it strikes."

"You didn't have to be so nasty to that poor man, his mother just buried."

He whipped around to seize her arm, his fingers biting like talons. "That poor man killed our daddy, can't you get that through your head, Cassie? He killed our daddy, and our granddaddy, and *his* daddy killed our two great-uncles, and caused our grandmother to die of a broken heart. I won't rest easy until either Kevin Moraghan, or one of his, pays in blood for those crimes, and neither should you!"

"It seems to me that all I've heard since I can remember is hate the Moraghans! Our hands aren't all that clean. Our grandfather was a notorious gunfighter for hire, and Daddy killed Brian Moraghan—"

His hand flashed out to deliver an open-handed blow to her cheek. "That ain't so! Daddy was somebody in East Texas, a duly elected sheriff. That Debra Lee murdered Brian Moraghan, killed her own blood, and Daddy was framed for it. Don't you ever forget that!"

Angered, Cassie rubbed her smarting cheek, and flared back at him. "Feuds between families is out of date nowadays. That's like something ignorant hillbillies do, something to joke about."

"To me, it's no laughing matter, and never will be. And I'd better not catch you laughing, or you'll get worse than what I just gave you. That's your trouble, Cassie, always thinking you're so high-and-mighty, better than the rest of us Dankers. Well, you ain't. To everybody in Nacogdoches, Dankers are trash, and you're included in the same chicken coop, don't you ever forget it."

Bud strode on, while Cassie hung back, her thoughts rebellious. He was right about one thing—she did think herself better than other Dankers. Cassie had always been a quiet, introspective girl, and, it seemed to her, completely out of step with the rest of the family. There were only two of them left at home now, along with their mother, living in an old house on the edge of Niggertown. The other children had all left home, and Cassie, now almost eighteen, intended to get away as soon as she could. They were virtual outcasts in Nacogdoches, thought little more of than the Negroes who were their near neighbors. The money they lived on came from what odd jobs Bud could find, demeaning usually, and Cassie took in washing, and found an occasional cleaning job.

Their mother had deteriorated rapidly after Tod Danker's death, going downhill physically, and although not yet sixty, she was close to being senile. Cassie had never known much affection from the woman, even early on, and she felt none in return, only pity. She would have left home already, but she knew there would be no one to tend her mother. Bud certainly would not, there was no love in him, only hate for the Moraghans—it drove him the way a giant engine was fueled.

Cassie felt no hate for the Moraghans, the Moraghan name was a respected one in East Texas. Even Brian Moraghan, who many decried as a despoiler of the land, was still accorded respect, all these years after his death. Sean and Nora Moraghan, of course, had been one of the first families to settle around Nacogdoches, and Debra Moraghan was now th wife of a circuit judge.

No, Cassie harbored no hate for the Moraghans, no matter Bud's rancor, his half-mad rantings. She would be happy to make the acquaintance of a Moraghan, to call one her friend.

But it was improbable that that would ever happen. It was unlikely they would even speak to a Danker if meeting one on the street, but would instead detour around, as they would a heap of steaming horse dung in their path.

Sighing, she plodded on, a slight, slender girl, with Danker brown eyes and Danker brown hair—but where most Danker hair was lank and lifeless as mouse fur, hers was shining and lustrous. And she possessed a bubbling

humor that dour Danker nature and dreary circumstances
had yet to fully subdue.

She quailed inside as she remembered the scalding
contempt evinced by Kevin Moraghan when he had learned
they were Dankers. The name Danker was like a curse on
most people's lips, and like a heavy yoke around her neck,
weighing her down.

"Nora's will is simplicity itself," Stony Lieberman
said. "She leaves everything to Kevin, or his heirs. The
only stipulation she dictated was that Moraghan should
remain in Moraghan possession as long as a Moraghan is
alive."

"Momma told me all that, just before she died," Kevin
said. "And she made me promise that I would never sell
it."

Lena said eagerly, "Does that mean that we're going to
be living here, Daddy?"

"Of course not, girl. I couldn't do that even if I wanted
to. I've spent all those years, while we all damned near
starved, building up that place. Now it's finally beginning
to pay off, I'm not about to leave it. Besides, I consider
the Valley my home now."

"It's not going to be easy to rent this place, Kevin,"
Stony said. "There's not enough land to farm."

"What about if I paid someone to live here and take
care of the place?"

"You could do that, certainly, if you want to go to the
expense."

"Well, hell, they could live here rent free, and there's
Momma's garden. Even when we were all at home, she
always raised more garden stuff than we could eat. With
that going for him, seems to me a man wouldn't need
much money to get by."

"True, but you're forgetting the horses."

"Horses?"

"The horses, Kevin, the race horses." Stony pulled at
his lip. "Your mother invested a lot of money the last few
years in breeding stock. She had a sort of dream about
building a racing stable. Racing, you know, is becoming

quite popular in East Texas. She told me once that maybe she could make Moraghan race horses well-known throughout Texas, and at the same time make the name Moraghan mean something again."

"You mean they're really worth something? She'd written me about the horses, but I thought it was sort of an old woman's fancy."

"Not at all. She's built up a strong bloodline. She hasn't raced many of them yet, but she was planning on it. Unfortunately, the fellow who bred and trained them died several months back. If he was still alive, there would be no problem. He could have lived here and raced the horses, sharing the profits with you. Nora fell ill around the time he died and never did get around to replacing him."

"There's nothing in the will that says I can't sell the horses, is there?"

"No, Kevin, there isn't."

Michael spoke up unexpectedly. "Daddy, why can't I stay here and run the place for a while? I've always liked horses."

Kevin gaped at him. "You? Stay *here*, son?"

"At least I can stay and see to the horses until I find a man we can trust. It seems foolish to sell the horses, when we don't know anything of their real value. And if we let a stranger stay here, he could allow the place to go to ruin. Grandmother wouldn't have liked that."

"But Michael, I need you at home, at the orchards."

Michael gestured negligently. "No, you don't, not really. You've always made the decisions, Daddy, you know you have. I've never been that crazy about fruit and produce growing, anyway. But the main thing is, I'd like to get away for a spell." His glance fell away. "You know I haven't been happy there since May Beth passed away."

Kevin nodded sympathetically. "I know that, son, but just the same . . . Kate, what do you think?"

"If that's what he wants, darling. He's a grown man." She sighed. "We'll miss him, but he's right about one thing, he's not all that needed at home. You know you have to see to everything personally."

Lena had been listening with mounting hope. "If Michael stays, I want to stay too!"

Both her parents stared at her. Kevin began to scowl, and said harshly, "Don't be ridiculous, Lena!"

"Why not?" Lena demanded. "Just for a while, a few months. I'm finished with school, and I'm not needed there, Mother, you have a housekeeper. I can cook and keep house here for Michael. He can't even boil water, you know that."

"No, it's out of the question, absolutely," Kevin said.

"Mother, please," she appealed to Kate. "Just for a while?"

"Dammit, girl, I just said no!" Kevin thundered.

"Sh-h, darling, simmer down." Kate touched his hand, her glance directed at Lena, and he calmed down, as he almost always did. "Dear, you *are* asking a lot of us. If Michael stays here, and you as well, we'll be all alone down there."

"Mother, that's not being fair. How many times have you told me that parents should not hold on to their children? Let the chicks try their wings, I recall you saying."

"Touché." Kate made a wry face. "However, you're a little young to try your wings, Lena."

"I'm nineteen. That's as old or older than Debra Lee was."

"The difference is, Debra didn't have our permission to leave. She ran off."

Debra stirred uneasily, said hastily, "Don't bring me into this. But if you do decide to let her stay, Mother, Daddy, I'm not too far away and can keep an eye on her."

"That's enough of this," Kevin said harshly. "The subject is closed." He turned to Stony, who seemed to be having trouble keeping a straight face. "Let's finish up with all this legal business."

"It's finished, Kevin." Stony spread his hands. "As I told you, Nora's was the simplest will I've ever drawn up. If Michael stays here and sees after the place, that certainly takes care of everything nicely."

"All right, Michael, you can stay," Kevin said heavily.

"But only until you have learned the value of the horses and can sell them without getting cheated. Race horses! I don't know what Momma was thinking of."

Lena said tentatively, "Daddy . . ."

"No!" He rounded on her. "You're not staying here and that's the end of it."

Kate gave her daughter a warning glance, and Lena subsided. She knew that Kate's was the final decision in such matters, never mind how much her father might rant, and Lena had the feeling that her mother might side with her. In her own way Kate was a rebel, a nonconformist.

# 3

Lena's surmise proved correct.

Two days after the meeting with Stony Lieberman, she stood on the front porch of Moraghan House, with Michael and Debra, waving good-bye to her mother and father as they rode away in Stony's surrey. Stony was driving them in to Nacogdoches for the start of the journey back down to the Valley.

In point of fact, it had been Debra who swung the balance in Lena's favor.

"Daddy, Mother, school will soon be out for the summer. I can stay out here for a while with Lena and Michael. It'll be good for the children to get out of town and away from that bunch of rowdies they play with. We've always spent a month in summer out here with Grandmother. And"—she had squeezed Lena's hand—"it'll give me a chance to get reacquainted with my brother and sister."

The three stood quietly until Stony's surrey rounded a corner on the river road and disappeared from view. The two Lieberman children scampered about the yard in play. The boy, Joseph, now nine, had Stony's lean figure, a touch of his craggy visage, and much of his father's solemnity, with the same habit of unexpectedly bursting into laughter at odd moments. The girl, Jennifer, at seven was unmistakably her mother's daughter—long, blond hair, laughing blue eyes, and a sunny disposition. She also had Debra's temper, could explode into a tantrum without warning.

"They're nice kids, Debra Lee," Lena said.

"I have to agree, don't I? Since I bore them." Debra smiled fondly. "Even though Joseph is too smart for his own britches, and Jenny is a little minx. Lord help the boys when that old girl grows up." She sighed, looked back at the house. "Well, I have to start cleaning this place, gather up Grandmother's things."

Michael said, "I think I'll check out the horses." With a flip of his hand, he started toward the barns.

"He's crazy about those horses," Debra said.

"About all we see in the Valley are mules. Debra Lee, I'll help you with Grandmother's things."

Debra laughed. "You don't sound too enthusiastic, sister. Why don't you wander around, get acquainted with the old homestead? You can help me later."

Lena turned her face up to the sun. "It's a warm day. I wonder how the water is in the river? I've been dying to go swimming ever since I got here, but I didn't think it would be proper, under the circumstances."

"Swimming? The water's probably warm enough but…" Debra frowned. "Can you swim, Lena? I certainly never learned down there. There was no water to swim in, only dust."

"Sure, I can swim," Lena said. "Things have changed since you left, Debra Lee. Water has come to the Valley."

"Well, I suppose it's all right," Debra said, still dubious. "The water in that old river is not swift, and not too deep, in most places. But you be careful, hear? There are a few places where it drops off suddenly, over your head. And what'll you wear? I don't know of anything suitable around the house."

"I can always strip down to my drawers."

"Oh, my!" Debra threw back her head and laughed.

"Wouldn't Mother and Daddy be shocked! Already I'm corrupting my little sister, letting her swim practically naked! But you know"—her laughter died—"Grandmother Nora wouldn't have objected. She told me that she often slipped down to the river on summer nights and swam without any clothes on. Too bad you didn't get to know her, Lena, you would have liked her."

As she made her way down toward the river, Lena's thoughts were defensive. It had only been a half-lie—there were watering tanks for the stock on the farm now, and she had often swum in them. Of course, the water never came much higher than her waist, and any swimming she had done would have to be classified as splashing, at best.

She walked along the riverbank, in the dappled shade of pecan and spreading oak. The river was not wide, and as Debra had said, flowed sluggishly, with pools here and there where the water, over the years, had carved niches out of the soft riverbank. The pools didn't look too deep, the water so clear she could see all the way to the bottom. Fish floated lazily, the smaller ones darting in quick spurts.

Lena stopped at one of these spots. Looking around, she saw that it was quite isolated. Heavy underbrush grew thick and high almost down to the water on the opposite bank, as it did on this side. Sunlight glinted off stone through the bushes in front of her. With some difficulty Lena pushed her way through, a thorn gashing the back of one hand.

Then she broke through into a sheltered nook. Rubbing the scratched hand, she looked around. At one time a large oak had fallen, and now lay half in and half out of the water. Lena stood on a large flat rock, sloping down into the water like a slide. An effective screen of bushes surrounded her on three sides.

Her breath caught—the perfect spot. She stooped and dangled her fingers in the water. It was cool and soothing as she plunged her still stinging hand into it. She stood, removed her slippers and stockings, then took off her long skirt and shirtwaist, and stood in her chemise and long drawers.

She darted a glance around then, breathless at her own daring, she shucked the chemise and stepped out of the drawers—tall, slender, with long legs, and high, firm breasts she had always considered too small. In the dappled sunlight her body had an alternately dark and coppery glow, the fluff of pubic hair the color of rust. She had her mother's red hair and coloring, but unlike Debra, whose skin always burned from too much exposure to the sun, Lena only had a tendency to freckle. Freckles, she had been told, by both boys and girls, were attractive, but she had always considered them a nuisance.

Lena knew that she was attractive to the male eye, but she usually disparaged her looks to herself, and to others, and was as yet not sure whether her beauty, if such it was, was an asset or a hindrance.

She sat down on the cool, mossy stone, extending her feet and legs slowly into the water. Then she let go her grip of the rock and slid into the water with a splash and a whoop of sheer exuberance. When she came to rest on the bottom of the river, the water came up over her breasts. The water felt deliciously cool, but there were several inches of mud under her bottom, and it felt slimy and unpleasant.

She stood up slowly, rinsing the mud away as she straightened, her back all the while to the bank. As she stood erect, a voice drawled from behind her, "A lovely sight, I must say. Who would have thought to see a nymph rising from the water in East Texas?"

Lena gave a startled yelp, whipped around just enough to see a man standing on the bank, leaning on the fallen tree. Thinking only of her naked state, she threw herself headlong back into the water. She went under and the momentum of her dive carried her a distance out. She fought to the suface, gasping for air and spewing water. Her feet reached for the bottom and found none!

She bobbed to the surface again, flailing about helplessly. Panic struck at her, and she forgot what little she knew about swimming. She splashed about frantically, going down deep this time, down until her feet sank ankle-deep in mud. In her panic she no longer knew which way the surface was. Her lungs beginning to burn, she tried to propel her way toward the surface—and could not. Her foot was caught in a tree root.

Dear God, she was going to die here!

And then hands were on her, tugging urgently. Pain shot through her trapped foot, as the pull exerted force on it. The blurred figure, which she could barely discern in the water, made murky by the disturbed mud, moved down her body. Hands found her foot, probing, and then jerked roughly.

Freed, she shot to the surface, lifted by strong arms. She was only half-conscious, her lungs a blaze of pain for lack of air. As her head rose out of the water, she gasped for breath too soon, and swallowing water, almost strangled.

Then she was on the bank, on her hands and knees, propped up by gentle hands, as she heaved and coughed. When the paroxysm had passed, the hands stretched her out on the rock. She was shivering, and the mottled warmth of the rock was welcome.

"Here," a voice said softly, "use my shirt. There's nothing else to dry yourself off with."

Lena's mind began working again, and she realized that a man was with her. And not only had he seen her naked, he had put his hands on her unclothed body. And yet, he had also saved her life.

With trembling fingers she dried herself as best she could with his shirt, and hastily pulled on her clothes, never once looking around, but she knew he was still there—she could smell burning tobacco. Her temper suddenly flared. He may have saved her from drowning, but he had also been the cause of her predicament.

Dressed, she faced about to see Mark Moraghan leaning against the fallen tree, smoking a cigarette. His trousers were sopping wet, apparently he had removed only his shirt and boots before diving in after her.

The dark hair on his head was plastered down, and the thick mat of hair on his broad chest glistened with water.

Before she could vent her outrage on him, Mark said, "Dammit, cousin, can't you swim?"

"No." She gulped. "Not really."

"What if I hadn't been here? You could have drowned!"

She finally let her anger out. "If you hadn't been here, hadn't frightened me, it wouldn't have happened! I had no intention of going into deep water."

He frowned at her, then began to smile. "You're right and I am sorry. But I couldn't resist. It never entered my head that you couldn't swim, for Christ's sake."

"How could I learn to swim, really swim, down in the Valley? There's ten times more sand there than water." Then, remembering the lie she had told Debra Lee, knowing that she was as much to blame for the mishap as Mark, Lena started to laugh. "You're right, Mark. It was a foolish thing for me to do."

His eyes began to sparkle with a wicked glint, his mouth curving in a lazy smile. "Of course, when I said I was sorry, I meant only that I'm sorry for frightening you, not for seeing you. That was a sight a man can't soon forget."

Her face flamed. "You're terrible! You should be ashamed of yourself!"

He arched an eyebrow. "It was not I who stood up out of the water naked as a babe."

"A gentleman would have looked the other way."

"A gentleman I am not, cousin, and lay no claim to such. Ask around. Anyone along the river, or as far as Nacogdoches, will attest to that. Even my own momma."

"That's not a nice way to talk about your mother."

"My mother is not always a nice person."

"I noticed that you were at Grandmother's funeral, but your mother and sister were not. Did your mother hate Grandmother that much?"

"It's not so much Grandmother Nora, although there was no love lost between them, but it's your father and Cousin Debra. Ma still believes that Debra killed Daddy."

"But it was Tod Danker, not Debra Lee! Everybody knows that."

"Everybody but Ma. But let's go into that another time. Or let's don't." He stood away from the tree to scoop up his damp shirt. "I understand you're staying on at Moraghan for a spell?"

"For a few weeks, anyway."

"Then I'll likely see you again, cousin. Now I'd sug-

gest you go up to the house and change out of those wet
things before you catch your death."

Shirt slung over his shoulder, Mark ducked through the
underbrush and was gone almost as suddenly as he'd
appeared.

Bemused, Lena stared at the thicket into which he had
vanished, half-wondering if he would magically reappear.
Her clothes were still damp, since she had not dried herself
thoroughly before putting them on. But instead of heading
for the house immediately, she picked a spot in the sun on
the sloping rock and sat down.

Mark Moraghan was the first male to ever ignite a spark
of interest in her. How different he was from the dullards
she had known down in the Valley! She knew he was
about Debra Lee's age, perhaps a year or so younger.
There was no denying his male attractiveness, yet it
seemed to Lena that something warred in his nature. He
appeared vital, intelligent, and had a sense of humor, a
wry wit, but at the same time there was a taint of cynicism
about him, a world-weariness, as though, almost against
his will, he found any activity boring, a waste of time.

It was too bad that he was her cousin.

Lena sighed and got up. Her clothes were dry now, but
her dress was wrinkled, and she was sure that Debra Lee
would notice. Consequently, she took a rather circuitous
route back to the house, wandering somewhat south,
following the course of the river for a bit, before cutting
back toward the house. When she did turn back, she
entered a grove of live oak. Emerging from it, she stopped
short. She was in a weed-grown clearing, and in the center
of that clearing stood a log cabin.

It was gray with age, much of the chinking had fallen
out from between the logs, and boards had been nailed
across the one window. Drawn by curiosity, Lena approached
it hesitantly. For some reason she couldn't define, the
cabin gave her an eerie feeling. Desolated out here, hoary
with age, it seemed enclosed in a bubble of brooding
silence, even the chittering of birds from the nearby trees
seemed muted. Yet the feeling she got was one of familiarity, not apprehension, and this was stranger still, since she

had not seen it, or even heard of its existence. Vaguely she
recalled hearing from her father that Sean and Nora Moraghan
had made their first home here in a log cabin, built by
Sean's own hands. Could this be it?

She pushed against the door, and it swung slowly open,
creaking. The interior was dim, the only light coming from
the cracks between the logs. She shoved the heavy door all
the way open before venturing inside.

The cabin consisted of one room. Crude, handmade
furniture was scattered about: a table, hardback chairs, and a
bed, bare of bedding, in one corner. At one end was a stone
fireplace, almost high enough to stand in without stooping,
and before it stood a cane-bottomed rocking chair.

What astonished Lena was the cleanliness of the cabin;
there were no cobwebs and very little dust, as though it
had been cleaned regularly. Yet she felt instinctively that it
was uninhabited.

She crossed to the rocking chair and sank down into it,
folded her hands in her lap. A strange calm descended on
her, and her mind seemed to empty of all thought. Head
resting against the high back, she dozed for a little. She
awoke with a start, shivering slightly. Although her outer
clothing had long dried, her skin felt clammy. Yawning,
she got up and left. Her limbs felt heavy, as if she were
walking in water, and her thought processes were slow.
And yet when she was only a few yards from the cabin,
she felt herself moving with a light step, and every sense
seemed keener than before.

She stopped, a little unnerved, and glanced back at the
cabin. It sat peacefully, bathed in sunlight, and there was
nothing even remotely threatening about it. Of course, she
hadn't felt threatened at all; it was just . . . well, strange.
She had never known such a feeling of peace. Also, she
had never believed in ghosts, yet there was *something* in
that cabin. However, if it was inhabited by ghosts, they
must be benign.

Laughing at herself, she set out at a brisk pace for the
main house.

\*     \*     \*

She found Debra on the front porch, rocking in Nora's old chair, with a pitcher of lemonade, watching her two children in the yard.

She glanced around as Lena came up the steps. "I got hot and dusty going through Grandmother's old trunks and made some lemonade. Fetch a glass from the kitchen if you want some—" She broke off with a frown. "God-almighty, girl, what happened to you? That dress is as wrinkled as if it had never been ironed, and there's mud all over the hem."

"I took it off to wade in the river, then slipped and fell, getting wet all over. I used it to dry off with, having nothing else. The mud . . ." Lena looked down at the splotch of dried mud on the bottom of the dress. "I reckon I must have dragged it into the mud. I'll wash and iron it, Debra Lee."

"I warned you to be careful."

Lena said hastily, "Oh, I wasn't in any danger, the water was shallow." She knew that if she told the whole story, told about Mark Moraghan, she'd receive the rough side of her sister's tongue, and likely Debra Lee would march over to scold Mark as well.

She sat down on the top step, and to divert Debra's thoughts from the swimming incident, she said, "Debra Lee, I stumbled across an old log cabin in a clearing between here and the river. Is that the cabin Grandfather Sean built when they first came to Texas?"

Debra nodded, smiling. "That's the place. It's been there since . . . oh, I think 1836 was the year. They lived there until Grandfather built this house before the war."

"It looks like it's been kept up, it could have been cleaned only days ago. Has somebody been living there?"

"No, Grandmother would never let anybody live there. She told me once that the only times it was used after they moved up here was when she and Grandfather had a spat, and he might storm off to spend the night there. But she had a sort of fetish about that old cabin and saw that it was kept up and cleaned every so often."

Debra smiled reminiscently. "I recall the fights she used to have with Maria, that's the Mexican housekeeper who

worked here for God knows how many years. She'd order
Maria to clean the cabin, and Maria would balk, saying,
why bother, nobody lived there. I remember hearing them
argue about it once. Finally Maria snapped that Nora kept
it like a shrine to a dead man. And Nora retorted that her
Sean was as alive as Maria's God, which horrified Maria,
and she quit for the umpteenth time. Our grandmother,
Lena, was not very religious. She was a lapsed Catholic.
Did you know that Sean Moraghan had been a Catholic
priest before he married her?''

Lena stared. ''No, I didn't know.''

''It's true. He had to leave the church to marry Nora. I
only learned that from Nora herself a dozen years ago.
Now don't be voicing it around, not many people know.
Although I reckon it wouldn't cause much of a scandal
after over fifty years.''

''Debra Lee, I know the bad feeling between Uncle
Brian's and Daddy's side of the family, but Mark . . . I saw
him here the night Grandmother died, and he came to the
funeral when his mother and sister didn't. Why are his
feelings so different?''

''Well, Mark's a strange one, for sure.'' Debra was
silent for a few moments, gazing off. ''He's got a reputation for being flighty, even wild. He's . . . what? Not too
much younger than I am, a year or so under thirty now.
But he's never married or settled down. He didn't get
along too well with Uncle Brian, and ran away from home
when he was eighteen . . .''

Debra got a strange look as she spoke of Brian Moraghan.
''When his father was killed, Mark came back, but he
didn't stick around long. I was living in Nacogdoches soon
after that, when I married Stony. Mark would stay away
for a year, sometimes longer, then drift back home for a
month, before he was off again. God only knows where he
was all that time, what he did. Mark's closemouthed about
himself. But one thing everybody agrees on—he's a woman chaser, he's broke more hearts between here and
Nacogdoches. Thank goodness, you're first cousins, Lena,
or he'd probably come around, trying to lift your skirts!''

That would hardly be necessary, Lena thought; not after

what happened today. Feeling her face begin to burn, she turned her head quickly away. She said, "He seems intelligent and well-spoken, as though he had a good education. More than just high school, I mean."

"He may have. I heard somewhere that he attended a semester or two of college during one of his absences. He's also well-read, I understand. He's even borrowed law books from Stony a time or two."

"It's too bad he doesn't apply himself to something."

"It's too late for that, I'm afraid."

Lena was silent for a few moments, thinking of Mark Moraghan. Then a forbidden thought nudged into her mind—she wished he wasn't her cousin. Falling in love with or marrying a cousin, especially a first cousin, was beyond the pale. How many horror stories she had heard about that—outcasts from decent folks, a sin against God and man, idiots for children.

She forced her thoughts away from Mark. "If you're ready to start on Grandmother's things again, Debra Lee, I'll help you now."

# 4

Michael Moraghan leaned on the rail fence and watched with deep pleasure the three colts frolicking around their mothers. Nora Moraghan's racing stable consisted of four mares, two stallions, and now the three colts.

God only knew what bloodlines ran in the animals—certainly no human did. There was a touch of Morgan, some Arabian, and even a strain of wild Mustang, Michael suspected. Since they were not thoroughbreds, they didn't possess the classic lines of the few purebreds he had seen, but he had worked with them enough by now to know that they possessed blazing speed, stamina, and great heart.

He had always had a fondness for horses, but now he

knew that he loved them; and he also knew that he was going to remain on Moraghan and race them, not sell them. Kevin would be furious when he learned of this, but there was little he could do about it. Oh, he could sell the horses since he had the legal title to them, but he could not force Michael to come back to the Rio Grande Valley. He was over twenty-one and then some, his own man now.

Michael had attributed his unhappiness at home to May Beth's untimely death, but he had come to realize these past few days here that there was much more to it than that. His father thrived on hard work, and he loved the land. All those years of struggle until he had finally made the land bloom down there had not beaten him down; he was proud of his achievement, and rightly so. But Michael did not have Kevin's love of the land, and he had plodded along in his father's footsteps all those years, working from dawn until dark, and he had felt no special pride when they had finally turned the corner.

He had not really been alive until he met and fell in love with May Beth. True, his nature had always been good-humored, but he had dimly realized that it was a defense, in a way, against the stultifying life of the soil. May Beth had been a creature of light, imbued with a rich, earthy humor. Slight, but with a full figure, with golden hair, saucy green eyes, she moved through his days with the awkward grace of a frisky colt, and he delighted in her love, glowed with it, until he had thought he would burst with happiness.

An outsider, a visitor from New Orleans, May Beth had come to Brownsville to visit an aunt and uncle for a few weeks. Michael and May Beth had met at a barbecue, and what followed was a classic example of love at first sight. They were married two weeks from the day they met, and moved into the old house, the adobe house Kevin had built when he first moved his family to the Valley.

For the first year, Michael floated in euphoria, sleep-walking through the days of hard labor, living only for the nights with May Beth, never suspecting the discontent that was growing in his wife.

Michael had been a virgin on his wedding night. He had

always been shy with women, well aware that virginity in a male of twenty-four was rare, even something to be ashamed of. However, he had never found a girl who attracted him enough to push him past his innate shyness, and the thought of visiting whorehouses, across the border into Mexico, with other youths of his age, repelled him.

May Beth, on the other hand, had not been a virgin on her wedding night, and made no apology for that fact. Michael's initial reaction had been dismay, but he'd had enough good sense to hide it, and it wasn't long before he realized that he had every reason to be grateful. She brought such a sensuality into his life, awakening a hungry sexuality in him heretofore unsuspected, and showing such an uninhibited delight in their lovemaking, that he knew he should be happy over her lack of chastity.

So the nights were such gardens of delight for Michael that he never once suspected her mounting unhappiness— until a night almost a year after their wedding.

They had just made ardent love, and now, passions spent, they lay content, May Beth's head on his shoulder, his arm under her head. Michael was weary after the day's hard work in the fields and their prolonged lovemaking, and would have drifted off to sleep but for the fact that his arm was numb from her weight resting on it, and he was fearful he would wake her if he moved the arm.

Then, to his surprise, she spoke. "Michael . . . ?"

He came fully awake with a start. "I thought you were asleep."

"Not yet."

There was a different note to her voice that made him uneasy. "May Beth, is something bothering you?"

She was silent for so long that he began to think she had fallen asleep after all. Then: "Darling, are you going to live the rest of your life in this Godforsaken place?"

Startled, he disengaged himself from her, sitting up to peer down at the blur of her face. "I reckon I've never given much thought to it one way or another. It's the only place I've known, outside of East Texas so long ago that I can scarcely remember. Why do you ask? Don't you like it here?"

"I hate it," she said vehemently. "And I should think you would, too."

"But why?" he asked, baffled. "True, it's not Eden. Even though Daddy thinks it comes close," he chuckled, "since it'll grow almost anything with water."

"But that's all it is, don't you see? A boring cycle of planting, tending, harvesting, year after year. I don't think I've seen anyone work harder than you and your father."

"May Beth, that's nothing at all unusual. A farmer's life, the life of any farmer, is mostly hard work. What's wrong in that?"

"But there has to be something else in life, Michael!"

"You're a city girl, sweetheart. It's natural you'd feel that way at first. But you'll grow used to it."

She raised her head. "It's been nearly a year, and I haven't yet. I don't *want* to get used to it, Michael. There has to be something better in life for us."

Stung, he retorted, "Then why did you marry me, May Beth? You knew what I was, what my life was like."

"I married you because I loved you, but I didn't realize what your life was really like. Not until I actually began to live with you."

Michael opened his mouth to say that his mother liked the life, and his sisters. Then he fell silent, remembering Debra Lee and her flight from the life here, and he recalled Lena's growing discontent. And he wasn't all that sure that his mother liked it that well. Kate Moraghan wasn't a complainer, and for the first time he wondered, thinking back to his childhood here, before Kevin brought water to the land—Kate's constant battle against the dust, and the endless hours of labor she put in each day just to keep this adobe clean.

But Michael also had to wonder if he could make a life for himself anywhere else. What else did he know? He had finished high school, his parents had insisted on that. Yet he knew nothing else but farming—what made it even worse, only orchard and produce farming, an endeavor that was unique to the Rio Grande Valley, at least in Texas.

May Beth ran her hand lightly over his chest, said, "I'm sorry, darling. I'm being a bitch, I know. After all, what

do I have to complain about? I have you, and that should
be enough for any one woman.''

"Not if you're going to be unhappy here. Let me think
about it. You did spring this on me kind of sudden like.''

Michael did think about it, hard. May Beth's question
gave him a whole new vision of his life here, and he
slowly realized that spending the remainder of his life in
the Valley was not an inviting prospect. While it was true
that he had known no other life, if he didn't leave while he
was still young, there would be no chance whatsoever to
start a new life somewhere else. On the other hand, there
was Kevin to think about. Michael was an only son, and
he knew that his father had always assumed that the land
would be handed down to him, and that he would take
over when Kevin died, or was too old to operate the place.
To flat-out leave here would hurt Kevin terribly, yet Michael
had his own life to live.

He confided none of this to May Beth, who did not
broach the subject again, either. When he finally reached
the decision to leave, after much inner torment and conflict, when he was about ready to tell her, the smallpox
epidemic swept through the Valley, and May Beth was one
of the first to fall prey to it. Within days she was dead and
in the ground, and he never had a chance to tell her of his
decision . . .

Now, leaning on the fence, watching the colts at play,
Michael was wracked again with guilt. If he had not taken
so long to make up his mind, May Beth would not be
dead. She could be with him now, perhaps gamboling
about with the colts in the small pasture. She had loved
horses, she had told him once.

Michael had talked of his agonizing guilt to his mother,
and Kate had scolded him: "I don't want to hear another
word of such foolishness, Michael Moraghan! There are
certain things in this life that we mortals have no control
over, and May Beth's death was one of them. You had
nothing to do with her getting smallpox, neither could you
have prevented it. If you had taken her away before the
epidemic, she could have been killed the very next day by
a runaway horse. I'm not all that religious, as you know,

but I do believe that we all have our time to go, and nothing can prevent it. I know how much you cared for May Beth, son, and I know your heart is breaking. But don't go adding to your grief by blaming yourself for her passing. It was her time.''

Logically speaking, he knew he shouldn't feel guilt, but it wasn't a matter that could be considered logically. Every time he even thought about her death, Michael's heart clenched. And while down there, he thought of her constantly. At least here, on Moraghan, she began to fade, just a little, and he knew it would slowly get better. For that reason alone, he was determined to remain. When the time came, he would simply have to convince his father of that . . .

''Pretty creatures, aren't they, Michael?'' a voice drawled by his elbow.

Turning, he saw his Cousin Mark approaching, a cigarette between his fingers trailing smoke.

''I happen to think so, yes,'' Michael said a little stiffly. He wasn't very familiar with Mark Moraghan yet, and he was never sure when the other man was sincere. It seemed to Michael that Mark had a habit of mocking everything, and everybody.

Mark smiled lazily. ''I wasn't funning. Young horses at that age are adorable. Grown up, they sometimes are beautiful, sometimes not. But the trouble is, grown or not, they all have about as much brains as a flea.''

Michael's gaze went back to the mares and colts. He said softly, ''Brainless or not, they're beautiful to me.''

''Like with a woman, eh? In the eye of the beholder?'' At Michael's sidewise glance, Mark held up a hand. ''Now, you'll have to admit, with all the mixed blood these horses have, they're not all that beautiful.''

''Perhaps not to you, but to a man used to mules, they are. And they have great heart and speed. I plan to win a few races with them.''

Mark arched an eyebrow. ''Do you now? Train and ride them yourself?''

''I know very little about race horses, but by cracky, I'll learn.''

Mark's expression was musing. ''I expect you will.'' He

leaned on his elbows on the railing beside Michael. "I've been to some of the racing meets in the East. There, you know, they hire riders, usually little bitty fellows. The less weight, the better." His glance measured Michael. "You're not all that slight, but you're not too big, either. And at the races around here, county fairs and such, I expect the riders come in all sizes. You have Uncle Kevin's approval of your plans?"

"Not yet. But I will. Either he goes along or I go my own way."

Mark grinned. "Independence time, huh?"

"I think it's about time, I'll be thirty before long. I probably should have left the nest a long time ago."

Mark's glance slid away. "That doesn't always solve things, Michael. I left home the first time when I was eighteen. I've knocked around a lot, seen most of the United States, and several other countries. The thing is, I keep coming back to East Texas. I really can't say why, but I do."

"I'm determined about one thing. I'm not going back to the Rio Grande Valley. Never again."

"Michael, where are you?"

At the hail they both faced around. It was Lena's voice, from the other side of the barn. Michael shouted, "Back here, sis."

In a moment Lena rounded the corner of the building, slowed to a halt when she saw Mark. "Mark . . . I didn't know you were here."

Stony had had a long talk with Kevin before the Moraghans went back to the Valley.

Kevin had been worried about Bud Danker's threat. "It may be just all blow, Stony, but the Dankers have always been a mean bunch. That's one reason I'm uneasy about leaving Michael and Lena on Moraghan. But what can I do, they're both grown now. I've warned them about Bud Danker, but I doubt either one of them took me seriously. The thing is, could you kind of keep an eye out? Maybe you could have a word or two with the sheriff in Nacogdoches, whoever he is these days. Ask him to keep an eye on Danker. Surely a word from you would carry some weight, being a judge as long as you have.''

"John Bradshaw was the man elected sheriff the last election. I ran on the same ticket with him, but I can't say I like the fellow very much. He runs a sloppy office. But I'll have a word with him, Kevin. I really don't think you have much to worry about. I think Bud Danker just wanted to vent his venom. If he'd really intended to do anything, I doubt he'd've warned you first.''

Two days after Kevin and Kate left for home, Stony paid a call on Sheriff Bradshaw. Bradshaw still used the office that had belonged to Tod Danker, and Stony felt a chill every time he visited the office—he could see again, too vividly, that afternoon when he and Kevin had accosted Danker, naming him Brian Moraghan's murderer. Faced with the undeniable facts, Danker had drawn a gun and Kevin had killed him. Stony imagined that he could still smell the stench of gunpowder every time he came into the office, which he did rarely.

Sheriff Bradshaw was in, lolling behind his desk. He was a big man, going to fat, moving as slow as molasses. His brain, in Stony's opinion, didn't move much faster. He took a fat, smoldering cigar from his mouth, his broad, red face registering surprise.

"Well, Judge! To what do I owe the honor?''

Stony perched gingerly on the hardback chair before the desk, holding his breath against the reek of cheap cigar. "It's about Bud Danker, Sheriff. If my memory serves, I've heard something about his being arrested. Am I right?''

Bradshaw cocked his head to one side, squinting, then shrugged beefy shoulders. "I've hauled him in twice, as I recollect. Both times for scrapping. Once was over a nigger whore. The second time he got into a fight in a saloon, pulled a knife on the other old boy.''

Stony said tightly, "But I don't remember him being brought up before me on charges. And I'm sure I would have remembered.''

"I let him go both times.''

"Why didn't you charge him?''

"Aw-w, hell, Judge! For fighting over a nigger whore?"

"How about the other time, when he pulled a knife?"

Bradshaw shrugged again. "Trouble that time was, nobody saw the knife but the other fellow, and the other fellow's a mean one himself. Now Bud said he didn't pull a knife. So, it was his word against the other fellow. Who you going to believe? It would have been a waste of county money, a waste of your time and mine, Judge. Never would have convicted him, no, sir."

Stony kept a tight rein on his temper. The man was too damned lazy to work up a decent case, he thought. This wasn't the first time, nor would it be the last. But he said nothing, just stared back at the sheriff.

After a moment Bradshaw's gaze dropped away, and he stirred uneasily. "What's your interest in Bud Danker all of a sudden, Judge?"

"You knew that Kevin Moraghan was up here for his mother's funeral?"

"Yup, I heard. Didn't stay long, I understand."

"He had to get back home. The thing is, Bud Danker and his sister showed up for Nora's funeral. Afterward, he made threats to Kevin."

Bradshaw frowned. "Now why the hell would Bud do a thing like that?"

"You must have heard about the feud between the two families. It goes way back, back to when Sean Moraghan first came to East Texas."

"I've heard, sure. Everybody knows about that." Bradshaw stared. "You mean that's what the threat was about? That old feud is still alive, at this day and age?"

Stony said tightly, "Apparently it's still alive as far as Bud Danker is concerned. You know that Kevin killed his daddy, right here in this very office?"

"Of course I know about that. You say old Bud threatened Kevin Moraghan? But I don't see what difference it makes, since Kevin has gone back home."

"Both his son and daughter stayed behind, out at Moraghan."

"You think Bud might do them harm?"

"It's not too likely, but anything is possible with a Danker."

Bradshaw snorted laughter. "Naw, I can't see it. My opinion, old Bud was just blowing a little. Anyways, what do you expect from me, Judge?"

"I thought you could sort of keep an eye on Bud Danker. After all, it's your job, as sheriff of the county."

"My job? Hellfire, Judge, my job is to catch people when they commit a crime, not before!"

"Your job is to protect the welfare of the people in this county."

"Protect their welfare? You know how many deputies I have, Judge? Four, all told. And I got a whole damned county to cover. Now, how can I spare a man just to keep an eye on trash like Bud Danker?"

Stony's temper slipped. He leaned forward, said, "You could get off your dead ass for once."

Bradshaw reared back. "Here now! What gives you the right to talk to me like that?"

Stony got to his feet. "I'm taking the right, Bradshaw. As a sheriff, you're a washout. I'm putting you on notice right now—if Bud Danker does anything to harm either Michael or Lena Moraghan, I'm holding you responsible."

Bradshaw, face flaming, stood up. "You got no right to hold me responsible for anything. Shit, just because you're a judge, don't mean you can come in here and roust me. I'm responsible only to the people who elected me."

"And if you don't do your job better, I'll see to it that they don't elect you for a second term. I have a lot of support with the electorate, and I can see to it that you lose, Bradshaw, believe me."

"Aw-w, shit, Judge. Now don't go flying off the handle like this." Bradshaw's voice took on a whining note. "We have to stand by each other. I don't think it's very neighborly of you to go about bad-mouthing me to the voters."

"Just do your job, that's all I ask."

Bradshaw's small eyes were venomous, but he nodded reluctantly. "I'll do what I can. I'll warn old Bud to behave himself, how's that strike you?"

"I don't know how much good it'll do. But at least he'll be put on notice." With a stiff nod, Stony left the sheriff's office.

Among Nora's things, Lena and Debra discovered three manuscripts, if they could be so called. They were plays— skits actually—written in Nora's neat, cramped handwriting, in schoolchildren's tablets.

Debra was little interested and wondered if they should be disposed of. Lena snatched them away from her. "No, don't do that! I want to read them."

Debra shrugged. "Fine with me."

Sitting on the floor, while Debra continued to go through Nora's trunks, Lena began to read. She started to smile, then laughed aloud.

Debra glanced over at her. "What in the world?"

"This play is funny, about a country bumpkin who blunders around, in and out of funny situations. Did you ever see this performed, Debra Lee?"

"Since I haven't even heard it, I can't very well say. But I don't remember anything about a country bumpkin."

"Let me read it and see if you remember."

Lena turned back to the beginning and began to read. At first Debra went about what she was doing, but before long she was seated cross-legged before Lena, completely engrossed.

Not, however, as engrossed as Lena. She became so caught up in reading the material that she completely forgot where she was. There were several roles in the play: the country bumpkin, an evil-hearted banker, a golden-haired heroine, her drunken father, her flighty mother, and a gambler and the stalwart lad, both vying for the heroine's heart. Lena *became* each character as she read the lines. The plot was slight, relatively unimportant, having to do with the black-hearted banker foreclosing the mortgage on the family homestead, and the yokel finally solving all the problems, and the stalwart lad gaining the heroine's hand. It was melodrama, pure and simple, yet it had its touching moments, and many funny scenes.

When Lena finished reading, Debra began to applaud.

Lena looked up with a start, blinking. "It's a good play, Debra Lee, but not *that* good."

Debra shook her head. "I wasn't clapping for the play, but for your reading of it. I've heard of somebody being born to something, but I've never observed it before. You, dear sister, are a born actress."

"Oh, you're exaggerating." Lena gestured negligently, but was nonetheless pleased. "But you aren't familiar with the play?"

Debra shook her head. "Nope, never heard it. In fact, thinking back, and I was very young, you must understand, I don't think I ever attended a play that Grandmother had written herself. I didn't even know she had written any, and I very much doubt that anyone else does either." She grinned. "It must have been Grandmother's private vice, like secret drinking."

Lena said, "Maybe she was afraid to show them to anybody, afraid of being laughed at."

"I don't know why anyone should do that. True, I know little about plays, theater, or such, but I think that this one should go over well, performed before an unsophisticated audience."

"Is it all right if I keep them?"

"Why not?" Debra got to her feet. "Somebody should keep them. I'm just glad you stopped me from throwing them away."

Michael was in the saddle on one of the mares, loping her around the pasture. Over the past few days, he had exercised the horses once a day, around the perimeter of the pasture, and their hooves had chewed up the grass, making a dusty track in the shape of a rough oval. Michael would be the first to admit that he had a lot to learn about riding. He had fallen off a number of times the first week, when the animals got a little frisky, and he still had to cling to the saddle when they pounded into a gallop. But he was grimly determined to learn.

As he brought the mare around the last lap, and began to rein her in behind the barn, he was surprised to see a man leaning on the railing, watching him intently.

As Michael drew the mare to a halt and slid awkwardly off, the man gave a bark of laughter. "You're a terrible rider, bub, you know that?" He spat a stream of brown tobacco juice. "You ride like a drunken Indian. Fact."

Michael was momentarily annoyed, then he relaxed with a laugh. "I can't argue with that, except I've never seen a drunken Indian ride. But I'm trying, give me points for that."

The man on the other side of the fence was short, wiry, totally bald, with a leathery face and faded, squinty blue eyes, laugh lines radiating out from the corners. He was close to sixty, Michael judged.

As Michael started to unsaddle the mare, the little man opened the gate and came around the fence toward him. Michael noticed that his clothes were worn and dusty, and he wore run-over cowboy boots. And his short legs were as bowed as a harp.

"You'd be Michael Moraghan?"

Michael nodded. "That's right."

"I'm Roscoe Barnes. Bandy to my friends, on account of . . ." The man grinned, gesturing to his bowed legs, and spat tobacco juice. "I heard in Nacognoches that you might be looking for a horse trainer."

"I might," Michael said warily. He slung the saddle over the fence, and began to rub the mare down, using a towel that had been hanging on the top rail.

"Here, let me do that, show you how it's done."

Bandy took the towel and began to rub the mare's sweaty flanks. The mare turned her head, eyes rolling at this stranger. Bandy began to talk softly, the words indistinguishable, and the animal immediately quieted.

Michael said, "From the looks of it, I gather you've had experience with horses."

"Fact. I know horses better'n some men claim they know women. I've even been accused of having relations with them. Now that's a flat-out lie, but I will say I'd rather bed down with a horse than some women I've known." He straightened up, spat a brown stream. "Started punching cows when I was fifteen, and that's a long spell, bub. But cowpunching ain't what it used to be, and I got pretty stove up a few years back, so I hooked on with Buffalo Bill's Wild West Show. Bill Cody, you know. Started working with him when he opened his first official Wild West, May 19, 1883, at the Omaha Fair Grounds, up in Nebraska. Fact.''

Bandy, finished, gave the mare a slap on the rump, sending the animal scampering across the pasture to where the other horses grazed. Wryly, Michael realized that the little man had rubbed the mare down in half the time it would have taken him.

Bandy bowlegged over to lean against the fence beside him. ''Stayed with Wild Bill until earlier this year, handling the bucking broncs used in his 'Cow-Boy's Fun' exhibition, also training the horses used in races.''

''Why did you quit? Or did you?''

''Oh, I quit. I did a good job and could've stayed as long as I cared to. Fact.'' Bandy sighed. ''But it just got to be too dad-blamed much for me. My joints creak these days like an old gate, and I ain't as spry as I once was.'' He peered around at Michael. ''Where you going to race these critters of yours, bub?''

''I hadn't given too much thought to that. I have to learn how to ride better first, before I race them anywhere. But I understand that horse races are becoming popular in Texas.''

''Heard something to that effect. Can't say myself. Haven't been back to Texas for a spell until I came back last week, from over to New Orleans. You ever been to New Orleans, bub?''

Michael felt a pull of sorrow—May Beth had been from New Orleans. He said, ''No, never have. Understand it's a great city.'' He was amused to hear himself speaking in the terse, choppy style of Bandy.

Bandy spat, said, ''Could be. But you couldn't prove it by me. Rained the whole time we were there. Fact. We, Buffalo Bill's Wild West, that is, came down this past year to play the World's Industrial and Cotton Exposition. Came down in a steamboat, down the old Mississippi. At Rodney Landing, we collided with another steamboat, and the whole shebang went to the bottom of the river.

"Have to hand it to Bill Cody. He salvaged the Deadwood coach and the bandwagon from the bottom of the river, and I had managed to save most of the horses. From somewhere, in only eight days, mind you, Bill Cody rounded up buffalo, elk, more wagons and other equipment, and we opened in New Orleans on time. Fact." Bandy turned his head and spat.

"But what happened to Bill Cody then, shouldn't happen to a mangy dog. It rained for forty-four days, without letup. I recollect that one day we sold only nine tickets. Didn't faze Bill Cody. He said to me, 'If nine people came out to see us in this rain, we'll show.' And he by God did.

"But all that rain was too much for my old bones. I ached from head to toe, just couldn't take it anymore. So when it was time for Bill Cody and his Wild West to move, I up and quit. Wandered over this way. In Nacogdoches I was told that you was in need of a man who knew horses. Well, that's me."

Bandy looked at Michael expectantly. Michael had already formed a liking for the little man, and he had the gut feeling that Bandy knew horses as well as he claimed. In addition, his yarning promised to be highly entertaining.

He said slowly, "I think you're the man I'm looking for, but I have to warn you, Bandy. I can't afford to pay very much, not in the beginning. When the horses start to race and win . . . well, we'll see."

"Don't need very much. Fact," Bandy said cheerfully. "Just food and a place to sleep, and a little something over for chewing tobacco. Maybe a bottle now and again. Not that I'm a boozer. But I do like a nip or two after a day's hard work."

"Then you're hired." Michael stuck out his hand, and Bandy shook it.

"Now," Bandy said briskly, "suppose we get started. You're the one needs work, more'n the horses, from what I've seen already. First off, bub, you have to learn to become part of the dadblamed critter you're riding. Between your bouncing ass and saddle on that mare, there was enough room to see clear over into the next county.

You have to learn to go *with* the horse, in a manner of speaking . . ."

In the middle of the week, Debra had to go into Nacogdoches for a few days, and Lena decided to go in and stay with her.

After supper the first evening, Debra said, "There's a medicine show in town, Lena. Have you ever seen one, and would you like to go?"

"I'd love to. And no, I've never seen one. No medicine show has ever been down in our neighborhood."

With a smile tugging at the corners of her mouth, Debra glanced across the table at her husband. "Stony?"

Stony snorted. "Now, you know better than to ask, Debra. A bunch of charlatans, selling snake oil. Someone wrote once, back in the early seventeen hundreds, a verse nailing such mountebanks to the wall. The lines went like this." He looked up at the ceiling, then slowly recited: " 'Before you take his Drop or Pill, Take leave of Friends, and make your Will.' That's even more true today than it was back then."

Debra said innocently, "But it's free entertainment, Stony, singing and dancing, and sometimes funny skits."

"It's pure balderdash."

Joseph set up a clamor. "I want to go, too, Momma!"

Stony turned a stern look on him. "No, you're not going, young man. I won't have you corrupted by such shenanigans. Not only are the products they sell fraudulent, but most of the skits I've seen them put on are racially biased, holding the black race up to ridicule. You go, Debra, if you want, you and Lena, but the children stay here with me. And don't argue with me, Joseph!"

Now that summer was upon them, the days were hot and humid, but the nights were still pleasant. The medicine show was located on a vacant lot about a half-mile from the Lieberman home, and as Debra and Lena neared it, people were converging on the spot from all directions.

As they walked onto the lot, Lena saw that it was already crowded. Several benches had been made by placing planks across soapboxes in front of the stage

wagon, and they were all filled by the time Lena and
Debra arrived. The stage wagon was stationed near the
back of the lot, and Lena could see other wagons and tents
behind it. Projecting from the stage wagon was a platform
about five feet high, and eighteen feet square, with slender
cross beams supporting a canvas roof. The rear half of the
stage wagon was hidden by a canvas backdrop, with a
legend spelling out DOC HOLLIDAY in huge letters across
the top. A smaller, lower platform ran out at right angles
from the big stage, forming a runway halfway down
between the rows of plank benches. Banners on both sides
of the stage, illuminated by torches, ballyhooed: "Doc
Holliday's Elixir of Life!"

Debra and Lena found a place at the rear of the crowd
just as the canvas curtain behind the stage parted, and a
tall, cadaverous man, dressed all in black, with a high silk
hat, and a pearl-handled revolver strapped around his
waist, stepped to the lip of the stage. As the crowd quieted
somewhat, he swept off his hat, exposing a shock of
snow-white hair, and bowed extravagantly, first right, then
left.

"Ladies and gentlemen," he said in a mellifluous voice,
"your kind attention, please!"

When the crowd did not immediately settle down to his
satisfaction, he plucked the revolver from the holster and
fired twice, aiming over their heads. Lena gasped and
caught Debra's arm.

Debra laughed. "Don't worry, Lena. Stony says he
doesn't fire real bullets. They're harmless."

"How does Stony know so much? I thought he didn't
attend medicine shows?"

"My dear husband knows a little about just about
everything, I've found. Also, he is sometimes a bit of a
phony. He *has* attended medicine shows. He was present at
the first two performances of this one. They need permits
to operate, you know, and Stony took it upon himself to
see that they weren't violating the terms of the license. He
still says they're charlatans, selling phony remedies, but
the thing is, as you'll see, they can't be charged with

promising something they can't deliver, because their claims for their products are so general.''

Lena turned her attention back to the stage as the man in black said, ''I am Doc Holliday, friends. No, friends and neighbors, I am not that Doc Holliday of Tombstone and the O.K. Corral fame. But he is a distant relative, and we share the same last name. He is a doctor of dentistry, whereas I am a doctor of nature, about which we shall talk later. Now, prepare yourself for dazzling entertainment, neighbors, presented to you absolutely free of charge! I now present the Holliday Players, featuring first that banjo picker of great renown, Bob Ketchum!''

From behind the curtain strutted a short man carrying a five-string banjo, which he was playing furiously. Propping one foot upon a chair, he played two rollicking pieces, then turned expectantly toward the curtain, and Doc Holliday's deep voice could be heard, ''And now, our own Little Susie!''

A short, slightly plump woman danced out, singing in accompaniment to the banjo. She wore a short dress, daringly short for the time, with dark hair tied up in ribbons behind her ears. Despite the shortness of the dress, the show of stockinged leg, she was surprisingly demure. Her voice was slight, with the sweetness of an innocent young girl.

As the banjo player finished with a flourish and Susie disappeared behind the curtain, Doc Holliday strode on stage again. ''Now, friends and neighbors, I am going to give you an opportunity to win grand prizes and buy a box of delicious candy at the same time! Our performers will pass among you, carrying a carton of delicious candies.'' As he talked, Doc Holliday came down the narrow runway exhorting the crowd, and around the sides of the stage platform came two men, the banjo player and another man in blackface. Baskets hung on straps around their necks, heaped high with cardboard boxes.

''For one thin dime, a tenth of a dollar, ladies and gentlemen,'' Holliday intoned, ''you may purchase a box of candy. In each and every box, my oath on it, will be either a small prize, or a ticket which will entitle you to a

more substantial prize from the stage, given to you by my
own hands. Three, mind you, *three* major prizes will be
given away here tonight, my solemn oath on it! Depending
on the extent of your good fortune, someone here tonight
is going to take home a dish set, a vanity set, or a fine,
cut-glass bowl. Now, buy one box of delicious candy, or
more if you prefer. The more boxes, the better chance at a
big prize!''

As the two men passed through the crowd, busily selling
the candy, and Doc Holliday continued exhorting the
audience to buy, Debra said in an undertone to Lena,
''Stony says that these shows are able to buy the candy so
cheaply that they make close to a hundred percent profit,
even after giving away a few prizes. Some medicine shows
sell cheap soap to start off, instead of candy, but no matter
what is sold, it's a cheap item. The philosophy is, a small,
inexpensive item will loosen the customers up, prepare
them for the higher price of the medicinal concoctions sold
later.''

After the pitchmen had passed through the crowd twice,
Doc Holliday asked everyone to open their candy boxes
and look for the prize coupons. In a short while, the
winners had claimed their prizes, and the crowd settled
down again, as Holliday motioned for quiet. ''Now, friends
and neighbors, prepare yourself to be mystified and
entertained by Madame Bella!''

With a flourish of music from the banjo, a woman
emerged from behind the curtain. She was dressed as a
gypsy, in a colorful costume. After a moment Lena recognized her as the woman who had sung earlier—Little
Susie.

''Ladies and gentlemen, Madame Bella is going to
astound you as she reads your mind! The men will pass
among you with a box of ordinary envelopes. Any one of
you who has a question about his or her life, select an
envelope, any envelope you wish, then write your question
on a slip of paper you will find in the box. Next, carefully
seal your question in the envelope.

''It will then be given to Madame Bella, who will place
the envelope unopened into the spirit cabinet. Later, she

will remove the envelope from the cabinet, press it to her forehead, and the spirits will aid her in reading the mind of the person who wrote the question. Madame Bella will be able to answer your question, then return the envelope still sealed . . .''

Debra whispered in Lena's ear, "But just before Madame Bella places the envelope in the spirit cabinet, she will rub a sponge dipped in alcohol across it. The alcohol will make the envelope transparent for a few seconds, long enough for Madame Bella to read the question, and dream up some kind of an answer."

Lena whispered back, "I suppose Stony told you how that is done, also?"

Debra had the grace to blush. "Well, yes. How he finds out these things I really don't know." She hastened to add, "He didn't feel that she was doing anything illegal, unethical perhaps, but nothing against the law, since no money changes hands. It's a mind-reading act, performed strictly for entertainment."

After Madame Bella was finished, Lena noticed that the audience seemed properly impressed by the mind-reading performance, and were placed in a more receptive frame of mind for the next item on the agenda.

Holliday, alone now on the stage wagon, held aloft a dark brown bottle. "Friends and neighbors, you see here in my hand a bottle of Doc Holliday's Elixir of Life. But before I tell you of its marvelous healing powers, let me tell you this." He drew the revolver and pointed it over the heads of the crowd, his face solemn. "Friends, hear me well! If I had a child and that precious child should fall deathly sick, and a man came to my town selling medicine, and I bought a bottle of it for my sick little one, and I found that he had lied to me, my friends, he would have to run for his life!" He flourished the revolver. "He would have to run, for I would shoot him down in the street like a mad dog. On the other hand, this bottle, Doc Holliday's Elixir of Life, is not a cure-all.

"No, sir, neighbors, this is nature's own medicine, gathered from the fields and the forests. It is made entirely from roots, gums, leaves, herbs, berries, and other elements of old Mother Nature. Buy a bottle and take it home, my friends. I will let you have it for a dollar a bottle, two bottles for a dollar and fifty cents! It will cleanse and purify your blood, it will calm your stomach and quiet your nerves. It will bring new life and vitality to your system. If my Elixir does not cure you, prepare to meet your Maker, for you're bound to die!''

Lena laughed. "He doesn't promise to cure? It seems to me he's promising to cure just about anything."

"But nothing specific, you see," Debra said. "He's not promising to cure any particular thing. Stony says that his Elixir is about sixty percent alcohol, so whoever takes it will feel good, at least for a time."

The two pitchmen were sent out into the audience with trays loaded with Doc Holliday's Elixir of Life, while Holliday paraded up and down the plank runway, exhorting the crowd. The pitchmen were doing a brisk business.

As a man and a woman got up from a bench and started to leave, Doc Holliday pointed a finger at them. "Hold there, neighbor! The evening's entertainment is far from over! After we have passed among you one more time, there will be a half hour of rib-tickling show, free for one and all. You do not have to buy my Elixir to remain, although your health will greatly benefit from it. My word on that, friends and neighbors!''

Lena and Debra did not stay for all of the final half hour of "rib-tickling show," for it was soon evident that Stony had been right. The after-piece was a skit with three performers: the Little Susie character seen earlier, the straight man, and Jake, the blackface comedian. Jake wore a comic tramp costume: huge "slap" shoes, gigantic trousers held up by extra elastic suspenders which made the comedian's breeches billow and bounce with every step, and a shirt of violent pink and green stripes. Jake was the butt of racially oriented jokes during the skit, as Stony had warned.

Debra said in a low voice, "Shall we go, Lena? I never could see the point of such humor."

Lena nodded, and they worked their way out of the crowd, heading for home. Lena said thoughtfully, "You know something, Debra Lee? Those plays that Grandmother wrote, they're something like that skit we just saw, without the blackface comedian, of course. But in his place she used the country bumpkin, and she wrote for laughs in much the same manner. Do you think she got the ideas from medicine shows?''

Debra shrugged. "I suppose it's possible. Medicine shows go way back. Oh, they've been changing over the years, but they've been around a long time, in one form or another.''

Lena was silent now, but her mind was busy, as she walked along beside her sister. Although she fully realized that the show they had just seen was sheer mountebankery, there was something about it that intrigued her. Even as clumsily done as some of the acts had been, the performers had held the audience enthralled. How exciting it must be to be able to do that, she thought; and it would be even more exciting to be really good at it.

Michael was humming to himself as the buggy rolled along the river road toward Nacogdoches. It was late Sunday afternoon, and he was due at the Lieberman's for Sunday dinner. Lena had been staying with Debra for a week, and Michael had promised to come for her today.

As the horse approached a sharp curve, Michael pulled back slightly on the reins. "Slow it down a little, okay? Easy does it, easy does it.''

It wasn't until then that he realized he had been humming. He was coming out of his shell now, he was happy here. Under Bandy's demanding tutelage this past week, he was even beginning to ride reasonably well.

"At least you haven't fallen off all week," Bandy had said with a grin. "Has to be considered progress.''

As the buggy rounded the curve, Michael loosened his grip on the reins, allowing the horse to pick up his stride again. The buggy went along the road at a fast clip, dust spinning out behind the wheels.

He was getting close to Nacogdoches now, about two more miles, he judged. And up ahead, on the right, he saw a figure walking alongside the road. It was a woman, carrying her shoes in one hand, bare feet sending up puffs of dust.

"Whoa!" Michael sawed back on the reins. "Hold up, now!"

He drew the buggy to a halt alongside the woman, who had stopped, turning a surprised face toward him. Michael saw that she was barely more than a girl, but quite pretty.

"Going into Nacogdoches, miss?"

She nodded mutely.

"It's still a far piece to walk. Would you like to ride on in with me?"

She hesitated before saying in a soft voice, "That would be kind of you, sir. Thank you."

She stepped to the buggy, put a foot on the step, and he leaned across to give her a hand. She sat down beside him, demurely tucking her skirts around her legs.

Michael snapped the reins, clucked to the horse. As the buggy started in motion again, he said, "I'm Michael Moraghan."

She gave him a startled look, biting her lip. "I'm Cassie Danker."

"How do you do, Cassie Danker? I'm pleased to make your acquaintance."

Her gaze clung to his face as the buggy picked up speed. After a little she said, "Didn't you hear me, Mr. Moraghan? I'm Cassie Danker. Don't you know who the Dankers are?"

"Oh, yes, I know who the Dankers are," he said dryly. "Do I ever know who the Dankers are!"

"Then I expect you'll want to stop and let me out."

"Why? If you can stand to ride with a Moraghan, I can stand to ride with a Danker. It seems to me it's about time this nonsense about an old feud is allowed to die a natural death."

# 5

Bandy gave the cinch a final tightening, and turned to give Lena a hand up into the saddle. When she was firmly settled in, he handed her the reins.

"Now you hold a tight rein, Miss Lena. This mare is too long in the tooth to be frisky. But a hoss is a funny critter." He turned his head and spat a brown stream. "Even the gentlest of them can be spooked by any little old thing. Hell, I've seen a hoss sent into a pitching fit by a grasshopper hopping across the road. Fact."

"I'll be careful, Bandy, I promise. And I want to thank you again for having patience with me, and for siding with me against Michael."

Bandy grinned. "Wasn't all that much, Miss Lena. That Michael, he worries about these critters as much as if they was his own children."

He slapped the mare lightly on the rump, and she started at a canter down toward the river road.

For the past week, when he wasn't busy with the other horses and with Michael, Bandy had been teaching Lena how to ride. It wasn't all that hard. According to Bandy, she was a natural. "Not like that brother of yours. I sometimes doubt that he'll ever be able to ride without holding on for dear life."

Lena liked Bandy, not only because she found the little man funny, a fund of outrageous yarns, but also because he was a kind man, good with horses, and very nice to her. When she had asked Michael if she could ride one of the mares, he had been against it.

"I'm training these animals for racing, Lena," he had said, "not for pleasure riding."

Bandy, overhearing, had laughed. "Now, bub, that one

old mare you've got there, she's too long in the tooth to ever race against anything faster than a chicken."

Michael had said stiffly, "She can still be used as breeding stock."

"I misdoubt any stallion would care to mount her, 'scuse me, Miss Lena. Even if that was to happen, she's too old to bear a colt. Fact."

"If that's the case, then I might as well get rid of her."

"Ain't necessary. She don't eat too much, she's company for the colts, and she's still fine for Miss Lena to ride."

In the end Michael had given in, grumbling that Lena could ride the mare, but only for a while. "Despite what Bandy says, I'll have to sell her soon. I can't afford to keep any animal around that doesn't pay its way."

The mare had a gentle, rocking-chair gait, for which Lena was grateful. She might be a natural, as Bandy claimed, but she was still uncertain in the saddle; two weeks was hardly enough time to make her an accomplished horsewoman.

It was well into June now, and the days were hot and muggy, but Lena didn't mind too much. Everything was green, and the smell of growth was in the air, a humid scent that set up strange, undefined yearnings in Lena.

After a mile's canter along the river road, the mare began to perspire lightly, a glistening of moisture on her flanks. Lena reined the animal in to a walk. The road here veered close to the river, and she could see the slow-flowing stream through the trees. As the mare rounded a curve, Lena saw another saddled horse, tethered to a pecan tree, grazing on the short grass along the riverbank.

Lena turned her own mount into the trees. Then she saw the figure of a man on the riverbank, a willow fishing pole in one hand. Smoke drifted up from a cigarette. Although she couldn't see his face, she knew who it was.

She dismounted quietly, tied off the mare, and then walked almost on tiptoe toward the man. She stopped a few feet away, pleased that she had been able to get this close without alerting him. She waited patiently, waited until the pole gave a sudden jerk, then called out loudly, "Mr. Moraghan, I do believe you have a bite!"

Mark jumped violently, looking back over his shoulder, mouth agape. In so doing, the pole fell out of his hands. "Dammit!" He made a lunge for the pole, but the fish on the other end had the bait in its mouth, and the pole was moving rapidly away. In a moment it was gone, disappearing into the water. Mark sat back, his shoulders slumped.

"Now we're even, *cousin*," she said in satisfaction.

Mark got to his feet, turning with a slow smile. "Oh, I don't know. I think I still have the best of the bargain. After all, what the hell's a fish, in comparison?"

Lena felt her face grow hot, and was furious with herself. "I thought you'd be gone by now. Everybody says you never stay around more than a week or so."

He took a cigarette from his pocket and lit it. "I decided I'd stay around longer this time."

"Why? Why is it different this time?"

"Can't you guess?" He came toward her, dark eyes intent, face quite serious. "I want to get to know you better, cousin."

He touched her cheek with the back of his hand, only the briefest of contacts, yet it was enough to start Lena's heart to hammering. "It may not take long. There's not all that much to know about me." She tried to control the tremble in her voice, but was unsuccessful.

"Maybe, maybe not. We'll see." The smile was back now, the serious moment gone as if it had never happened.

Lena felt that she had to get away from the threatening intimacy of the moment. She said, "Well, I was just riding by and saw the horse, then saw you, and thought I'd say hello. I'd better be on my way."

"I'll ride along with you for a piece. You've seen to it that I've lost my fishing pole, so there's no reason for me to stay here. If you don't mind, cousin?"

Lena did mind—she was frightened by the riot of bewildering emotions that raged through her every time she was in his presence. But she certainly could not tell him that. She pretended indifference. "Why should I mind?"

In a short while they were riding at a trot along the river road. After a couple of miles Mark pulled up, and Lena reined the mare in alongside his pinto. They rode along at a walk now.

Lena said, "Debra Lee said that you come and go, Mark, that you left home the first time at eighteen. Where do you go? And why?"

He was silent for a little, smoking. She stole a glance at his face. He was staring straight ahead.

Without looking at her, he said, "I could say that it's none of your business, but I won't, since I know you'll be hearing about me from all sides. As to where I go, anywhere and everywhere. I've been in most of the states in the Union, and I've traveled to Mexico, the Hawaiian Islands, and the Orient. On those trips I work as a deckhand on freighters. On my next trip I'm thinking of going to Europe. I've never been there. As to why, that's harder to answer."

He shifted in the saddle, thumbing the cigarette into the dust of the road ahead of them. "It's interesting, seeing other countries for the first time, other people and their customs, but that's hardly an answer. I know that in time I'll become bored, and every place will seem the same. The first time I left home, I was disgusted with Daddy and the things he was doing. We never did get along. But then after he died, I kept it up. It had become sort of a habit. There doesn't seem to be anything here for me, you see? Each time I come back I think I may settle down, but I never do. It isn't long before I become restless again, and take off."

"Have you ever thought of getting married?" She had blurted the question without thinking.

He laughed abruptly, glancing at her. "No, cousin, I haven't. The woman's eternal answer to a man's problems. Get married, settle down."

She said defensively, "Well, if you had a family, responsibilities, you would *have* to settle down."

"Not necessarily. Many men with families and responsibilities find them too much of a burden, and take off anyway."

"A man who would do that isn't much of a man."

"Maybe, maybe not. It all depends on the viewpoint.

But to answer your question a little more definitely, no, Lena, I haven't considered marriage, not really, and for one simple reason. I've never met a woman I would consider living with for the rest of my life.'' His voice turned sour. "And even if I did find one, how would I support her? Daddy saw to that. He wasted Moraghan, there's nothing left. I have nothing to offer a woman.''

"That sounds an awful lot like self-pity, Mark. You can always get a job. Other men do.''

"A job doing what? Digging ditches? That's about all I could find around here.''

"Even so, if a woman loved you, she wouldn't mind.''

Mark reached across between them to take her hand. "Love conquers all, is that it, cousin?''

She snatched her hand away. "Why do you have to mock everything, Mark?'' She drummed her heels, and the mare jumped ahead, breaking into a gallop.

In a moment Lena heard hoofbeats, and Mark's mount moved up alongside her. He reached across to catch the mare's reins, and pulled the animal to a halt.

"I am sorry, Lena. I didn't mean to mock you, not really. I suppose it's a habit I've built up over the past few years. I can't help myself sometimes. If you will forgive me, I will try my damnedest to curb my tongue in the future. All right?''

Michael leaned on the railing fence, watching Bandy put one of the stallions through its paces in the meadow. He was gradually coming to realize how fortunate he was to have Bandy working with the horses. The little man had endless patience with them, and his knowledge of horses was close to incredible. He had completely taken over the training of the race horses, and yet he still found time to tutor Michael in the finer points of riding. There was a county fair scheduled two weeks hence over in Palo Pinto County, and the program included horse races. Michael planned to enter two of his horses in the races. He and Bandy were leaving in a week...

"Mr. Moraghan?'' a voice said softly.

Michael turned to see Cassie Danker standing behind

him, a sway-backed mule beside her. At his glance she colored and looked down shyly.

"Well, hello!" Michael moved toward her. "Cassie, isn't it? Cassie Danker?"

She took a step back, then seemed to brace herself, her chin coming up. "Yes, Mr. Moraghan."

"Please." Michael gestured. "My father is Mr. Moraghan. I'm Michael."

She blushed again, her gaze skittering away. "I was riding out this way, and I . . ." She took a deep breath, small breasts thrusting at him. "Bud, he keeps making threats. I don't know whether he means them, but it's—" Her voice became a plaintive cry. "It's not right! I know how angry Bud would be at me, but I had to warn you."

"Thank you, Cassie," Michael said gently. "I know how much pain it must cause you, to do this, and I appreciate it. Let's hope that it comes to naught, his threats, because I certainly agree with you. It's all wrong, that old feud."

Now she looked at him fully, her eyes like those of a frightened doe. "Maybe you wouldn't tell about me riding into town with you last Sunday? Or about my being here today?" Her voice caught. "If Bud finds out, he will be furious with me."

"It will be our secret, if that's the way you want it. But it seems to me you're old enough to choose your own friends. And I would like to be your friend, Cassie, if you will have me."

Her face lit up momentarily, then darkened again. "You don't know Bud. He loses his head when it comes to the Moraghans, and if he learns that we're friends, he might go around the bend."

Michael frowned. "You're afraid of him, aren't you?"

She nodded mutely.

"You're afraid he might beat up on you?"

"If he gets mad enough."

"If he ever does that," he said harshly, "you let me know, hear?"

She shook her head violently, her hair whipping back and forth across her face. "No, no, that would only make it worse—'' She stopped at the sound of approaching footsteps, and turned.

Lena came around the corner of the barn, slowing when she saw Cassie. At the sight of her, Cassie let out a small cry, jumped on the mule, heels drumming. The mule bolted into an awkward gallop, rounding the barn and out of sight.

Lena said, ''Do you know who that is? Cassie Danker!''

''I know who it is, sis,'' Michael said crossly. ''I gave her a ride in to town last Sunday.''

''Daddy warned us to have nothing to do with the Dankers. I heard her brother threaten us at Grandmother's funeral.''

''That was her brother, not Cassie. For God's sake, Lena, what harm can a slip of a girl like that do to us? She hates that old feud, she just told me so.''

''Still, she's a Danker. Why are you defending her so?'' Lena peered at him. ''You're not sweet on her, are you? A Danker?''

Michael felt heat touch his face. ''What if I am? It's my affair!''

''But a Danker, Michael!''

''How about Mark? First cousins, no less. How do you think Daddy would look upon that?''

Her face froze in astonishment, only her eyes enormous and beginning to tear. ''What do you mean? What a terrible thing to say, Michael!''

He felt impelled toward cruelty. ''I'm not blind, sis. I've seen the way you look at him.''

Crying openly now, she started to turn away.

Swept by contrition, he caught her arm. ''I'm sorry, Lena. I don't know what made me say that. It's just that my whole life up to this point has been dictated by my family. I'm trying to free myself of that. Besides, there's nothing going on with Cassie Danker. Good God, I've only seen the girl twice in my life. A buggy ride into town, and just now.''

Lena looked into his face for a moment, biting her lower lip. With her free hand she knuckled the tears from her eyes.

"Forgive me, Lena," he said in a gentle voice. "I shouldn't have said what I did. I have no more right to criticize your personal life than anyone else."

"Do I really look at Mark that way? I didn't realize . . ."

"Forget it, sis." He shrugged. "It's probably all in my imagination."

It had never entered Lena's head that any interest she had in Mark Moraghan was anything other than that of one relative toward another, but Michael's jibe was an insidious seed that sprouted and grew. It haunted her, was in her mind constantly, and no matter how much she tried to tell herself otherwise, she knew there was some truth in it. She *was* strongly attracted to Mark. Was it because of the forbidden aspect of it? Was it because Mark was the first really attractive man she had ever known? Was it because he treated her more like a sweetheart than a cousin?

She eventually decided that it involved all of these things, to a certain degree, yet it was more than that. When Mark began to inhabit her erotic dreams at night, Lena knew that she had to find out; either that or flee like a coward back to the Valley. One thing she definitely had to know—was he attracted to her in the same way?

Her opportunity to find out came on the Fourth of July. The farmers along the river, she learned, always had a picnic on the Fourth, and she was invited as a matter of course, as were Debra Lee, Stony, and Michael. The Liebermans could not attend, and Michael would be gone that weekend, attending his first horse race at the fair in Palo Pinto County.

Lena had not seen Mark for almost two weeks, and she was afraid that he might have gone off on one of his journeys. Steeling herself for a chilly, perhaps even hostile, reception, she saddled up her mare and rode over to Mark's house.

There was an air of neglect about the place, the front yard rank with weeds, and what had once been a fine, two-story Colonial house—in Brian Moraghan's day—was now badly in need of paint. Lena tethered the mare to the picket fence and went up the steps to the broad veranda.

She raised and lowered the brass knocker, and could hear its clatter reverberating inside the house, giving off a sound of emptiness. Listening intently, she heard no sound of footsteps. After a little she banged the knocker again, louder this time. Finally she heard the shuffle of footsteps. Taking a deep breath, Lena moved back a step, composing herself. She forced a smile to her face when the door opened.

The big blond woman filled the doorway. She said sullenly, "What do you want?"

"Mrs. Moraghan? Anna Moraghan?" Lena said brightly.

Anna Moraghan shifted a little, and behind her Lena could see a slender girl, blond as the woman in the doorway, hovering like a ghost. She seemed so insubstantial that for a moment Lena had the fancy that she hovered several inches off the floor, that she was, indeed, a ghost.

The woman in the doorway spoke again. "What do you want?"

"I'm Lena, Aunt Anna—"

The big woman stiffened. "You're that Kevin's brat! Don't call me aunt, I don't claim any kin to Kevin or any of his." She gestured. "Now I'll thank you to get off my porch, and my property."

"I'm here to see Mark, not you."

"Mark! What have you to do with my Mark? You like that whore sister of yours?" Anna opened the door wider and came at Lena in a lurching gait, one huge hand upraised.

Lena, taken completely by surprise, stood rooted to the spot. Then the big woman was seized from behind, and a man's arms wrapped around her, halting her.

"All right, Ma, all right now, that's enough."

Mark held his mother for a moment, then warily let her go. Anna stood slumped now, the venom drained out of her. She said in a dead voice, "Get this slut off my property, Mark. I'm going in for that old rifle of your daddy's. If she's not gone when I come back, I'll kill her. So help me I will!"

Mark took Lena's arm and led her off the porch. "We'd better do as she says. She might not do it, but you never know with Ma these days." His tone was bitter. "Much as I hate to say it, she's not always right in the head. Let's go out to the barn. I'll saddle my horse and ride along with you for a piece."

He untied Lena's mare and started toward the barn. Lena, still shaken by the encounter with Anna Moraghan, said tremulously, "I hadn't seen you in so long, Mark, I thought you might have left again. That's one reason I rode over."

"If you'd waited another day or two, I probably would have been gone. I've been seriously thinking of it. I can only stand so much of Ma these days. Did you see Betsy standing there right behind Ma?"

"Yes, I saw her. She looked almost like . . ."

"Like a ghost, is that what you're going to say? You're right, she does. When we were growing up, Betsy was rowdy, a tomboy. I remember we all three used to play together, Debra Lee, Betsy, and me, and we played rough, I can tell you. Well, since Daddy was killed and Ma turned strange, she has managed to plant some of her own craziness in Betsy. It's gotten to the point where Betsy won't even go out of the house. And as for going out with a fellow—forget it. She's long past the point where she should be married, with a family of her own. Now, of course, she never will. What man would have a woman who has about as much life to her as a stick, who's afraid of her own shadow?"

They had reached the barn now, and Mark led the way into the dim manure stink of the interior. Lena held the mare while he went into a stall and saddled his pinto.

He was talking all the while. She couldn't recall his talking so much, and it seemed to her that it was compulsive.

"You were wondering why I take off every so often, now you know the reason. Yet I feel guilty all the while I'm gone and I have to come back, hoping, I suppose, that Ma and Betsy have changed. But it's not going to happen, I'd know that if I had any sense."

The pinto saddled, he stopped to light a cigarette before leading his mount out of the stall. "I haven't shut up since you got here, have I, cousin?" He grinned at her. "I don't

even know why you rode over, bearding the dragon's den,
so to speak."

Lena gave a start. "Oh! I'd almost forgotten the reason
myself. You know about the Fourth of July picnic?"

"I know about it," he said easily. "It's been going on
as long as I can remember. And you wanted to know if I'm
going? I really hadn't planned on it, but now that I know
you're thinking of going, cousin, I do believe I'll change
my mind."

She made a startled sound. "What are you, a mind
reader?"

"That's one of my nice traits." He came toward her. "I
would be delighted to escort you to the picnic, cousin."

Lena put together a lunch for the picnic: cold fried
chicken, German potato salad, cole slaw, cold biscuits,
plus a peach cobbler she made from a jar of canned
peaches she found in the cellar. She had a natural talent for
cooking, but she had always viewed it as a tedious chore.
However, she was happy as she rattled around the empty
house, preparing the picnic lunch. Debra Lee and her
children were in Nacogdoches for the weekend, Michael
and Bandy were halfway across the state at the fair, and
Lena was alone. She was glad to be alone, and certainly
glad that Michael wasn't there, upset about her going to
the picnic with Mark.

She had come to partial terms with her relationship with
Mark. She would wait and see what developed, at least
until she learned how he felt. Strangely enough, now that
she had worried at it for several days, a romantic attachment to her first cousin didn't strike her as all that terrible.
She suspected that women were much more practical than
men about such matters—all too many of the sexual taboos
handed down from generation to generation were initiated
by men.

Lena laughed, bringing herself up short. She was thinking like an experienced woman of the world, not like a
virgin who had never even felt a male hand caressing her.

She was waiting in the front yard, the horse hitched to

the buggy, the picnic basket in the back, when Mark rode up.

"You didn't have to do that, cousin. My not having a buggy of my own to take us to the picnic is bad enough, but at least I could have hitched it up for you."

"I wanted you to see that I'm far from just a helpless female."

"I don't know about the helpless part, but you are a woman, no arguing that." His gaze assessed her in frank admiration.

Inordinately pleased, Lena felt herself flushing. With the picnic in mind, she had bought a new outfit in Nacogdoches: a frothy silk dress in an off-color pink that swirled around her ankles like cotton candy when she walked, long white gloves, and a floppy-brimmed straw hat, and tiny white slippers that peeked coyly out from under the hem of the dress. Strangely enough, for the first time in her life she believed a compliment paid her by a man.

"You do indeed look mighty pretty, Lena. I hope you didn't hitch up the buggy wearing that outfit?"

"Oh, no, I did that before I dressed up."

"Then let's be on our way, shall we?" With a half-bow, he gave her a hand up into the buggy, then went around to get in the other side. With a flick of the reins he started the buggy down the drive toward the river road.

There was no specified time for the picnic to start, but traffic had been heavy on the river road since midmorning, and now well past noon, it was still heavy. The picnic was held every year in a wedge-shaped park, formed by a lazy U-curve in the river, on land given to the county years ago by Sean Moraghan, with the proviso that it be turned into a park. It required little maintenance, just a scything of the tall grass before any scheduled event, and a ritual, annual painting of the bandstand in the center.

Long before they reached the park, they could hear the popping of firecrackers, even the discharge of a few firearms.

"I wonder how many accidental shootings will take place this year," Mark said. "I wasn't here last year on the Fourth, but I understand that two people were wounded by stray bullets, including one bullet in the leg of a fellow who was running for the state legislature. Now that, I would say, is a good thing. If it happened more often, less politicians would show up for these things, to bore us all to death.''

"That sounds pretty cynical, Mark," she said, smiling. Without thinking, she touched his knee. "Don't you like politicians?"

"They're all windbags and bores," he retorted, casually moving his knee away. "Except maybe your brother-in-law. He's not going to be here this year?"

"No, he won't be there." She was smiling. "He said he isn't up for election this year, so why should he put himself through all that torture?" She sobered, remembering. "Actually, there's more to it than that. The doctor has quarantined them at home this weekend. Joseph has come down with the mumps, and nobody can come and go to their house but the doctor. That's why I'm all alone this week. Debra Lee isn't even allowed to come out to Moraghan."

Mark looked sidelong at her. "And Michael?"

"He and Bandy are over to the Palo Pinto County Fair. It's Michael's first horse race. When he found out I was going to be all alone, he wanted to stay home, but I talked him out of it. He's been looking forward to this race for weeks."

They rode along in silence now. Lena was too mortified to speak again immediately. What had prompted her to tell Mark that she was at Moraghan all alone? She had gone out of her way to make a point of it, and he certainly must realize that. Why had she done such a thing?

The traffic along the river road had thickened considerably, and Mark was forced to slow the buggy to a crawl as they reached the picnic area. He had to drive on past the park for a quarter mile before he could find a spot to leave the buggy and horse. Then, with Mark carrying the picnic basket, they joined the people on foot, making their way back to the park.

They were fortunate enough to find a spot under an oak tree near the edge of the river, where they could spread out the tablecloth when it was time to eat. For the moment they were content to sit back and watch and listen, Mark lazily smoking a cigarette, and Lena leaning back against the tree, legs folded up under her skirts.

A three-piece band was playing patriotic tunes in the small bandstand. Children and dogs ran about, screaming and barking. Games had already started up among the adults: potato-sack races, tugs of war between unevenly matched teams, wrestling matches.

Lena said, "Aren't you going to join in any of the games, Mark?"

"Nah, I'm not much for games—"

He was interrupted by a whiskery individual, who sidled up to squat alongside him. "Moraghan," the newcomer said in a stage whisper. "Would you like a jug of wild mustang? One dollar for a quart fruit jar full."

Mark slanted a glance at Lena. "Sure, why not, Clint? This is supposed to be a day of celebration, correct?" He took a dollar bill out of his trousers pocket and gave it to the bearded man.

With alacrity the man got to his feet and disappeared into the trees toward the main road. In a very short time he was back, his hands cuddling a bulge under his coat. He squatted beside Mark again, and Lena saw the fruit jar change hands. Mark held it out to her after the man left. It was filled to the brim with a liquid as clear as water.

"Did you ever sample wild mustang wine, Lena?"

"No, I never have. But I've heard of it. It's made from wild mustang grapes, isn't it?"

"Right. And it's potent stuff. Whoever thought of the expression 'kicks like a mule' was sure as hell thinking of wild mustang." He grinned, held out the fruit jar. "Have a snort, cousin?"

Lena hesitated briefly. She had drunk very little of anything alcoholic, not because her parents disapproved of it but simply because there was little alcohol in the Valley. No wine was made there, and what liquor was available was brought in; consequently it was quite expensive, except for the tequila brought from across the Mexican border, which Lena could never bring herself to like.

"Why not?" she said, feeling suddenly reckless. She

took the fruit jar from him, and tilting it up, took a tentative swallow. It had surprisingly little taste, and what taste there was was tart, pleasantly sour. She took another swallow, then still another.

"Whoa now! Didn't I tell you that stuff was potent?" He wrested the fruit jar from her grasp.

"Didn't do a thing for me," she said airily, and giggled.

The rest of the afternoon went by in spurts and starts, at times slowly, and at other times speeding up hilariously. The raucous games were played all around them, the band played loudly if not too well, and the parade of office-seekers spoke one after another.

Lena didn't understand a word they said. By the time she had taken her third helping of wild mustang wine, she was drunk, gloriously drunk, and everything outside of her immediate vicinity existed in a rosy haze, all sounds were muffled, and she heard only what Mark said.

Everything he said was either terribly funny or achingly sad, and she loved him wildly.

This thought popped into her head like a revelation, and it sobered her for a few moments. She watched him, his face more animated with the liquor, less bitter and less cynical, and he gestured extravagantly as he told her some tale of his travels—she didn't listen to the words, just to the sound of his voice.

The knowledge that she loved him moved her close to tears, because she knew that any love of theirs was doomed from the beginning. She reached out for the fruit jar, and was surprised to discover that it was nearly empty. She drank, and the brief spasm of melancholy passed.

"Lena . . ." She was aware of his touch on her hand, and the warmth of his breath on her cheek. "You're drunk, and I must take the blame. I should have known better than to feed you that white lightning."

"Not your fault," she mumbled. "You didn't . . . didn't pour it down me."

"I might as well have. Here, eat something. I've already put it out."

Lena ate hungrily, the wine had made her ravenous. But the food did little to alleviate her intoxicated condition, it only succeeded in making her sleepy. The next thing she knew she was being shaken awake, and helped to her feet.

"Let's go home, Lena. You don't have far to walk, I managed to drive the buggy up close. Can you make it?"

She blinked around. It had gotten dark awfully sudden, she thought. There were still many people in the park, and the band was still playing. Torches flickered here and there like enormous fireflies. As Mark supported her toward the buggy, a gunshot sounded off to the right, and Lena flinched, crying out in alarm.

In the buggy, on the way back to Moraghan, she slept again, her head on Mark's shoulder. He kept the buggy at a slow pace, and except for a couple of times when a wheel rolled over a bump in the road, she wasn't jostled.

Then he was shaking her gently. "Wake up, Lena. We're here. Hang on until I can come around and help you down."

She sat up, half-asleep, until he came around the buggy and helped her to the ground. She tried to stand upright, and sagged against him. He laughed, deep in his throat, and scooped her up in his arms and started toward the house.

One arm around his neck, she spoke against his throat, "I'm awful, Mark. I'm sorry. I'll never drink again, I swear."

"Famous last words. How many times have I said that?" He was laughing. "Cousin, it's all a part of growing up, getting drunk at least once. 'Course, I suppose that's more true of boys than girls."

They were inside the house now. "Which one is your bedroom?"

A faint note of alarm sounded in Lena's mind. She refused to listen to it. "The last door on the left down the hall."

He had to put her down to light a wall lamp, and didn't pick her up again. Instead they made their way down the hall with Lena leaning against him. He fumbled the door open, and started to light the lamp just inside the room.

"No," she murmured. "Don't light it. Just leave the door open."

First she had let him know that she was in the house all alone, now she had just given him a more blatant invitation. Even in her befuddled state, Lena was aware of what she was doing; and she couldn't use her condition later to excuse what she knew was about to happen.

Mark helped her to the bed. She sat on the edge of it while he removed her shoes. Still kneeling before her, he looked up, his face a barely recognizable blur in the dim light coming in from the hall. "Are you all right, Lena? You're not going to be sick, or anything?"

"No, I don't think so," she said weakly.

"Do you want me to . . .? He motioned, indicating her clothes.

"Yes, please," she whispered. "If you would be so kind."

She lay back on the bed, and he removed her stockings with trembling fingers. Lena turned on her side while he unbuttoned the row of buttons running down the back of the dress. Feeling almost boneless, she sat up while he removed the dress.

He stood up, and became a bulking shadow with the light behind him. "There, you can sleep now."

"The rest? Please, Mark?" A part of her was appalled at the brazenness of her behavior. And when he did not respond at once, she said, "Mark?"

A gusty sigh came from him. "Jesus, Lena! Do you know what you're asking of me? I'm flesh and blood, you know."

"I know, Mark, but it's all right, really it is."

Then she felt his hands on her, quickly stripping away the rest of her garments. His mouth was on her breasts, caressing the nipples, and a sweet agony seized her. The nipples became taut and full, aching with need. His knuckles brushed across the juncture of her thighs, and Lena arched off the bed, groaning.

"Ah, Lena, Lena!"

His hands and lips left her, and she moaned, bereft. She raised her head and felt immense relief when she saw that he was still in the room, removing his clothing. Lena had never seen a naked man, and her curiosity demanded that she look. There was enough light in the room to show her that Mark was slender and more symmetrical than she had thought a man would be. She had also thought that a naked man would be inordinately hairy, but this was not true of Mark—he seemed almost hairless.

And then he turned, and she sucked in her breath as she saw the proud thrust of his aroused organ. Often she had daydreamed of this moment with a man, yet she had never gotten beyond this point in her dreams, oddly enough, and questions tumbled through her mind. She was a virgin. Would the pain be too intense? More importantly, would she be able to accommodate that swollen part of him?

He was on the bed beside her, his mouth on hers. At the touch of his manhood on her inner thigh, a weakness invaded Lena's loins, and her legs yawned open for him, and there was very little pain, and she had no difficulty taking his hardness into her.

It was everything she had imagined it would be. In those few timeless moments, as her body strove toward completion, there was no feeling of guilt, only a yearning for the sparks of sensation throughout her body to coalesce, come together in the very core of her being.

Her hands stroked his supple back, glorying in the rippling strength of the muscles there. She had always feared that her ignorance would show when this moment came, but an ageless instinct took over, and her body knew intuitively what to do.

Her heart was hammering furiously now, and she could feel the ultimate ecstasy gathering in her. And then it happened—a sunburst of rapture that wrung a sharp cry from her. Almost at once a mighty shudder took Mark, and he groaned aloud.

"Yes, dear Mark, yes!"

She arched her hips, making a bridge holding him off the bed, holding him inside her until his final tremor of passion had receded. Then she sighed, and slowly eased back down onto the bed.

The combination of the potent wine and the abrupt release of sexual tension sent her into a state of relaxation close to swooning.

She felt his fingers stroking her cheek, and heard his stricken voice saying, "I'm sorry, Lena. Jesus, I *am* sorry!"

She murmured, "Don't be, Mark. There's nothing to be sorry for. It happened, we both wanted it to happen..."

And then she was asleep.

When she awoke, Mark was gone. She fumbled across the bed, and experienced a sense of desolation at his absence.

She lay still, assessing how she felt. There were some twinges of guilt, but she doubted that any guilt she felt was stronger than she would have felt in any case. After all, she had been a virgin, and unmarried, and she well knew that sexual relations between unmarrieds was considered taboo by her elders. At least for the women. It seemed to Lena, even as inexperienced as she was, that it was not considered so for men. To attain an unchaste state as soon as possible, and by any means possible, was to be desired by the male.

Had the flavor of the forbidden made it more enjoyable? She would have liked to believe otherwise, but she was honest enough with herself to realize that the forbidden aspects *had* added spice to it.

She suspected the contrary with Mark, suspected that he had left her bed laden with guilt, and her suspicions were borne out three days later when she received a letter from him, postmarked Nacogdoches.

She opened it with trembling fingers, and read the single sheet with mounting dismay:

Dear Cousin,

There is nothing that I can say to you that will ease the guilt that I feel, and I do not dare beg your forgiveness, for what I did was unforgivable.

I seduced you, my own cousin, and that is incest, a powerful taboo recognized as so by people in general, and religion in particular. I am not very religious, so that part does not concern me. But we would stand in disgrace should any of our relations learn of this, or other people in general. My own disgrace does not bother me too much, since I can always escape to where I am not known. But you, dear cousin, being a woman, cannot do so so easily. Be assured that no one shall ever learn of this from my lips, and I am sure that you are so mortified by what I did that you will never tell.

I cannot even plead drunkenness as an excuse for my behavior, since I was not so intoxicated that I did not know what I was doing. Perhaps in time you may see your way clear to forgive me. I can only hope that that time will come.

Meanwhile, I am once again taking the coward's way out, by absenting myself from East Texas. This time I intend to remain away for a longer period of time. When I do return I sincerely hope that you are married to a good man that you so richly deserve, and are happy. You must know that I still respect you, and blame myself totally for what happened.

> Yrs. respectfully,
> Cousin Mark

Foolish, foolish man!

Angrily she crumpled the letter up and threw it across the room. But in a few minutes she was up and searching for the wad of paper. As she smoothed it out and began to read it again, she noticed that it was daylight.

As Lena finished the letter, a thought came to her, something that she had been told would occur. She hastened to the bed, and threw back the top sheet. Yes, there it was. The bottom sheet was blood-spotted.

Hastily, she stripped the bed. Debra Lee and her children were coming back to Moraghan soon, perhaps today. She had to change the linen on the bed and wash out the blood, before Debra Lee happened across it.

# 6

Michael was ecstatic. He had entered two horses in two races at the fair, and had won one. In the second race he had come in third, which wasn't all that bad, either.

But the knowledge that he had won, actually *won* a race, was the best news he could possibly have had. The purse had been small, scarcely more than enough to pay his and Bandy's expenses, and the entrance fees, but Michael had proven to himself that not only were his horses worthy of being raced but he was capable of bringing home a winner.

"Don't get too carried away, bub," Bandy said disparagingly. "I've seen better critters than that bunch of nags you raced against lined up in slaughterhouses, due to become dog meat. Fact."

Bandy's pessimism didn't dampen Michael's spirits. Besides, he knew Bandy well enough by now to know that the little man had an ingrained superstition—"Don't pay to look on the bright side too much. Man can go blind that way."

When their little band of horses and the buggy reached Moraghan, Lena and Debra Lee, and Debra Lee's two children, came out to the barn to meet them.

Michael leaped down from the buggy and scooped Lena up in his arms and danced her around. "I won a race, sis! I won!"

"Put me down, you idiot!" Laughing, Lena pounded on his shoulders. "So you won a race, is that any reason to go crazy?"

Stung, he said, "I think it is, yes." He set her on her feet. "I should think you'd be glad for me."

"I am, Michael, I'm happy for you. Michael . . . a letter

75

came from Daddy while you were away. He wants to know when we're coming home. He says it's been over a month, and he wants to know when you're going to sell the horses and come home."

He said slowly, "I'm not going back down there, Lena. Not ever. And I'm not selling the horses. Especially not now that I've had my first winner."

"But Daddy has title to the horses, Michael."

"I know, and I'll just have to convince him not to sell them. You can help me, sis. Will you?" He took her hand. "We'll both write him a letter, telling him that I can make the Moraghan racing stable pay."

"Racing stable?" She started to smile, then sobered. "All right, Michael. I'll make a bargain. I don't want to go back, either. So if you'll help me, I'll help you."

He studied her intently. "I'll do what I can, Lena, but I don't know how much good it'll do. What if we can't talk him into letting you stay? What then?"

"What will *you* do?"

"Oh, I'll be staying anyway. If not on Moraghan, then somewhere else."

"It's the same with me. I'm staying, too."

"It's not quite the same, Lena. I'm a man, and you're not even twenty-one yet."

Her head went back in defiance. "It doesn't matter. I'm old enough to know my own mind."

Debra cried, "Stop it, you two! Will you just listen to what you're saying? You're not giving a single thought to Mother and Daddy."

Michael said, "Did you, Debra Lee?"

Debra winced. "I know, I deserved that. But the circumstances *were* slightly different. And you two were still left at home when I ran away. Now, they'll have nobody."

"Debra Lee," Michael said gently, "this may sound harsh and uncaring, but I do have my own life to lead."

"Well, so do I!" Lena cried.

He nodded reluctantly. "Yes, Lena, you do, although I still think you're a trifle young to be making a decision like this."

Debra threw up her hands. "Do what you like, the pair of you. Just don't make me a part of it."

Michael was strangely restless after the horses had been taken care of. He needed someone to talk to, someone who would be pleased to hear of his triumph, minor though it might be. Clearly his sisters weren't particularly interested.

Finally he hooked up a fresh horse to the buggy and headed for Nacogdoches. It was still early—they had camped last night only three hours from home—so he reached Nacogdoches in late afternoon. Cassie Danker had told him that she did housework for a banker's family in town on Thursdays, and this was a Thursday.

He was lucky—as he drove the buggy down the tree-lined street past the banker's house, he saw Cassie trudging up the street two blocks away.

He stopped the buggy beside her. "How about a ride, lady?"

She glanced around and her tired face lit up momentarily. Then fear shadowed her eyes, and she looked about worriedly. "I don't think it would be wise, Mr. Moraghan. If Bud was to find out—"

"Cassie," he said in annoyance, "you can't live in dread of your brother forever. Come on, hop in."

She hesitated for a moment more, and then with that defiant set of her chin he was becoming familiar with, she climbed up onto the seat beside him.

Michael started the horse moving. "Cassie, have supper with me. There's a little café on the road east of town. I've eaten there once. It has the best fried chicken I think I've ever eaten. How about it? Nobody will know us out there, if that's bothering you."

"Mr. Moraghan—"

"Dammit, Michael!" He struck his knee with his fist. "Please, Cassie, will you call me Michael?"

"It don't . . . it doesn't sound right." She refused to look at him.

"It sounds better than mister, believe me."

"All right . . . Michael."

"There! That didn't hurt too much, now did it?" He

took her hand and squeezed. "Tell me, have you been by Moraghan recently?"

"Not since the one time I was there. I was afraid Bud would find out."

"The reason I asked, I've been gone almost two weeks. I took some horses over to the Palo Pinto County Fair. Cassie." He could contain his jubilation no longer. "I won my first race, and came in third in another!"

"I'm glad, Michael. That must have made you happy."

He stole a glance at her, and saw that she was smiling at him, a smile clearly genuine. "It did, it made me about as happy as I've ever been." He remembered May Beth and fell silent, recalling the happiness he had experienced during their brief time together.

"What is it, Michael? What's wrong? You look like a cloud just passed over your face."

"I was thinking of my wife," he said in a low voice. "She's dead, you know. I was thinking how happy she would have been for me. You know something?" He brightened. "I somehow knew you'd also share my happiness, that's the reason I came looking for you, as silly as that probably sounds. My sisters, they couldn't care less."

"I don't think it's silly at all," she said softly. "I'm glad you came looking."

"Somehow I knew you would be."

"Tell me all about it, Michael."

On the way to the restaurant he told her about it, how it felt to be a winner, how it felt to be out in front of the pack, and not following along in his father's footsteps.

It was not yet dark when they passed through the center of town, and neither of them saw a man staggering out of a saloon to stand gaping after them. The man muttered under his breath, "Cassie? Cassie and a Moraghan? I must've drunk more of that rotgut than I thought. Must be seeing things."

By the time they reached the eating place, they were at ease with one another, and Michael was especially pleased that Cassie was not as wary of him as she had been on the other two occasions. She was relaxed, natural, and even took his arm as they started into the restaurant.

Just on the threshold of the restaurant she suddenly held back, her face registering dismay. "This all happened so quickly, I forgot. Michael, I've been cleaning house all day. My dress is dirty, and I'm badly in need of a wash."

"No excuses now." He tightened his grip on her arm. "You look fine, Cassie. They have a washroom here, you can wash up before we eat."

She whispered, "I never realized this was . . . I've never eaten in such a fine eating place."

"Then it's high time you did. Come along."

Cassie made Michael let her off a quarter mile from the house. "I don't want to risk Bud seeing us together."

She saw Michael's lips set stubbornly. "I think he should know, Cassie. I want us to do this again, if you're willing. We can't sneak around like a couple of criminals."

"Please, Michael. Not just yet. And I would like to do it again, if you want. I enjoyed myself and it was a great supper."

Facing him, she held herself poised for just a moment, wondering if he would try to kiss her. On the few dates she'd had with boys they were all over her the minute they could get her alone, but she was accustomed to that—she was Cassie Danker, after all. However, it was different with Michael, he was too much of a gentleman to try something like that.

And he didn't. He got out of the buggy without touching her, and came around to the other side to give her a hand down. Perhaps he would kiss her now? Again, he didn't. He took her hand, pressed it, and said, "I had a grand time as well, Cassie. And I do want to see you again."

Despite the fact that this proved that he didn't consider her trash to be mauled at will, Cassie felt a pang of disappointment as the buggy whipped away. It would have been nice if he had kissed her good night, she thought wistfully.

She turned and walked down the rutted lane toward the house. She felt good about herself. It was the first time a man had ever taken her to supper in a nice place, the first time a *decent* man had ever taken her out, just for the pleasure of her company. And a Moraghan!

She hugged herself in delight, scarcely able to believe it.

She walked on toward the house. There was only a dim light on in the kitchen, which was a relief, since it probably meant that Bud was not home. As late as she was, he would be sure to question her if he had been home.

She unlocked the front door and started down the short hall.

As she passed the open door to the sitting room, a voice lashed at her out of the dark, "Cassie! Come in here!"

She hesitated, rebellious. It was Bud's voice, and he was upset with her, and he had no right to be, no right at all! She was entitled to her personal life.

With a sigh she went into the sitting room just as a lamp flamed weakly. The room stank of whiskey. Bud stood up from the worn divan, his shadow elongated and menacing in the lamplight. "Where have you been? You should have been home hours ago, Cassie."

For just a second she toyed with the thought of telling him the truth, but she knew it would be a grievous mistake. She improvised, "I met Maude Dorn on my way home, and she asked me to stop off and have supper with her—"

"You're lying, Cassie!"

Before she had time to dodge, his fist came at her out of the gloom, striking her alongside the cheek. The blow knocked her back against the wall, and she slid limply to the floor. Her head rang, and she could taste the brassy flavor of her own blood in her mouth.

He loomed over her, glaring down. "Bobbie Dean came by a couple of hours ago. He said he saw you in a buggy with that Michael Moraghan, going east out of town. Is that true, Cassie? Now don't lie to me again or I'll—"

"Yes! Yes, I was with Michael!" She was yelling suddenly, filled with a fury such as she had never known. "I'm my own person, you can't tell me what to do!"

He reached down, caught her by the arm, and yanked her cruelly upright, holding her against the wall. "I can't tell you what to do, is that it?" His breath was rank with cheap whiskey.

"No, you can't! You can beat up on me all you want, but I'm going my own way from now on, and there's nothing you can do, Bud! When you're like this, you're sick in your mind.''

"Nothing I can do about it, huh?" he said darkly.

The one hand still holding her, he shook her violently, the other drawn back. Then he said in disgust, "Aw-w, you're not worth the strength. But I'll show you what I can do about it, Cassie."

He let her go, turned, and left the room. In a moment Cassie heard the front door slam. She was dizzy now and stood swaying.

"Cassie? Is that you, girl?"

"Yes, Momma, it's me." With an effort she forced herself to stand erect as her mother shuffled into the room, wearing an ancient, tattered bathrobe, her gray hair wild and uncombed, her face puffy with sleep.

In a whining voice Sue Anne Danker said, "How can a person sleep with all the shouting? Did I hear Bud yelling in here? If he keeps it up, I'll have to tell his daddy on him."

"Momma, Daddy's no longer with us. He's been dead for ten years," Cassie said wearily.

"Tod's dead?" Sue Anne Danker said querulously. "Why wasn't I told?"

"Come on, Momma. Let's go back to bed now."

With gentle hands Cassie took her mother's arm and led her from the room.


Bud Danker was almost insensate with rage when he bolted from the house. How could Cassie betray him like this? For years, since his daddy's murder, Bud had tried to instill hatred for the Moraghans into the minds of his brothers and sisters. They had all finally left him, scattered all over Texas, and were mostly indifferent to the Moraghans. Only Cassie had remained behind, and Bud had thought she shared his hate for the Moraghans. Now it seemed that he had been wrong all along.

But how could she go so far as to go for a buggy ride with a Moraghan? To be seen in public with one? His face twisted in agony, and he paused on his way to the barn in back of the house, bending over to retch.

Finally he straightened up and staggered on to the barn. He'd drunk too much of the rotgut Bobbie Dean had brought him, while waiting for Cassie to sneak home, and now he was weak and sweaty.

He made it into the barn, and climbed up the rickety ladder to the loft. In one corner, hidden under a pile of moldy hay, was a trunk. Bud put his key into the padlock and opened the trunk.

He struck a match and lit the lantern he kept up here. Holding the lantern high, he dug into the trunk, reaching down under the pile of clothes. Everything in the trunk had belonged to Tod Danker—clothes that he had worn, and other mementos, including the Colt and gunbelt that Bud now took out.

He stared at it, running his hand lovingly over the blued steel of the barrel. He never let a week go by that he didn't take the gun out of the trunk and polish it.

Bud would never forget that day ten years ago. He'd been fifteen at the time, and on his way downtown to visit with his daddy, in the sheriff's office. He was button-busting proud of his daddy. To think that a Danker could become a sheriff! Bud made it a habit of visiting almost every day.

On this day he knew something was wrong the minute he rounded the corner and saw the crowd gathered before the jail building. Bud began to run, and was breathless, his heart pounding with dread, by the time he reached the edge of the crowd. He wormed his way through, pushing people aside without apology.

He finally made it to the door of his daddy's office, and found his way barred by one of his daddy's deputies. "I don't think you should go in there, Bud."

"It's my daddy, ain't it? Something's happened to him, I know it has! I have a right to go to him! Let me past!"

"I reckon you do have that right, Bud." The potbellied deputy stepped aside, and Bud brushed past him.

In the office he found his daddy on the floor behind his desk, and several men milling about, among them Kevin Moraghan and Stonewall Lieberman. Bud rushed past them to crouch by his dead father. After he was recognized, he was left alone. He heard enough to know that

Kevin Moraghan had killed his daddy. Tod Danker had always railed against the Moraghans, but Bud had paid little heed. Now he saw with stark clarity that his father had been right—the Moraghans were their mortal enemies. In that moment Bud swore to himself that he would somehow pay the Moraghan clan back for his father's death.

Soon, Stonewall Lieberman and Kevin Moraghan left, and two men came for the body of Tod Danker. While no one was watching, Bud had removed his father's gunbelt, gently pried his father's fingers loose from the Colt, and wrapped gun and gunbelt in his coat, placing it to one side.

"We have to take your daddy now, sonny," one of the men said gently.

Bud turned a tear-streaked face up to him, nodded, scooped up the bundle his coat and the gun made, and stood back against the wall.

The men who took the body away took no notice of the fact that the sheriff's weapon was missing, and by the time notice was taken, Bud already had it hidden away in the house. He was questioned about it, but he lied steadfastly, denying any knowledge of the missing gun. Since the matter wasn't all that urgent—there had been three witnesses to the fact that Tod Danker had been armed and had drawn his weapon—it was not pursued further, and Bud had the gun.

Since that day, when he could spare the money for ammunition, he would ride out into the country and practice. He never let anyone in on his secret, and his practice was always solitary, without supervision. Even after all these years of practice, he still wasn't very good. At fifty feet he could hit an empty whiskey bottle about one out of three shots.

But a man was larger than a whiskey bottle, and in Bud's estimation, he could kill Michael Moraghan if he could get as close as fifty feet to him.

He sat huddled against the trunk, caressing the barrel of the Colt, bloody images in his mind: Michael Moraghan spouting his life's blood; Michael Moraghan dying on the ground, pleading for mercy; and he, Bud Danker, putting him out of his misery with a bullet between the eyes, as he would a horse with a broken leg. Or maybe he wouldn't show mercy, maybe he would just squat by the man and watch him die. He had no thought of snuffing out Moraghan's life with one shot; he had to suffer for what he had done.

Bud finally climbed down out of the loft, the gunbelt strapped around his waist. He saddled one of the mules and rode out, rode east toward Moraghan. It was long after midnight by the time he reached his destination. There was a quarter moon, and it was a cloudless night, so he could see fairly well. He tied the mule off in the grove of trees about a half-mile from the house, and then crept into the barn. A horse snorted softly, and Bud froze, hand gripping the butt of the Colt. When he heard no sounds of alarm, he slowly relaxed, and sneaked down to the end of the barn, where he found a pile of hay. He squirmed down into the hay, making himself comfortable. He had heard that Michael Moraghan was training his horses to race, so he would be out to the stable before sunrise to exercise his animals. Bud intended to be ready for him. The barn door was less than thirty feet away, and the moment Moraghan stepped through that door, he was a dead man. Bud realized now that his fantasy of Moraghan dying slowly was not feasible. There were other people in the house, and a gunshot would alert them. No, if he was to get away, Bud knew that he had to kill Moraghan with the first shot.

He settled himself in, determined to remain awake and alert. But the combination of a lot of alcohol and the long ride out here proved too much. He nodded, dozing, jerking awake from time to time, and then he was sound asleep.

He awoke to the sound of hoofbeats, and realized at once that he had slept too long—it was already sunup. And the hoofbeats had to mean that Moraghan was already exercising his horses.

Bud got up, shook the hay off himself, and crept slowly to a door in the side away from the house. He peered out and saw Moraghan galloping a horse on the other side of the small pasture. Bud saw that the pasture was being used as a race track, and that Moraghan would be riding past the barn shortly.

Bud hurried to the rail fence only a few yards from the side of the stable. Making himself as small as possible, he rested the Colt on the second rail from the top, cocked it, and waited as Moraghan and his horse galloped around the turn and came charging down the dirt track toward the barn.

A sense of elation filled Bud. Moraghan would have to come past him, not six feet away! He couldn't miss.

Then the horse and rider were there, almost upon him. Just as Bud started to pull the trigger, a voice yelled behind him. The sudden sound startled the horse, and it began to rear up. Bud fired pointblank, and Moraghan tumbled from the saddle. He hadn't missed!

He barely took note of the fact that the horse stumbled a few steps forward, and fell with a thud. Bud was already turning, remembering the voice behind him. He saw a bowlegged little man charging toward him, yelling, "Hey! What the hell you doing, you asshole!"

Bud swung the Colt around to bear. He squeezed the trigger. Nothing happened. He had forgotten to cock it! He flipped the hammer back with his thumb and fired. As the Colt spat flame, the little man was falling.

Bud was already turning away. Jamming the Colt into his belt, he began to run at full speed toward the trees where he'd tethered the mule.

At least he had gotten Moraghan, he wasn't sure about the other man. He would have to go on the run now. Too many people knew about his threat to the Moraghans; and if the little man back there wasn't dead, he probably could identify him.

But it really didn't matter. He had accomplished his aim—there was one less Moraghan in the world. There was nothing for him here now. Being an outlaw wasn't a bad life; his grandfather and great-grandmother had been outlaws. He might even drift down to the Rio Grande Valley and kill Kevin Moraghan.

He felt vindicated as he ran on, he felt ten feet tall.

Lena was just sitting down to breakfast when she heard the first gunshot, out by the barn, and was up and running in the instant, ignoring Debra, who was calling after her.

The second shot sounded as she burst through the back door. When she had covered half the distance to the barn, she saw the figure of a man running from behind the barn toward the grove of trees. It was some little distance, but she was sure that it was Bud Danker.

Then she was at the end of the barn, the running man lost from sight. The first thing she saw as she rounded the building was Bandy clawing at the pasture gate. She ran at him, calling, "Bandy, where's Michael?"

He turned a white face to her. "He's on the ground, Miss Lena. I don't know if he's dead or not."

Then he had the gate open, charging through, Lena right on his heels. Lena felt her heart surge with relief when she saw Michael sitting up, a dazed look on his face. Several yards away the stallion he had been riding was also on the ground, legs thrashing.

Lena kneeled beside her brother. "Are you all right, Michael? Are you hit?"

Still wearing the dazed look, he shook his head. "I don't think so. The bullet must have missed me. But my leg, I think it's broken. I broke it when the horse threw me."

Kneeling beside Lena, Bandy laughed shakily. "He's a lousy shot, whoever he is. He missed me head-on, but I think you can consider yourself lucky, bub, that you're such a lousy rider. Your falling off that hoss saved your hide. Fact. Feller with the gun likely thought he'd done for you."

"The fellow with the gun, Michael, was Bud Danker. I got a glimpse of him running and I'm sure of it."

"Bud Danker? You're really sure, Lena?" It was Debra, arriving out of breath.

"Pretty sure. I only saw him the one time before . . ."

The downed horse neighed, a piercing sound of pain. Bandy got to his feet and walked over to the animal. After a moment he stood up from examining the horse, his face set and angry. "This Danker feller did his damage all right, bub. The bullet hit the horse. The knee is shattered. I'm going to have to put him out of his misery."

"Are you sure, Bandy?" Michael said in distress. "Can't he be saved?"

"Nope. That leg will never heal." He started for the barn. "I'll get my old rifle."

"Wait, Bandy," Debra said. "After you do that, you'd better ride into Nacogdoches and send a doctor out for Michael's leg. Find my husband and tell him what happened here. Lena, help me get Michael up to the house."

Cassie Danker was in the sitting room, mending an old dress, when she heard the heavy tread of footsteps on the porch. She was concerned about Bud, he had not been home since the bitter scene last night. It wasn't that unusual for him to stay out all night, but she had a bad feeling about it. He had been walking the thin edge of madness when he'd stormed out last night.

She was at the front door by the time the knock sounded, and she opened it immediately. The big, beefy man with a star on his vest and smoking a stogie she recognized as Sheriff Bradshaw. The tall, skinny man looked vaguely familiar, but she couldn't put a name to him.

"What is it?" she asked fearfully. "Has something happened to Bud?"

"Now why should you think that, girl?" the sheriff asked in a harsh voice.

She gestured helplessly. "I don't know. It's just that he, he hasn't come home . . ."

"When was the last time you saw Bud?"

"Last night. About ten o'clock." Something warned her not to say anything more.

"Did he tell you where he was going?"

"No. No, sir, he didn't."

"Now don't lie to me, girl," Sheriff Bradshaw rumbled. "I don't take kindly to being lied to. Now, what I'm wondering is, why you'd think something might have happened to that old boy just because he's been out all night? From what I hear, that ain't nothing unusual for him. Now . . ." In a move surprisingly quick for such a heavy man he seized Cassie's wrist and squeezed. " . . . I want you to tell me the truth. Did he tell you what he was up to?''

Cassie gasped out, ''No, no, sir, he didn't.'' The sheriff exerted more pressure. ''You're hurting me!''

The other man spoke up. ''That's enough of that, Sheriff. This girl is the innocent party in all this. No need to come down on her so hard.''

''Innocent party, shit! A Danker don't know what innocent means.''

''That may well be, but let her go.''

''You telling me how to do my job, Judge?'' the sheriff growled, but he let go of Cassie's wrist.

''If my telling you not to abuse people unnecessarily is telling you how to do your job, yes, I am.'' To Cassie he said, ''I'm Stonewall Lieberman, Judge Lieberman, Miss Danker. Your brother has made threats against the Moraghans. Early this morning, a man took a shot at Michael Moraghan—''

Cassie couldn't restrain a gasp of shock. ''Michael! Is he badly hurt?''

''Actually the bullet missed him, but the horse he was riding was wounded and had to be killed. In falling off the horse Michael broke his leg, but he'll mend.'' Stony tugged at his long nose. ''The thing is, his sister saw a man running away, and she's sure it was Bud Danker.''

''Oh, dear God,'' she said faintly.

Stony continued, ''He has made threats, as you know. To him, that old feud is still very much alive and flourishing. Now the thing is, he probably thinks he killed Michael, and if so, he likely has hightailed it for good. That might be better for everybody concerned, Miss Danker, even you. Do you have any idea where he might run to, if he has run?''

''No idea at all, Judge Lieberman. Bud has never even been out of the county, neither one of us has.''

Stony gave his nose a tug. ''I see.''

''But we'll run him to ground, no matter what hidey-hole he picks. 'Scuse me for butting in, Judge,'' Sheriff Bradshaw said with elaborate sarcasm. ''But I do have my job to do here. I'm putting you on notice, girl. If he gets in touch with you, or you have word as to his whereabouts, you pass it on to me, hear? You don't and I find out, I can jail you for aiding and abetting a fugitive. Come along, Judge, this ain't getting us anywhere.''

He stomped off, blowing smoke from the rank cigar. Stony gazed after him in disgust, then faced around to tip his hat to Cassie. ''Good day to you, Miss Danker.''

As he started to turn away, Cassie spoke on impulse. ''Judge Lieberman, can I have a word with you?''

He stared at her gravely. ''Of course.''

''It's about my momma. You see...'' She hesitated. ''She's not been right in the head since Daddy was killed. I've been taking care of her as best I can. But if Bud has gone away for good, it's going to be too much for me to handle. By myself I don't know if I can earn enough to pay the rent on this old place, and put food on the table for the rest of us.''

''Yes, I know the condition your mother is in. You're wondering if I can find her incompetent and declared a ward of the county, is that it, Miss Danker?''

''I know it sounds mean and coldhearted, but I don't know what else I can do,'' Cassie said miserably.

''There are hard decisions some of us have to make sometimes, in this life.'' His look was understanding. ''It could even be that it would be in your mother's best interests, Cassie. All right, I'll grant your mother a competency hearing sometime next week. If the court finds that she's incapable of caring for herself, she will be placed in a home.''

''You don't think it's awful of me, Judge Lieberman?''

''Not at all. I don't see that you have a great deal of choice. I've never been one to believe that one person should ruin his or her life to care for a parent for God knows how long. But what will *you* do, Miss Danker?''

''I haven't thought that far yet. But I'll manage some way. Almost anything would be an improvement over the way I've been living since Daddy was killed.''

On Wednesday of the following week, Stony found Sue Anne Danker incompetent to see to her own affairs, or even tend to herself, and ordered that she be sent to the county home.

Cassie had been in court, but by the time the issue had been resolved, and her mother taken away, she had quietly slipped out. Stony had wanted a word with her, he was concerned about her future. He found himself liking the girl, he admired her spunk, and he knew she was emotionally torn up over what had been necessary to do for her mother, and by her brother's actions. It had been over a week since the shooting incident, and there had been no word of Bud Danker. It was the opinion of Sheriff Bradshaw that he was gone for good, but Stony was not so certain of that.

Stony recessed court early and rode his buggy out to Moraghan. He had wired Kevin about the incident, and a letter for Michael had come in the day's mail. Stony was reasonably sure what the letter was about, and he knew he was in for a rough time at Moraghan. He had taken the coward's way and not told either Michael or Lena about the telegram he had sent to Kevin.

He found Michael on the front porch, his injured leg propped up on the railing, sitting where he could see Bandy working with one of the horses in the pasture. As Stony's buggy clattered up, Lena and Debra came out of the house to stand alongside Michael's chair.

Debra met him at the top of the steps, embraced him briefly.

"How's the patient?" Stony asked heartily—too heartily.

Lena answered, "Grumpy as an old bear." She rumpled Michael's hair affectionately.

Stony bounced Kevin's letter against his palm. "A letter came today from your daddy, Michael."

Michael reached out for the letter, almost reluctantly.

"Before you read it," Stony continued, "I think I should tell you that I wired Kevin about what happened here."

A sound of dismay came from Lena, and Michael scowled blackly. "Why ever did you do a thing like that, Stony? Daddy'll be wild, yelling for us to come back down there."

"I'm sorry, Michael. I saw it as my duty, pompous as

that may sound. The last thing Kevin asked me was to see that nothing happened to you two. I feel responsible for what happened.''

"It wasn't your fault," Michael said. "What could you do about some crazy fellow taking a shot at me?" He inserted a fingernail under the flap of the envelope and took out two sheets of paper.

Stony sat down on the porch steps. "I feel responsible, nonetheless."

Michael quickly scanned the letter. He groaned. "Both he and Mother have written. Daddy is thundering for both of us to come home at once. And Mother is practically begging." He crumpled up the sheets of paper and threw them over the railing, his face set. "Well, I'm not going! I've found what I wanted here, and no crazy Danker is going to run me off. And dammit, there's nothing Daddy can do, except maybe sell the horses out from under me."

Stony said softly, "He won't do that, Michael. Not when he calms down and realizes that you mean what you say. I'll write to him, tell him that Bud Danker has apparently vanished off the face of the earth. Sheriff Bradshaw is convinced he'll never show his face around Nacogdoches again."

"You think so?" Michael said eagerly. "Well, I purely hope so. I wouldn't want a complete break with my folks. But I will if I have to."

Lena said, "I'm not going back down there, either."

Stony stared at her. He gave his nose a tug. "I don't know as you have much choice, Lena. I don't think Kevin, or Kate either, would stand for you staying up here, not after what's happened."

"But you think they might let Michael stay? Why? Because he's a man and I'm a girl? That's not fair!"

"That's part of it, but Michael is . . . what? Twenty-eight now? And you're only nineteen, Lena."

"I'll be twenty in a month." Her chin set stubbornly. "And I'm not going back."

"Like I said, you don't have a choice. I'm sure that Kevin is quite capable of roaring up here and dragging you back."

"He can't if I'm not—" She bit off the words and whirled away, storming inside, the screen door slamming behind her.

Stony made a helpless gesture, and said ruefully, "It seems I'm not too popular around here today."

Debra patted his arm. "Don't worry, darling. She'll calm down and accept the inevitable." She grimaced. "After all, what else can she do? She's a woman, right? Godalmighty, maybe someday men won't boss us around all the time." She went into the house after Lena.

"Michael, there's something else happened this week that might interest you," Stony said. "The Danker girl, Cassie, asked me to hold a sanity hearing for her mother, which I did. Well, the poor woman isn't rational, no question about it. I had her sent to the county home. The girl hated to do it, but she had no—"

Michael was agitated. "Cassie? But what happened to her? Cassie, I mean? What's she going to do?"

Stony shrugged. "I asked her that, and she said that she'd get by somehow. She said that with her brother gone, she just couldn't manage her mother on her own. I feel sorry for her."

"But where did she go?" In his agitation Michael tried to sit up, his injured leg falling off the railing. "Dammit to hell and gone!" he roared, his face twisted in pain. "Of all the times to have something like this happen to me!"

"Michael, don't get so upset. Like I said, I'm sorry for the girl, but what can anybody do? Besides"—Stony smiled slightly—"if it hadn't been for Bud Danker taking a shot at you, you wouldn't have a shattered leg, Cassie wouldn't have to see her mother committed, and—"

"No, no, you don't understand, Stony," Michael said, rocking back and forth, nursing his leg. "There's more to it than that. I've seen Cassie a couple of times. She's a fine girl, despite her being a Danker."

"I'm sure she is," Stony said, puzzled. Then a light dawned. "You mean you've been *seeing* her, like man and woman?"

"Well, not quite that, but close, I reckon. The thing is,

Bud must have learned about it. That's why he tried to kill me, you see?''

Stony frowned at him. ''Far be it from me to interfere in your personal life, Michael, but do you think it wise to get involved with a Danker? Certainly your father wouldn't approve, at all!''

''You see, that's what I mean. I've been tied to my folks too damned long, Stony. I have a right to choose my own women, whoever they might be. And if I go back down there, it will never change.''

''You mean Kevin picked out May Beth for you?''

Michael wagged his head. ''No, no, that's not it. They happened to like May Beth, although I'm sure Daddy would have let me know if he hadn't. But the thing is, down there my choices are limited. That's why Debra Lee left, you know.'' He smiled suddenly. ''Did it ever occur to you that you might never have met her again, if she hadn't run off from down there?''

Stony nodded solemnly. ''Oh, yes, that has occurred to me, many times.''

''Listen, Stony, are you going to Nacogdoches in the morning?''

''Yes, I have to be in court tomorrow afternoon. I'll be leaving before daybreak.''

''Then I want to ride in with you. I want to see if I can find Cassie, before she up and leaves town.''


There was one way that Lena could avoid having to go back to the Valley—run away from Moraghan before her father came for her.

When the idea first came to her, she was appalled, but the more she thought about it, the more it appealed to her. After all, she thought wryly, there's a good precedent, as Judge Lieberman would say—Debra Lee had run away.

There were numerous barriers in her way. She had very little money, enough for perhaps a two-hundred-mile stage-coach ride, and she had no job skills. She remembered that Debra Lee had been in somewhat the same position, and she had ended up running a brothel in Corpus Christi. Lena wasn't prepared to go quite *that* far, but she grew more determined to leave.

It had been edging into her mind since the day she found that Mark had left, with no indication of where he was going or how long he would be gone. What if she became pregnant as a result of their lovemaking? If she returned to the Valley and had a child out of wedlock, she would never live down the shame.

When the letter came from her parents demanding that she and Michael return home, not enough time had passed for her to tell if she was pregnant or not.

The thing that finally decided her was a small advertisement appearing in a Fort Worth newspaper, to the effect that Doc Holliday's Medicine Show was appearing for one week in the outskirts of Fort Worth.

Lena packed her few possessions, taking particular care that she had the three plays that Grandmother Nora had written, sneaked out to the stable early in the morning, saddled the mare she always rode, while Bandy was in the house having breakfast, and rode away in the early morning mists, heading for Nacogdoches and the stagecoach station. She left no note in the house, but she did intend to leave a note with the mare, and instructions to the stage agent to see that her brother was notified of the animal's whereabouts.

# 7

Michael waved away Stony's offer of assistance, and managed to swing himself down off the buggy seat. When his injured foot hit the ground, pain lanced up it and it almost collapsed beneath him.

Using the improvised crutch he had brought along, he levered himself painfully toward the Danker house. This was the first time he had seen it in broad daylight, and it was a sorry sight: peeling yellow paint gave it a scabrous look, one front window had been broken and patched with criss-crossing planks, and the porch sagged and creaked under his weight.

What with the creaking porch and the thump of the crutch, Michael figured that he had made enough noise to alert anyone inside, yet there was no sound. His heart sank. Had Cassie already left for parts unknown?

Sweating profusely from the effort, he made it to the door, and leaning on the wall, he thumped the door with the handle of the crutch. When there was no immediate answer, he thumped again.

"I'm coming!" Michael felt a wave of relief as he recognized Cassie's voice.

The door opened, and began to immediately close again when she recognized him.

"Cassie, don't you dare shut the door on me! If you do, I'll lay siege to this place, camp on your doorstep, until you talk to me! Now, come on, let me in."

The door opened slowly, reluctantly, and Cassie stepped into the doorway. "Not inside, Michael."

"Why not?"

"I'm ashamed to have you see it. Last winter we were so short of fuel, no money to even buy wood, that Bud chopped up some of the furniture and burned it in the fireplace."

She closed the door and stepped close to him, her face concerned. "Are you all right, Michael? I heard about Bud trying to kill you. What can I say?"

"No need for you to say anything, Cassie," he said gruffly. "And I'm getting along fine. The doctor tells me it'll take a while for the leg to heal, but I'll be as good as new in the end. Have you had any word of Bud?"

"No, he's probably gone for good."

"Well, I thought he might write to you."

"Bud can't read or write," she said steadily.

"Oh, I see. Well . . ." He cleared his throat. "The reason I'm here, Stony told me about your mother and that you would be alone now. What do you plan to do?"

"I haven't really made any definite plans yet. I do have some brothers and sisters scattered around within a radius of a hundred miles. Some I haven't seen in years. Bud wouldn't let me keep in touch with them. He said he no longer recognized them as related, since they just took off to get away from Momma. But who can blame them for that? What I'm doing to her is even worse, I reckon."

"Now, you're not to talk like that, Cassie. Stony has told me about your mother, and you're doing the only thing, under the circumstances. There's no reason all the burden should be on your shoulders." He broke off, peered at her closely. "You're not thinking of leaving Nacogdoches for good, are you?"

She pushed the hair out of her eyes with a distracted gesture. "I don't know, Michael. I don't know as there's anything for me here. All I've ever done is scrub work for other people, cleaning up their messes. And now that Bud is on the run for trying to kill you, people will think even worse of me."

"Cassie, I want you to listen to me now. I don't want you to go away. We need some time to get to know each other. I want you to pack your grips and come out to Moraghan with me. You can stay there until we see which way things go."

Her brown eyes gleamed with hope briefly, then went dull. "I can't do that, Michael. Living out there with you like that. It would be the scandal of East Texas."

Michael grinned tightly. "I don't care, if you don't. Besides, my sister is staying there for a while yet, and my older sister spends some time out there. Cassie . . ." He took her hand, his voice softening. "I care for you. I was beginning to think that I would never get over May Beth dying. Now I'm starting to, and you've been a part of that. I realize I'm rushing things, for both of us. That's why I want you to stay at Moraghan, so we can get better acquainted. Maybe we'll come to see we never would make it together. But if you leave for good, then we'd never know, would we?"

"Michael, I'm a Danker. Are you asking me to marry you?"

"No, not right now. I'm not ready for that. We have to get to know each other first."

She frowned at him. "You didn't listen to me. I'm a

Danker. My brother threatened to kill your daddy, and he tried to kill you. What would your family think of me living in the same house with you, much less us ever marrying?"

He said doggedly, "My family has nothing to do with it. And you have nothing to do with any threats or killing. You hate this feuding business as much as I do, you told me so."

"That's true. But—"

"And if you're thinking I'm asking you out to Moraghan to be my woman, not true. I promise never to touch you until we're man and wife. Now, will you come out to Moraghan with me?"

"I shouldn't. I have a strong feeling it's a terrible mistake," she said with a sigh. Then her smile broke, sudden and brilliant. "But I will, I will!"

"Fine and dandy. Now pack your grips. I'll be waiting in the buggy with Stony."

"I don't have any grips, Michael."

He said impatiently, "Then put your things in boxes, anything. I don't care."

He turned and began crutching his way across the porch, and then hobbled across the yard to Stony's buggy.

He heaved himself up onto the buggy seat. As Stony picked up the reins, Michael said quickly, "No, wait! Cassie is coming with us. I've talked her into moving out to Moraghan, for the time being at least. If I can use your buggy, Stony, I'll take us out, and send Bandy back in the morning with it."

"Michael." Stony stared at him, tugging at his nose. "I suppose there's no use my asking if you know what you're doing?"

"Not the slightest. Whether I know what I'm doing or not, it's the only way I can keep Cassie around. I want to get to know that girl better, Stony."

"If Kevin learns of this, nothing on heaven or earth will keep him from storming up here and taking you and Lena home by force. He might even be so upset he'll sell Moraghan, despite Nora's wishes."

"He might take Lena, he won't take me back," Michael

said grimly. He turned a pleading look on his brother-in-law. "He doesn't have to know right away, does he? All I want is time to get to know Cassie. If nothing else will do it, I'll marry now, if she'll have me. That way nobody can say anything about it. But I'd rather wait, to be more sure of myself, and of Cassie."

"Did you ever think this way may not be fair to her?"

"Not fair! In what way? She'll have a place to live and food to eat, and she can work off her keep if she wants to. Oh . . . maybe you think I'm moving her into my bed. No, Stony, I won't lay a hand on her until she's my wife, if that ever happens."

"No, that wasn't what I was thinking, Michael. But whether you'll be taking her to bed or not, people will think you are, and that's what I mean by not being fair to her."

"Perhaps you're right, but I know what Cassie's answer to that would be. People have a low opinion of Dankers, anyway, so how could another bit of gossip hurt her?"

"Well, I've said all I'm going to say, Michael. You're well past the age of consent, you're your own man now—"

He broke off at the slam of the screen door, and they both turned to see Cassie trudging across the yard, a stuffed flour sack slung across her shoulder. Stony got down to come around the buggy and help her up onto the seat beside Michael.

"Thank you, Judge Lieberman," she said shyly.

Michael said, "Is that all you're taking, Cassie?"

"All I'm taking are my clothes, and a few other personal things. Nothing else in that old house belongs to me. Let whoever rents it next have the things left."

Climbing into the buggy, Stony clucked to the horse, and the buggy was underway. "I'm due in court, Michael, so I'll drive to the courthouse, and you can take it from there. If that's all right with you?"

"Fine with me, Stony."

They had to pass the stagecoach station on the way to the courthouse. As the buggy started past, a man ran out of the station, waving a letter, and yelling, "Judge! Judge Lieberman!"

Stony sawed back on the reins, and the vehicle skidded to a stop in the dusty street.

The station agent puffed up to them. "Judge Lieberman, your sister-in-law took the stage out of here this morning. She left a saddled mare out back, and said this letter was for whichever one of her family comes for the animal."

"Lena?" Stony said in disbelief. "Lena took the stage?"

"If that's her name." The agent held out the envelope, and Stony accepted it. "How about the horse?"

Stony said in a dazed voice, "Somebody will take it off your hands before the day's over, Sam."

The agent turned and reentered the station. Stony gingerly held the envelope out to Michael. "You'd better read this, Michael. I have a feeling it's for you, anyway."

Michael took the letter, opened it, and ran his gaze over the short note enclosed. "Jesus! It's from Lena, right enough, without any salutation to anyone." He cleared his throat, read aloud:

> I do not intend to stay around for Daddy to come up here and drag me back to Brownsville. I am going off on my own, and I intend to prove to everyone that I can manage my own life. I will write from time to time, to you, Michael, to Debra Lee, and to Mother and Daddy.
>
> You can easily find out that I bought a stagecoach ticket to Fort Worth, but it would be a waste of time to try and catch me there. I am not staying in Fort Worth, and will be gone by the time anyone can find me.
>
> I hope everyone will forgive me, in time. I feel that I have to do this. Do not worry about me. I can take care of myself.
>
>                              All my love, Lena.

Michael snorted. "Take care of herself! She's nineteen years old, for Christ's sake! Hardly more than a child, and she's never been out on her own."

"I'm not quite eighteen, Michael," Cassie said. "But I can take care of myself. She might do better than you think."

"She's an innocent, Cassie. Your life has been harder, you've had to learn how to survive." He glanced at Stony. "Do you suppose it would do any good to chase after her?"

Slowly Stony shook his head. "I don't think we could catch her, not if she doesn't stay in Fort Worth like she claims. We could wire the authorities in Fort Worth, and other towns around, and they might find her. But do we want that? She's committed no crime, Michael."

"You're probably right. Daddy told me that's why he didn't have the law look for Debra Lee when she ran away." He laughed suddenly. "We Moraghans are good at running away, aren't we? I have to wire Daddy about her running off. God, I hate to think how he'll react."

Stony flicked the reins, starting the buggy in motion. "I'm going to be late for court if I don't hurry. You drop me off, then take the buggy for what you have to do. It won't be necessary to have Bandy drive it back to town. I'll ride over on the weekend, or sooner if I can get away. You'd better send the wire to Kevin, Michael, it'll be better coming from you. And tell Debra not to worry too much. By this time she's probably beside herself wondering what's happened to Lena. Tell Debra that I said to remember back to when she did much the same thing, and it turned out all right in the end."

"It's come full cycle, hasn't it, darling?" Debra murmured against her husband's shoulder.

Stony raised his head, trying to see her face in the dark. They were in the back bedroom at Moraghan, the one that had been Nora's. "I'm not quite sure what you mean, sweet."

"Well, Lena has run off, just like I did. And a Danker has tried again to kill one of us. Thank God it failed this time!"

"I suppose you could make a case," Stony said thoughtfully. "But then it's been my experience that this often happens in families, children repeating what other family members have done.''

"Right after that mess with Tod Danker, Bud's father, Grandmother Nora wondered to me if there was a curse on the Moraghans, with all the things that have happened."

Stony said curtly, "I don't believe in curses."

"I don't either, but it is strange, you'll have to admit. Even Brian ran off twice, you know. He ran away the first time to join the Texas Rangers, and then later to fight in the war.'' Her voice was musing. "I suppose it could be said that *I* got it from him, since he was my father. But the same can't be said for Lena.''

"What do you think Kevin will do about her? Do you think he will come up here?''

She said slowly, "I doubt it, Stony. After all, what can he do? Lock the barn door, after the horse is gone? What can any of us do?''

"There's one thing we could do, of course. Since Lena has broken no law, the law will not be interested in finding her. But Kevin could hire the Pinkertons to track her down. It might be expensive, but they're good at it.''

She shook her head. "No, Daddy would never do that. He didn't in my case, he won't in hers. If they found her, what would happen? They could bring her back home by force, but that would make her even more determined to run away again, the first time she had the chance. I know I would have if I had been dragged back. If Daddy's not wise enough to realize that, Mother certainly is.''

He sighed pensively. "I suppose you're right.''

"I think I'll come home with you tomorrow, Stony, for good. With Lena gone, there's no reason for me to stay out here." She hugged him tightly. "I miss you, being out here so much.''

"God knows, I want you home, Debra, but do you think it's wise now, what with Cassie staying here?''

"All the more reason for me to go home. I'll just be in the way here.''

"It'll cause even more talk, with Michael and Cassie alone out here, unmarried.''

She made a low sound of amusement. "That's another

thing about the Moraghans. We've never given a hoot for what people think. Godalmighty, I sure didn't!''

"Well, I'm glad for one thing."

"What might that be, my darling husband?"

"You're past the point of running off."

"Don't be too sure about that. I just might, if you're not nice to me," she said in a teasing voice.

"Nice in what way?"

"Like making love to me right now." She fastened her teeth around one of his nipples and bit down gently.

"Ouch!" He pulled her face up to his, and said against her mouth, "I never realized we had that particular problem. The opposite, in fact. If the people knew what went on in the privacy of the Lieberman bedroom, they'd be shocked out of their drawers."

"Speaking of drawers, I'm not wearing any, if you had been interested enough to notice."

"Oh, I've noticed."

His hand was under the sheet, cupping her mound.

"Then do something about it," she said roughly. "Make love to me now, darling! Remember that first time, in my sporting house in Corpus Christi?"

"Yes, indeed, I remember. I'll never forget it."

She groped for his hardness under the sheet. "Do me like that now!"

He rose and Debra squirmed under him, adjusting herself to him. In a moment a small cry escaped her. "Ah, yes, like that! Stony, darling Stony! I love you, love you to pieces!"

While it was true that Bud Danker could neither read nor write, there was nothing wrong with his hearing, and he heard two men in a saloon in Beaumont passing the time over schooners of beer. Bud had been brooding over a bottle of whiskey when he heard one of the men say, "Yup, I passed through Nacogdoches just last week..."

Bud glanced furtively at the pair at the next table. Then he slowly relaxed. He did not know either man, so there was no reason he shouldn't remain where he was and eavesdrop. He soon learned that both men were traveling drummers, and the one doing most of the talking hit Nacogdoches several times a year.

"... heard one rather weird bit. You know the history of the Danker family, don't you, Henry?"

"Sure thing. Meaner than a sack of snakes. What have they been up to now? I thought they had tamed down some since Tod was killed."

The other man laughed. "Tamed down is pretty much the way of it, I reckon. The only old boy left at home is Bud Danker, and if what happened is any sign, he's about as dangerous as a defanged rattler."

"Why do you say that? What happened?"

"Well, you know the bad blood that's been between the Dankers and the Moraghans for God knows how long?"

"Sure, I know about that, everybody does."

"Well, it apparently has flared up again. Bud Danker, he snuck out to the Moraghan place, and took a shot at Michael Moraghan, who was on horseback. It seems old Bud is such a terrible shot he missed Michael entire and shot his horse! The only thing happened to Michael is, he has a broken leg which he got from being tossed from his horse. And that ain't all ..." The drummer glanced around the saloon. "The Danker girl left at home, Cassie I think her name is. You know what she's gone and done ...?" He leaned across the table to put his mouth to the other man's ear.

Bud was no longer interested, he had heard enough. Blind with fury, he got up and staggered outside, into the humid summer heat and tidal stink of Beaumont. He had failed! He hadn't killed Michael Moraghan after all. The impact of his failure was such that his stomach heaved, and he stumbled to the side of the road and vomited up the greasy breakfast he'd eaten, along with the cheap whiskey.

Finally, eyes streaming, belly sore, he made his way around the side of the saloon and climbed aboard the mule. But when he picked up the reins, he couldn't decide which way to go. Should he ride back to Nacogdoches and make another try for Michael Moraghan? But if Moraghan was laid up with a broken leg, he would be hard to get at, and

Bud was certain that the law would be laying in the weeds waiting for him to come back.

But what if he went the other way, to the Rio Grande Valley? Nobody would be expecting him to head in that direction, and he wasn't known down there; therefore, it should be easy as pie to get close enough to Kevin Moraghan to put a bullet into his heart. Kevin Moraghan was the one, anyway. Let Cassie fool around with Michael, if she was sorry enough to go that way. Kevin Moraghan had killed his daddy, he was the one with the most to account for.

His decision made, Bud headed the mule west out of Beaumont. He doubted that the old mule would make it to Brownsville, and even if the animal could, it would take forever. He needed a horse. He also needed some cash money. Paying for his breakfast and the bottle in the saloon had left him with a few sorry coins in his jeans.

His first problem was solved late that afternoon as he rode the plodding mule along the wagon road toward Houston. The road closely followed the coastline, and the afternoon breeze off the Gulf was welcome, slightly reducing the stifling heat. And up ahead he saw a fine-looking horse standing in the meager shade of a stubby palm tree.

As he approached, Bud could make out the figure of a man sleeping in the shade, head propped on his saddle, a wide-brimmed hat across his face.

Bud quietly dismounted, dropped the reins to the ground, drew the Colt, and held it close to his side out of sight. He walked slowly and quietly toward the sleeping man. The man slept on, undisturbed.

In a moment Bud stood over him, barely breathing, undecided. Should he kill him? Or just thump him over the head with the Colt, rendering him unconscious?

Then the man twitched, muttering, deciding his own fate. Bud triggered two quick shots into the prone man's chest. The body jumped, blood spouted, and then the man was still.

Bud loosed an exuberant shout. His heart was pounding, his breath coming heavily. This time there was no doubt— he had killed his first man! Intuitively he knew that he would never doubt himself again; he was blooded now, and would be invincible henceforth.

Belatedly, he looked around. There was no one on the road, and the hot, drowsy afternoon seemed totally undisturbed by the two shots.

Bud went down to one knee and quickly rifled the dead man's pockets. He was disappointed at the result—less than twenty dollars. That would be insufficient to get him all the way down to the Valley. But there would be other wayfarers he could kill and plunder on the way, or small country stores, and now he had a decent horse.

He rolled the body off the saddle, scooped up the saddle, and cinched it onto the big pinto the man had been riding. Bud mounted up, not even sparing the mule a final glance. Even the saddle on the mule was shabby.

He rode tall down the dirt road, at least two feet higher than he had been on the mule. He reloaded the Colt as he rode, humming tunelessly under his breath.

Bud killed his second man a few miles west of Corpus Christi—the keeper of a country store. The man had been alone when Bud came in, and offered no resistance when Bud pulled the Colt, but Bud shot him anyway. He was aware now that he received a sharp jolt of pleasure from killing. As he watched the quivering death throes of the storekeeper sprawled across his counter, Bud felt something very much like an seizure in his loins. He did not have an orgasm—maybe next time?—yet his pleasure was intense.

He filled his saddle bags with food from the store, found close to a hundred dollars in the dead storekeeper's pockets, and took a sack of grain from the back of the store. To be on the safe side, he rode down the road a ways, to a small stream, before feeding and watering the pinto.

As the days passed, and the miles went by, Bud advanced farther into the smothering, enervating heat of the Rio Grande Valley. Why on earth would anyone wish to live here? The landscape was flat to the horizon, dotted with mesquite and cactus and, as he proceeded farther south, an occasional small herd of cattle.

Even when he reached the lush greenery of the fertile

Valley itself, Bud didn't like the country. It was simply too hot, too damnable hot. He made a few casual, cautious inquiries, and eventually arrowed in on Kevin Moraghan's produce and citrus fruit acreage. Bud was surprised at the size of it, and at the number of Mexican laborers working in the orchards and fields.

This fact gave him pause. How was he going to get close enough to Kevin Moraghan to achieve his purpose when Moraghan was always surrounded by workers? Bud lurked behind a hedge of oleander bushes, thinking about it. The solution finally came to him.

Apparently designed as a windbreak, the oleander bushes had been planted in a neat row along the north side of the orchard. They were high as a man's head, brilliant with red, white, and pink blossoms at this time of the year. Bud had noticed that some of the male workers left off picking from time to time to repair to the oleanders to urinate, hidden from the other workers, many of whom were women.

Bud waited until a man approximately his own size wormed his way between two oleanders to urinate, his huge-brimmed sombrero pushed back, held by a string round his neck. Bud crept up behind him, then struck him twice, quickly, on the back of the head. The man went down without a sound. Bud sent a glance back into the grove; apparently the attack had gone unnoticed.

Bud dragged the limp body to the far side of the oleander hedge, and hurriedly stripped off the man's colorful serape, sombrero, and heavy leather sandals. Bud sat down in the dirt and removed his boots with a grimace. He hated to dispense with the boots—he likely wouldn't have time to come back for them—but high-heeled boots in the orchard would be a dead giveaway. Well, hell, he could get another pair without too much trouble.

He stood up, the serape draped over his shoulders, its folds hanging down below his waist to conceal the gunbelt, and the wide sombrero tilted far down in front, partially obscuring his face. He pushed through the oleanders, and began walking toward the area where Kevin Moraghan was supervising the fruit pickers. The soft, plowed earth between the rows of trees felt strange under Bud's feet, in the unaccustomed sandals.

No one noticed anything untoward as he approached, his hands hidden under the serape, one hand on the butt of the Colt. Kevin Moraghan had his back turned, and Bud walked up to within three feet of him.

In an atrocious Spanish accent, he said, "*Señor* Moraghan?"

Kevin turned, frowning. "Yes? What is it?" He tried to peer under the sombrero. "Do you work here? Or are you looking for a job? I'm not hiring right now—"

Bud had taken his left hand from under the serape to push the sombrero back, far enough to reveal his face. Kevin went slack-mouthed with astonishment. "You! What are you—?"

Bud's other hand came up holding the Colt. He brought the muzzle up level, only inches from Kevin's heart, and fired point-blank, twice.

# 8

In the 1880s Fort Worth was the dominant one in the twin-sister relationship with the city to the east, Dallas. Cowtown, as it was known far and wide, was the hub of the cattle industry still. It was not the boom town it had been a few years ago, perhaps, yet it was lively, kicking up its heels, like an aging tart, displaying a last burst of gaiety. Fort Worth—"Where the West Begins."

Lena got off the stagecoach just short of noon, after a long ride from Nacogdoches. She was hungry, and spent a dollar of her remaining few for a large breakfast of ham and eggs, red-eye gravy, hot biscuits and jam, at a small café adjacent to the stage station.

Then, carrying her meager possessions in a straw suitcase, she had found in the attic at Moraghan, and with instruc-

tions from the café waitress as to how to get to the lot
where Doc Holliday's Medicine Show was playing that
evening, she set out across town.

She was awed, almost intimidated, by the bustle of
buggy, carriage, and horse traffic on the Fort Worth streets,
and the scurry of pedestrians along the sidewalks. She'd
never seen so many people at one time in one place. It was
into August now, and the moist heat was oppressive, the
sun blazing down from a clear sky, made brassy and
shimmering by the heat. The heat carried the fetid stink of
the distant stockyards and meat-packing plants. She had
been told told it would be prudent to avoid the section of
Main Street called Hell's Half Acre—it was a district of
saloons and brothels. Many cattle drives ended in Fort
Worth, and Main was peopled by gamblers, whores, and
criminals who preyed on the thirsty, roistering cowhands
with money in their jeans.

At least the location of the medicine show was some
distance from Hell's Half Acre, and the stench had
disappeared by the time Lena reached the lot late in the
afternoon. The canvas front was down on the stage wagon,
and the other wagons and tents behind the show wagon
baked in the heat.

Lena approached the other wagons hesitantly. There
seemed to be no one about. She knew medicine show
people worked late at night, but at the same time she
didn't know how they could sleep in the heat. Then she
went around one wagon, and found several people seated
around a table, eating and drinking listlessly. A strip of
canvas had been fastened to the wagon on one side,
extending out to two poles stuck into the ground. The canvas
strip provided scant shade.

Of the people around the table—a half dozen in total—
she recognized only the white-haired Doc Holliday, and the
banjo picker. There was only one woman present, a tall,
rather thin woman, sitting beside Holliday, who had his
shirt off, displaying a brawny chest, covered with thick,
gray hair like an animal's pelt.

Doc was the first to notice her. His dark eyes lit up with
curiosity. ''Well, ma'am, who might you be?'' He got to

his feet and made a courtly bow. "Whoever you are, for the Lord's sake, come in out of the sun before your brains broil."

Lena ducked under the canvas, setting her straw bag down, and took the seat he offered. The others around the table were studying her with curiosity, the tall woman with active hostility.

"My name is Lena Moraghan. I saw your medicine show in Nacogdoches, and I've come to join up."

Doc grunted. "How'd you know Agnes had left us?"

Lena frowned. "Agnes?"

"Our Little Susie *and* Madame Bella. She packed up and left us this morning. No reason I can think of."

The tall woman snorted. "No reason! There's plenty of reason, Doc, and you know it. One reason is I told her to pack up and get, or I'd claw her eyes out!"

"All right, Lucy, no need to go into that before strangers." Doc batted a hand at the woman without taking his eyes from Lena. "The thing is, Miss Moraghan, how did you know she'd left us?"

"I didn't, Mr. Holliday. I saw your show in Nacogdoches, like I said, and decided I wanted to join up."

His black eyes were sardonically amused. "You have any medicine show experience?"

"No, but I can learn, and I can sing and dance as well as your Little Susie."

"Can you now? No experience and you walk up here as bold as brass and ask for a job?"

Lucy said, "Send her packing, Doc. She's probably run off from home. She means nothing but trouble for us and we don't need more trouble."

"Be quiet for once, will you, Lucy?" To Lena he said, "That true, you run off from home?"

"That is my affair, sir." Her head went back. "I am of age, my own woman. And I will cause you no trouble, that I promise you."

Chin propped on his hand, Doc studied her for a few silent moments. Lena took note of the fact that there was more than a professional interest in his eyes, and she felt a brief qualm of uncertainty. She had the strong feeling that

Doc Holliday was a practicing lecher, and that that was the reason Little Susie-Madame Bella had left so suddenly. On the other hand, Lena was determined to make it on her own, and to do that she could not let male lechery deter her.

"You're pretty enough, that's for sure," he said musingly. "How talented you are, time will tell. But what the hell, Agnes wasn't all that great."

The woman named Lucy said warningly, "Doc, am I going to have to put up with another one?"

He turned his face toward her, and Lena saw that his look was baleful. "Now you just shut up, Lucy. By Christ, I'm still running this shebang. Besides, I have to have someone to take Agnes's place, now don't I? What do you expect me to do, hire some old hag? That would go over good, wouldn't it?" He switched his gaze back to Lena. "I'm going to give you your chance, Lena. Maybe you'll work out. The life of a medicine show is hard, get that straight right now. And the pay ain't all that great. You get paid a percentage of the take. If we do good, you do good. Now, you'll want to meet the rest of our little troupe. The woman here with the big mouth is my wife, Lucy. Bob Ketchum is our banjo picker, and the short fellow there is Andy Jacks, our blackface comic, Jake . . ."

The other two men, Jack Wrightman and Ed Marks, were roustabouts, doubling on occasion as candy butchers and medicine hawkers. Before the introductions were completed, Lucy Holliday got up and stalked away to one of the wagons.

Doc looked after her for a moment, then turned to Lena with a careless shrug. "Don't pay any mind to Lucy, Lena. I don't know why I took her on the road with me, anyway. She refuses to work and she gets huffy about any woman working the show with us. But she's generally harmless. If she comes around to you like she did to Agnes last night, without me knowing about it, don't listen to her. You ever have any complaints, come to me about it, hear? By George, I ramrod this show." He got to his feet. "Come along, I'll show you your sleeping wagon. After it cools off a little, I'll run through with you the things you have to do during the show." He grinned. "There're a few gimmicks I'll have to show you, with the Madame Bella act, and I'll give you the skits you'll be doing with Jake."

The quarters that were to be Lena's took up the rear half of one of the boxy wagons. It was cramped, with a narrow cot for sleeping, a tiny dressing table, and a few hooks on the sides for her clothes. It was hot as an oven, and Lena was perspiring profusely by the time she had stowed away her few belongings. She was driven out of the wagon by the heat, and sat on a camp stool in the meager shade of the wagon, reading the skits that Doc had given her. The skits were the broadest comedy possible, and soon Lena was absorbed in figuring out how she could improve them. She found lines, whole new scenes, popping into her mind, much funnier and less crude than the original. She quickly scribbled her ideas down onto a tablet, using the basic framework of the skits Doc had given her.

So absorbed was she that she gave a great leap when Doc's voice drawled at her, "My, my, you're writing up a storm. Who to, the folks you left behind?"

Something warned her not to reveal what she was doing this soon. Looking up at him looming over her, she said, "Something like that, yes."

He squatted on his haunches in the shade beside her chair. "Must be something pretty rotten back where you came from to cause you to join up with a medicine show. Like I said, it's a rough life, Lena."

"But it can pay well, can't it?"

"Sometimes, but more often than not, no. Sometimes you can have a good year, maybe gross thirty or forty thousand, which I did two years ago. But last year was a lousy year, which is the reason I'm on the road right now. Summer, Lena, ain't a good time to be on the road. Harvest time, that's the best. In the summer doldrums people just don't have those extra dollars to spend. Come cotton-picking time in Texas, or other Southern states, or the wheat harvest in the fall in the Midwest, all the way up to the Canadian border, that's a different story. People have extra money in their jeans and they're easier to shake loose from a few dollars. But some towns are terrible, even after harvest time.''

"Why is that?''

"There could be any number of reasons. The town could be played out, too many medicine shows. It might have a sheriff who is hostile to medicine shows in his town. It could be a town that, for some reason unknown to anybody, is dead set against us. These towns are known as 'graveyards of medicine shows.' And one thing that happens all too often is that some cheapshot artist has been through recently selling snake oil.''

"Selling snake oil?''

"Yeah. Selling stuff made in washtubs out of whatever is handy and then peddled as a cure for everything that ails man, woman, or child, when in fact it cures nothing. In fact, sometimes it even makes the taker sick. A snake-oil artist like that burns a town for the rest of us. He's out for a quick dollar, never intending to come through that town again.''

Lena smiled skeptically. "And you don't operate that way, Mr. Holliday?''

"Nope, I've never found it necessary. My tonic is not a cure-all, but it can help alleviate many ailments. Just ask the people who buy my product. Sure, some people aren't happy with it, but then a man can never satisfy all the people. I make more people happy than I do unhappy.'' He grinned lazily. "I may gimmick up the show a bit here and there, but that's to entertain the folks. My product is as honest as the next man's.''

"Is Doc Holliday your real name?''

"Not exactly,'' he said unashamedly. "The Holliday part I kind of adopted for my own. Real name is Jones. Now how would that look on a show banner? But the Doc part, that's real enough. I'm entitled to use that for my own.''

"Why is that?''

His grin widened. "Because I'm a real-life veterinarian.''

Lena stared. "A veterinarian!''

"Yep. That's what I started out in life as. But I got fed up with treating sick cows and horses. Besides, there was no money in it, and certainly no fun. With a medicine show I sometimes make a pot of money, sometimes I go hungry, but it's always a barrel of fun, by heaven, it is. And before you ask, no, I don't spread the word around, so don't you do so, either. How would it strike the suckers out there if they knew I'd once been a horse doctor?''

"I have no reason to tell anyone." She thought of telling him that she would be quiet about his secret in exchange for his keeping hands off, but she didn't. She had the strong feeling she would have trouble with him eventually, but if she made such a threat at this time, he'd likely send her packing.

Doc got up, uncoiling to his full height. "Let's amble over to the stage wagon. The sun's down far enough now so that it should be in the shade. I'll call Bob over and we'll see if we can find a couple of songs you can sing with him. Then we'll rehearse you with Jacks in the skit we're using tonight. Finally, I'll fill you in on how to run the Madame Bella number. I'll tell you, Lena, I hope this works. I was worried when Agnes came up missing this morning. This is a plum location here. Last night's show was pure velvet, and I was worried that it might be a bloomer tonight without some female pulchritude to flash before the suckers.''

That evening, after Doc's opening words, Lena came on stage with Bob Ketchum. She was dressed demurely, her long hair in braids, and in a long velvet dress out of the show's wardrobe trunk. It *was* cut a little low above her bosom, showing the swell of her breasts, and she might have been embarrassed under different circumstances, but something happened that she had not anticipated—she was absolutely frozen by stage fright. All she could think of was those hundreds—no, thousands!—of faces staring up at her.

Dimly, she could hear Ketchum plucking the banjo strings, and she knew she was supposed to sing, but she couldn't remember a single word of the song they'd rehearsed that afternoon.

Then Doc had her by the elbow, and his lips were at her

ear. He hissed, "Sing, damn you, Lena! Sing or you're fired as of this very moment!"

She gave a start, wrenched her stricken gaze from the audience, and the words came back to her. Hands folded before her, looking at the stage planks beneath her feet, she sang the sentimental piece in a clear, sweet voice.

She was awful, she just knew she was! But when she had finished, a storm of applause rose from the audience— "A good tip tonight," Doc had said earlier behind the curtain, peering out at the crowd.

Lena was already growing familiar with medicine-show terminology. "Tip" meant crowd, "plum location" meant an audience that spent freely, as opposed to "bloomer," which meant a crowd that spent little. It was an arcane language, a private communication, that hinted at dark secrets, an alliance against the rest of the world, and Lena felt grateful to be privy to it. It gave her a feeling of belonging, of being a member of an inner circle, and now that she was past the spell of stage fright, she realized that she was going to love her new life. Without knowing how she knew, she knew that she would never again be afflicted with stage fright.

Behind the curtain, Doc grinned at her. "Froze up out there, didn't you?" At her nod he chuckled. "Don't let it get to you, honey, it happens to most people, the first time. Some never get over it."

"It won't happen to me again," she said simply.

His eyes widened. "No, I suppose it won't. The applause did it, I imagine?"

"Yes. I thought I was so terrible they'd hoot me off the stage. But they didn't, Doc!" She clutched at his arm. "They liked me!"

"I could say that they're so starved for entertainment, especially of the female variety, they'd applaud anything, and that's true enough. But you're good, Lena, damned good. One of those rare ones, who was born a singer, born an entertainer. You're going to be just fine."

He cocked his head, listened to the silence as the applause died, and then he was gone with a flip of his hand, back onto the stage. She listened for just a moment,

listened as he began his spiel. Then she went behind the
canvas that was rigged in the back of the stage wagon for
her costume changes, and got into the Madame Bella
costume.

Tonight's mind-reading act would be slightly different
from the performance Lena had witnessed in Nacogdoches.
Doc had told her, "The spirit-cabinet gimmick is a little
too complicated, Lena, until you've had more instruction.
The one we'll use tonight is easier and baffles people just
as much, especially if they know little or nothing about
carbon paper. The people here in Fort Worth are a little
more sophisticated than the suckers back in Nacogdoches,
but since this is the blow-off night, I think we can risk it.
Most of 'em are drawn here tonight because this is the
night the results of the talent contest are announced."

"Blow-off," Lena had learned, meant one of two things—
either the last night of a show stand, or an additional
entertainment where admission was charged. Usually the
after-show was a little bawdy. Doc Holliday's Medicine
Show did not offer an after-show.

After Lena, wearing the Madame Bella outfit, took her
place at the small table on the stage, Doc called the
audience to attention. "Ladies and gents, you are now
going to witness an amazing demonstration of mind reading by Madame Bella! Jake will pass among you with a
tablet, the magical tablet. You may write your name and
any question you wish Madame Bella to answer on a sheet
in the tablet. Jake, without looking at what you have
written, will then tear off the sheet of paper, and return it
to you. When several questions have been written down,
the pad will be brought to Madame Bella, so she can get a
psychic reading from it, and then she will answer your
questions."

Jake passed through the audience with the tablet, people
wrote their questions and signed their names, and then
Jake came to the stage to hand the tablet up to Lena. She
sat down at the table, which had a dropcloth wrapped
around it, and held the tablet in her lap. Each time a tablet
sheet had been scribbled on, Jake had inserted a slip of
carbon paper beneath the sheet, and then surreptitiously

pocketed the second sheet, and each question and signature stood out boldly for Lena to read.

Hands hidden from the audience by the cloth, Lena leafed through the slips of paper. In a clear, carrying voice, she spoke the words Doc had written out for her: "Ah, the mental vibrations are very strong tonight! The mind waves from each of you who have written are coming through clearly." She closed her eyes, head thrown back, hand over her eyes. "Mrs. Carter. Mrs. Reba Carter. You are worried about your daughter being still unmarried at twenty-four. You wonder if she will ever marry. I see a man in her future, a handsome young man, well-off. He is asking for her hand in marriage and she accepts."

A loud gasp came from the woman who had written down the question, followed by a scattering of applause. Lena waited for quiet before going on. Doc had told her to use her imagination with her answers, but always keep her responses cheerful, optimistic, no matter what the question might be.

"Mr. Bert Thomas, you ask if your hog will be fat and sassy come hog-killing time. Mr. Thomas, I see a fat hog hung up, scalded white. You will have many hams and tasty ribs, and enough spicy sausage. You will eat well for most of the winter. I see you sitting down to a mess of backbone. But a word of caution, Mr. Thomas . . . do not eat too much of that fresh backbone. You know what that can do to the digestion. If you plan on eating too much, I would advise you to buy a bottle of Doc Holliday's Elixir of Life before leaving here tonight."

A gust of laughter swept through the audience, and voices hooted: "Don't worry about it, Bert! Me and my family will traipse over at killing time and help you eat that old hog!" "Buy a case of Doc's Elixir, Bert, I'll carry it home for you!" "Better get your privy in good shape, Bert, afore killin time!"

Lena waited for the hilarity to subside, then read another question and improvised an answer. She didn't feel particularly guilty about the fraud involved. It was harmless entertainment, who was hurt by it?

. Then she came to a question that gave her pause: "My daughter ran away last month. Will she come home soon?"

The question hit too close to home. Her throat closed up, and tears burned her eyes, as she suddenly felt a longing for her own home so sharp it was like a physical pain. She hesitated, staring down at the question, almost forgetting where she was.

Then Doc was speaking, moving smoothly toward her. "I'm sorry, folks. Reading minds is very hard on Madame Bella. We mustn't overtax her. And we have a lot more show for you, including the results of the talent contest."

He had Lena by the hand, urging her to her feet, hustling her behind the curtain. Once they were hidden behind it, he said in a low voice, "You were good, by Christ! That bit about the hog was great, honey!" Then his voice changed. "But why did you freeze there at the last? I thought you said you were over the stage fright?"

"I am." She looked at him with moist eyes. "It wasn't that . . ."

"Oh." He nodded in sudden understanding. "The question, right? About the girl running off from home?"

'Yes, that's what did it." He had startled her with his flash of insight. In the beginning she had thought he was a charlatan, strictly a con artist, but she was beginning to perceive that there were unsuspected depths to Doc Holliday.

"Don't let it get you down, honey." He chucked her under the chin with a forefinger, grinning. "We've all run away from home at one time or another. You get over it, take my word for it. Well,"—he became brisk—"get ready for the skit, Little Susie. We're doing that earlier than usual, the talent contest winners being brought on last, since that's what drew the big tip tonight. If you do as well in the skit as you just did, we're home free tonight!"

Although Lena had some ideas about changes, improvements, in the skits she'd read that afternoon, she had decided not to attempt changes until she was more familiar with the skits and her role in them. So she played her part straight on this night, wearing the Little Susie outfit, hair in plaits halfway down her back, acting the straight part to Andy's buffoonery in his Jake costume. She played the bewildered, naïve country girl, recoiling from his tomfoolery, eyes cast down, dragging her toe across the stage. But near the conclusion of the skit, when Jake fell to the stage, supposedly stumbling over his own feet in the awkward, floppy shoes, she drew back from him, and added a bit that drew a roar from the crowd—she hiked her long skirt nearly to the knee, exposing her shapely limbs sheathed in white stockings.

There was a brief suspension of sound, a moment of shocked silence, and Lena feared that she had gone too far. Then a concerted roar came up from the crowd—mostly from male throats, she was sure—and loud applause and bawdy shouts followed.

Letting her skirt fall back into place, Lena made a slight, demure bow, and then ducked behind the stage curtain. Doc swept in a moment later, grinning from ear to ear.

"Great, honey! By God, that was something!"

A voice said acidly behind Lena, "Vulgar, you mean. Vulgar, in low taste. I knew this little snip was trouble the minute she walked onto the lot."

Doc scowled blackly. "That'll do, Lucy! This girl is the best thing ever happened to this show, and all you can do is throw cold water!"

Lena had faced around to see Lucy standing behind her, her lips set primly, hands crossed over skimpy bosom.

Lucy sneered. "The greatest thing, Doc? You looking forward to getting into her drawers? Probably won't be all that hard to do, is my guess."

"By Christ, that's enough now!" Doc blazed. He took two quick steps and slapped her across the mouth, not too hard. Lucy stepped back, eyes widening in shock. Her hand flew to her mouth. In a whining voice she said, "You hit me."

"Yes, and I'll do it again, Lucy, if you don't button it up. Maybe I should have taken the back of my hand to you before this. A man once told me that the only way to keep a woman or a dog in line is to beat them regularly. Maybe that's good advice."

Eyes dry, Lucy drew herself up. "I will not stand to be beaten, not even by my own husband!"

He eyed her thoughtfully. "No, I don't expect you would, and I don't relish whomping on a female, anyway. But there is one thing I can do, woman. You give me any more trouble and I'll pack you off home. By heaven, I will! I don't know why you tagged along, anyhow. Any person around a medicine show has to pull his own weight.''

His wife gave him a look of flashing venom, turned, and pushed through the back entrance of the stage wagon.

Doc stared after her, then said with a sigh, "I'm sorry for that, honey. If she tries to give you any trouble when I'm not around, be sure and let me know. I'll by God send her packing.''

Without thinking Lena said, "How long have you been married, Doc?"

"Huh?" He gave her a startled look, then began to laugh. "You mean, this time? This is the third one, honey. And we've been married four months, four months I've sorely regretted. Sharing her bed is a chore, believe you me. You know why I married her? I was busted, after that lousy season last year that I told you about. She was a widow lady with some money. Without her money I would never have made it on the road this season. But believe me, honey, you pay for what you get in this life, and I'm paying for marrying Lucy for her money. Too damned much, dammit to hell!''

Andy Jacks stuck his head around the stage curtain. "Doc, what's holding things up? They're getting antsy out here.''

"Oh, hell! I'm sorry, Andy. Got busy here for a little. Be right there." As Andy's head disappeared, Doc reached out to touch Lena's hand. "Don't let any of this get under your hide, Lena. We're going to have a hell of a season, I can feel it in my bones. You're an asset to the show, believe it.''

By the time Lena had changed out of her costume, Doc had finished his Elixir pitch and sent the men through the audience. She watched from behind the curtain, and saw that Doc had been right—they were having a good night. Doc's Elixir of Life was selling almost as fast as the men could pass the bottles out.

Doc handled the crowd masterfully, milking them for the last dollar, until he finally sensed their beginning restlessness.

With a sweeping gesture he cut off the sale. "No more selling tonight, folks. It's time for the finals of the talent contest." Consulting a slip of paper in his fist, he read off three names, the three finalists in the contest.

He had told Lena a little about the contest that afternoon before the show. "It's all a means of hyping sales, or bringing more people back night after night, which amounts to the same thing. Different shows do it different ways. Some have a most beautiful girl contest, others the most popular. That can get you into hot water sometimes. But with a talent contest, the competition is based more on merit, less apt to cause bitterness among the contestants. At least that's been my experience." He laughed suddenly. "Not that there is any great talent out there. But at least they're all more or less equal in that respect. And the judges are selected from among the townsfolk, so we can't be accused of chicanery. Tonight, the three finalists are two singers and one dancer. I wouldn't advise you to witness the performances, Lena. I sure as hell wouldn't if I didn't have to!"

Lena knew that each finalist tonight would perform her specialty, then the three judges would vote on a winner, who would receive an elaborate set of dishes, which Doc had told her cost about five dollars wholesale. "But look at the honor of winning! Which I hope will last at least until we can get out of town."

As the first girl began to sing, Lena recognized the reason for Doc's warning—the girl was awful. She had all the tonal quality of a crow.

Lena fled to the wagon where she was to sleep. Even there, she could still hear the voice. But she'd had little sleep since leaving Nacogdoches, and the excitement of the evening now took its toll. She washed her face and hands, got undressed, and fell onto the cot, where she went to sleep within minutes. She awoke once during the night to the sound of hammering, and knew that the men were dismantling the stage and the benches, and loading the wagons. Doc had told her that they would be ready to leave Fort Worth by first light.

She awoke the second time to find the wagon in motion. Daylight filtered through the side windows of the wagon.

She got dressed quickly, and made her way to the front of the wagon. She was surprised to see Doc driving the team, reins held loosely in his lap, as he drank from a tin cup.

At her sound of surprise he glanced around. He looked tired, his eyes bloodshot, a faint stubble of beard on his face. "Hi, honey. Sorry if I woke you."

She climbed out to sit beside him. "I didn't expect you to be driving. Where's . . .?"

"Lucy?" His grin was sardonic. "It seems I don't have to send her packing. She took it on herself to leave. Without even saying good-bye. How about that? Here." He handed her a tin cup from under the seat, and then held up a blackened coffeepot. "I made this just before pulling out. Not too hot, but at least it's still warm."

She poured the cup half full of coffee and drank gratefully.

Doc said, "We'll stop and whip up some breakfast out of town a ways."

"Where are we heading?"

"West. To Mineral Wells. That's our next show spot."

They rode along for a little in silence. They were already in the outskirts of Fort Worth. The sun was coming up behind them; it was going to be another hot day. Yesterday Lena might have been troubled by Doc's wife leaving, making her the only woman in the troupe. Eventually she was going to have to fend off his advances, or accept them, she knew that. But she also knew this man better now, and the prospect of his sexual advances did not bother her all that much.

She put such thoughts out of her mind for the time being, and said, "I'm sorry if I've brought trouble between you and your wife, Doc."

"What trouble?" He yawned widely. "Lucy was the troublemaker, honey, not you. As hardhearted as it may sound, she served her purpose. Now that I'm on the road, I'll stay out until the season's over. I owe her, but I should be able to pay her back after the season's over." He patted her knee, in a purely fatherly fashion. "Especially now that you're with us."

A thought had nudged into her mind just before she went to sleep last night. And although it was probably premature, she put voice to it. "Doc, did you ever think of starting up a tent show, offering pure entertainment, none of this medicine peddling? You've got the core of it already, with me, yourself, and the other fellows. All you'd need would be to add a few more actors and performers to your troupe, and buy a tent. I'm not talking about this season, it's too late for that, but we could do it next year . . ."

# 9

Michael brought Kate back to Nacogdoches with him following Kevin's funeral. Debra had accompanied him to Brownsville for the services. Kate had wanted to bring Kevin's body back to Moraghan for burial, but it simply was not possible. It had been difficult enough to postpone the services until Michael and Debra could make the long journey down to the Valley.

Stony had been presiding over a trial and had remained home with the children. He met the stagecoach as it pulled in.

Kate was in black. She as somber, and looked drawn and pale, but she was dry-eyed—she had already done her weeping for Kevin.

Stony took her into his arms. "Dear God, Kate, I am sorry, sorrier than I can ever say."

She nodded against his shoulder, her voice muffled. "I know, Stony, I know." She stepped back, tears threatening again.

Stony kissed Debra, shook hands with Michael. "I have a surrey waiting."

As they walked up the street to the surrey, Michael said, "Have you heard anything from Cassie, Stony?" He had begged Cassie to go with them down to the Valley, but she had adamantly refused. "Michael, how do you think your mother would feel, me attending your daddy's funeral, when it was my brother who killed him?"

"We don't know for sure that it was Bud. All the telegram said was that some stranger shot Daddy down in the citrus orchard."

"Who else could it be? It had to be Bud. I'm as sure of that as I am about anything. And I'm not going down with you, Michael, don't waste your breath."

At the time, Michael had been too distraught about his father's sudden death to give it much thought, but all the way back from Brownsville, he had been plagued by one thought—Cassie had not promised to be there when he returned.

Now Stony said, "Not a word, Michael. Of course, I haven't been out to Moraghan since you and Debra left."

Michael fell silent, sneaking a sidelong look at his mother. She showed no reaction. With much trepidation he had told her about Cassie on the way up. It was better that way than letting Cassie's presence at Moraghan come as a complete surprise.

Kate had shown little bitterness; of course, they still didn't know, for certain, that Bud Danker had killed Kevin. She had said, "Cassie Danker? Isn't that the girl I saw with her brother at Nora's funeral?"

"Yes, Mother. But she's different from Bud as night from day. She hasn't a mean bone in her body, she's sweet-natured as can be. She doesn't hold any grudge against the Moraghans."

"That's a switch," Kate said dryly, "since she's a Danker."

"And she's pretty, too, Mother," Debra said.

"Oh? Are you sweet on her, son?"

Michael said stiffly, "I think that's my own affair, Mother. I'm a grown man now."

She gave him a slow, penetrating look. "Yes, Michael, I can't argue with that. But a Danker . . ."

She had fallen silent, staring straight ahead, and Michael had been more than glad to drop the subject.

Now, everybody in the surrey and headed for the Lieberman house, Stony said, "I don't know if this is the time to bring this up, Kate, but I've had some word from the authorities, including the Texas Rangers, about Bud Danker."

Kate sat up straight. "Now is as good a time as any, Stony. Have they caught him?"

"No, but they've pretty well established that it was Bud killed Kevin. It seems he left a trail of blood across half of Texas. He killed a man outside of Beaumont and stole his horse. At least he was seen later riding the dead man's horse. And he's been definitely identified as the man who killed a storekeeper the other side of Corpus Christi. Also, he was seen down in the Valley, asking questions about Kevin. So they're pretty sure it was Bud who gunned Kevin down."

"Lord God, must we always be plagued by the Dankers?" Kate sighed. "Then I presume they don't know where he might be?"

"No, he seems to have disappeared. After Kevin was killed, a man answering his description did rob a country store well north of Brownsville, pistol-whipping the proprietor, taking his cash and a new pair of boots. The storekeeper said that the robber was wearing a pair of Mexican sandals, and I understand that's how Bud got close to Kevin, disguised as a Mexican laborer."

"Yes, that's how it happened," Kate said in a dead voice. "There were some men picking not ten feet away, they never knew anything was wrong until the gun went off—" She choked up for a moment, then went on resolutely, "After Kevin fell down dead, this man ran. He had a horse tied off on the edge of the grove. And they did find a pair of boots he left behind in his hurry. Oh, dear God, Kevin! My poor Kevin!"

Debra, sitting on the seat beside her, turned to take Kate into her arms. "There, Mother, it's awful, I know. Godalmighty, I know! But they'll catch the bastard in the end. He'll hang for what he did!"

Kate pulled herself away, staring stonily ahead. "I hope they never catch him. I hope he just vanishes off the face of the earth."

Michael gaped at her. "Mother, do you know what you're saying?"

"Yes, I know what I'm saying. Will catching him, hanging him, bring Kevin back? There's been enough violence, enough killing, between the Dankers and the Moraghans. Maybe this will put an end to the feud. Don't you see, son? If he's executed, who knows but what one of his brothers, or sisters, or even one of their children, will think he has to avenge Bud's death, blaming the Moraghans. It happened with Sonny Danker, it happened with his son, with Tod, and now with Bud. Dear God, let there be an end to it!" Her voice was like a cry of pain.

They all fell silent now, as the Lieberman house came into view. The children came tumbling out of the house, running to the surrey with cries of welcome. After they had climbed all over Debra and had been properly kissed and hugged, they sobered when they saw their grandmother. They tried to hide behind Debra. Kate, smiling wanly, knelt and held out her arms. Debra shoved them around in front of her, and they advanced on Kate shyly, and then she had them both hugged tightly against her. Over their heads she looked up at Debra with moist eyes.

"You see, Debra Lee?" Kate said in a husky voice. "We can't have these children caught up in this stupid feud when they grow up! We have to see to it that it never happens again!"

Debra swallowed. "You're right, Mother, and I was wrong. There has to be an end to it."

Stony cleared his throat. "Well! You all go into the house while I put the horse and surrey away. It's soon suppertime. Knowing about what time you'd get in, I asked Mrs. Atkins if she'd stay and fix supper. You must all be starved. I know stage-station grub isn't all that great."

A short time later they were all seated in the parlor. Stony had made drinks for them. Even Kate was having a glass of watered bourbon. The children were in Kate's lap.

Debra said, "That's enough now, you two. Go out in the yard and play until suppertime. We old folks want some peace and quiet."

After the children were outside, Stony took a swallow of his drink, said gravely, "What are your plans, Kate? Is this just to be a short visit or are you staying around for a while?"

Kate said slowly, "I may stay permanently."

Stony arched an eyebrow in surprise, pulled at his nose. "This is a switch. What about the ranch, farm, whatever you call it, down there?"

"At the moment Juan Mendoza, the Mexican foreman Kevin hired a half-dozen years ago, is running it. He knows almost as much about running it as Kevin did, certainly a devil of a lot more than I do. He's honest, a good worker. Whatever profits there are, I'll get my proper share. What else could I do? I talked it over with Michael, he said he had no desire to run the place. I certainly can't do it alone."

"But you've always said you loved it down there."

"Now that Kevin's dead, I've learned that I don't, not really. I always said that for his benefit, I reckon. There is no way I'll stay down there alone, with Kevin killed not a half-mile from the house. The memory of that would always hurt. Michael doesn't want to live there with me, and I guess Lena made it clear she doesn't, either. No, my real home is up here, on Moraghan."

Stony nodded, taking a swallow of his drink. "Will you sell the acreage down there?"

"Maybe, maybe not. I haven't made up my mind yet, and there's no tearing hurry. I may hang on to it. It'd be a shame to let it go, after Kevin worked so hard to make it pay. Maybe Michael or Lena will change their minds, or maybe one of their children, if they ever have any, might take over the orchards and run them. Speaking of Lena, has there been any word of her at all?"

"I'm afraid not, Kate. Since Kevin and you wired that you didn't want her chased after, we have no clue as to her whereabouts."

"That's another reason for me to stay here. If she's all right, if she comes back, it'll be to Moraghan, not Brownsville, I feel certain of that. I want to be here when

she does." Kate sighed heavily. "More than likely she
doesn't know about Kevin."

"I'm sure she doesn't, Kate, or she would have come
back, or at least gotten in touch."

Kate said, "It was mentioned in the Brownsville paper,
but the odds are against her seeing that."

"We'll be hearing from her soon, Kate, I know we
will," Stony said.

"I purely hope so, I wouldn't want to lose her, too.
That would be too much."

Michael chafed to rush out to Moraghan, to see Cassie.
But it was night and Kate was weary from the long journey
up from Brownsville. He didn't want to leave her, didn't
want her to have to go out to Moraghan by herself. So, he
fretted to himself, spent an almost sleepless night, and was
able, without being too obvious about it, to get them on
the road right after breakfast the next morning.

He hadn't fooled Kate for an instant. She said, "You
really must be stuck on this girl, Michael. You've been
itching to get started out here since we got into Nacogdoches
last night."

"You're right, Mother, I have," he admitted sheepishly.
"And I suppose you're right about the other, too. I am
stuck on her. I wasn't all that sure until I'd been away
from her all this time."

"Debra Lee told me something that shocked me, son.
The pair of you have been living on Moraghan alone
together, without being married. Do you think that's wise?"

He stiffened. "It doesn't bother me. Nor does it bother
Cassie."

"Well, that's all right for you, I'm sure, but there are
others involved."

"The Moraghan good name, you mean?" He laughed
scornfully. "You mean, like Grandfather Sean being a
defrocked priest? Like Debra Lee running a whorehouse in
Corpus Christi?"

"That's enough, Michael!"

He plowed on, "Or like you being pregnant with her

before you married Daddy? Or like her being Uncle Brian's, not Daddy's . . .''

She slapped him ringingly across the face. "I'll not listen to this!"

"It's true enough, isn't it?"

In a dead voice she said, "You'd better turn this buggy around and take me back in to town. I can see that it was a mistake coming up here."

"Mother, I'm sorry," he said wretchedly. "I shouldn't have said those things, but I'm tired of being picked at. 'She's a Danker, Michael! It's a disgrace, living in sin like that with her!' Well, Mother, that part isn't true, we're not living in sin. We keep to our own beds." His sudden laugh was wry. "God knows, I might as well have bedded her, since everyone seems to think I have. I've thought about it, don't think I haven't. But you know *why* I haven't, Mother? Because I know Cassie wouldn't stand still for it, not until we're legally married. That's the kind of a girl she is."

They rode along in tense silence for a mile or so. Then Kate gave a sigh, visibly relaxing. "I'm sorry I slapped you, Michael." She laughed. "You are a little long in the tooth for that."

"It's all right, Mother, I deserve it. I shouldn't have said all those things."

"They are true, just like you said. What I can't figure is how you knew all that. Some of it you obviously would know, but the rest?"

He shrugged. "I've heard bits and pieces here and there, Mother, I don't really remember. It's hard to keep family secrets secret, you know that."

"We're not a very nice family, are we, Michael?"

"We're a very nice family, all in all," he said stoutly. He reached across to take her hand. "And Cassie will be a fine addition to the Moraghan family. You'll like her, you'll see."

Cassie wasn't there, of course. Michael had had the strong feeling all along that she would be gone.

Bandy came out of the barn to meet them as they drove up. Michael said, "Mother, I'd like you to meet my horse trainer, Roscoe Barnes, called Bandy. Bandy, this is my mother, Kate Moraghan."

Bandy removed his sweat-stained Stetson. "Pleased to meet you, Missus Moraghan. Fact."

Michael was looking toward the house. "Bandy, where is Cassie?"

"Well, bub . . ." The little man cleared his throat, looking sidelong at Kate. He jerked his head. "Word in private, bub?"

Tense with forboding, Michael moved over to one side with Bandy. Speaking in a hoarse whisper, never looking at him, Bandy said, "The girl left. Three days ago. She had been in to town in the buggy the day before for groceries. Said she wanted to fix a real good coming-home supper for you and your ma. I was busy when she got back from town. When I finally came in to the house, I found a cold supper waiting for me. I didn't see the girl, but I just thought maybe she was tired after a hard day and went to bed early. But after I exercised the horses early the next morning and came to the house for my breakfast, I found she was gone. Don't know whether she left the night before, during the night, or what. Don't know how she got to wherever she was going. She didn't take a horse or buggy, that's for sure. Fact."

"She just took off . . ." Michael's throat closed up. "Without a word of any kind?"

Bandy was taking an envelope from his pocket. "Found this on her pillow when I went looking for her. Addressed to you, bub."

Michael closed his hand around the envelope. He started to open it, then glanced over at Kate, who was waiting patiently where they had left her, staring at the house. "Bandy, would you take Mother's things into the house?" At the little man's nod, Michael raised his voice. "Mother, Bandy will take your things in. I'll be in in a bit, I want to check on the horses first."

He strode toward the stable, eyes burning with unshed tears, the envelope clutched tightly in his fist.

He went around to the other side of the stable and leaned on the rail fence, staring at the horses in the pasture, the letter still unopened in his hand. He stared blindly at first, but gradually the horses came into focus, and as always the sight of them brought a measure of calm to him. The colts frisking around their mothers even caused him to smile.

Finally he straightened up, and slit open the envelope with his thumbnail. The letter was brief, almost cruelly so:

Dear Michael:

I will be gone by the time you read this. It will do no good to come after me. You might find me, but I will not go back to Moraghan with you.

It was all a mistake from the beginning. I knew that it would be, but I went along against my better judgment. Please do not think that you are to blame for my leaving, Michael. I care for you, much more than I should. But we can never have a life together, darling Michael. You are a Moraghan and I am a Danker. That will always be between us, that and the fact that Bud killed your father. You would never be able to forget that, no matter how much you might tell yourself now that it does not matter. It does matter, to me and to you.

I hope I have not hurt you too much. Please take care of yourself. Be good to yourself, you deserve it. You are a grand person, Michael, and I will always love you. I have loved you from the first moment I saw you. I did not realize how much until I penned this letter.

Good-bye, Michael
Cassie

He let the hand holding the letter fall to his side. He already felt an emptiness, an ache of loneliness, that he suspected would grow worse. If Cassie had realized how much she loved him in writing the farewell letter, he realized how strong his own feelings were by reading it.

Ah, Cassie, Cassie! Why did you do it? He knew her reasons, of course, and she was probably right—it might never have worked out for them. Yet she could have given it a chance, *they* could have given it a chance.

A futile rage seized him, and he hammered his fist against the railing until the pain cut across the edge of his anger.

And worse than anything, he had not made love to her, had not even tried. At least he could have had the memory of that to keep with him. How many would believe they had never shared the same bed? He laughed aloud, a bark of bitter laughter. He remembered his words to Kate a bit ago—"Because I knew Cassie wouldn't stand still for it, not until we're legally married." But how did he *know* that? He had never tried, maybe she wouldn't have rebuffed him. That could even be one reason she had left, she might have figured that he didn't want her sexually.

He read the letter again: "... the fact that Bud killed your father." How could she be so sure of that? Had Bud gotten in touch with Cassie during his, Michael's, absence? But how could he have? He couldn't read or write, and surely even Bud wouldn't be crazy enough to venture back here!

It was true that Bud Danker could neither read nor write, but that wasn't too uncommon in that day and time, and there were people to be found in almost any city who would write letters for a fee.

The day Cassie took the buggy into Nacogdoches for groceries, she had no thought of leaving Moraghan. She was not looking forward with any great relish to facing Kate Moraghan, or living in the same house with her, but she was prepared to endure it for Michael's sake.

Her grocery shopping done, she was on her way back to Moraghan, passing the post office on the way. Apparently her presence in town had been noted by the postmaster, for he was waiting in front as she started past. He came toward the buggy, waving a letter over his head. Cassie sawed back on the reins.

The postmaster, a scrawny, red-faced, tobacco-chewing individual, put a hand on the buggy seat and leered up at

her familiarly. "Hidy, Cassie. Heard you were living out
to the Moraghan place instead of your own house—"

She interrupted him. 'It's not my own house, Mr.
Parker, it's rented."

"Whatever," he said with a shrug. "Anyways, this
letter came for you. I was wondering how to get it out to
you when I saw you riding past."

He held out the letter, and Cassie took it from him.
"Thank you, Mr. Parker. I do appreciate it."

She dropped the letter onto the floorboards of the buggy,
flicked the reins, and the buggy jumped ahead so unexpectedly
that the postmaster had to leap back out of the way to keep
from being knocked off his feet. He shouted a few curses
after her.

Cassie was reluctant to open the letter. It had to be word
of Bud and could only contain bad news. She didn't stop
until she was a good ways out of town. Finally she pulled
in under the shade of an oak alongside the road. Picking
the envelope up from the floorboards, she turned it over
and over in her hand. Finally, she opened it with a wildly
beating heart. The envelope was postmarked Fort Worth
and there was no return address. Inside was a single sheet
of paper, with only a few lines written on it in a flowing
hand that struck Cassie as being feminine.

It was couched in vague language, offering no clue, to a
stranger to Bud, as to the identity of the sender:

Dear Sister:
    Am writing to let you know I am fine. I hear that I
messed up with that fellow you know there, but I set
matters aright down south. I have done honor to the
family name, and no longer will we have to feel
shame. We can hold our heads up high and proud
now. I promised you that I would do it and I did. Will
leave word at the White Elephant Saloon on Main
Street in Fort Worth, should you want to get in touch
with me.

There was no signature, no name at the bottom of the
page.

Despair was a heavy weight on Cassie's shoulders as she read the letter again. There was no doubt in her mind as to what the phrase "I set matters aright down south" meant. Bud had killed Kevin Moraghan. She had thought as much, now there was no longer any doubt whatsoever.

How could she face Michael now? Worse, how could she face his mother? Michael had told her that he intended to bring his mother back to Moraghan, for a short stay if not permanently. She could not face them, she simply couldn't!

She had to go now, before Michael returned. Perhaps it was for the best anyway. She had known, far back in her mind, that it would never work out, but she had allowed Michael to lull her into false hopes. A Moraghan and a Danker? It was not fated to be. Even if Michael could somehow convince himself to overlook Bud's killing his father—and she strongly doubted that he could—it would rankle, eating away at him like a slow-growing cancer, and eventually he would come to hate her.

No, it was time to go, before he came back.

She had just about enough money for a stagecoach ticket to Fort Worth . . .

She laughed suddenly. That was where Lena had gone. She couldn't go to Fort Worth anyway, not at this time. The postmaster would be sure to have noted the postmark on the envelope and he would guess that it came from Bud. If she went to Fort Worth now, she would likely lead the law right to Bud. Maybe she could look him up later, after the furor had died down. She had a sister in Houston, one she had been on good terms with. She would go to Houston for the time being. She didn't think Michael would come after her, he had too much pride for that.

Mind made up, she clucked to the horse, setting the buggy in motion. She put herself to planning exactly how she would slip away from Moraghan without alerting Bandy.

# 10

Mark Moraghan disembarked from the tramp steamer in New Orleans. He had been at sea for almost nine months, a voyage all the way around South America and back, and for the first time in his many travels, he was homesick. He was not fooled; he knew that his longing for home had nothing to do with his family or his home per se—he longed to see Lena. She had been in his thoughts constantly during the long voyage. He was hopelessly in love with her, and that was exactly what it was—hopeless.

Even as he left the ship, duffle bag slung over his shoulder, Mark still hadn't made up his mind whether or not he would go to Nacogdoches. He could ship back out on the same freighter, which would be leaving port again in a few days. And he had been told that he could sign on with another ship sailing in the morning. What purpose would it serve to see Lena again? It would only make matters worse, for both of them. Besides, Lena had probably returned to Brownsville by this time. Or even worse, she could have taken his sage advice and found some fellow to marry.

Mark had always loved New Orleans, he considered it the most cosmopolitan of cities, and he loved the bustling wharf area, with its exotic odors—the rich aromas of coffee, bananas, and other fruits from the tropics. He was fascinated by the polyglot mixture of races: black, white, and yellow. The cries of street vendors rang in his ears as he gravitated toward the French Quarter, only a short walk from the docks.

He hadn't had shore leave since Rio, he had a wallet swollen with back pay, and he was ready for what the French Quarter had to offer. Strong drink, perfumed wom-

en, some of the best food in the world, an expensive hotel
with a hot bath, silken sheets, and a good barbering—not
necessarily in that order. Mark had strong appetites, and he
could deny them only so long. In the embrace of a talented
whore he could at least forget Lena for an hour or so.

He checked into the Royal Orleans, the most elegant
hotel in the Quarter, ignoring the desk clerk's raised
eyebrows at his rough seaman's duds. Of course the man
unbent a little when Mark took out his thick wallet and
began plucking out bills to make the required payment in
advance.

When he had registered and was given a key, Mark
slipped the desk clerk a ten-dollar bill. "Send a barber up
to my room in an hour, will you, my good man?" he said
grandly, hiding his grin until he turned away to follow the
black man with his duffle bag.

It was nearly dusk when he emerged from the hotel,
barbered until the skin on his face burned, and dressed in
his one good suit—a gray-stripe, with a white shirt and
flowing cravat, and black boots polished to a high gloss.

Firing a cigarette, he strolled up the street to Antoine's,
got a table by himself, and dined sumptuously. He had two
whiskies before the meal, and lingered a long while over a
pony of brandy after he was finished eating.

After paying his bill, he bought an unaccustomed cigar
and strolled along the streets of the Quarter, smoking. It
was early yet to find a woman for the night. He enjoyed
the swirl and color of the quarter's night life as he made
his way along Bourbon Street, waving off the prostitutes as
they swished up to him.

As he turned down a side street off Bourbon, his
attention was caught by a poster pasted over the window of
an empty store: "Come One, Come All! Grand Opening,
Week of May 20-26, The Holliday Traveling Players! Fun
and Frolic for Everyone. Melodrama to Wring Your Heart-
strings! Laughter to Bring Tears to Your Eyes! This Week's
Drama, NELL'S DILEMMA, Featuring Toby and Little Nell!
Thrilling Olio!"

Smiling, Mark was about to move on, but then he did a

double take. At the bottom of the poster were two photos—
one of a man in an exaggerated rube costume, the other
was of a woman, a girl really. It was on this picture that
Mark's attention was riveted. He struck a match and
peered closer.

It was Lena, it had to be Lena! It was either Lena or a
girl who bore an uncanny resemblance to her. Mark
ruminated, staring at the picture until the match burned his
fingers. The date mentioned on the poster was this week,
tonight was the next to the last performance, and the time
the curtain rose was listed as eight o'clock. Mark pulled
out his pocket watch. It was seven forty-five. He still had
time to make it, since the location of the tent show was
only a few blocks distant.

Suddenly he made up his mind. Throwing away the
cigar, he began walking briskly in the direction of the
show tent. It was on a vacant lot, with the earthen levee
hulking up ominously in the night, holding back the surge
of the Mississippi. It had been a rainy spring, he had been
informed, and the Mississippi was mightily swollen, the
water dangerously near the top of the levee. It had not
rained today, but the night had a humid, sullen feel to it,
and lightning laced through the sky as Mark neared the
show tent.

It was a few minutes short of eight as Mark bought his
ticket. He paused before the tent entrance, staring up at the
banner stretched high across the front. Among the faces
painted there was Lena's—or her double. He shook his
head in disbelief. It seemed inconceivable to him that he
should come across her in such a manner.

Mark went into the tent, which was about half full. The
tent, he estimated, would hold about six hundred people—
four hundred in the rows of benches front and center, and
another two hundred in the cheaper bleacher seats in the
rear. Mark had bought a ticket in the fourth row—he
wanted to be close enough to the stage so there would be
no danger of his not recognizing Lena, if it was indeed
her.

Two candy butchers were working the aisles as Mark
searched for his seat. One approached Mark, and he parted

with a dime for a box of candy to keep the butcher from bothering him further. Sitting down, he opened the box, took out a piece of candy, unwrapped it, and popped it into his mouth. It was tough and had very little taste. As the coal-oil lamps on the tent poles dimmed, he removed the wad of candy from his mouth and dropped it onto the sawdust-covered floor, his gaze riveted on the curtain as it began to rise.

The set was that of a farm kitchen, and two characters were on stage—the farmer's wife and Toby, the hired hand, an exaggerated rustic type, with loud clothes, a frizzy wig of hair the color of carrots. From their conversation the audience was informed that the farm was heavily mortgaged, and the farmer had recently died, leaving a wife and daughter. The mortgage payments were past due, and the banker was threatening foreclosure.

Then the daughter, Nell, came on stage. Mark leaned forward, holding his breath. It was Lena Moraghan, there was not the slightest doubt. Her long hair was in braids, her clothes were simple, and her face scrubbed, giving her an innocent look. But it was Lena.

Mark leaned back, scarcely following the action of the play, pondering on how Lena could possibly have come to be involved in a tent-show operation. He had received no communications from home, and knew nothing of what had transpired during his absence.

Gradually he began to focus on the play. The plot line was simple, melodramatic, but it was a heart-tugger. *Nell's Dilemma* involved two young men: the banker's son and a neighboring farm lad. Nell loved the farm lad desperately, but if she married the banker's son, her mother would not lose the farm. If she married the farm boy, the mortgage would be foreclosed at once. Mark was a little surprised that such a play would be performed before a sophisticated New Orleans audience, and there were occasional hoots of derision, but as the play progressed, the crowd grew quieter, absorbed in it, and even Mark was caught up in the drama played out before him.

As the third act drew toward the play's climax, it became clear to Mark why the audience was enthralled.

Despite the melodrama's trite plot line and the black and white of its main characters, it was absorbing because of two performances—Lena's and the man who portrayed Toby. Lena was innocence personified, with a purity of soul that shone like an angel's halo. Could this be the same woman he had made love to? It was hard to believe. She delivered the simple lines with an intensity and honesty that added an element of reality to them, to the point when, in the third act, she rejected the rich banker's son for the poor farm boy, the audience stood up and cheered lustily, and Mark saw tears glisten in the eyes of those women near him.

And although the character of Toby was a buffoon, a rustic clown, the actor playing him gave an underlying dignity and a broad dimension to the role, and the gales of laughter he induced by his bumbling antics were not in the least disrespectful.

It was Toby who resolved the situation in the end, by discovering a satchel of hidden loot on the farm, the proceeds from a robbery of the town bank, and there was enough reward for the recovered loot to pay off the mortgage. This revelation brought down the house, and the curtain fell to thunderous applause.

When the actors made their curtain calls, Mark applauded along with the rest. He waved a hand over his head, trying to catch Lena's eye, but if she noticed him, she gave no indication.

As some people started to file out, Toby stepped to the forefront of the players and held up his hands for attention.

Stepping out of character, he said in carrying voice, "Ladies and gents, your kind attention, please! As a special added attraction, The Holliday Traveling Players is pleased to announce an olio performance, starring our players. Bob Ketchum, the fellow who played the bank robber in our play, is a banjo picker supreme. He will honor us with several solo selections. Lena Moraghan, who played Nell, will sing several songs for you, accompanied by Bob Ketchum on his banjo. Bessie Carson, who played Nell's mother, will perform a mind-reading act for your enlightenment and enjoyment. Andy Jacks, who played the banker, will do a dazzling juggling act. I personally will try to mystify you with feats of magic.

"The olio will be performed in about twenty minutes, as soon as our players can change costumes. The men will now pass among you with tickets. Just twenty-five cents, folks, for this extra added attraction. When the tickets are sold the men will then pass among you with candy, popcorn, and cold lemonade for sale, for those of you who are hungry or thirsty."

On cue, two men emerged from around the stage wagon, and began working through the audience, most of whom remained. It struck Mark that such was the instant popularity of the players that the crowd was willing to part with money to see them in roles other than their stage characters. Mark, who still had not made up his mind if he was going backstage to speak to Lena, dug twenty-five cents out of his pocket and bought a ticket. About two-thirds of the audience remained for the olio.

Mark waited impatiently for Lena to appear on the olio program, but she was last, which struck him as appropriate when he heard her sing. The others were mediocre, with the exception of the banjo player, who was a marvel, long fingers a blur as they flew over the strings. The juggler dropped two Indian clubs, misjuggled a flaming torch and almost set the backdrop on fire, and was rewarded with groans from the audience. The magician was not too adroit, and tried to cover up his ineptitude with a patter of not particularly funny lines borrowed from his Toby character, and the mind-reading act was only a little better.

Lena, however, was worth the admission price, and Mark didn't think he was unduly prejudiced, given the enthusiastic response from the audience.

She came out in a peach-colored dress, her long auburn hair loose and flowing. The dress was cut daringly low, revealing a swoop of bosom, and Mark remembered vividly those full breasts bared to his gaze, the nipples sprung to full arousal under his stroking hands. Lena had shed her virginal appearance now, and exuded a certain sexuality, yet it was not overly blatant.

Her voice was obviously untrained, but was sweet and

clear. She confined herself to a repertoire of Stephen Foster songs: "Oh, Susannah," "Camptown Races," "My Old Kentucky Home."

The applause was thunderous, demanding an encore, and she obliged with "Dixie's Land," cajoling the audience to join in, and soon voices rose, hands clapped in time, and feet stomped. Mark couldn't remember ever having heard a more rousing rendition of "Dixie."

Lena was called back twice for bows, to cries of, "More, More!" But, smiling, she begged off. When the curtain was finally lowered, applause was still sounding.

Mark waited until the tent was almost empty before he ventured toward the back of the stage. The stage, he saw, was made by two wagon beds stationed end to end. He expected to be intercepted any second, but he managed to make his way around the stage wagons without incident.

He heard laughter and voices, and he finally came to a sort of dressing area between the stage wagons and the back of the tent. The show people were milling about, talking animatedly, exchanging congratulations. Several were having drinks, including the man who had played Toby. He was standing off to one side, talking to Lena. Neither saw Mark as he approached.

"I tell you, honey, I stunk up the place. I don't think I'll ever get the hang of this magic stuff. I can talk St. Peter into opening the pearly gates for the worst kind of sinner, but when it comes to my hands, I'm about as graceful as a jackass!"

Lena patted his arm. "It just takes practice, Doc, and we haven't had all that much practice, any of us. You'll be all right down the road. The play went well, don't you think?"

Doc brightened. "It went smooth as silk, honey. But much of the credit is due to you. Lena, they ate you up out there."

"You weren't so bad yourself. I told you all along you'd make a better Toby than Andy ever would—" She clapped a hand to her mouth and looked around. "Good heavens, I hope Andy didn't hear me say that!"

Her gaze found Mark and she stared, a tiny frown creasing her forehead.

"Lena?" Mark took a tentative step toward her.

"Mark! Oh, my God!" she shrieked, and ran at him.

He folded her into his arms, glorying in the feel of her, in the scent of her. Over her shoulder he saw the man she'd called Doc staring at them. His face showed hurt, edged with anger. As their glances met, the other man tossed off his drink, making of it a gesture of defiance.

Now Lena drew back a little, and rained kisses on his face. Breathlessly she said, "Where did you come from, Mark? Where have you been all this time? How did you find me?"

He laughed. "First, I just got off a ship that docked this afternoon. Second, I've been at sea for nine months. And third, I saw a poster advertising Holliday's Traveling Players, with a picture of you on it. Now it's your turn, cousin... how in the holy hell did you ever get with a traveling tent show?"

Her eyes, clinging hungrily to his face, glowed. "It's a long story, Mark, a *very* long story. Mark..." She took his hand and turned. "I want you to meet Doc Holliday. Actually"—she grinned impishly—"his real name is Hoyt Jones. Doc, this is a cousin of mine, Mark Moraghan."

Doc began to smile. He stepped forward to pump Mark's hand, saying heartily, "Pleased to meet you, Mark Moraghan. Any relation to Lena is always welcome. Nobody knows how much I owe this little old gal." He threw a proprietary arm around her shoulders.

Lena moved away from him without being too obvious about it.

Mark said, "Can we talk, cousin? We have a lot of catching up to do."

"Of course we'll talk! But I have to get out of these clothes first. Then you can take me to supper, Mark. I'm starved. I can never eat before a performance, I'd throw up all over the stage."

"I'd be happy to take you to supper," he said, not bothering to tell her he'd already eaten.

"I'll see you later, Doc," Lena said.

Taking Mark's hand, she led him through the back tent flap. "My wagon is back here, Mark. You can wait outside for me while I make a fast change."

"I still can't get over it, you being with a tent show." He shook his head. "How long have you been away from Nacogdoches?"

"Since a short time after you left. I had a choice, running off or going back down to the Valley. Daddy was threatening to come up and drag me back."

"You ran away?"

"Yep." She laughed quickly, swinging their locked hands between them. "You see what kind of an example you set, Mark? I didn't join this show then, it didn't exist. Doc had a medicine show that came through Nacogdoches. I joined them in Fort Worth, and then convinced him to start up this show. We've been here in New Orleans all winter, putting it together. Here, this is my wagon." She drew him to a halt, giggled suddenly. "I've come up in the world, Mark. A whole wagon to myself. With the medicine show I only had a part of one, a small part at that. Wait here for me, I'll only be a couple of minutes."

She grazed his cheek with her lips, then darted up the steps into the wagon. Light bloomed through the small side window. Mark lit a cigarette and leaned against the wagon, smoking moodily, wondering how wise it had been of him to let his presence be known. What would Lena expect of him? Nothing had changed since he had run from her like a thief. For nine months he had been alternately wracked with guilt and afire with need of her. It would never work for them—the old taboos were too strong. No matter how he looked at it, it still came up incest.

He stood upright, throwing away his cigarette, as the tent flap folded back, and all the members of the troupe poured out, still laughing and chattering. They began to separate, going off to different wagons.

Mark saw the man called Doc stop a short distance away, staring at Lena's wagon. Mark was concealed in shadow, but the light from the wagon splashed across the other man's face. He had an unguarded, melancholy look, and Mark had to wonder what relationship existed between them. He had called Lena honey, and his manner toward her was possessive. Were they lovers? True, Doc was considerably older. But when had that ever been any great obstacle? Clearly Doc was an experienced man of the world, while Lena was . . . what? Nineteen, twenty now?

Mark laughed abruptly, deep in his throat. What business was it of his? He had no rights over Lena, one way or another. Her private life was her own affair.

The wagon door swung open and Doc Holliday hurried off. Lena came down the steps to Mark, hooking her arm in his.

"Where are you going to feed me, Mark? I warn you, I eat like a horse after doing a show."

"How about Antoine's, and a mess of oysters?"

"Aren't we being a little elegant? That has to be pretty steep."

They started up the street toward the French Quarter. "I can afford it, I have nine months pay in my back pocket." He looked down into her face. "Do the folks back in Nacogdoches know about you being with the tent show?"

"Nope." She shook her head, her hair swinging back and forth. "They haven't the least idea of where I am or what I'm doing. I haven't written them yet. But Nacogdoches is on our schedule, in about a month. I thought I'd surprise everybody there. They're going to be scandalized, I'm sure, but I don't care. I'm happy with what I'm doing. Besides, Grandmother Nora used to perform plays on Moraghan, in the little schoolhouse. Did you know that, Mark?"

"I remember hearing something to that effect, yes."

"She even wrote some plays. The one we did tonight? That was hers originally. I rewrote it a little, brought it up-to-date, and added a few lines, some additional scenes."

He grunted in surprise. "So you're not only an actress but a playwright as well."

"Well, let's just say I'm in the learning stages of both."

"One thing I don't understand, Lena . . . I'm not an expert on tent shows, or anything having to do with the theater, but it seems to me that your show tonight would go over better in small towns, places like Nacogdoches, or even smaller."

"Oh, we realize that, but like I said, we've spent the winter in New Orleans putting the show together. So we decided to open it here."

"Well, I must say it went over better than I would have expected, given the relative sophistication of the audience. You didn't have a full house but those who came certainly seemed to enjoy it."

"And I thank God for that!" She tightened her grip on his arm. "If we had failed dismally, I think Doc would have closed it down before we ever got on the road. I had to talk myself blue in the face before I could convince him to put together this tent show. He's been spooked all week, like a cat dancing on a hot stove. He kept telling me he was doing just fine with the medicine show, so why change. I think tonight may have finally convinced him."

And what did you do besides talk to convince him? Mark thought, but didn't dare put it into words. They were in the Quarter now, crossing Bourbon Street. They walked a half-block in silence, before Lena suddenly stopped and swung him around to face her.

"Aren't we going to talk about it at *all*?"

"Talk about what, cousin?" he said with feigned ignorance.

"Don't play dumb with me, Mark! You know perfectly well about what. About why you left so suddenly."

"Didn't you get my letter?"

"Of course I got your letter, but—"

"I should think that would have explained everything."

"It explained nothing!" she said in exasperation.

"Lena, we're first cousins, blood cousins," he said with exaggerated patience. "For blood cousins to have...uh, carnal relations is a sin."

"Says who?"

"The Bible, the church, society, just about every damned body you can name."

"As our Nell would say, balderdash! The reasoning of the male mind often baffles me. And you never told me you were all that religious, Mark. Not the way you act the cynic.''

"I'm not. The contrary, in fact. But it's what others would think and say, our families and neighbors.''

"Since we've both left our families, more or less, I fail to see how that matters. As for friends and neighbors, we could always live some place where we're not known.''

He recoiled slightly. "Lena! You're talking like I've asked you to marry me and you've accepted.''

She got a startled look. "I am, aren't I?''

And then, without warning, she dissolved into helpless laughter. In a moment he joined in, and they leaned against the nearest building, still convulsed with mirth. Then Mark noticed that passersby were giving them a wide berth, with odd looks.

With an effort he got his laughter under control, and took her arm firmly. "Come on, cousin, we're making spectacles of ourselves.''

They walked on toward the restaurant, more at ease with each other now. As if by mutual consent, they steered clear of any conversation about their personal concerns during the meal. It was now quite late, and Antoine's was relatively uncrowded. They had a table to themselves in an isolated corner. Lena ate with gusto, while Mark drank wine and merely picked at his food.

He asked Lena about her life with the medicine show, and how that had evolved into the tent show.

"I suppose it all had its beginning in my mind when I came across Grandmother's old plays,'' she told him between bites. "I was intrigued by the idea of performing before an audience. Then I saw Doc's medicine show in Nacogdoches, and when I decided to leave Moraghan, I came directly to Fort Worth, where his show was playing, and got a job. I was lucky there, the woman who had been working with him had just quit and he hired me. My career, if I can give that name to it, almost ended before it began. That first night, when I appeared before an audience for the first time, I got stage fright. Mark, I was absolutely petrified!'' She laughed, almost choking on a bite of food.

"What happened?''

"Doc jarred me out of it. I was supposed to sing, but when I froze up, I forgot every word to the song. Doc whispered in my ear that he would fire me if I didn't sing. So I sang. Since then I haven't been bothered by stage fright. Doc might seem to be nothing but a con man, but he's much more than that. He has a great insight into people. I suppose you have to have that to be able to con people into buying medicine that does them very little good."

"Didn't that part of it bother you?"

"Not a great deal. After all, it did make them feel good for a time, since it was about sixty percent alcohol."

"That's no excuse, cousin, and you know it."

"Is it?" Her eyes glinted at him. She dabbed at the corner of her mouth with a napkin, and leaned back. "You know what our biggest competition was, with the medicine show? And probably will be with this tent show, as well. Revival meetings. Any time we set up in a town where a revival meeting was going on, we didn't make enough to pay expenses. Usually Doc would just give the order to fold and we'd move on."

"So?" He spread his hands. "What does that have to do with what we were talking about?"

"It has this to do with it. In most of those revivals, there was some evangelist selling miracles from the pulpit. Saving souls, speaking in tongues, laying on of hands. In Doc's words, selling snake oil. The evangelist would convince seriously ill people that he had healed them. They would leave the meeting feeling cured, and the next day go right back to being the same, or worse. Now, is that any better than selling medicine like we did?"

Mark shrugged. "On that basis, I suppose not. But then that is in the nature of the pot calling the kettle black. All right, all right!" He was laughing as he held up his hands. "I'll concede the argument. Besides, I have no right to carp at the ethics or morals of others. Do you want some dessert, Lena?" He indicated her empty plate.

"Good heavens, no!" She sighed. "I've eaten too much as it is."

Mark beckoned a waiter over with the check. After the

bill was taken care of and they were on their way out, he said, "Do you stay at a hotel, or do you sleep on the show lot?"

"Right now, I'm staying in a boarding house where I've been all winter. When we're on the road, I'll be sleeping in my wagon." She took his arm outside the restaurant. "Did you know what low opinion most people have of those of us in any kind of show business? In most towns along the road, you aren't accepted in hotels or rooming houses. If you don't have a wagon to sleep in, you're out of luck."

"You've placed yourself in a different category, cousin, by getting into show business. I wouldn't let it worry me too much. Is your boarding house too far to walk, or shall I hire a hack?"

"Mark . . . where are you staying?"

He blinked at her. "The Royal Orleans."

"Oh, my, we *are* living high! Mark . . ." She moved a hip against him. "I don't want to go to the boarding house. Not tonight."

He was silent for a moment, but he was acutely aware of her nearness and of what she was offering. Even as he thought of it, he felt a powerful arousal, to the point of embarrassment.

Instinctively he knew that if he spurned her, she would be hurt, perhaps irreparably. He seemed to have no choice. Yet, even as he said "Then how about my hotel room?" a part of his mind was hooting at him—*now* who was making excuses?

Lena had known that Mark would not make the first move, and even though it was outrageously brazen of her, she felt that she had to suggest spending the night with him, or she would end up alone, and Mark would go haring off again.

So, when he made his suggestion, she tucked his arm close against her side, and said, "I think I'd like to see your hotel room, Mark."

She noticed, as they walked through the ornate lobby of the Royal Orleans, that Mark kept glancing about apprehensively. But as far as she could tell, no one seemed to notice anything untoward.

Mark's room was on the second floor, and they didn't speak all the way down the corridor; in fact, they hadn't spoken, Lena realized, since she had agreed to go to his room.

Before the door to his room, Mark fumbled the key out of his pocket, and said, "Well, this is it." He made no move to put the key into the lock.

Lena said brightly, "Yes, this is it." And then: "Don't you think you'd better open the door, Mark? We'd seem a little strange should anyone come along, standing out here like two lost children."

"Oh! You're right, Lena," he said with a sheepish grin, and keyed the door open.

Lena moved into the room. While not a suite, it was quite large, and decorated in excellent taste. Gas lights burned on the walls, highlighting the large bed. She glanced at him slyly. "You got a room with that large a bed just for yourself, Mark? Or do you have some female acquaintance here in New Orleans?"

"It was the smallest they had available," he said gruffly. He stood in the center of the room, hands hanging limply, as if he didn't quite know what to do next. He took a cigarette out of his pocket and lit it.

Lena moved briskly about, turning out the lamps. When they were extinguished, there was still a fair amount of light spilling in through the window. Without a word to Mark, she stood by the bed and began removing her clothes. She was unembarrassed by it; somehow it seemed a natural act, performed without guile or shame.

In her undergarments she turned to glance at Mark. He stood unmoving, but his gaze riveted on her. She said impatiently, "Well?"

He started to speak, then gave a yelp of pain as the cigarette between his fingers scorched his flesh. "Dammit to hell!" He hurried to the bed table to put out the cigarette.

Lena began to laugh, and he turned his glare on her. "That's not funny, Lena! It burns like the devil!"

"Oh, poor baby." She stepped to him, put his hand to her lips, and cooed, "Does it hurt bad? Here, let me kiss away the pain."

He jerked his hand from her grip. "Don't talk baby talk to me, I don't like it!"

Her temper sparked. "Then don't act like a baby, if you don't wish to be treated like one!"

He got a startled look. "Was I acting like that?"

"Yes!"

He said ruefully, "I'm sorry, I guess I was, at that. It's just that I'm in an unusual situation here."

"What's unusual about it? It isn't as if it hadn't happened before," she said with an impish grin.

"That other time was . . . well, sort of inadvertent."

"I didn't think it was inadvertent at all. I thought it was kind of nice." She took his face between her hands and kissed him lightly. "Dear Mark, I've missed you terribly, and I've often thought of that night. I felt awful when I found you gone. And if you're thinking that I *might* insist that you marry me, now that you despoiled me, disabuse yourself of the notion. After all"—she laughed softly— "I'm a show business person now, and everybody knows about our morals."

"You think I haven't thought about you? Not a day has passed that I haven't thought of you, Lena, and that one night we had together."

His resistance was suddenly gone, and he put his arms around her, his mouth rough and demanding on hers. In a moment she tore herself away, pushing him back. In a husky voice she said, "Get undressed, Mark."

Turning away now, she stripped the covers off the bed, and stretched out on her back. She resisted any urge to watch him disrobe, for she knew he was uneasy enough already. In a short time she felt his weight come down on the side of the bed, and only then did she look at him. She was already fully aroused, moist and ready for him. Without a word she reached out and pulled him down to her. As the length of his body touched hers, there was no doubt about his own readiness.

She urged him to her, and when he raised an eyebrow in question, she murmured, "Yes, Mark, now. Don't wait!"

She opened her thighs to him, he positioned himself over her, and went into her with a gusty sigh, and Lena rose eagerly to meet him.

It was quick and satisfying, her ecstasy excruciating in its intensity. She cried out piercingly, cradling him between her thighs, and he came as she was still shuddering mightily.

As they lay quiescent, his head on her shoulder, she said next to his ear, "Not that it's any of your business, Mark, but I want you to know something. You were my first, you already know that, but there have been none since that night. So far, I haven't lived up to the loose reputation of show people."

His laughter was wry. "I don't know whether to be flattered or scared to death."

"You know, actually the morals of show people aren't all that bad. I've learned that. Most of the women with tent shows or medicine shows are married, as well as many of the men. And due to the reputation we have, undeserved or not, those who aren't married are very careful to lead exemplary lives. There's very little sleeping around. I'd venture to say that we live more sinfree lives than any church folks. Oh, you may come across a toper now and then, medicine shows especially seem to attract drunks. But that's about as far as it goes—"

"Lena." He put his fingers over her mouth. "You're chattering away like a chipmunk, did you know that?"

She was silent for a long moment. "I was, wasn't I?" She laughed abruptly. "I reckon you weren't the only one nervous tonight. But it's all right now. Isn't it?"

"Yes, Lena, everything's fine," he said with his face averted. He moved around to sit up against the headboard, lighting a cigarette. In the flare of the match his face looked secretive, withdrawn.

"Mark, what are your plans now? Are you going back to Nacogdoches for a while?"

He didn't answer for a few moments, and his voice was low when he finally spoke. "I really haven't decided yet,

Lena. I'm sure things haven't changed there for me.
There's a ship I can ship out on in the morning, but I
haven't made up my mind yet."

"I don't suppose you'd consider going on the road with
the show? We can use another man to take Larry Brown's
place. He plays the male lead opposite me. He's changed
his mind about going out with us, and we need a
replacement."

"Me? On the stage?" he said incredulously. "You can't
be serious, cousin!"

"Why not? I happen to believe you could turn into a
very good actor. You're good-looking enough, you have
stage presence, and you're certainly bright enough to learn
the lines. Look at me, I had no stage experience, and I
happen to think I'm pretty darned good. After all, acting in
a tent show doesn't require all the talent in the world. Of
course," she raised up to grin down at him, "you'd be
playing opposite me, and we pledge to marry at curtain
fall. Maybe that would bother you?"

"That's not it. I just don't think I'm cut out to be an
actor. Look, that's enough talk. Come here."

He reached out and drew her down to him, silencing her
with his mouth. He began to make love to her again. This
time neither was in a great hurry, and it was prolonged,
nothing like their previous times. They explored each other
minutely, discovering their touch points of passion, and
when they finally joined together and spiraled toward a
mutual explosion of rapture, it was deeply satisfying for
both.

After it was over, Lena nestled down in the crook of his
arm with a sigh of contentment.

She slept soundly, well into the morning, and she was
awakened by the sound of a ship's horn in the harbor not
too far away. She had learned a little about ships during the
winter here in New Orleans, and she knew that the
mournful sound heralded a ship's departure.

She stretched lazily, and groped along the side of the
bed for Mark. She raised her head and said drowsily,
"Mark?"

He was gone. Jolted fully awake, she sat up in bed. The hotel room felt strangely empty. Her gaze was drawn to the corner of the room where she had seen Mark's duffle bag last night—it was gone, too.

She knew instinctively that he was on the ship sailing out of the harbor. Leaping up, she flew to the window and peered out. But the harbor was not visible from the window, only the small park across the way.

Shoulders slumped, she stood at the window for a long time, staring blindly down at the people on the street. She blinked back the sting of tears. Strangely, she felt neither anger nor surprise at his flight, but only a sense of great desolation.

# 11

The Holliday Traveling Players sloughed the tent after the Saturday evening performance, and moved out early Sunday morning, the wagons rumbling off the lot. They were headed for Port Allen, across the Mississippi from Baton Rouge, over seventy miles away. They would only be able to show for four days in Port Allen, since it would take them three or four days to make the journey and set up the tent. Henceforth their schedule had been arranged so that they could always give at least five performances in every city and town along their route, but Doc had wanted to get well out of the New Orleans area before they gave another performance.

They had been able to find a replacement for Larry Brown—a brawny, handsome lad by the name of Lee Woodward. He had no acting experience and, in Doc's words, "He has all the wits of a guttering candle, but he's pretty enough to set all the female hearts to fluttering. Watching him, they'll all be wondering how it'd be like for him to get in their drawers, and that should be enough, never mind how dimwitted he is.''

Now, as they pulled off the lot, Lena sat alongside Doc on the seat of the office wagon, the other wagons strung out behind them. Doc had said nothing to Lena about her being out all night, which had surprised her a little. It was possible, of course, that he didn't know, but she doubted that very much—little went on around the show that he wasn't aware of.

As the wagons strung out, settling down to an even pace, Doc reached under the seat for the pot of coffee he'd brewed just before they left the lot. He gave her the pot and two tin cups. ''Pour some for us, will you, honey?''

She poured the cups half full of coffee and gave him one. As they drank, she gazed around. Now that they had climbed up on a level with the levee, the brown spring waters of the Mississippi could be glimpsed through the trees. It had been a wet spring, and she was just as glad to get out of New Orleans. The water was creeping dangerously toward flood level. But today was bright, the sky swept clean of clouds, and it was going to be a warm, pleasant day.

''Well, honey, here we go, off and running,'' he drawled. ''Happy with the way things went so far?''

''Very. How about you?''

''Well . . . I'll confess something to you. I was against this from the start, but you're a pretty convincing lady, you know.'' He glanced over at her with a twinkling smile. ''But I think I'm going to like it. We may go bust somewhere down the road, but it'll be an experience, by Christ it will!''

''You're a fraud, Doc. You liked all that applause, don't you think I know that?''

He looked abashed. ''Maybe, maybe not. But whether I like it or not ain't the important thing here, making it pay is what counts.''

''It'll pay,'' she said confidently. ''It'll pay. The people through Louisiana, Texas, Oklahoma, and Arkansas are hungry for entertainment, especially the smaller towns without theaters. And it's practically a virgin field at the moment. I'll make a prediction right now. In the next twenty to forty years, tent shows like ours will become thick as fleas."

"That could well be. But medicine shows have already proven themselves," he said in a grumbling voice.

"Now Doc, don't start up again. I thought we'd thrashed that all out. Besides, you're running your candy butchers, aren't you? That should keep you happy, satisfy your appetite for milking the suckers.

"In that regard, I have an idea. Since the candy makers put code numbers on the boxes which hold gift certificates for the large prizes, I think we should see to it that the candy boxes holding certificates should be passed out to the most deserving people in the audience, poor widows and others who can hardly afford the admission price *and* the money for a box of candy. It shouldn't be too hard to learn who they are. A little snooping in advance should do it."

He glanced at her with a sardonic grin. "All heart, ain't you, honey?"

She shrugged. "It shouldn't matter all that much to you, and it'll buy us a lot of goodwill, well worth the effort in my opinion."

They rode along in silence for a few minutes. Then he glanced at her sidelong. "Speaking of heart, what happened to that fellow who came to the tent the other night? Some relative of yours, ain't he?"

"A cousin," she said coolly, looking him full in the eye. "And why did heart make you think of him?"

"Oh, I don't know," he said uncomfortably. "It's just that you two seemed pretty close. At least that's how it struck me."

"We are pretty close, Doc." It was on the tip of her tongue to tell him that she had spent the night with Mark in his hotel room, but at the last instant she changed her mind, why she was not quite sure. "In Nacogdoches Mark and his folks live only a few minutes from Moraghan, our old home place."

Lena waited for him to ask her why she stayed out all

night, but he didn't mention it, although it seemed to her that he was on the verge of speaking several times.

As they rode on, the silence more comfortable now, Lena wondered why she hadn't told him about where she'd spent the night. She was as bad as Mark! And yet, if she had spent the night with another man *not* her cousin, would she have told Doc? It wasn't likely. It was none of his business, and she was entitled to a certain degree of privacy.

The site the advance man had selected for their Port Allen location was closer to the levee than they liked.

Theirs was the first wagon to reach the lot. Doc got down from the wagon seat and stood with his hands on his hips, staring up at the bulk of the earthen levee towering above them. Lena climbed down and stood beside him. Somehow, instead of being reassuring, the levee had an ominous look.

Doc was scowling. "I'm going to have to have a word with Charlie, I'm not all that happy about this location."

Charlie Dobbs was their advance man, traveling ahead of the show at least three weeks in advance. It was his task to rent lots for their tent, plaster the towns with show posters, take care of any permits necessary, and arrange for publicity, and wine and dine the city fathers to further public relations. Charlie was another old-time medicine-show man that Doc had recruited.

Lena said, "It could be that this was the only lot available. I'm sure he did the best he could, Doc."

"I saw other vacant lots on the way in."

"But you know how show business people are regarded by many townsfolk. Harlots and thieves and general no-goods. The owners of those other lots probably refused to rent to Charlie."

Doc snorted, but said nothing more, as the other wagons began pulling onto the lot. He got busy supervising the placement of the stage wagons, and the unloading and erecting of the tent. It was the middle of the afternoon, and they would have to push hard to have the tent up before dark. Townspeople had gathered, mostly children of various ages. Doc recruited a number of the older boys and several men to help put up the tent, to be paid in show passes.

Since there was nothing Lena could do at the moment, she wandered away, finding a path up the side of the levee. She stood for a long while staring down at the swirling brown waters. The river churned with floating logs and every kind of debris imaginable. The water level was only about two feet below the top of the levee. A shiver of apprehension shook Lena, and she felt cold in spite of the sultry heat. Hugging herself, she glanced up at the sky. It was clear, not a cloud in sight. If it didn't rain during their stay here, maybe it would be all right. She knew, however, that heavy rains along the river up north could bring a roaring flood crest down the river, without a drop of rain falling here.

She faced around to look down at the bustle of activity on the lot. Sledgehammers rang out as the tent stakes were being driven into the rain-softened ground. The tent was already spread out, the tent ropes being tied loosely to the slanted stakes. Soon, she knew, the center tent poles would be in place, and the tent would go up, the canvas side walls to be hung last.

Doc was everywhere, directing operations. She watched him scurry about. Bareheaded, that thick mane of white hair flew in the breeze like a flag. Even without sleep since the night before, he was as energetic as a man half his age.

She recalled her thoughts on that day last summer when she had joined the medicine show in Fort Worth. It had been her conviction that day that he would be after her, trying to get her into his bed. It hadn't happened, and she was beginning to think that her estimation of him had been in error. She had grown quite fond of Doc Jones, a.k.a. Holliday. Gradually she was discovering that there were many qualities about him to be admired. There had been times over the past few months when the awakening urges of her body made her think she would not be averse to having him in her bed. This last flight of Mark's had made her see that any hope she might have harbored about their ever marrying was futile. She was not only disillusioned with Mark but deeply angry.

With an annoyed exclamation at herself, Lena broke off such speculations and started down the steep levee grade. Just as she reached the edge of the lot, the tent rose in the air, like an enormous, burgeoning tan mushroom.

Doc was standing back, hands on his hips, shouting orders. As she ranged alongside him, the tent reached its full height, and the roustabouts raced about, tightening the side ropes on the ground stakes.

Doc sighed with satisfaction and turned to her. "Well, honey, we'll soon be ready. You've been up all night, I'd suggest you sleep for a few hours. We're going to have to rehearse tonight, especially with Woodward. Even then, we'll be lucky he doesn't forget most of his lines tomorrow night."

She touched his arm. "You've had no more sleep than I have, Doc. How about you?"

"No time, Lena," he said brusquely. "I have to keep on top of things until the tent is finished. You go on now, honey." He grazed her cheek with the tips of his fingers. "I'll wake you when it's time to rehearse. Maybe I'll get you up a little early and we'll have supper together. I noticed a clean-looking café up the street. If that's agreeable to you?"

"I'd like that, Doc."


People flocked to the lot early the next evening, and as Lena peered out at the audience a few minutes before curtain time, she saw that they had a full house. It was a noisy, boisterous crowd—the best kind, Doc maintained. "If your tip is quiet, it means they're prepared to be critical. But if they're noisy, even a little rowdy, they're happy, ready to like whatever they're given!"

Lena knew they would quiet down the instant the curtain rolled up. She was already made up and in her costume for the play. She was supposed to be on stage when the curtain went up, along with her stage mother.

The play tonight was titled *Toby's Last Stand*. The setting was the parlor of the ranch house of the ranch owned by Lena's widowed mother. They had five plays in their repertoire—the three Nora Moraghan had written and two Lena had written herself during the winter months in New Orleans. All five, naturally, had rural settings, but this one was slightly different in that it took place on a ranch, with the threat of an Indian raid always imminent, from a band of renegade Indians egged on by the villain, who sold them guns and redeye. It had been chosen for tonight's performance because it had fewer lines allotted to the character portrayed by Lee Woodward.

There was one other slight difference. Near the climax of the play Lena had inserted a short speech for the villain, written in a slightly satirical vein. It was Doc's contention that the lines would either be over the head of the audience, or they would resent them. She and Doc had fought over the lines all winter, with Lena finally winning out.

Tonight would be the first public performance of this particular play. Doc's Toby role was that of a bumbling cowpuncher, who would not only thwart the Indians but rescue Lena from the clutches of the villain.

Lena was nervous as the curtain rose, as was Bessie, playing her mother, but from the complete silence of the audience, Lena knew they had their full attention, and her nervousness disappeared. The humorous lines and situations evoked the hoped-for laughter, and the tense, dramatic moments brought them to the edge of their seats. When Lena or Doc were in desperate straits, shouts of encouragement rose from the audience. Lena was gratified.

When the curtain fell at the end of the first act Lena, hurrying backstage for a costume change, met Doc in his Toby costume, on his way to making his between-the-acts candy pitch.

Beaming, he paused for a moment. "It's going over great, honey! Don't you think so?"

"I know so. If I were that kind of a person, I'd say I told you so."

"Say it, say it! I won't mind." He skidded a kiss off her cheek and hurried on.

The controversial line came in the next to the last scene in the play. Lena was alone in the bunkhouse when she was cornered by the villain. He backed her into a corner, a rope in his hand—he was bent on tying her down and having his way with her. He had been pursuing her with lustful intent throughout the play, Lena barely escaping his clutches each time. This time, it appeared that there was no possible escape.

The villain advanced on her, leering, twirling his mustache. Lena feigned despair and overwhelming terror, cringing back into the corner, and then she screamed shrilly.

The villain paused, and then said plaintively, "Why do you fear me so, my beauty?"

There was a brief suspension of all sound. Lena held her breath, fingers crossed behind her back. Then the noise she had been waiting for erupted—an explosion of laughter that buffeted them. Lena had told Bill Carruthers, the villain, to freeze absolutely still until the laughter—if laughter there was—had begun to subside. The third act had been moving steadily toward the play's resolution, with almost no laugh-evoking lines—Toby hadn't been on stage for several minutes. It had been Lena's contention that a laugh was needed at this point to release the tension.

"But not at the expense of poking fun at the play, Lena," Doc had maintained, "and that's what you're doing here."

"The audience isn't all that stupid, Doc. Give them credit for *some* intelligence, and sophistication. They won't mind a touch like this, especially if Bill can make them see that he actually feels that way. Why *should* she be afraid of him?"

As the laughter began to fade, a voice shouted up out of the audience: "She has good reason to be afraid of you, you bastard! And if you'll step outside the tent with me, I'll give you something to be afraid of!"

Laughter rose again, and Lena was exultant. It had worked as she'd hoped!

The rest of the play went well. Doc, in his Toby character, devised a strategem that shouldn't have worked but did, foiling the renegade Indian attack, and the villain at the same time. At the curtain he and Lena received a resounding ovation. Together on stage, holding hands, they bowed repeatedly. Lena glanced at Doc covertly. She usually received an ovation to equal his, and she often wondered if he resented it. If so, he had never said a word to her, and certainly he was beaming happily now.

She hurried offstage after her final bow to change for the olio program. It was already apparent that most of the people in the audience would remain for the after-show.

As they ate a late supper at a small café up the street from the show lot, Doc was more relaxed than she had seen him since she had cajoled him into the tent show endeavor. He was chattering away, picking at some minor things that had gone wrong, but not really critically.

"Doc." She interrupted his stream of chatter. "All of that will smooth out when we get everybody more settled into their roles. Now I want the truth—aren't you glad we went into this?"

"Well . . ." He leaned back, seeming to consider the question with a sober countenance. But he couldn't keep up the pretense. A broad grin broke across his face. "I reckon I might as well confess, hadn't I? Yeah, I'm glad. I'm having more fun than a roomful of monkeys. But you know me, I always look to the profit side. And it's beginning to look as if it's going to pay off. If no disaster strikes."

She had to laugh. "Always with the pessimism, huh, Doc? You know, I've always heard that con men are all optimistic by nature."

He arched an eyebrow. "That's what you think I am, a con man?"

"Not now so much, but all medicine men are con men, now admit it."

His frown didn't last long and he laughed ruefully. "You're right, of course. As for my being a pessimist, the world tends to make a man one. I've learned that if you always expect the worst, you're pleasantly surprised when it doesn't happen."

The waitress came with coffee, and they were silent until she had left. Then, staring down into his cup, Doc said in a low voice, "I haven't told you yet, Lena, but Lucy's divorcing me. In fact, it's final this week."

She made a sound of surprise. "No, you hadn't told me. On what grounds?"

"What grounds? Honey, anything you name, she could have used. But she's claiming desertion, and I can hardly deny it."

"You did pay her back?"

"Yep, every dime I owed her."

"So you're even with her, in a manner of speaking." She took a sip of coffee, leaned back. "I'm curious, why did you wait all this time to tell me?"

He shrugged. "No particular reason, honey. I wasn't even sure you'd be interested. I don't know if this is the right time to get personal, Lena, but I reckon you know that I care for you a great deal."

She said carefully, "Exactly what is that supposed to mean?"

"Dammit, Lena!" In a burst of anger he slammed his cup down, sloshing coffee onto the table. "It means exactly what I said, I care for you a great deal."

She said slowly, "I'm not sure it's a good idea for us to get involved. It could cause talk. You know we have to live in a glass house, so to speak."

"Who said anything about getting personally involved?" he growled.

"Why else would you mention it? Or . . ." She stared at him. "Or is this some kind of a back-door proposal? I have no intention of getting married any time soon, Doc, and sure as the dickens I'm not interested in being the fourth Mrs. Holliday. Or is it the fifth?"

"Women!" he said in a snarling voice. "Say a nice word to one and she starts shopping for a wedding dress. Well, for your information, I'm never going to get hitched again. My record in that department is lousy and I won't chance it ever again."

She gave him a sly look. "Not even if you go broke and need money to go on the road again?"

He winced. "That's a low blow, Lena." He shoved away from the table, and got to his feet. Without another

word he strode to the counter, taking out money to pay
their bill.

Laughing, Lena gulped a mouthful of coffee, and caught
up with him at the door. She caught his arm, said soberly,
"I'm sorry, Doc, that *was* mean of me. And I wish you to
know that I'm flattered that you care for me. I care for
you, too, in a way."

He barely acknowledged her words with a nod, his gaze
going past her out the window. His face registered dismay.

She turned around to look out. It was raining, not hard,
but it was coming down steadily.

"I don't like the looks of this," he said darkly.

"Oh, don't be such a gloom, Doc." She took his arm.
"It may stop any minute."

The rain did stop by morning, and a pale sun shone
through a high overcast. The rain left the lot muddy, and
Doc had the roustabouts bring in several wagons of straw
which was spread across the ground before the tent.

The clouds darkened as the day progressed, and it began
to rain again by showtime that evening. The crowd was
smaller, the tent only half full, and they seemed sullen,
depressed by the rain, and their response to the play and
the olio was disappointing.

Immediately after the olio, Lena went to her wagon and
to bed, skipping supper. It was still raining and she could
hear it striking the panes of the wagon windows as she
went to sleep.

She awoke suddenly as the wagon rocked, and she
realized someone had entered. She sat up, clutching the
bedclothes about her. "Who is it?"

"It's me, Lena." It was Doc's voice, urgent and driving. "Get dressed, honey. I want you to drive the wagon
out of Port Allen. I've hooked up the mules already. The
levee has broken through north of town and it may go any
minute."

Lena was already out of bed, shucking her nightgown
and fumbling for the dress she wore out on the road. "But
what about the tent and the rest of the wagons?"

"The tent is already coming down. I'll hook up two

other wagons, so the other two women can drive them off. All of you keep going until you find high ground out of town. The road to our next location veers west away from the river, you should be safe there."

"But shouldn't I stay here and help?"

"What can you do here, honey? No, you'd only be in the way. Get your tail out of here the minute you're dressed."

"But how about you and the other fellows, Doc? The tent's not worth risking your life for. We can always get another."

"What with?" he said bitterly. "If the tent goes, we're out of business, you know that. Don't worry, we'll have some warning. If the levee above us starts to go, we'll hightail it out of here. Now, get a move on!" Turning on his heel, he left the wagon.

By the time she was dressed, Doc was just finishing hooking the teams up to the other wagons. The rain was coming down hard. At least the wagon seat was partly sheltered by an overhang. Wrapped in a slicker, Lena huddled on the seat.

Doc came splashing over, his slicker flapping. Past him Lena could see the tent lying on the ground, and the dim figures of the men untying guy ropes and pulling up stakes. She knew that the rain-soaked tent was going to be hard to manhandle onto the wagons.

Doc yelled up at her, "Move out, honey! Get as far away as you can and wait for us!"

Lena leaned down. "You be careful, hear?"

His teeth flashed in a grin. "Don't worry about me. I'll be fine!"

As Doc watched Lena drive the wagon off the lot, water splashing as the wheels bounced through puddles, he knew that he had been speaking out of bravado, and she probably realized it. If the levee went suddenly, they'd never escape in time. But what else could he do? Everything he had was sunk into this show. He had lied to Lena when he'd told her that he had repaid Lucy all the money he owed. He hadn't, only half. But since they had started out so well, he was hoping to earn enough soon to repay her in full before she could get around to getting an attachment against the show.

He faced around, staring up at the levee, dimly seen through the sheets of rain. Mud oozed down the bank, glistening like spreading oil, but he couldn't see any unusual amount of water pouring down.

He shook himself angrily, and charged at the downed tent, his slicker spreading like wings of some prehistoric bird. He yelled, "Move your asses, dammit! Get those stakes up!"

He joined the laboring men, pulling the loosened stakes up in a fury. In a moment he straightened up to shout, "Bob, you and Andy take what men you need and get that tent loaded. That's the most important thing. If we lose a few stakes, we lose 'em."

Bob Ketchum took all the men who were regulars with the show, leaving two with Doc, a pair of townies he had been able to rustle up on the street with an offer of ten dollars cash.

He turned to them. "You men! You know how to hitch up a team and wagon?" At their combined nods he said, "Start hitching up the wagons then."

As they hastened to do his bidding, Doc went at the stakes again, yanking them out of the ground as fast as he could, pausing every so often to carry an armload to the stage wagons. His back was aching, and his hands soon burned with splinters embedded in them from the wooden stakes. He ignored all the discomforts and worked on, glancing about from time to time. The men had the tent unlaced now, and were rolling up the three sections of water-soaked canvas. Doc saw that the other two were coming along well with the teams. Three of the remaining six wagons, including the two stage wagons, were hitched and ready to go.

Bob Ketchum called over, "Doc, can you give us a hand here?" They were trying to lead a section of canvas onto one of the stage wagons. "With all this water the canvas weighs a ton."

Doc hurried over to them. He stooped to get his hands under the canvas. "All together now! Heave!"

With a concerted effort they managed to swing the canvas up onto the wagon, and turned to another section.

In a short time they had all the canvas loaded. As Bob and Andy started to lash it down, Doc said, "Never mind that. As heavy as it is with water, it'll stay on. Let's finish gathering up the stakes."

They had about half the stakes loaded, when Doc heard a yell. Facing around, he saw a man pounding up on a horse.

The rider reined in his mount. "You people better get to hell and gone out of here! A chunk of the levee broke loose a few blocks north of here. If the levee goes all the way, this lot'll be under six feet of water faster than shit through a goose!"

Doc nodded, shouting back, "Thank you, friend."

With a wave of his hand the man rode off. Doc sent a glance around the lot. The men hitching the teams had yet another wagon to go—the office wagon—but at least the canvas and about half of the stakes were loaded. Cupping his hands around his mouth, Doc shouted at the men with the teams, "You fellows forget the last wagon. Get over here for your pay, then hustle out of here." He turned to the others. "Get on the wagons and let's move it. Leave everything else."

He was already moving toward one of the stage wagons. The two townies converged on him. He handed over two ten dollar bills, and scrambled up onto the wagon seat. Standing, he sent a glance north along the levee. He blinked against the rain. Was that a wall of water he saw heading this way? If so and if it hit the lot before the wagons could move off, they would be at the very least mired axle-deep in mud. At the worst the wagons would be overturned and all of them drowned.

He picked up the reins. "Ho, you damned mules! Move! Move it!"

Lena and the other women drove the wagons as fast as the mules could pull them, taking the road out of town in a

westwardly direction, toward the town of Opelpusas, their
next show location. They were still traveling at dawn.
Lena craned around, looking back the way they had come.
There was no sign of the other wagons; of course, she
hadn't really expected there would be as yet. She halfway
expected to see floodwaters surging after them. The road
was full of horses and vehicles, all heading west. Apparently the possibility of a break in the levee had frightened
others.

With her head out from under the overhang, neck
twisted to look back, she suddenly realized something. It
had stopped raining! Looking up, she saw that the sky was
clearing, and to the east the rising sun suddenly broke
through. The wet landscape was already beginning to
steam. How ironic! The rain stopping would be too late to
save the men back there if the levee broke.

At midmorning they began to climb a slight incline.
Lena saw a sort of park off to the right alongside the road,
large enough to accommodate the wagons. She called
back, getting the attention of Bessie Carson, driving the
second wagon, and motioned to the park area. She drove
her wagon off the road, and got down to wait for the others
to pull in behind her.

Bessie got down and hurried toward her wearing a
worried frown. Her husband, John, was a roustabout and
one of the candy butchers. "You think they're all right,
Lena?"

"We can only hope, Bessie." Lena hastened to add,
"But I'm sure they're fine. Doc is not a man to take
unnecessary chances. I thought we'd wait here for them. If
we can find enough dry wood, maybe we can build a fire
and have coffee and a hot meal ready for them when they
do show up."

All the wood they were able to find, even dead wood,
was rain-soaked, and after repeated tries, they still didn't
have a fire going. In exasperation Lena broke up one of
the wooden camp chairs, making kindling, and they finally
got a fire started. Piling wet wood on the blaze caused it to
sizzle, but the wood slowly caught and the heat soon dried
it enough to make a respectable fire.

They went about making pots of coffee and began preparations for a meal, down to the point where they could put the food on to cook the minute the wagons hove into sight. During all their preparations, Lena paused frequently to peer down the road. There was no sign of the wagons.

Weary and spent, Lena placed a chair by her wagon and leaned her head back against the wheel spokes. She dozed for a time, to be awakened by Bessie shaking her shoulder. "They're coming, Lena, they're coming!"

Lena came up out of the chair, racing to the side of the road. In the distance she could see the show wagons. It was too far to count the wagons, but she experienced an immense relief. At least most of them had made it!

They started the food cooking, one or the other of them running to the road to look down the grade from time to time. And finally Lena was able to count the wagons—one was missing. She could see the extra mules plodding behind the lead wagon. But the approaching wagons were near enough now so that she could see Doc on the seat of the first one.

She was waiting at the side of the road when he guided the wagon into the camp area, the others following him.

When he had pulled the wagon to a complete stop, Lena stepped to it, standing on tiptoe to grip the seat. His boots and trouser legs were caked with dried mud and his unshaven face looked gaunt, the eyes staring down at her with infinite weariness.

"Are you all right, Doc?"

He scrubbed at his whiskery chin and dredged up a wan smile. "That all depends on how you look at it, honey. I'm all in one piece, but I'm by God weary to the bone."

"How about the others?"

"About as tired as I am, I reckon, but nobody's hurt. I think Andy sprung an ankle, but he can get around all right. We lost one wagon, the office wagon, and a number of tent stakes."

"Yes, I noticed the missing wagon. What happened?"

Lena stepped back as he climbed down to the ground. "The levee broke just before daylight, and water came pouring down on us. But we did get some warning from a fellow riding by. We didn't have time to hitch up the office wagon and we left it behind. The water was coming in as we pulled off the lot and we almost got trapped. I looked back once and saw the office wagon hit by a wave of water, tumbling it over. We were by Christ lucky that the lot was lower than the road. The roadbed was high enough so that the water was only about a foot deep over it as we drove off.''

She nodded somberly. "Even so, I'd say we were *real* lucky. The wagon and the stakes we can replace, but if we'd lost the tent we'd have been in real bad shape, not to mention how lucky you all are to still be alive.''

"You're right there, we'd be up shit creek. But we have to kiss good-bye to the rest of the week's receipts.'' He was plunged into gloom. "We were doing fine, but now there won't be enough money to pay the week's wages.''

"I don't think we have to worry too much about that. They'll all wait a week. As long as we have enough food to get us into next week, we'll be fine. Now, come on.'' She took his arm. "We have hot food waiting. I'm sure you haven't eaten a bite?''

"Nope, didn't have time. I wanted to get as far away from that infernal river as possible.''

They started toward the cooking fire. The other men, after the two married ones were properly greeted by their wives, were busy unhooking the mules.

Doc said, "Since we have plenty of time now to get to the next lot, we might as well spend the rest of the day and night here, and get some rest. We'll get an early start in the morning.''

The women had heated kettles of water, and the men lined up at two wash basins. By the time all were washed, the food was ready: hot biscuits from the Dutch oven, heaping platters of ham and eggs, jars of jams and jellies, and an abundance of coffee.

Lena sat with Doc in the shade of her wagon as they ate. Finished, Doc lit a cigarette and smoked, in a better mood now. He leaned back against the wagon wheel. "I guess

you're right, honey, we could be a hell of a lot worse off."
He grinned at her. "That optimistic enough for you?"

She laughed and touched his cheek lightly. "Don't get
*too* optimistic, Doc, I wouldn't know how to take it."

His eyes began to droop and shortly he was asleep, the
cigarette burning down between his fingers. Gently she
took it from him and ground it out. She shook him lightly.
"Come on, Doc, you'll sleep better in a bed."

He came awake with a start, knuckling at his eyes.
"Yeah, you're right. But I need a bath first. I smell like a
river catfish."

"Why don't you use the tub in my wagon? While you're
getting ready I'll heat some water."

He glanced at her sharply, as if trying to read something
in her face, then slowly nodded. He went into Lena's
wagon, and she heated two kettles of water. She lifted
them onto the rear steps of the wagon one at a time, then
opened the door.

Doc's startled voice came at her. "Don't you know
enough to knock? I'm starkers in here."

She laughed softly. "I've seen naked men before."

She set the kettles inside, then climbed up the steps. She
had told Bob Ketchum to fetch several buckets of cold
water from the water barrels. As she turned around, she
saw Doc cowering back against the wagon wall, a large
towel wrapped around his waist.

Lena laughed again. "Come on, Doc! A man your age
shy?"

He straightened up with a show of indignation. "I'm not
all that old!"

"Of course you're not, Doc," she said soothingly.

By the time she had dumped the hot water into the large
galvanized tub she had bought to take with her on the
road, Bob Ketchum arrived with the buckets. Lena poured
in the cold water a little at a time, testing it until she
calculated it was the right temperature.

She stood back. "There, that should be about right."
She stepped over to close the door, and turned back. Doc
hadn't moved from his place against the wall. "Well, get
in, for Heaven's sake! Don't let it get cold."

"Ain't you going outside?"

"I hadn't thought of it." Her sudden smile was mischievous. "I thought you might need me to scrub your back."

"What will the others think?"

She gave a slight shrug. "I've decided to stop worrying about what anybody thinks."

He peered at her in the dimness. "What the hell! If you don't care, why should I?"

Straightening, he dropped the towel, strode to the tub, and climbed in, having to double his knees up to his chest to fit.

A little startled by the suddenness of it, Lena stood blinking, uncertain what to do.

"Well?" he said impatiently. "I thought you were going to scrub my back?"

With a shrug of her own, she found a washcloth and a bar of strong yellow soap. She scrubbed his back a little more vigorously than was necessary, but he didn't voice a complaint. Eyes closed, he said blissfully, "Ah, honey! That feels good, by Christ, it does!"

Although she was momentarily tempted, she didn't venture around to the front, where she could occasionally see his genitals bobbing in the sloshing water, but confined herself to his back. When she was done with that, she stepped back and said, "Now, *you* can finish the rest."

She gave him the washcloth and bar of soap, and retired to a camp stool at the front of the wagon.

After a bit Doc stood up, began to dry himself. "I should have brought some clean clothes from my wagon. I hate to put these filthy duds on."

"Why not just sleep here?"

He stopped what he was doing, his head swiveling around slowly. "Do you realize what you're saying?"

"I realize. It's time, wouldn't you say? Besides, I'm sure the others think we're doing it already."

She felt very indebted to this man, and the thought earlier that he might have died back there in Port Allen made her realize how fond she was of him. She was a healthy woman, with strong, newly aroused appetites— Mark had done that much for her, if nothing else. She had

committed herself to show business, and she resolved then
and there to stop hoping that Mark would come to his
senses. So why save herself for him? The phrase caused
her to smile to herself, it sounded like a line out of one of
their plays.

She stood and began removing her clothes. She was
glad of one bit of foresight—in furnishing the wagon she
had purchased a large bed instead of a cot.

Doc finished toweling himself and got into the bed.
Naked, Lena joined him. Doc was trembling with passion,
and he brought her to orgasm quickly, managing to hold
back until she was pleasured before letting himself go.

A few moments later he said with heaving breath, "So
much for glass houses. But I know how we can take care
of that." He raised his head to gaze down at her. "Why
don't we get married, honey?"

She made a sound of surprise. "I thought you said
you'd never marry again?"

"A man can change his mind, can't he? My divorce
from Lucy will be final next week. *Will* you marry me?"

And that was how they became lovers, and how Lena
became Mrs. Hoyt Jones the following week in Opelousas,
Louisiana. Doc insisted that his real name be used on the
marriage license.

# 12

By the time Bud Danker had been gone from Nacogdoches
a year he had killed six men, four more after he left Kevin
Moraghan dead in that citrus grove down in the Rio
Grande Valley. He had become proficient enough with a
Colt so that he qualified now as a gunfighter for hire—a
title that pleased him immensely.

The West had tamed down considerably from the violent
days following the Civil War, yet there was still employ-

ment for a man who was good with a gun, and had no
compunction about killing. Bud had drifted across Texas
and into New Mexico, where wars between nestors and
cattlemen still raged from time to time, and Bud had hired
out his gun a number of times.

In between cattle wars he drifted back to Texas, always
gravitating to Fort Worth. One reason for this was the hope
that Cassie might have left word for him at the White
Elephant Saloon. There was never any word, and he had
about given up on her. But the main reason he returned to
Fort Worth repeatedly was because the place was booming
again as a cattle town, since the Texas and Pacific Railroad
had reached there.

It was because of the Texas and Pacific that Bud met
Jim Courtwright.

Bud was at loose ends and prowling the saloons along
Hell's Half Acre. He had just ridden in from New Mexico
with a good-sized roll from his last job, and he wouldn't
have to seek employment for a while. Need of money,
however, wasn't what drove him to hire out his gun. He
knew now that he loved killing, he had a strong need for
it, a greed for it. Although he occasionally sought out a
whore when he was flush and between jobs, he had
discovered that he didn't like women all that much. He had
come to realize, dimly, without analyzing it, that killing
was as much a sexual thrill as a sexual connection with
any woman. For instance, the saloons in Hell's Half Acre
all had shacks out back for purposes of prostitution, and he
hadn't visited one yet.

It was midsummer in Fort Worth, and it hadn't rained
for a month. The streets steamed with heat, and dust roiled
up like a choking smoke cloud. Bud drifted from one
saloon to another, drinking a beer in each one, leaning on
the bars. A trail drive had just come in to town, with cattle
to be shipped out on the train, and the saloons along Main
Street thronged with thirsty, rowdy cowhands.

It was just dusk when he went into the Occidental
Saloon, and he was lazing on his elbows on the bar when
he noticed that a hush had settled over the crowded saloon.
He looked around and saw a tall man, over six feet,

standing just inside the batwings, looking over the room with cold black eyes.

The man leaning on the bar next to Bud nudged him with an elbow. "Know who that fellow is, friend? That's Jim Courtwright. Hammer-Thumb Courtwright!"

Bud stared in awe. He had never seen a famous gun-fighter at close range before. Most of them were gone now, shot down or hung by the law. Ben Thompson was dead, Wes Hardin was in prison, Billy the Kid had been gunned down by Pat Garrett, and Bill Longley had been hung.

The man beside Bud said, "I seed Long-Haired Jim in a gunfight once, seed him draw. Fastest man I ever saw. He don't have to take a back seat to anybody, including Wesley Hardin, or the Earps."

Bud made a sound of impatience, never taking his gaze from the man in the entrance. He knew who Jim Courtwright was, everybody in Texas knew who he was. Several times, in New Mexico and in El Paso, Bud had come along shortly after Courtwright had been there and left his mark.

Now Courtwright moved on into the saloon, making his way down the room to an empty table in the rear. He was dressed in fringed buckskins. He wore two pistols with the butts reversed forward, not for a cross-body draw, Bud knew, but for a single-gun, right-hand pull. He had coal-black, shoulder-length hair, a heavy mustache adorned his upper lip, and he had a swarthy complexion that gave him an Indian look.

Courtwright took a seat at the table, his back to the wall, his cold gaze sweeping over the saloon. A barkeep hastened from around the bar, carrying a bottle and a glass over to him. Courtwright's gaze met Bud's, lingered for a moment, then moved on. Bud turned back to his beer. He would have liked nothing better than to go over and shake Courtwright's hand, but he didn't have the temerity to do so.

He continued to lean on the bar, working on another beer, covertly glancing over at Courtwright's table from time to time. Finally, after a half hour and two small sips of whiskey, Courtwright got to his feet and started out. Bud hastily swallowed the last of his beer, bounced a silver dollar onto the bar top, and followed Courtwright from the saloon.

He had nothing in mind, he hadn't the least idea as to why he was following the gunfighter. Something indefinable had nudged his brain, prompting the move. It was full dark outside now, and the street thronged with drunken cowboys. Up ahead he saw Courtwright's tall figure making his way along the board sidewalk, under the flickering gaslights. He did not weave in and out of the crowd, but walked a steady course, looking neither left nor right, forcing the men in his path to step aside. One cowboy, weaving, head down, did not see him, and Courtwright gave him a shove, pushing him aside, and strode on.

Bud was close enough to hear the cowhand cursing at the receding back of Jim Courtwright. Then he fumbled his gun out of his waistband, and leveled it in unsteady hands, aiming at Courtwright's back.

Later, Bud was never able to figure out exactly why he acted as he did. In normal circumstances he would not have so much as raised a finger to help another human being in trouble. But now, without even thinking about it, he drew his Colt and snapped off a shot. His bullet struck the drunken cowboy in the shoulder, sending him reeling back against a storefront, his gun clattering to the planks at his feet.

Out of the corner of his eye Bud saw Courtwright wheel and draw his gun, all in one fluid motion, falling into a slight crouch. His alert gaze took in the scene in a single, raking glance. He straightened up, holstering his gun, and came toward Bud. The wounded cowboy, holding his shoulder, went lurching up the street, moaning.

Courtwright stopped before Bud. "I'm much obliged to you, friend. A man tends to get a touch careless after a few drinks, forgetting to be on the lookout for backshooters. And it ain't often that a fellow like you is willing to step in and lend a hand. I'm Jim Courtwright." He held out his hand.

"Bud, Bud Danker." They shook hands. Courtwright's grip was strong.

"Well, Mr. Danker, I want to thank you again. I have a

good memory for favors. If I can ever help you in any way, don't hesitate to ask.''

Bud, still slightly dazed by his unthinking intervention and more than a little intimidated by a man of Courtwright's caliber shaking his hand, could only nod mutely.

"Mr. Danker, I was just about to have a bite to eat at the café around the corner. I'd be most honored if you would join me.''

Bud nodded again, and they fell into step together. Over chicken-fried steak in the small restaurant, Courtwright became garrulous. He told Bud that he was in Fort Worth to go to work for the Texas and Pacific Railroad as a special constable. "Actually, I'm going to be operating as a strikebreaker,'' Courtwright said with a cold smile. "The railroad's having trouble moving their trains with this damned strike on. It ain't a job I'd take under most circumstances, but I'm suffering from the shorts right now. I've been having some trouble with the law of late, and haven't worked much, as you probably know.''

Bud knew the story. A few years ago Courtwright and another gunfighter had been employed by an old friend of Courtwright's, General John Logan, now a United States senator from Illinois. General Logan was a rich, powerful man. Among his holdings was the J L Cattle Ranch in the American Valley in New Mexico. He had been having trouble with nestors on his range, especially with two Frenchmen, the Lalonde brothers. Logan met with Courtwright and hired him to run the nestors off his land. Courtwright took the job, taking an old crony along with him. In the ensuing gun battle, Courtwright and his friend killed the Lalonde brothers. There was an immediate uproar from the farmers in the area, and Courtwright and his companion fled New Mexico. Courtwright returned to his favorite town, Fort Worth, confident that nothing would come of it, once he was back in Texas. In that he was wrong. A warrant was issued for him, along with the necessary papers to extradite him from Texas back to New Mexico. Courtwright was arrested and lodged in the Tarrant County jail. Word of his arrest spread quickly, and such was his popularity among the people of Fort Worth that a mob was formed. When Courtwright was taken from the jail that evening by three lawmen and escorted down Main Street into a restaurant for supper, the mob accosted them in the café. The officers were overcome. The shackles were removed from the prisoner, and he was given a saddle horse and a .45. He headed for the Mexican border, and had remained there for some time.

Although Bud knew the general outline of the story, he saw that Courtwright was in a talkative mood, and he was more than happy to listen. He was especially intrigued that the story involved the cattlemen-nestor feud in New Mexico, since Bud himself had so recently been in the middle of that conflict.

He said, "Are you still wanted by the law?"

"Naw." Courtwright grinned. "I stayed down below the border until recently, until I figured things had cooled down. I went back to New Mexico and gave myself up. And I had figured rightly. What few witnesses there were had scattered to the four winds, and the climate had changed. I went on trial, but the jury couldn't agree on a verdict. So, I'm free as a bird."

In an abrupt movement Courtwright pushed his chair back and got to his feet. "I want to thank you again, Mr. Danker, for potting that backshooter for me. You ever need a favor, don't hesitate. No, don't get up, finish your coffee." He waved a hand. "I have to see someone. Almost forgot."

On his way out Courtwright stopped and paid the bill. Then, settling his hat on his head, he marched out of the restaurant.

Bud watched him until he was out of sight. This had been the best day of his life, save that day he had shot Kevin Moraghan dead. And what a thrill it would be to someday work in tandem with such a famous man as Jim Courtwright!

He drank coffee, staring out into the street, thinking pleasant thoughts—a rare occurrence in his life. After a bit his thoughts turned to Nacogdoches, not in homesickness, but in rumination about Cassie. He missed Cassie. He had no time for any of the rest of the Danker clan. Certainly not for his mother, who was crazy as a loon. But Cassie had always been close to him, maybe it was because they were closer together in age than the other Dankers. He was sorry now that he had abused her that last night. He shouldn't have done that.

Would he ever see his little sister again?

Cassie was working as a waitress in a waterfront café in Galveston. The work was hard, she was on her feet ten hours a day, and the pay wasn't much. But by skimping on everything but the bare necessities, she was putting away a few dollars. After almost a year working at Big Red's Café, she had a tidy little nest egg. Exactly what she was saving toward she wasn't sure, yet it seemed the wise thing to do, and she had always been thrifty by nature.

In fact, she should have been reasonably content. She was independent, and earning money; as little as it was, it was more than she had ever earned in her life. What few dollars she had made in Nacogdoches had always either gone for food, or Bud had taken it for his own use.

However, she was often dispirited, especially early in the morning, with another long day before her, among strangers. The fishermen and sailors who patronized the café were a rough lot, but the burly ex-seaman who owned the café was a kind man in his gruff way. More than once he had laid a rolling pin alongside the head of someone who got rowdy with Cassie. A big man in his fifties, Red Baker had never touched her, which had puzzled Cassie in the beginning. Then, after one episode, when a drunken sailor had mauled her before Big Red came to her rescue, he had told her, "Reckon you've often wondered why I haven't tried to haul down your drawers, Cassie. I'll tell you, it ain't from lack of wanting. It's because I can't do it anymore. I was castrated some years ago, like a butchered hog. I was squiring this old girl, you see. She didn't bother to tell me that she was married. Her man caught us in an, uh, indelicate moment. In fact, I didn't know he was there until he had me hog-tied and hobbled. Then he worked me over and I ain't been any good to a woman since. I caught up to him, later on, and fixed his wagon, but that's another story.

"Thing is, Cassie, I won't touch you, and as long as you work here, I'll see to it that no other fellow does, either."

Cassie knew that much of her bad moods came from simple loneliness. She was over nineteen now, at the age where she needed a man. But every time she saw one that she even remotely liked, the image of Michael flashed across the screen of her mind, and she knew that she would not only be miserable with another man, but would make the man miserable as well.

Would she never get over Michael Moraghan? It would seem that a year would have made it easier, but sometimes she thought that the passage of time only intensified her longing for him.

She was standing at the café window, staring out into a foggy morning, just having opened the front doors for business, when Red's voice startled her: "What's up, Cassie girl? You look like a lost soul standing there like that."

She faced around with a start, managed a pale smile. "Sometimes I feel like one, Red."

His bulging brown eyes were sympathetic. "You thinking of some old boy? Or just home?"

"Both, I guess." She had never told him of her past, nor had he asked. Normally reticent, Cassie had a sudden urge to unburden herself. Haltingly at first, she told him about the Danker-Moraghan feud, about Bud and Michael, and her sudden, panicked flight. There were no customers in the café until she had finished, and then two bleary-eyed sailors came in for cups of coffee.

When they had left, Red said, "I've been mulling over what you told me, girl, and I think you behaved foolishly. Why run from this Moraghan fellow? Seems to me he's gone on you. I'll bet that he would have proposed eventually, and you'd have had a good life for yourself."

She shivered, hugging herself. "I couldn't, not after what Bud did. And how could I face his mother, after Bud had killed her husband?"

"I remember reading something about that in some paper, your brother on a killing binge. He's a bad'un, no doubt about that, but I don't see how that affects you, Cassie. If your fellow didn't care, why should you?"

"I've gone over and over it in my mind. I was afraid that he would, in the end. Wouldn't you, Red, if you were in his place?"

"Not if I cared enough for the girl. I figure a man marries the woman, not her family."

"But my circumstances are different! How many times would a man be marrying into a family that had killed his grandfather, his uncle, and his father?"

"Not very many, I reckon."

All of a sudden she was weeping—the first time. And she didn't really know if she was crying for Michael, or for herself.

"Aw-w, sugar, don't do that," Red said in distress.

"I'm sorry, Red," she said angrily. "I'm not a crybaby usually." She wiped the tears away, got to her feet, and moved around behind the counter as the door banged open, announcing a customer. Passing Red, she whispered, "Much obliged, Red, for listening."

On Moraghan, although Michael still missed Cassie, still loved her, the year that had passed since her disappearance had helped to ease some of the pain. He was still confident that she would eventually return to Nacogdoches. If she really loved him, he couldn't see her doing anything else.

Meanwhile, he had found his place in the world. The fame of the Moraghan horses had spread throughout Texas. Under Bandy's tutelage Michael had become an expert rider, and he won about two races out of three nowadays, racing at county fairs and rodeos, even at a country crossroads, if he could find a horseman willing to race him.

From his winnings, and the sale of several of the colts at prices inflated by the growing renown of Moraghan horses, he had judiciously bought another dozen horses, both as competitors and for breeding stock, always relying heavily on Bandy's advice. Bandy was almost one of the family now. Kate had taken to Bandy at once, and Michael had a hunch that a romance might blossom between them, as soon as her grief had receded, and he was not at all displeased.

Just two mornings ago, at breakfast, after Bandy went out to feed the horses, Kate, out of the blue, had dropped a revealing remark: "No disrespect to your father, Michael, but I am not a woman meant to live alone."

He had replied innocently, "But you're not living alone, Mother."

"Don't be dense, son!" she had said sharply. "You know very well what I mean."

She had turned away to the cookstove, but not before he had seen color pink her cheeks. Wisely he had decided to keep his mouth shut.

Kate seemed to be content enough on Moraghan, keeping house and cooking for the two men, and she was quite proud of the success Michael was enjoying. Stony and Debra brought their children out almost every weekend, and Kate took great joy in her grandchildren.

One cloud hung over their happiness—there had been no word from Lena. She had been gone well over a year, and she could just as well have vanished off the face of the earth.

Consequently, Michael was in for a surprise one afternoon in early July. He was out at the pasture watching Bandy work one of the new horses when he saw Stony's surrey coming up the road. He was at the front gate when the vehicle came to a stop. Kate came out of the house to join him. Debra and the children were also in the surrey.

Michael tightened with apprehension—the Liebermans almost never came out except on the weekends. He steeled himself for bad news until he saw that Debra was smiling broadly as she jumped down to the ground. She was carrying a large envelope, which she waved at them.

"Guess what?" she said excitedly. "Godalmighty, this is from Lena!"

Kate gasped and said in a rush, "Is she all right? Where is she?"

Debra laughed. "I haven't opened it yet, Mother. It's addressed to Michael."

She handed it to him, and Michael opened it with trembling fingers. Inside was a large poster, folded several times, and a single sheet of paper, covered with writing on both sides. Puzzled, he unfolded the poster before reading the letter. It was an advertisement for a traveling tent show—The Holliday Traveling Players, with several pictures on it. At the very top of the poster was the legend "Appearing in Nacogdoches the First Week of August." Still puzzled, he looked at the poster more closely.

"My God, look!" he exclaimed. "It's Lena!"

He showed it to Kate, jabbing a forefinger at one of the pictures.

"You must be mistaken, son." She snatched the poster from him and peered closely at the picture. "It is, it is Lena!"

Michael switched his attention to the letter, began to read it aloud:

Dear Michael and Debra Lee:

At last you are receiving word of your wayward sister. First, I am fine and quite happy. I am acting, as you can see by the poster enclosed, and I am *good* at it! I must have inherited it from Grandmother Nora, or else, as Doc claims, I was born to it. More about *him* later. I have not written until now because I wanted to wait until I knew for sure how I was going to be as an actress. Also, Doc and I just started our first Toby show this spring, and recently we have scheduled Nacogdoches for a week. I wanted you to know that I was coming, so nobody would die of shock when I showed up without warning . . .

The letter went on to explain, briefly, Lena's medicine-show experience and the past months with the tent show.

Suddenly Michael broke off reading with a gasp. "Good God, Mother, she's married, Lena's married!"

He resumed reading:

The man I have been writing about, Doc Holliday, actually Hoyt Jones, and I got married back in May.

Doc is an older man, but he is a good man, and I am sure you will all take to him . . .

Kate said, "She doesn't say anything about loving him." Michael read on.

I'll be in Nacogdoches a day in advance of the opening night for the show, and I hope that I can see you all, if I have been forgiven. Of course, I want you all to see the show as my guests. I am also writing to Mother and Daddy, so they will know in time to come up, if they want to come up and see me. Our route is not anywhere near the Valley.

Love to all, Lena.

Kate drew in her breath. "Dear Lord, she doesn't know about Kevin!"

"She had no way of knowing, Mother," Michael said quietly. "I'm sure she would have come, or at least been in touch with us if she had known about Daddy."

"Working in a tent show," Kate said wonderingly. "I don't know as I approve. That hardly seems the life for a decent girl."

Debra said, "I can't say I'm too surprised. Right after Lena started staying up here, we were going through some of Grandmother's old things and we found some of the plays she'd written. Lena read one aloud to me, playing all the parts. Godalmighty, it was spooky, listening to her, like she'd been doing it all her life. And Grandmother did put on plays, Mother, and act in them. You've told me about it."

"Yes, but that was *here,* down at the old schoolhouse, not running around the country like some gypsy. But I do recall"—Kate began to smile—"that Nora shocked folks sometimes by some of the plays she put on in that schoolhouse."

"Well, I'm sure that Lena isn't doing anything shocking, or she and her husband wouldn't be making money at it."

"And that's another thing, this fellow she's married. An older man."

"And what's wrong with that? Older men marry much

younger women all the time. Sometimes it's better that way."

"And using two names. That sounds sneaky to me."

"Oh, Mother!" Debra sighed. "Haven't you ever heard of people using stage names?"

"But why Doc? Is he some kind of a doctor? And Doc Holliday, isn't that the name of a gunfighter out West?"

"I believe that Doc Holliday is dead, Mother," Michael said.

"But this one could be related to him, with a name like that."

Debra gestured in exasperation. "Mother, this isn't like you at all. It's a stage name, an assumed name. Lena wrote that."

"I just don't know..." Eyes vague, Kate ran her fingers through her hair in a distracted gesture. "My little girl. I thought I'd never see her again." A sob shook her. "And now she's a married woman." A startled look passed over her face. "Why, she might even be pregnant!"

Debra and Michael laughed, and Debra said, "If she is, Mother, I'm certain she would have made sure to mention it."

Listening, Michael felt a pang of deep regret. If he had only made Cassie pregnant before she left, she would have to come back to him.

# 13

Lena was not pregnant. She had learned a few days after marrying Doc that she never would be, not by him at any rate.

"I reckon I should have told you, honey," he had said abashedly. "I can't father children. A doctor once told me that it has something to do with a childhood illness. I'm right sorry, Lena, I know that women have a need to bear children."

"Not all women, Doc," she had said with a light touch on his arm. "I'm an actress now. If I got pregnant and had to raise a child, how could I keep on acting?"

That part was true enough, she didn't want children, not now. Yet his belated confession had hurt her. She would want to have children some day, before she was too old, but she still would have married him if he had told her before.

Over the two months they had been married, she had suffered other disappointments. Doc was a flawed man. Oh, he loved her, she hadn't the least doubt of that. He was gentle and kind, and very considerate of her, he worked hard, he made a great Toby character, and he ran the tent show capably enough.

Yet he had changed since their marriage. There was something in his manner now almost fawning, as though he was afraid he would say or do something to offend her. Before they were married, he often argued heatedly with her about matters pertaining to the show, but now he rarely spoke a cross word to her about anything. When she snapped at him in an irritable moment, he would more than turn the other cheek—he would assume a wounded look and suffer her hard words in silence. It infuriated her so much at times that she wanted to scream at him to show some spunk, to flare back at her. In short, she ached for a good fight to clear the air.

This strange relationship carried over into their bed. She had not really expected the passion and ecstasy she had experienced with Mark, whose very touch could set her ablaze; but in bed Doc's approach to her was tentative, almost as if he was prepared to stop and withdraw if she so much as uttered a negative word. At first Lena thought it might have something to do with his age, but whenever she played the aggressor, she could bring him to a pitch of passion. Yet that was not a role she was prepared to play, it seemed somehow degrading. And for a woman of her time to play the sexual aggressor was unseemly.

As a result their sexual relations had deteriorated to the point that night after night would go by while they lay tense and sleepless side by side, neither speaking, neither making the first overture.

Not only was Lena hurt by this, she was sorely puzzled, and yearned to talk to Doc about it, but the few times she had made the attempt, he refused to discuss it and turned his back on her.

But aside from the unhappiness of the disappointing

relationship with her husband, Lena was content. She had been born to be an actress, she knew that now, and realized that she wouldn't be happy doing anything else. She had escaped the dreary life of a housewife to some clodhopper down in the Valley, and she was grateful for that. She reveled in the applause and adulation of the audiences they played to. The tent show was even more successful than she had ever dreamed. They played to full houses in every town—their fame having preceded them. Even the weather had been kind. Since the near disaster in Port Allen, there had been very little rain.

And then, as if the gods had decided that things were going too smoothly for the Holliday Traveling Players, they had a terrible week. It happened in Henderson, their second town in Texas, the week before they were to play Nacogdoches.

There was the usual crowd of sightseers when they arrived on the lot and started to erect the tent, so no one had an inkling of anything amiss. But on opening night, just as Lena finished dressing for the show, Doc, already in makeup, appeared at their wagon in a state of agitation.

"Something's wrong, Lena. We only have about a third of a tent. Hell, we're not even going to make the nut tonight!"

Lena said thoughtfully, "Maybe it'll pick up the rest of the week. Tonight could be a fluke."

He shook his head. "I don't know, I just have this feeling that we've finally struck the hard times I've been worrying about."

Laughing, she stood to kiss his cheek. "My darling pessimist! Maybe Henderson is one of those towns you told me sometimes happened with medicine shows. Maybe this place is a graveyard for Toby shows."

"Naw, it's not that," he said gloomily. "Those towns had usually been soured on medicine shows by being burned too often. This ain't true in our case. As you've said yourself, there's never been a Toby show through these towns before. Hell, we should have more people in there tonight just out of curiosity, just to see what it's all about."

"Well, we'll survive one bad night, or even a bad week." She patted his arm. "Now, come on. We have a show to do, even if there was only one person in there."

The whole evening was a disaster. Lena learned for the first time what it was like to perform before a meager audience. The first thing she saw when the curtain went up was all those empty seats. They seemed to symbolize rejection and failure. The audience was noisy and sullenly silent by turns, and laughed very little.

It affected Lena's performance, no matter how hard she tried, and she soon saw that it affected all the performers. They were all terrible, and Lena wouldn't have blamed the audience if they had started raining rotten fruit and vegetables on the players.

She felt an immense relief when the final curtain fell. There was only a mild scattering of applause, and she was even relieved about that—they wouldn't have to take curtain calls.

She said to Doc, "I was awful."

"We all were," he said glumly. "We stunk up the place." He heaved a sigh. "I'm not going out there to pitch for the olio. They might hand me my head. There'll be no after-show tonight. I doubt if we'd sell any tickets anyway."

The next evening Lena was just sitting down at her dressing table when Doc stormed into their wagon, face grim as death.

She stared at him in surprise. "Doc, you haven't even started making up yet. What's wrong?"

He reached down for her hand, drew her to her feet. "Come with me. I want to show you something."

"I can't! I have to get ready to go on."

"I've already told Andy to tell the people that the curtain will be late rising tonight. What the hell difference does it make, anyway? There's hardly anybody out there."

"But we've always made it a point to start on time."

"Well, tonight we ain't. I want to show you why nobody's coming."

He hauled her out of the wagon. To all her questions he would only say, "You'll see."

He walked with long strides up the street, walking so rapidly she had to half-run to keep up. They went two blocks south and turned west. The block they were now on was lined solidly with buggies, wagons, horses, every kind of vehicle.

Then, on a vacant lot at the end of the block, Lena saw another tent, the sidewalls up, light streaming out, and she could hear the sound of singing. In consternation she said, "You don't mean there's another tent show in town?"

"Not in the way you mean, no. It's worse than that."

A few people were still straggling in. Doc and Lena mingled with them, finding seats in the back row.

"So that's it, a revival meeting!" she muttered in his ear. "I should have guessed when I saw the tent and heard the singing."

He nodded. "But even that's not the worst of it, as you'll soon see. Listen to this hellfire-and-brimstoner when he gets going good."

There was a small platform at the front of the tent, with a pulpit. Now a tall, scrawny man with lank black hair and snapping black eyes stepped to the pulpit. He held up his hands, palms out, and a hush fell over the crowd.

"Let us pray," he said in a deep, rumbling voice.

Heads were bowed as he led the assemblage in a lengthy prayer. Finally he raised his head to say, "Amen, praise the Lord." His fiery gaze swept slowly over the audience. For a moment Lena was sure that he was staring directly at her, and she had a cowardly urge to flee the tent.

"To those of you with us for the first time tonight, I am the Reverend Eli Walker, here to bring the word of our Lord to you. I had a vision that I was to travel about the countryside battling sin and wickedness, to bring your souls to our Lord, and to drive Satan from your hearts!" His voice was hypnotic, rising and falling with a zealot's thunder. "I see a number of empty seats here tonight. Do not think that those absent tonight are fooling the Lord, brethren. The Lord knows even the flight of the tiniest sparrow." He raised one hand high, then pointed it dramati-

cally in the direction of the tent show. "No, sir, brothers
and sisters, the Lord and I know where the missing
members of our flock are tonight!" Another dramatic
pause. "They are following Satan's lead. They are attending that tent show up the street. Painted, near-naked
women, and men made up and capering like the fool.
Harlots and mountebanks! Thieves and jezebels! The
handservants of Satan, brethren! Instead of sitting here
seeing to the salvation of their eternal souls, they are
reveling in that tent of iniquity!"

"Oh, for God's sake," Lena muttered. "I can't believe
what I'm hearing! Tent of iniquity! I may burst out
laughing any minute."

"I've been told that he's been preaching like that for
three days before we arrived here, telling everyone that
they would be eternally damned if they went to our show
instead of his revival meeting."

"Well, I seem to recall you saying revival meetings
were stiff competition to your medicine show."

"But in those days, if that happened, I could just hitch
up our wagons and move on to some place else. Now we
have a schedule to follow, and we have a payroll five times
what I had on the medicine show. Everyone there worked
on commission anyway, now everyone's on salary."

The Reverend Eli Walker had calmed down considerably
now and had opened his Bible on the pulpit, outlining the
content of his sermon.

"Let's go, Lena, I've seen and heard enough." Doc
was already getting to his feet, pulling her up with him.
Mutters of complaint were heard and dark looks came their
way. Doc strode on, unheeding. Outside, he let his breath
go with a gusty sigh. "I'll have Charlie's ass for this,
booking us opposite a revival meeting. He knows better!"

Lena didn't speak. She held back, her footsteps dragging, deep in thought. He plowed on ahead a few steps,
then stopped to look back over his shoulder. "Come on,
Lena! We do have a show to put on, as you so carefully
pointed out."

She caught up with him. "I was just thinking, Doc.
Since this *has* happened, why not take advantage of it?"

"Take advantage? How, for God's sake?"

"Well, we've all been working our tails off since New Orleans. A few days of rest would do us all good."

He got a look of shock. "You mean, close the show?"

"That's just what I do mean. We're not making expenses here, the way it is. Close the show after tonight. If any tickets have been sold in advance, refund the money."

"There *was* no advance sale," he said darkly. "That should have warned me right there."

"Well, then?" They began walking on. "We've been making good money, we can afford a few days off."

Doc still looked dubious. "That certainly wouldn't make us any friends here, if we come through here again."

"Then we simply won't come through here again." She took his hand and swung their hands between them. "Our next town is Nacogdoches. If we close now, we can go on ahead, and have a few extra days with my family." She became gloomy. "If Daddy and Mother have forgiven me enough to come all the way up to see me. I wrote them, but that's one thing about traveling like this, mail never catches up with you. I don't know whether they got my letter or not. But Debra Lee and Michael surely did. Can we do that, Doc?" She looked up at him with shining eyes. "It would make me happy. I've been gone from there a long time."

"What's this 'we' stuff?" he said gruffly. "You can go, of course you can, honey, if we decide to close for the rest of the week. But you know I can't leave the show for that long."

"What do you mean, you can't? Do you think the whole show would fall apart if you weren't around for a few days?"

"Somebody has to be in charge, even if we're not operating."

"Either Andy or Bob can handle things. What's going to happen in a few days, for heaven's sake? I want you to meet my folks, you're my husband. And you promised!!"

"I promised we'd come in a day early, have supper with them, but no more than that."

Lena stopped to stare up into his face, but he was

looking off and refused to meet her gaze. "Why, Doc, I do believe you're timid about meeting them!"

"I'm old enough to be your father, Lena, you know that. They probably won't approve of me at all."

"They'll approve of you or to the devil with them. You're my husband. And why this age business all of a sudden?" she said teasingly. "Every time before, when I've even hinted at the difference in our ages, you've bristled like an angry porcupine."

"That was just between us. Anyway, it may have been a mistake, us marrying," he said dully. "But I loved you so damned much, I thought the age difference wouldn't matter all that much. But I'm afraid that it does."

She said lightly, "You haven't heard me complaining, have you?"

"You have reason to, you know how it's been in . . ." His color rose. "Between us in bed."

Lena pulled him to a stop and faced him. "That's what the trouble is, your age?"

"I reckon so. The first week or two, I was like a young man again, but Father Time caught up with me."

"I don't believe you," she said bluntly. "There's something else. Not another woman, I'm as sure of that as anything, but *something*."

"We shouldn't be talking like this, Lena. It's not proper talk between a man and a woman."

"Horse feathers!" she snorted. "We're husband and wife. It's *time* we talked about it."

"All right, then, I'll tell you!" he said almost angrily. "I've been a rounder all my life, a woman-chaser. I've long since lost count of the women I've bedded, and most of them have been tramps."

"It'd make things better between us if I were a woman of that sort?"

"Of course not, Lena! But you were pure, a virgin that first night in your wagon. I feel . . . impure whenever I touch you in bed."

"You really believe that I was a virgin?" she asked in disbelief.

"Of course you were."

"Then all that experience you just told me about hasn't taught you a thing, Doc Holliday! For your information, I was *not* a virgin that night. And you're stupider than I thought if you think differently."

"I don't believe you, you're lying just to make me feel better."

"Believe it. To make it even worse, it was with my own cousin, the man in New Orleans, Mark Moraghan. I spent the night with him there, and we had done it before, long before I met you."

Doc got a stunned look. "Your own cousin?"

"That's right. So, you see, you're not the first man who's bedded me!"

"Lena, I've never heard you talk like that."

"Maybe that's where I made my mistake." She was so angry she was trembling. "That's the way all your other women talked, isn't it? Now who's impure?"

"Honey, I would never think that of you." He tried to take her hand.

She evaded his grasp, and started off, almost running, tears burning her eyes. She heard his footsteps pounding after her.

He caught her arm and held her fast. "I'm sorry, honey, for everything. I'll do what you ask. I'll close the show after tonight, leave Bob Ketchum in charge of moving to Nacogdoches, and we'll leave tomorrow to visit with your family, if that's what you want."

She smiled slowly, her anger appeased. "I want that very much, Doc."

Since the road they had to travel to Nacogdoches passed near Moraghan, they went there first. The thought crossed Lena's mind that there was a slight possibility that Mark might be home. How would he react to her being married? But then he had once told her she should forget about him and marry, so he would be content.

They were on horseback, not in a wagon. Doc had talked of buying a buggy, but had not as yet gotten around to it. As they reined in before the house, Lena saw Michael and Bandy working with the horses in the pasture.

Doc stared at the horses with a low whistle. "That's a fine-looking bunch of animals."

"Michael must be doing well. He's acquired more race horses since I left."

Michael had seen them. He dismounted, gave his horse over to Bandy, and came striding toward the house, just as the door opened. Kate stood framed in the doorway, looking out at them.

Lena got down quickly and ran toward the house. "Mother!"

Kate advanced to the edge of the porch, and said uncertainly, "Lena? Is that you?"

"Yes, Mother, yes!"

She flew up the porch steps and they were in each other's arms. Kate hugged her fiercely. "My baby! I was afraid that I'd never see you again!"

Lena stepped back. "Didn't you get my letter?"

"Yes, Michael's came three weeks ago, but . . ."

"Well, if it isn't little sister!" Michael came up the steps with lunging strides, beaming broadly.

"Michael!"

They embraced, and then Michael put his arm around both women. "It's nice to have you two together again!" His glance was drawn to Doc, still astride his horse.

Lena raised her voice. "Darling, get down and come up here. I want you to meet my folks."

Doc got down, taking his time, and slowly came up onto the porch. "Mother, this is my husband, Doc Holliday." Lena grinned. "Actually, as I wrote you, his real name is Hoyt Jones. Darling, meet my mother, and my brother, Michael."

Doc dipped his head slightly. "I'm delighted to meet you, Mrs. Moraghan. And Michael."

The two men shook hands warily. Lena's attention was distracted by Bandy, who came bowlegging up the steps.

"Miss Lena, it's grand to see you again. Fact."

"The same here, Bandy. I saw Michael riding out there. Can he stay on now without falling off?"

Bandy said solemnly, "Most of the time." Then he broke into a broad grin. "He's become a fine rider, Miss

Lena. Wins more races than he loses. Thought I'd never live to see the day."

Lena had turned to peer through the screen door with a frown. "Mother, where's Daddy? Didn't he come up with you?"

Her mother looked stricken, exchanging a quick glance with Michael, and a cold feeling crept over Lena.

Kate took her hands in hers. "Kevin is dead, Lena," she said in a choked voice. "Your daddy is dead."

The shock was numbing. Lena swayed and would have fallen but for Kate's support. "How . . . how did he die?"

"Bud Danker came down to the Valley and shot him."

Lena said tightly, "Did they catch Bud?"

Michael answered, "Not yet. I'm not even sure the law is still looking for him. Certainly not very hard."

Lena stared at Kate almost in accusation. "Why wasn't I informed?"

Michael answered again, this time with a thread of anger in his voice. "How were we to do that, Lena? You're a fine one to ask that of us."

"Oh." Lena's shoulders slumped as she remembered. "You're right, of course. I'm sorry. If there's any fault here, it's all mine. But it should have been in the newspapers."

"It was in a few," Kate said. "But they were all local, here and down in the Valley. It didn't make any big-city newspapers. Your father was a fine man, dear, a respected man, but hardly well-known enough for the news of his death to be known all over."

"When did it happen?"

"Not long after you ran away, sis."

"And all this time I've been enjoying myself, having a fine time, and Daddy was dead. You know what my fondest dream has been? That Daddy could see me on stage and approve." Her grief came then, overwhelming in its intensity. Eyes streaming with tears, she whirled away and beat on the veranda post with her fists. "Those damned Dankers! Must they kill every Moraghan in existence before they're satisfied?"

Doc stepped up to put his arms around her shoulders,

and said gently, "Take it easy, honey. Easy now. I know how you must feel but this won't help any."

Kate said briskly, "I expect you're all tired and hungry. Where did you come from today?"

"From Henderson," Doc replied. "We closed the show early up there."

"Then you must be starved. I'll start supper, I was about to, anyway." She looked at Bandy. "Bandy, perhaps they would like a drink. Would you see to it?"

Bandy rubbed his hands together. "I sure will, Kate."

Lena, her tears dried, was a touch surprised—her mother and Bandy seemed on rather familiar terms.

Kate went into the house, and the others started after her. Lena held Michael back with a touch on his arm. "Michael, how is Cassie taking what Bud did? I know you were . . . uh, seeing her before I left."

"She left, Lena." Michael was plunged into gloom. "After Bud left, Cassie had to have her mother committed. I persuaded her to move into the house here. But then, when the news came that Bud had killed Daddy, she was torn up. When Mother wrote that she was coming up here, Cassie apparently couldn't face her. I love her, Lena. I was going to ask her to marry me, but she left before I could get around to it."

"Oh, Michael, I *am* sorry." She placed her hand gently on his arm. "But maybe it's best this way, did you ever think of that? After all, she is a Danker, and after what her brother did to Daddy . . ."

"That was her brother, Cassie had nothing to do with it. But that's why she left, she was ashamed."

"That still doesn't erase the fact that she is a Danker. To take a Danker for your wife, to have one in our family. It wouldn't be right."

Michael twisted about in sudden anger. "You've done better, I suppose, dear sister? Marrying a man twice your age, and some sort of a gypsy showman in addition?"

She flared back. "You have no right to say that! You don't know a thing about Doc. He's a fine man, if you'll let yourself get to know him. And if he's a showman, so am I. I've chosen it as my life now."

Michael sighed, raised and lowered his shoulders. "I'm sorry, Lena. But it's a sore spot with me, everybody always pointing out that Cassie is a Danker. And I don't think anyone has to worry. It doesn't look much like I'll ever see her again." He held up both hands. "Peace, sis?"

She laughed. "Peace, brother. Now let's go in. I could use that drink Bandy promised." She linked arms with him and they went into the house.

Bandy was sent into Nacogdoches to take word to the Liebermans. Stony drove Debra and the children out to stay the week. After the first day at Moraghan Doc overcame his uneasiness, and soon he was getting on well with everyone. Even Michael came around. He told Lena, "I like your man, Lena. He's a good husband for you, I can tell."

Lena wasn't at all surprised. She knew very well how charming and likable Doc could be when he made the effort. He regaled the whole family with tales of his days with medicine shows, editing out the more unsavory episodes.

Much to Lena's surprise, there were very few recriminations from any members of her family about her running away. The only ones who even mentioned it were Debra and her mother.

"I can understand your running off, Lena," Debra told her. "I should, since I did the same thing myself. I felt the same way you did, I had to get away from down there. I'm only sorry you didn't get to see Daddy before he was killed."

Close to tears, Lena said, "Oh, God, so do I! If I could only know he forgave me, that he still loved me."

"He forgave you, Lena, Daddy was a very forgiving man."

When Lena said much the same thing to her mother, Kate said gently, "Of course he forgave you, dear. He was worried about you, of course, but when he got over his first anger, it was all right. Kevin was a man quick to anger, but also quick to forgive, especially those he loved. And he loved you until the end, don't you ever believe otherwise."

"If only I had let you know where I was, so you could have let me know of his death."

"I doubt you could have made the funeral, Lena. It would have taken you too long to get there." Kate smiled slightly. "Kevin never much believed in funerals anyway, he always said they were barbaric rituals, conducted for the living, not the dead."

Despite these reassurances, Lena was still troubled by guilt. It would have been a happy week, with all her people together, but for her guilt and grief. She grieved in private, often walking or riding down to the river, or to the old cabin, to sit for long periods, sometimes giving way to tears, but she made the effort to show a happy face to the others.

Her relations with Doc plagued her. It had been her hope that things would improve after their talk, but there was not that much change in their relationship. During the week at Moraghan they shared the bedroom in the back that had once been Nora's. It would have been a boon to find solace and relief in his embrace, to be able to forget everything, if only in a few minutes of passion. But it was not to be. Only once during the week did he turn to her, and it was as it had been before—a tentative coupling on his part, leaving her unsatisfied. But she would be damned if she would make the first overture!

There had been no mention of Mark, and Lena couldn't bring herself to ask after him. It would have been a perfectly natural question, of course, but she was afraid she might give herself away, remembering that Michael had suspected something between her and Mark once.

The show was due to arrive in Nacogdoches on Thursday, and they were scheduled to open on Monday night. Doc left Moraghan that Thursday, to go in to town to oversee setting up the tent, and to make preparations for their Monday show.

As he prepared to leave for town, she said, "I'll have Bandy saddle a horse and I'll ride along—"

He said quickly, "No, honey, you stay out here with your folks. I can handle everything that needs doing."

She was shaking her head. "You didn't let me finish.

I'll just ride a ways with you, then stop off along the river.''

As they rode away together, Doc said, "I've noticed you riding off somewhere by yourself almost every day since we've been here. Where do you go?"

"Oh, I have a place down by the river, where I used to sit and daydream. Now I go there to sit and do my grieving for Daddy. Either there, or to the old log cabin that Grandfather Sean built when he and Grandmother first came to Texas. I'd rather grieve by myself than mope around the house, making everybody else miserable.''

He reached across to take her hand. "I'm right sorry about your daddy, Lena, I hope you know that.''

She gave him a wan smile. "Of course I know that, darling.''

"In fact, I've been thinking . . ." He cleared his throat. "Maybe we should stay shut down this coming week as well. It hardly seems fitting, you going back on stage so soon after learning about your daddy's death.''

"You'd give up a whole week's receipts, just for me, Doc?"

He looked embarrassed. "It would hurt me to the quick, I admit, but I don't want you back on stage until you're ready.''

"That's sweet of you, Doc, but I'm ready. I *need* to be back on stage, the sooner the better. Besides, Daddy's been dead for over a year. If we don't open next week, it will mean we'd have to move on without showing in Nacogdoches at all, since we *do* have a schedule to keep. If that happens, my family wouldn't get to see me on stage at all. No, I'll go on Monday night.''

"If you're sure that's what you want.''

She nodded decisively. "It's what I want.''

They had been riding along the river road for some little time now. Lena reined in her horse. "I'll turn off here, darling. My secret place is just down there, in that clump of trees.'' She nodded toward the river.

Doc reined in beside her, taking her hand. "I'll come back out again on Sunday, after we're all set up, to fetch you back in to town.''

"You don't have to, Doc. I can ride in with Stony, he'll be coming out on Sunday anyway, for Debra Lee and the children."

"I'd rather we rode in together."

"All right, darling." She stood up in the stirrups and leaned over to kiss him lightly. "Take care now, and I'll see you on Sunday."

"You, too, honey." He cupped her face between his hands, his eyes luminous. "I love you, Lena, don't be forgetting that."

Startled, she stared at him with widening eyes. "I won't, darling. I love you too."

She sat her horse as he rode away. Just before the bend in the river road, he looked back and waved. She returned the wave, kneed her mount down toward the river.

She tied the horse off and forced her way through the thicket to the tiny glade. She had been surprised and pleased when she'd come down here earlier in the week—it had looked as if it had been undisturbed all the time she had been away, just waiting for her return.

Lena sat on the sloping rock, removed her riding boots and stockings, then let her feet dangle in the water, leaning back on her hands, face turned up to the sun.

It was very quiet and restful, only the sounds of insects and the gurgle of the water as it pushed past the bank. She thought of very little, her mind almost a blank. This was something she could do nowhere else, only here. There was a mystical quality about the glade, or perhaps it only existed in her imagination. Yet it had the ability to heal the mind and spirit, of that there was no doubt.

Shortly after lunch on Sunday, Lena rode again down to the river, and her private sanctuary. This would be the last opportunity to avail herself of the benefits of the glade. She had left word at the house that if Doc came back he was to be told that she would return in plenty of time for the trip in to Nacogdoches.

Once again, she let her bare feet dangle in the water, her face turned up to the sun. By now she had decided there was something actually hypnotic about the combination of the glade, the cool water rushing over her feet, the sun on her face, and the quiet, enabling her to put herself into a half-trance, going deep into herself, so that few outside stimuli penetrated her consciousness.

Consequently, she gave a great start of fright as a voice spoke behind her. "I must say that marriage must have wrought a change in you, cousin. The last time I was here you rose out of the water like a nymph."

She twisted around and had to clutch at the rock to keep from sliding into the water. "Mark!"

"Hello, cousin," he drawled. He was leaning negligently against the fallen tree, smoke spiraling up from the cigarette in his hand. "I guess I owe you an apology. I had no intention of frightening you again. I made enough noise barging in here to awaken Sleeping Beauty."

"I . . . I was daydreaming and didn't hear a . . a thing," she stammered. She was stunned by his unexpected appearance, her mind a rage of conflicting emotions— dismay at his being here, yet at the same time flooded with gladness. She got hurriedly to her feet. Her feet slipped on the wet rock, and she would have tumbled into the river if Mark hadn't jumped forward and caught her. Her heart began to beat erratically at his touch on her arm. Without being too obvious about it, she shook his hand off and backed up against the tree trunk, breathing unevenly. "I didn't know you were at home. I thought you were at sea."

"I came home two days ago," he said without expression. "I got word that you were on Moraghan. I asked after you at the house and they said you'd gone riding. I guessed you'd be here."

Getting herself more under control, Lena said, "The last time I saw you, you spoke as though you'd never come back home."

His glance slid away. "I don't really know why I did. Nothing has changed. Ma hasn't changed one iota, and neither has my sister. I don't think my sister has been out of the house since I left the last time. I heard about Uncle Kevin, Lena." His glance moved to her again. "I'm sorry about that, truly sorry. I always liked him."

"Thank you." She stared at him, her temper beginning to stir. "You said you asked after me at the house. The way you left me in the hotel in New Orleans, I got the impression you never wanted to see me again. Was I wrong about that?"

"Ah, Lena. It's not that I didn't want to see you again, it's just that not under that . . . that kind of circumstances."

She said coldly, "You could at least have said good-bye. Or perhaps left some money on the dresser. Isn't that the way it's done with girls men pick up for the night?"

"Lena, don't talk like that," he said in shock. "It wasn't anything like that, and you know it. But if I had said good-bye, it would have meant a scene. Neither of us wanted that."

"You've never seemed to care much about what *I* want, Mark."

"It was not right, Lena—"

"I know, it's a sin. God knows you've told me that often enough. I still think it was a despicable thing to do, leaving me like that, without a word of any kind. At least the time before you sent me a letter."

He threw his cigarette into the river with an angry twist of his wrist. "I can't see why you're carrying on. I notice you didn't wait very long to get married."

"I was only following your advice, Mark," she said evenly. "You told me to find a good man and get married, remember? So that's what I did."

"I suppose I should offer congratulations, although it galls me to do so."

"Why should it? You never loved me, you made that quite clear."

"That's not true, dammit!" he said harshly. "I do love you, Lena, and I suppose I always will. But it would never have worked for us. You're not stupid, I don't know why you can't see that!"

His confession of love set up a trembling inside her, and that made her angrier still. "You never gave it a chance to work, Mark. But it doesn't matter, I belong to another man now."

"Is he good to you, cousin?"

"Yes, of course he is!"

"Good for you in bed as well?" His voice became mocking, his eyes turning smoky. "Is it as good for you in bed as it was with us?"

"What a foul thing to ask! And why should you care?"

"Then it isn't!" he said on a rising note of triumph. Before she divined his intention, he had moved close, taking her by the shoulders. "Does he make you feel like this?" he asked, as he kissed her.

She was on fire instantly. Despite her firm resolve not to give in to him, she could not muster the necessary resistance. Her blood flowed hot and thick as honey, and she felt her knees go weak. The sexual desires so long unsatisfied by Doc threatened to overwhelm her. She realized that she would sink to the ground with Mark on the instant, if it was his wish.

Then his hands began to roam over her body, and she tore her mouth from his. She whispered fiercely, "No, Mark! I will not give in to you! Everything is different now. I will not betray Doc. It is not right—"

His laughter grated. "I wouldn't think of compromising you, cousin." His voice was bitter with self-mockery. "I just wanted to prove to you that whatever it is between us is still there, and I think I succeeded in doing that."

Still, he did not let her go. He held her tightly against him, his grip almost cruel, and she could feel his muscular body against hers, could feel his erection through his trousers, and she wanted him. Oh, God, how she wanted him!

Then she went rigid with horror. She was staring past Mark's head, and she saw Doc emerge from the thicket around the glade. He skidded to a stop and stood very still, his eyes wide. Color rose in his face.

Lena began to struggle against Mark's arms. "Let me go! Let me go!"

Doc said tonelessly, "It's a little late for that, isn't it, honey?"

"Oh, Jesus!" Mark let his arms fall, and turned slowly, his face guarded. "Hello, Mr. Holliday."

Doc grunted. "So it's you, the relative. I can't say I'm too surprised."

Lena said, "It's not the way it looks, Doc."

"Ain't it, honey?"

"No, I swear it's not. Mark caught me unawares and he . . . well, he . . ." She stopped, unable to continue the lie she had started. She had been about to say that Mark was trying to rape her, but she would not do that to him, no matter what.

"Was it just a welcome-back kiss between relatives, honey? Is that what you're trying to say? It struck me as more than that. If I hadn't happened upon the scene, as we say in show business, the pair of you would have been on the ground in another minute. Or . . ." He grinned without humor. "Or are you trying to tell me that he was about to force himself upon you? Is that it?"

"That's about it, Mr. Holliday," Mark said easily. "If there's blame to be placed, blame me. Like Lena said, I came upon her unexpectedly. I reckon I've always been taken with her. I just couldn't help myself. I guess it's a good thing you came along, you saved me from doing something I would always regret."

"Oh? Seems I'm in the wrong getup here." He gestured to himself. "I should be in my Toby outfit. That's Toby's routine, saving the virgin from the villain's clutches. But then you're hardly a virgin, are you, honey?" His gaze honed in on Lena, sharp and merciless. "You see, Mr. Moraghan, Lena is honest, I have to give her that. She's already told me about how you two have carried on in the past. So how can you expect me to believe differently this time around?"

Mark turned to Lena. In a stricken voice he said, "You told him about us?"

Ignoring him, she looked steadily at Doc. "What's different this time is that I'm married. You're my husband."

"And you wouldn't put the horns on me?" Doc laughed raggedly. "You expect me to believe that, honey? One thing you should have learned with me—never try to con a con man."

"It's the truth," she said doggedly. Then her temper

flared. "Another minute and I would have sent Mark packing. If you hadn't sneaked up on us like that—"

"Sneaked? *Sneaked!* Hell, I made enough noise for a buffalo. The way you two were trading spit, a tornado wouldn't have disturbed you a bit."

"Mr. Holliday," Mark said, "if there are no objections, I'll leave now. Unless you're going to challenge me to a duel, or some such nonsense?"

Doc looked at him balefully, slowly shook his head. "You can go, Moraghan. There'll be no duels or anything of the sort. In fact, I'll be glad to see the last of you."

Mark gave Lena an unreadable look. "I suppose you won't believe me if I say I'm sorry for what happened, but I am, I really am. Good-bye, cousin."

"Good-bye, Mark."

He was already in motion, worming his way through the thicket, and soon disappeared from sight.

Lena looked at her husband. "Well, Doc? What happens now? Will you be glad to see the last of me?"

He studied her in speculation. "I want you to know one thing, Lena. Despite what you may think, I wasn't spying on you. I was on my way back to your house and I remembered your telling me that you sometimes came down to this place along the river. I turned off the road, and seeing your horse, I knew you were here. I want you to believe that."

"I can't see that it matters, one way or another." She shrugged. "I believe you, for what it's worth. But you haven't answered my question. Does this end it between us? If it does, I'll go on back to Moraghan and you can ride back in to town. I'm sure you can find someone to take my place with the show."

When he still didn't answer, she picked up her boots and stockings and started past him. She might pick up a few burrs in her bare feet, but she wanted to get out of his sight as quickly as possible.

"No, I don't want you to go!" he said explosively. He caught her arm as she started past, and pulled her against him.

"What are you doing, Doc?" She laughed uncertainly.
"Are you going to beat me?"

His arms were around her firmly, holding her still. He
cupped a hand behind her head and brought her mouth to
his. Astonishment rendered Lena still for a few moments,
her mind working furiously to figure out what he was
about. Then she knew, and she was caught between laughter and anger.

When she got a chance to speak, she said, "Here, Doc?
Right here?"

"Right here."

"In broad daylight, right out in the open?" She knew
she was being cruel, but she couldn't help taunting him a
little. "It should be in the dark, and with some slut. But
then I guess that's what I am in your eyes now. Isn't that
right, Doc?"

He closed her mouth with his and pulled her down to the
ground with him. The brief encounter with Mark had
aroused her, and Doc was equally aroused, she found out
in the next moment as he rose up, his trousers down, and
mounted her. He entered her with an exhalation of breath.

She had already decided not to fight him—he was her
husband, after all—but she also decided not to cooperate.
He could do what he wished with her, she determined to
lie as still as the log behind her head.

This determination melted away almost at once. This
Doc was different from the one she was accustomed to. He
made love to her in a controlled frenzy, with a fierceness
and directness she hadn't seen in him before, and her
treacherous body, almost against her will, began to rise
and fall with his. It was close to rape, yet it wasn't. Rape
was an act of anger, and while Doc might be feeling some
anger still, there was a strong sexual emotion rampant in
him, a hunger and a need for her that he had not evinced
before.

And whether it was the lingering passion aroused by
Mark's embrace or the unexpectedness of Doc's lovemaking, she experienced a powerful, gripping orgasm as he
exploded within her. She rose, clinging, her pelvis grind-
ing against him.

As the storm passed, she said with an explosion of breath, "Whoo! I'm not sure, until I sort this thing all out, what brought this on, but it was nice, darling." She smoothed at the silvery hair as his head rested on her shoulder. "I can only hope that this wasn't a one-time thing."

He raised his head to look into her eyes. His face had the soft, unfocused look of satiated passion, all his anger drained away. "I told you more than once that I loved you. Did I convince you this time?"

"You convinced me," she said in a soft voice.

He moved over to stretch out beside her, lying on his side. Lena could feel the wild pounding of his heart against her breast.

She sensed that it had a lot to do with his catching her in another man's arms. Perhaps it had taken that to convince him that she was not the unsullied woman he thought her, that she was flesh and blood. But why should she search for reasons? It was what she wanted, wasn't it? Why did she feel a need to search for reasons?

Just accept, foolish girl, she thought wryly, and be grateful. She had the feeling that this new closeness would continue between them, and it gave the future a rosier outlook.


# 14


Mark Moraghan had left Nacogdoches the day Doc stumbled upon him with Lena, and a year passed before he set foot on Texas soil again, and that was at Galveston. During the year he had gone around the world three times, touching the States only in New Orleans, and immediately shipping out again.

But he was weary of traveling. However, he did have to make a living some way, and the only thing he knew was the sea. Since he had never become more than a deckhand, he had never earned much money. Several times, officers, taking note of his superior intelligence, had told Mark that his talents were wasted as an ordinary seaman, and had offered to tutor him so that he could try for his officer's papers. Mark simply wasn't interested. The sea didn't appeal to him that much, and he didn't wish to make a career of it.

After disembarking at New Orleans this time, he had taken a job as a deckhand on a rusty old freighter that plied the waters of the Gulf, carrying miscellaneous freight to the various ports along the Gulf coast, going all the way down to Brownsville.

Mark had heard no word of his family, and certainly nothing of Lena. Often, he wondered if he hadn't made the mistake of his life in turning his back on her. God knows, he saw things every day much worse than marrying his own cousin! Well, it was too late for second thoughts. He'd made his own bed, she'd chosen hers, and now he would have to lie in his alone.

The coast freighter was lying overnight in the Galveston port, so Mark went ashore late in the afternoon, mainly in search of a good supper. The work on the ship wasn't hard, since the captain wasn't much for painting or rust scraping, but the food was atrocious. Mark was glad that the ship docked every day or so, so he could search out decent places to eat.

Two blocks from the dock, he came upon a small café—Big Red's Eatery. It didn't look like much, but a glance in the window told him that it was clean, even the windows showed regular washings, and cleanliness wasn't a common virtue among waterfront cafés. He decided to try it.

The café was about half full, and Mark took an empty table toward the rear. The tables had neat red-and-white tablecloths, and everything in sight was polished and shining. He felt better about his choice. The menu was a chalkboard on the wall. A look at it told Mark that he was home—good old Texas food.

There was one waitress in the place, a slight, slender girl with long, lustrous brown hair. She moved with a lithe grace and buoyancy that surprised Mark, since he was sure that she had been at work in here all day. She wore a clean brown dress, only the bright red apron around her narrow waist showed food stains.

She finished serving two sailors three tables away and came down to Mark's table. He saw that her eyes were brown, and at the same time he was struck by something annoyingly familiar about her.

She smiled wearily. Now that he could view her up close Mark could see that she was indeed tired, and he was surer than ever that he'd seen her somewhere before.

"What will you have, sir?"

Mark leaned back, smiling. She attracted him, and he wondered if he should try. He'd made a quick trip to a whorehouse in New Orleans, but that had been several days ago, and the thought of a woman who'd cost him no more than a supper and perhaps the price of a hotel room was appealing. "What do you recommend, miss? I've found that I often end up with the best by asking that question of a waitress. Of course, sometimes it can go the other way."

She smiled again, this time more warmly. The first smile had been the automatic house smile—she hadn't really focused on him.

"Red is a very good cook. Everything is good. As the menu says, tonight's speciality is fried chicken. It is very good."

"Then you'd recommend it?"

"I would. It's what I'll be having for my supper."

"How about a gizzard or two? I haven't had chicken gizzards in so long I've almost forgotten how they taste. In restaurants they usually throw them away."

"Red throws nothing out if he can help it. In fact, I'm sure he has more than one, since most people don't care at all for the gizzards. Should I ask him?"

"You do that. I'll eat all the chicken gizzards he has around." As she nodded and started off, he called after her. "Oh, miss, would you bring me a cup of coffee right away? With cream and sugar? On board ship we usually have to drink it as black and bitter as gall."

"Certainly, sir. Right away."

He watched her walk away. Although the dress she wore was loose and almost to the floor, he could see the sensual sway of her hips, and he sensed rather than saw that there was a nice body under all that covering. A pleasant warmth began in his loins as he contemplated the possibility of seducing her. His experience with women was such that he usually could tell in advance as to his chances of success. In this instance he wasn't quite sure yet, but it was pleasant to contemplate. What could he lose by trying?

Yet there was that haunting familiarity about her that still puzzled him. When she came back in a few minutes with a steaming cup of coffee, he studied her more closely. He was surer than ever that he had seen her before. She seemed uneasy by his scrutiny, and left his table quickly.

He drank the coffee leisurely, wondering if he should ask right out if they had met before. But that was such a stale approach, if he did intend to ask her out.

When, a few minutes later, she came carrying his food, he almost had it. She set the dishes out before him—a plate of fried chicken, mashed potatoes and green beans, and a bowl of thick gravy.

"Red found a half-dozen gizzards for you, you'll notice," she said in her light voice. "I hope you enjoy them, sir."

"Thank you, miss."

As she started to turn away, a man down the room called out to her, and she stood poised for a moment, head turned slightly toward the man's voice.

As he studied her profile Mark had it—the Danker girl! He exhaled a breath in astonishment—it had been caught by the coincidence. Yet it probably wasn't all that much of a coincidence. He'd heard she had left Nacogdoches in a hurry after Bud's murderous rampage, and Galveston was a busy port town. He was sure it was easier for a woman to find a job waiting tables here than in many towns in Texas. Apparently she didn't have a glimmer of who he was. Of course, there was no reason why she should, he'd never seen her more than two or three times.

He began eating. True to her promise, the food was

excellent, as good as any home-cooked chicken he'd ever eaten. He ate slowly, debating with himself whether or not he should make himself known to her. What purpose would it serve? If she knew the whereabouts of her brother, it wasn't very likely that she would reveal it to a Moraghan.

From time to time he glanced her way. She was a hard-working girl, a very efficient waitress, and there was a decorum about her, surprising in a waitress, especially one serving rough, randy seamen. There was nothing the least bawdy or forward about her manner, qualities he wouldn't have been at all surprised to find in a Danker. Mark grinned wryly at himself. He knew he wasn't being fair to her, dumping her into a basket with the rest of the Danker clan, but dammit, her brother *had* killed Uncle Kevin.

She seemed to sense when he had taken the last bite and was there immediately. "Anything else, sir? We have pecan pie, peach cobbler, or pound cake, all made here on the premises."

"I think I'll have the peach cobbler."

When she came back with the cobbler and set it before him, Mark said, "Your name is Danker, isn't it? Cassie, I believe?"

She froze, all the color draining from her face. She swallowed, staring at him, brown eyes wide with fear. "How did you know?"

"I'm from Nacogdoches. I'm a Moraghan, Mark Moraghan."

"Oh, dear God," she whispered, and started to turn away.

He caught her hand. "No, don't go. I don't mean you any harm, Cassie. I wasn't looking for you or anything like that. It just happened. I'm working on a ship plowing up and down the coast, and we're docked here for the night. Does anyone in Nacogdoches know where you are?"

She shook her head so violently her hair whipped from side to side. "No one."

"I thought not. Did you know that my cousin Michael is about out of his mind not knowing where you are?"

"I'm sorry if I hurt Michael. I wouldn't hurt him for the world, but I had to leave as I did, after Bud . . ." She swallowed again.

"I know, after he killed Uncle Kevin. But Michael doesn't hold you in any way responsible for that."

"Maybe not now, but he might in the future."

"I think you're selling him short."

"It wasn't Michael so much as his mother," Cassie said. "She was coming to Moraghan. I just couldn't face her after what Bud did."

Mark suddenly felt sorry for her. She was completely sincere, he felt it in his bones. "Well . . . I can see how you might feel that way."

"Have they caught Bud yet?"

He stared. "You don't know anything about him, where he is?"

"No." She hesitated. "Not really. He wrote me before I left Nacogdoches, gave me a place to get in touch, but that was a long time ago and I—"

"Don't tell me." He held up his hand. "I don't want to know."

She summoned up indignation. "I wasn't going to tell you. I despise what he's done, but I wouldn't betray him."

"He hasn't been caught, Cassie. At least not the last I heard."

She stared at him with a flicker of hope in her eyes. "Are you going to tell on me?"

"Where you are, you mean?" He shook his head. "If this is the way you want it, Cassie, I won't cause you any trouble. Anyway, you're not wanted for anything. Except by Michael." He smiled suddenly. "And there's nothing illegal about that." He reached into his pocket for his fold of money, peeled off enough for the bill, and gave it to Cassie. "Good luck, Cassie, whatever you decide to do."

She smiled, a shy, sweet smile, and he could easily see why Michael was in love with her. "Thank you, Mr. Moraghan. I do appreciate your keeping quiet."

Mark quickly ate his cobbler and left the café, leaving

Cassie a dollar tip. He started back toward the ship, without thought of stopping anywhere else. It wasn't until he started up the gangplank that he recalled his earlier thoughts about seducing Cassie. He laughed shortly. Strange, but all considerations of that sort had fled his mind once he had learned who she was.

A month later Mark got off the freighter in Brownsville, his duffle bag over his shoulder. He was thoroughly sick of the water, even the relatively serene Gulf, and he considered himself well quit of it. He asked directions to the Moraghan place, and then set out on foot. It was a long walk. He could have rented a rig, but walking on solid ground was a treat after so long on the rolling decks of a ship.

He spent the night in an alfalfa field, the scent of it sweet in his nostrils. It was July now, and the days were scorching in the Valley, cooling off just enough at night to make sleeping outdoors pleasant.

The next morning he walked on, breakfasting off a package of jerky he had bought in Brownsville. It was the middle of the afternoon when he finally stepped onto Moraghan land. There were no signposts so indicating, but the citrus fruit trees here were green and thriving, in better condition than any of the other orchards he had seen, so it had to be Moraghan land.

This surmise was confirmed a mile down the road. He saw several men working between the rows of trees, hoeing weeds and cleaning out the irrigation ditches. He turned off the lane and went over to them. He saw that they were all Mexican. "Is this the Moraghan place?"

They all looked at him blankly, but one squat, heavyset man came toward him warily. He wore a straw sombrero that shaded his dark features. A heavy, drooping mustachio hid his mouth, and his dark eyes glinted at Mark from under the sombrero. "*Sí, Señor,* this is the Moraghan orchards."

Mark stuck out his hand. "I'm Mark Moraghan, Kevin's nephew."

"And I am Juan Mendoza, *Señora* Moraghan's foreman.'' He accepted Mark's handshake guardedly, his eyes squinting in suspicion.

"Oh . . . you think I'm here to take charge.'' Mark grinned engagingly. "Nothing could be further from the truth, Mr. Mendoza. Aunt Kate doesn't even know I'm here, and I know damned little about running a fruit ranch.''

Juan Mendoza visibly relaxed, but his eyes still looked a question.

Mark gestured. "I thought maybe there was some job I could handle here. I'm a seaman by trade, but I want to get away from ships for a spell.''

Juan got an astonished look. "You are searching for a job? Here, *Señor*?''

"Yes. If you'll have me, if there's any place I might fit in.''

"We can always use another man. There is always work.''

"But again, to be frank, I know nothing about it.''

For the first time Juan smiled. "*Señor* Moraghan, there is nothing difficult to learn. All a man needs is a strong back and a willingness to work hard.''

"That I have. Swabbing decks either gives a man a strong back, or it kills him.''

Juan hesitated, then said slowly, "The pay is not much, *Señor*. If you expect . . .''

"No, no, I expect nothing more because I'm a Moraghan. You pay me what you pay the others.''

"The main house is empty, although my Maria cleans it regularly. You may use one of the many bedrooms there.''

Mark shook his head. "I'd rather not have privileges not granted to the other workers. I can bunk in the bunkhouse with them.''

"It would be better this way, *Señor*. All the workers are of my race, and speak very little of your language. They would be uncomfortable with you bunking with them. The main house, please.''

That evening, after Mark had settled in and eaten a light supper, he sat down to write a letter to Michael. He had debated with himself about this, in view of his promise to Cassie, but he had finally decided that he owed Michael the familial courtesy of letting him know about Cassie.

Anyway, he was reasonably confident that Cassie had left Galveston almost immediately.

Dear Cousin Michael:

I hope all are well on Moraghan. I have some news to pass on to you that you may find of some interest.

First, I am now employed on Uncle Kevin's fruit ranch. I became weary of the sea, and wish to stay on solid ground for a while. You may tell Aunt Kate that everything is fine here. The man she left in charge, Juan Mendoza, is doing an excellent job. Also, tell her that I am not here to interfere with him in any way, or to try to ramrod it over him. I'm just a hired hand, like the other men here, and I aim to keep it that way.

The other bit of news, Michael, concerns Cassie Danker. A month ago I was in Galveston, and came across her. She was working as a waitress in a waterfront café called Big Red's Eatery. I have not written you sooner because she made me promise that I would not reveal her whereabouts to anybody. I am now breaking that promise because you are family, and deserve to know, and because I know you do not intend her any harm.

I have no way of knowing whether or not she is still working there. If she is not, I reckon you will be upset with me for not writing you sooner. I just could not make up my mind until now. I suppose it has something to do with my now living on Uncle Kevin's place. I feel closer family ties than I have in a while.

Tell Debra Lee and hers that I asked about them. Also . . .

Here he hesitated for a moment, pen poised over the paper. But if he didn't mention Lena, Michael would think it strange.

Also, give my best regards to Lena if you see her any time soon.

My best to everybody, and I will write again soon.
                                        Your cousin, Mark

*   *   *

Michael left for Galveston early the morning after Mark's letter arrived. He would have left immediately, but the stage heading south didn't depart until the following morning, and a stage would be faster than a horse, since it went straight through, changing teams en route. With a horse he would have had to rest the animal or risk killing it.

The only one he told about the purpose of the trip was his mother. He showed her Mark's letter, and then said, "I'm going after Cassie in the morning, Mother, if she's still there. I'm going to ask her to marry me and bring her back here, if she'll come."

Kate smiled softly. "All right, son."

"You won't mind, my marrying a Danker? You won't mind living in the same house with her?"

"We've discussed all that, Michael. I bear no animosity toward the girl, just because she's Bud's sister. If this is what it takes to make you happy, God bless you. And if anyone should be upset about the two of us living here, together, it should be her. No young woman likes her mother-in-law living in the same house with her, especially not right after getting married."

"No, Mother, you'll live here," he said firmly. "Moraghan is more yours than mine. If Cassie objects, and I'm sure she won't, knowing her as I do, we'll just live somewhere else."

"If that happens, how about all your horses, son? You love this girl enough to give them up?"

He burst into laughter. "That's two different things, and I can always find a place for them." Abruptly he was plunged into gloom. "She probably won't have me, anyway."

Kate reached out to touch his face. "Any woman would consider herself fortunate indeed to have you for a husband, son."

Michael reached Galveston in the early afternoon, and went at once in search of Big Red's Eatery. He found it without difficulty. Since it was the middle of the afternoon, the restaurant was far from crowded. Michael felt a pull of dismay when he saw the only waitress in the place—blowsy, bright red hair, in her forties.

He took a seat at the counter and ordered a cup of coffee. When it was served, he asked, "Is Big Red here?"

"Sure, sugar. Big Red's always here. He does the cooking." She bellowed, "Red! Front and center!"

A big man, with weathered features and hair almost as red as that of the waitress, came from the rear, wiping his hands on his apron. "Yeah, what is it, Gladys?"

"Gent here wants to see you." The waitress jerked a thumb at Michael, and went around the counter to answer a hail from one of the tables.

Red squinted at Michael suspiciously. "What is it you want, stranger?"

"I'm looking for Cassie Danker. Is she still working for you?"

The big man's face tightened, his lips thinning.

Michael said hastily, "I don't mean Cassie any harm. I'm Michael Moraghan, from her hometown."

Red began to smile. "Yeah, I've heard the name! Cassie told me about you. As for an answer to your question...naw, she no longer works here." He motioned with his head, without lowering his voice. "Do you think she'd be working here if Cassie was still around?"

Michael sighed despondently. "I was afraid she'd be gone by the time I got here. Where did she go, can you tell me that?"

"I haven't the slightest, young fellow. She left no forwarding address. She did say that she thought you might come looking. She told me that if you did, to please pass on this word: Don't try to find her, it won't do you a damned bit of good, the cuss word mine, of course. And I know Cassie well enough to know that she means it, Mr. Moraghan."

# 15

Hell's Half Acre.

Cassie, walking down Main Street, carrying her meager

possessions in a straw suitcase, was intimidated by what she saw.

Drunken men and painted women strolled the street. The women openly flaunted their profession. Saloons lined the street: Waco Tap, The Occidental, Friends, The Red Light, Our Comrades, The Cattle Exchange. She had never seen so many saloons in one place in her life. Although it was only a little past noon, the saloons were all doing a roaring business. The batwing doors were in constant motion.

Then she came to a full stop: The White Elephant. That was the one Bud had written her about. If she ever came to Fort Worth in search of him, she was to leave a message here.

She hesitated for a little, summoning up enough courage to go inside. Finally, clutching the suitcase in both hands, she ventured into the dim interior. It stank of beer and stale whiskey. She paused just inside, stepping out of the doorway, uncertain about how to proceed. A man in the rear toiled at a piano, sending waves of tinny music across the room.

Scantily clad women danced with men on a cleared space near the piano. At tables scattered throughout the room men played cards and drank. At a bar that ran along one wall of the room other men leaned on their elbows, drinks in their hands, while two sweating bartenders labored busily.

Cassie took two hesitant steps toward the bar, and then a man had her by the arm. "How about a little dance, girlie?"

She turned in fright to find herself staring into the red face of a cowboy, his breath strong with liquor. She tried to jerk her arm out of his grip. "I'm not here to dance!"

He leered. "Then what are you doing here? Want to go out to one of the cribs in back? How much, girlie?"

"No, no!"

She pulled her arm free, and lost her balance, stumbling back against the bar. The drunken man lurched toward her, and was intercepted by a short, immaculate individual in black. "All right, cowpoke," he said in a soft voice. "You heard the lady say no. Now back off." He jabbed the man in the chest with a forefinger, and Cassie saw the cowboy literally cringe in terror, and then bolt away.

The small, dapper man turned toward Cassie. His eyes were an icy blue, his face clean-shaven. He was so small he couldn't weigh much more than a hundred and thirty-five pounds. In that same soft voice he said, "What *are* you doing in here, miss? You strike me as if you just came in from somewhere out in the sticks."

"I'm looking for Bud Danker. He told me to leave word here at the White Elephant Saloon, if I ever wanted to get in touch with him."

The little man shook his head. "I know of no Bud Danker. Now, you'd better get out of here before you get hurt. This is no place for a lady"—his mouth curled in a sardonic smile—"as the saying goes."

Cassie nodded mutely.

He returned her nod, stiffly, and turned away.

As Cassie stood gathering up courage to make a dash for the batwings, a voice said softly behind her, "I know old Bud."

She turned quickly to see one of the bartenders leaning over the bar toward her. "You do? Then why didn't that man . . . ?"

The man's glance scuttled back and forth around the room. He beckoned her closer, said in a voice little more than a whisper, "For reasons of his own, Bud is using another name right now. But I'm in touch with him from time to time. I'll pass the word on to him."

"I'm his sister Cassie. He wrote me to leave word in this saloon if I ever wanted to find him."

The bartender nodded. "I'll tell him as soon as I see him. Where'll you be?"

Cassie said uncertainly, "I don't know. I just got in to town. Can you recommend a place?"

He looked her up and down. "Well, you don't want one of the hotels. They don't take single women, anyways, most of them. There's a boarding house, with decent prices, good food and clean linens. Martha Bennett's. Outside, you turn right, go two blocks, turn right again, and it's three more blocks down. You can't miss it. I'll tell old Bud you'll be staying there.''

"I'm right grateful to you, sir." She started to turn away, then paused, turning back. "Who was that man who came to my aid?"

The bartender bared yellowed teeth in a grin. "That's Luke Short, young lady, probably one of the best gunfighters in the whole state of Texas. He owns this here place. He's a hard man, but fair, and he doesn't approve of nice ladies in his saloon. I'd advise you not to come in here again. I'll get in touch with Bud, never fear."

Cassie was troubled as she left the saloon. Why was Bud using another name? Of course, it could be because he was wanted for killing Kevin Moraghan.

Sadness swept over her, as it always did when she thought of that. In one way she was reluctant to see Bud, because he *had* killed Michael's father, and she certainly would let him know of her displeasure. Yet he was her brother, and she well knew how obsessed he was with the Moraghans, how caught up in that old feud he was. Maybe it was all out of his system now, she certainly hoped so.

When she had fled Galveston, this was the only place Cassie could think of to come. Fortunately she had saved up enough money so that she wouldn't have to look for a job until she was good and ready.

Following the bartender's directions, she trudged down the street, carrying the suitcase in both hands.

Bud Danker was riding high these days. He was making good money, and he was working for Jim Courtwright, a dream come true, something that he would never have thought would happen a year ago. But best of all, he was a big man in Fort Worth—many people feared him.

His only regret was that he was known around town under an assumed name. Courtwright had insisted on that, so now Bud Danker was known to most people as Brad Dalton.

After a bloody gun battle at Buttermilk Junction in which Jim Courtwright had participated, and where several railroad strikers had been killed, four Texas Ranger companies had been sent in, and the strike had finally come to an end. Jim Courtwright had returned to Fort Worth, rented an office near the old courthouse, and opened the T. I. C. Commercial Detective Agency. Actually, what Courtwright was selling was protection, not detection. A recent reform movement had become very active, and Fort Worth had enacted a stiff ordinance against gambling. Professional gamblers were being hauled into court, paying heavy fines. Courtwright offered protection against such harassment for a high weekly fee. He hired a couple of professional thugs to assist him. If a saloonkeeper didn't enroll in Courtwright's protection plan, his "assistants" would harass their establishments with more drastic tactics than mere court fines.

Soon after Courtwright's operation began, Bud, who had been over in New Mexico again, returned to Fort Worth. Learning of Courtwright's operation, Bud went to see him.

It was the first time Bud had seen Courtwright since the night he had saved the man's life, and he was uncertain as to how he would be greeted. He found Courtwright alone. "Mr. Courtwright, I don't know if you remember me."

"Of course I remember you, Mr. Danker. I never forget a man who saves my life." He stood up to shake Bud's hand and gestured him to a chair. "What can I do for you, sir?"

"Well, you told me that if you could ever do me a favor," Bud said hesitantly, "I should come to you."

"I meant it then and I mean it now. I never forget a promise. What favor are you asking of me?"

"I heard about your detective agency. I'd like a job with you. I'd like nothing better than to work for Jim Courtwright."

"Well, now, I'm downright flattered, Mr. Danker." Courtwright resumed his seat and stared at Bud keenly. "You say you've heard about my agency. Just exactly what *have* you heard?"

"Well, I . . ." Bud cleared his throat, flustered.

Courtwright waved a hand, smiling slightly. "You've

heard that I'm running a protection game, instead of strictly a detective agency, am I right?"

"Well, yes."

Courtwright nodded. "I don't deny it, not to my friends. I tried the side of law and order for a long time, and I've soured on it." His voice turned bitter. "You know, when I was marshal of Fort Worth, I wasn't allowed to do my job properly. I got conflicting orders from almost everybody over me. They wanted me to stop the flow of blood but not the liquor. I was told not to arrest drunks until they'd spent all their money. I was often sent out of town on some wild-goose chase, just to get me out of everybody's hair for a few days.

"I wasn't hired to enforce the law as such, I was hired to see that everything ran smoothly for the crooked gamblers and those of that ilk that fleeced the cowboys in town on a spree. And for that I was paid a pittance. Even when I worked as a constable during the railroad strike, I got the wrong end of the stick. Many people blamed me for the Buttermilk Junction massacre, never taking into consideration that the strikers fired on us first. They had Winchesters and we were armed only with pistols. Well, I've decided to turn the tables on them. From now on I'm getting *paid* for what I do."

Courtwright grinned wolfishly. "And I am providing a service. The only trouble is, some of the saloonkeepers refuse to believe they need my protection. For that reason I do need another man, one who has some power of persuasion. The two I have now are fine for what they do, but I need a man who is slick about what he does."

Bud was thrilled to the core. He was going to work for Jim Courtwright! "In making them see the light, how far can I go?"

"Well . . ." Courtwright leaned back, making a steeple of his hands, peering over them at Bud. "I'll leave that pretty much up to you. A little harassment might cause them to think they do need my protection. But I want nobody killed, understand?" He leaned forward, leveling a finger at Bud like a pistol. "A little roughing up, maybe, even a little destruction of property, but nobody killed."

Bud felt a pulse of disappointment, but he nodded. "I understand, Mr. Courtwright."

Courtwright nodded in satisfaction. "Good! We understand each other, I think. You're on my payroll starting today."

"I want to thank you, Mr. Courtwright." He had been hoping the man would tell him to call him by his first name, but he didn't dare do so without permission.

He stood up, as did Courtwright, who leaned across his desk, extending his hand. They shook, and Bud started out.

Before he could reach the door, Courtwright said, "One more thing, Mr. Danker. I have learned something about you since we met. You're wanted by the law, I believe, for killing one Kevin Moraghan down near Brownsville. Is that correct?"

Bud tightened up. "Yeah, but that was because—"

Courtwright batted a hand at him. "I don't wish to hear about it. I have killed men myself." His smile was cold. "But there are no warrants current on me. What I had in mind is, I think it would be a mistake for you to do a job for me under your own name. It would be better for both of us if you assume another name. Soon, you will become well-known around Fort Worth. If anyone you were pressuring to sign up with my agency learned you were wanted, a word to the right people and you'd rot in jail. Or even be hung. Now, I'm sure you wouldn't want that, Mr. Danker."

So now, to all but a few, he was Brad Dalton. Bud wasn't happy about it, but he had sense enough to recognize the wisdom of Courtwright's suggestion.

Through various tactics—intimidation; the hiring of thugs to stage a fight in a particular saloon, resulting in expensive damage; veiled threats of even worse to come—Bud brought several recalcitrant saloon owners under Courtwright's protection. The one man in Fort Worth who so far had refused to go along was Luke Short. Bud had confronted Short in the White Elephant once, and had been thrown out for his trouble, and Short had promised to gun him down if he came around again. Short had a reputation as a deadly gunfighter, some even said he was faster than Jim Courtwright, and he was absolutely fearless. Bud had to admit, to himself, that he was afraid of Short, yet he kept mulling over ways to bring the man into line. So far, he had failed to devise a scheme that would not place him in personal danger.

However, he wasn't giving up. He had an ace in the hole, he knew one of the bartenders at the White Elephant, Dick Raymond. He slipped Raymond a few dollars now and again to keep him posted on Short, with the additional promise of a substantial reward if he, Raymond, was instrumental in getting Short to come into the Courtwright fold.

Bud also had a few ideas of his own. If they could sell protection to the saloon owners, why not include other businesses in Fort Worth? The shop owners should be much easier to persuade than saloonkeepers.

But when he had broached the idea to Courtwright, the man was against it. "No, Mr. Danker. It doesn't pay to get too greedy. Greed has been the downfall of many men. Besides, I am more comfortable with saloonkeepers and gamblers, having been a gambler at times myself. The saloonkeepers can't afford to have too much light shone on their activities, since many of the things they do to make a dollar go against the grain of the so-called upright citizens. If we put pressure on legitimate businessmen, they might persuade the city authorities to stop my operation. As it is, I'm left pretty much alone."

For the first time Bud lost some of his respect for Jim Courtwright. In his opinion, the man was either getting too old and settled in his ways, or his ambitions were too small. So Bud had set himself to finding ways and means of selling protection to the other businessmen on his own. And he had no intention of sharing his profits with Courtwright. Why should he, since he would be doing it all on his own? He had no fears of the businessmen running to the authorities. They were all frightened little men, scared of their own shadows. He would put the fear of God into them, and they would fold before him like willow branches in a high wind.

He strolled along Main Street, smoking a cigar, a habit he'd recently acquired. Now that he was affluent he dressed better—black frock coat, with a ruffled silk shirt, a flowing cravat, a white Stetson, and hand-tooled boots. The only item on him that was old was his daddy's Colt, holstered on his hip. It had served him well, and he was confident that it would continue to do so. He was superstitious about that old Colt and would never part with it.

He was headed for the White Elephant, not to go inside but to wait for Dick Raymond to come out. Raymond's shift was about up.

Bud leaned against a storefront several doors up from the White Elephant, smoking, watching the doors of the saloon. Shortly Raymond emerged. He looked both ways along the street. Bud stood away from the wall, with a wave of his hand. Raymond saw him and came hurrying up, smiling.

Bud said, "You look like the cat that just ate a big, fat bird."

"I have news for you, Bud." Raymond rubbed his hands together.

"News?" Bud perked up. Maybe Short had done something today that he could get a handle on. "What is it?"

"A girl came into the place today looking for you."

"A girl?" Bud frowned, puzzled. "Looking for *me*?"

"Yep. She said . . ." Raymond lowered his voice, looking around. "She claimed to be your sister."

"Cassie? Here?" Bud said in astonishment.

"That's her. I don't see much family resemblance." Raymond grinned. "She's a pretty girl, your sister."

"Where did she go?"

"I gave her the name of a boarding house, Martha Bennett's. You know the place." Raymond shrugged. "Whether she went there or not, I don't know. She came in about three hours back, so she's had time to get settled, if she's there."

"Thanks, Dick," Bud said exuberantly. "Cassie finally here! I can't believe it!" He started to stride away, then paused to ask, "Anything to tell me about Luke Short?"

Raymond shook his head. "Nope, today was no different from any other. If I was you, Bud, I'd give up on Short. You mess around with him and he'll have your liver for breakfast.''

Bud gave a curt nod and hurried off. It was just short of suppertime when he bounded up the steps to the boarding house. He could smell the good odors of food cooking as he knocked on the door. It was opened a few moments later by a plump, harried-looking woman, her face rosy from the heat of the cookstove. She frowned at him. ''I don't take in men boarders, mister.'' She started to slam the door in his face.

Bud said quickly, ''Wait! I'm not looking for lodgings. There's somebody here I want to see. Cassie Danker. I'm . . . uh, related to her. Is she staying here?''

''She just moved in. I'll tell her you're here. But you wait out here, on the swing over there, if you want.'' She motioned to a porch swing. ''No men callers allowed inside the house.''

''That's fine, I'll wait.''

Bud moved over to the porch swing, but didn't sit down. He was too anxious. He fired a cigar and waited. It was only a few minutes before the door opened again. He took two quick steps toward it. ''Cassie?''

It was Cassie, right enough. She peered at him uncertainly, her gaze searching his face. In the two years since he'd seen her, Cassie had matured. She was a grown woman now, and a beauty, far prettier than any of her sisters had been.

''Hello, Bud,'' she said quietly.

He took both her hands in his. ''Little Cassie,'' he said wonderingly. ''You've changed quite a bit, I must say.''

''So have you.'' She disengaged her hands from his grip and stepped back. ''You're looking mighty prosperous, for one thing.''

''I'm doing fine, sis,'' he said expansively. ''I'm working for a big man here in town, Jim Courtwright. Maybe you've heard of him?'' At her negative head shake he went on, ''Well, he's a mighty important man in Fort Worth. He operates a detective agency, and I'm doing important work for him.''

"Bud"—she broke into his feverish chatter—"why did you kill Kevin Moraghan?"

"You know why, Cassie!" He made a violent gesture. "Because he was a Moraghan!"

"He'd never done you any harm."

"Kevin Moraghan killed our daddy, how many times have I told you that!"

"You tried to kill Michael, too. He's never done anything to you."

"He's a Moraghan, ain't he? Any time I get a chance to kill a Moraghan, I will. Just like I'd step on a centipede."

Cassie's eyes filled with tears. "I'm so sick of all the killing. I'm the sister of a killer. How do you think that makes me feel? I'm ashamed."

Into Bud's mind swam the images of all the others he'd killed since Kevin Moraghan. How would she feel if he told her about them? He longed to tell her, to gloat, but he sensed that if he did, he would alienate her forever, and she was the only blood left to him, certainly the only one he cared spit for.

"I reckon I can't expect you to understand, Cassie, you're a woman. But a man, if he is a man, has to avenge any killing of his own blood. I couldn't rest easy with myself if I didn't."

"That's sick, Bud! You're sick in the mind!"

"Now, that's going too far, Cassie!" He caught her arm in an iron grip. "How about Sean Moraghan killing Daddy's two brothers? How about Kevin Moraghan killing Daddy? Does that make them sick, too?"

She choked out, "I don't know! I just know that it's ruined my life!"

"Aw, come on, sis! Your life ain't ruined. You're a pretty girl, a real beauty. Someday you'll find some old boy you like, you'll get married, and bear me some nieces and nephews." He squinted at her. "If you're still sore about me beating on you the last night I saw you, I'm right sorry about that. I was mad at the world that night, and didn't realize what I was doing."

She gestured wearily. "I'm not still mad about that, I've practically forgotten it."

"Anyway, I'm glad you're here in Fort Worth, little sister." He became expansive. "Things ain't like they were in Nacogdoches, I've got money now. You *do* intend to stick around?"

"I suppose, I have nowhere else to go," she said drearily. "I reckon I can find a job waiting tables. That's what I was doing down in Galveston."

He grunted. "In Galveston? You mean you had left Nacogdoches? How about Momma?"

"I had to put her in a sanatarium. She got real bad after you left, Bud."

He shrugged. "It's for the best, she had turned loony long since. But about you getting a job, that ain't necessary. I can take care of you now. You can live in a good place, eat the best food, wear the best of clothes." He threw his arms wide. "You don't have to live in a place like this."

In throwing his arms out, his coat had fallen open, revealing the gun on his hip.

Cassie stared at it. "Why are you wearing a gun, Bud?"

"That? That's Daddy's old Colt." He caressed the handle of the gun. "Everybody wears a gun, sis. I'd feel naked without it."

She said caustically, "Is that part of your job, wearing a gun to work for this big man you told me about?"

"Now, don't you worry your pretty little head about such matters, Cassie. You don't need to know nothing about my job."

"Don't talk to me like a child, Bud! I'm grown up, in case you hadn't noticed."

"Oh, I noticed," he said. "But you're still a woman, and women don't inquire into a man's business."

The door opened and the landlady poked her head out. "Supper's on the table, Miss Danker."

"I'll be right there, Mrs. Bennett. We'll talk more another time, Bud."

She started past him and he seized her arm, then said in an injured voice, "But I thought we'd go to some fancy place for supper, Cassie. We haven't seen each other for a long spell. Don't go away on me now."

"Another time, Bud." She jerked her arm out of his grasp. "I've had a long day and I'm tired."

She went on into the house, leaving Bud staring after her in frustration. His anger boiled up. To hell with her, then, if that was the way she wanted it! He gave his gunbelt a hitch and strode down off the porch.

When the Holliday Traveling Players arrived in Nacogdoches for the second year in a row, it was a festive occasion for the Moraghans. Kate and Michael came in to town to spend the week at the Liebermans', with the intention of seeing every night's performance.

There weren't any spare days this trip. The show arrived late on a Sunday and began to set up, so they could be ready to open on Monday.

It had been a good year for Lena and Doc, in many ways. The show had made a tidy profit, enough to repay all the money Doc owed Lucy, and enough to keep them in comfort during the winter months in New Orleans. And they had played to packed tents in every town this season so far. Their fame had spread, and their performances were eagerly awaited.

Since that rather startling scene on the river when Doc had discovered Lena in Mark's arms, their relationship had improved markedly. Lena knew that she would never feel for Doc the overwhelming passion she felt for Mark, but she was content enough. Doc's lovemaking was no longer tentative, and he was quite robust in bed for a man his age. More so than most, she suspected. One thing did bother her a little, something she would not have thought a year ago—she wished Doc wasn't sterile, so she could have a child by him. She knew now that it was possible for a woman in her profession to have children, and never miss a performance. After all, they were only on the road from the first of May until some time in October.

As the office wagon entered the outskirts of Nacogdoches, Lena was looking forward to seeing her family. She and Doc had spent two weeks at Christmas on Moraghan, but that had been all the time she could spare. She had devoted most of the winter to rewriting and polishing the old plays,

and had written two new ones. Lena knew now that she
was doubly blessed—she had a felicity for writing as well
as for acting.

Michael was waiting on the road in to town, astride his
horse. The office wagon, as always, was in the lead.
Michael's face bloomed in a broad smile and he kneed his
horse alongside the wagon seat as Doc pulled the mules to
a halt.

"Hello, sis!" He doffed his hat, nodded to Doc. "And
Doc. How are you all?"

"Michael, I'm delighted to see you!" Lena said. "And
I'm fine, everything is fine."

"Good season so far, if nothing happens to upset the
apple cart," Doc said. Then he smiled broadly. "In fact,
it's been a helluva year. How are you, Michael?"

He leaned out with his hand extended, and Michael took
it.

Lena looked at Doc fondly. He had changed to the point
where he was hard put nowadays to find something to
grouse about. She linked her arm in his. "Things have
been going so well that even old gloom and doom here can
find little to complain about."

"Glad to hear it," Michael said. "Look, Mother came
in to town with me. We're both spending the week with
Stony and Debra Lee. We don't intend to miss a single
show. Mother's waiting at the house. Why don't you ride
back with me, Lena?" His glance went to Doc. "If you
can spare her, brother-in-law?"

"Sure thing. You go on, honey," Doc urged. "We'll
manage to limp along without you."

Lena acquiesced with an eager nod. Michael maneuvered
his horse into position, wrapped a strong arm around her
waist, boosted her across, and she settled down behind
him on the horse, her arms around him.

Michael said, "We'll be expecting you for supper, Doc.
Around seven, all right?"

"I'll be there." Doc waved, flicked the reins, and
started the office wagon in motion.

Michael kept his horse at a sedate walk all the way to
the house. "Is everything truly all right, sis?"

"Truly, Michael, it really is. We are so well-known now that most performances are sold out well in advance. How is everything on Moraghan?"

"Fine and dandy. Your show may be becoming known, but so are the Moraghan horses," he said with pride. "I'm still winning more than my share of races, and I can sell any foals I breed, at good prices."

"I'm happy for you, brother." Lena gave him an affectionate squeeze. "Have you heard anything more about Cassie?" While at Moraghan for Christmas, Michael had told her about his quick trip to Galveston only to find Cassie gone.

"Not a word," he said glumly. "I've just about given up hope."

She said casually, "How about Mark? Is he still on our old place down in the Valley?"

"Still there. I would never have believed that Mark would stay in one place that long. Maybe our cousin has finally settled down."

"I wouldn't bet on it," she said tartly. She added quickly, "How is the romance between Mother and Bandy?"

"Not much further along than it was, I'm afraid." Michael laughed. "In their case, the course of true love doesn't run smooth. Mother wants Bandy to give up chewing tobacco. A filthy habit, she says. That was about a month ago. Bandy stormed away in a huff, and they don't speak to each other nowadays except when absolutely necessary."

"Then he won't be in to see the show?" she said in disappointment.

"Oh, he'll be there, but on the sly, he told me. He'll come in to see a couple of shows, but sit off by himself."

Lena laughed softly. "It's a little weird, thinking of Mother and Bandy. Oh, I do hope she gets married again. And I like Bandy, but you must admit they're exact opposites."

"I know. Bandy talked to me about that once. He's never been married, he's knocked about from pillar to post all his life, and he's never amounted to a whistle in the wind. His words, not mine. But I'm not about to say a word to Mother. She was nice enough to accept Cassie into the family, if that ever happens, so she can marry whomever she damned well pleases.''

"I agree, Michael. She accepted Doc readily enough,'' Lena said slowly. But I wonder how she'd take to Mark as a husband, she thought wryly. Now why did I think of that? That's never going to happen!

They were in front of the house now. Michael slid down and helped Lena off the horse. By that time the front door was open. The children came running toward them, with Debra and Kate remaining on the porch. Lena squatted down to give each of the children a quick hug. Then she took one by each hand and went up onto the porch, while Michael led his horse around to the barn in back.

"Hello, Mother, Debra Lee.''

She and Kate embraced, and then Lena skidded a kiss off Debra's cheek.

Kate said, "Where's your man, Lena?''

"He's getting the tent set up, everything ready for tomorrow. He'll be here in time for supper.''

"Good! That'll give us a chance to talk, catch up on what's been happening." Kate laughed. "To you, I mean. Not very much ever happens around here.''

Debra said, "Mother, you and Lena sit out here on the porch where there's a breeze, and I'll bring you something cool to drink.''

Kate said, "Sure I can't help you in the kitchen, Debra Lee?''

"No, everything's cooking. It mostly needs just watching over.''

Kate and Lena took the two rockers side by side on the porch. With a straight face Lena said, "You say nothing's been happening to you, Mother, but that's not the way I hear it.''

"What do you mean?''

"How about Bandy? Aren't you two sweet on one another?''

"That Michael! He's been talking too much again.''

"Mother, I can't see anything wrong with you finding a

man." Lena patted her mother's arm. "Daddy's been dead a while, and you're far from an old woman."

"Sometimes I feel like an old woman," Kate said with a sigh. "As for Bandy, I just don't know. I like the bowlegged rooster well enough, I reckon, but I sometimes believe he thinks more of horses than he does of women. And he has a few nasty habits he has to give up first, such as chewing tobacco, and drinking too much. Besides, why hasn't a man his age ever been married? There has to be some reason."

"Maybe he just never found the right woman."

"And I'm the right woman? Pshaw, Lena! That I find a little hard to swallow."

"Maybe he's at the age where he realizes he'll end up a lonely old man if he doesn't find somebody." The thought of Mark popped into Lena's mind, as it often did when her thoughts turned to marriage and men. Would there ever be a time when Mark didn't enter her thoughts at unexpected moments?

Kate was saying, "Well, we'll see how it goes. It's no earth-shaking problem, in any case . . ."

Michael came around the side of the house, just as Debra came out with cold drinks, and nothing further was said about Bandy.

Lena said, "Where's Stony, Debra Lee?"

"He had an important meeting this afternoon. We didn't know what time you would arrive. He'll be back in time for supper."

Michael sat down, leaning back against a porch post, and the conversation became general, with Debra popping in and out of the house to check on supper cooking. Lena was caught up in what news there was around Nacogdoches.

The only news of any import came from Debra. "There is some movement afoot to run Stony for the state legislature, Lena. That's what the meeting is about this afternoon."

Lena arched an eyebrow. "And what does Stony think?"

Debra shrugged. "He is some interested, and naturally flattered, but if he was elected, it would mean that we would either have to move to Austin bag and baggage, or he would have to be away from home when the legislature sits. He's not too crazy about that.''

"And how do you feel, Debra Lee?"

"Well . . ." Debra's eyes brightened. "It would be a feather in his cap, certainly. Stony's been a judge for quite a while, and even he agrees that it's a dead end. He's getting a little tired of it. So, if he gives up his judgeship, he will either have to run for some other office, or return to private law practice."

Lena said, "It would be nice, one of the family in the state legislature."

"It could even lead to the governor's chair," Michael said. "It's happened before."

Debra snorted softly. "Now, Michael! You know what Stony would say to that? A Jew, the governor of Texas?"

An uncomfortable silence fell, which Debra broke with another snort. "You see? Godalmighty, just mention it and everybody gets as embarrassed as if a cow chip, fresh and steaming, had been served up on a platter for supper."

"Debra Lee!" Kate said in a shocked voice. "There's no call to be common, for heaven's sake!"

"Hah!" Debra flounced into the house.

"You know, she's right. Until it's mentioned," Lena said thoughtfully, "I never think of Stony as a Jew."

Another silence fell. Then Kate said briskly, "Lena, you haven't said very much about yourself and the show."

"I'm fine, Mother, and the show's doing great, far better than we ever hoped for to start off with. People are looking forward to our arrival everywhere we go."

Michael said, "I noticed on the side of the wagon that you're no longer billed as Lena Moraghan, but as Lena Holliday."

"That was my idea. Doc wanted it left like it was, but I told him that I was proud to be his wife, and I wanted people to know it. Besides"—she made a face—"tent-show people are considered sinful enough. If I didn't use my married name, people might think we weren't married, but living together in sin."

"I hate to believe that people are nasty-minded enough to think that," Kate said.

"Then you don't know people, Mother. Besides, show people are in a different class. Doc once said that we live in glass houses and that's pretty much true. By the way, I've written two new plays that I want you all to be sure and see while we're here, one especially." Her smile was a touch wry. "It's scheduled for the last night, so I can be out of town before you decide to lynch me."

"Why is that, sis?" Michael asked. "What's it about, the play? Tell us!"

"No, you'll know soon enough." She broke off as she saw a horse coming along the street. "There's Doc."

"Just in time," Debra said, as she came out onto the porch. "Stony's about due too."

Lena said, "Before I forget it, we're going to play a week in Fort Worth, late in October, after our regular season is over. We don't usually play in towns as large as Fort Worth, but we've become so well-known that the mayor sent Doc a letter asking if we would appear there for a week at the end of the season. The thing is, it isn't all that far. Why don't you all plan on coming to Fort Worth for that week?"

# 16

Bud Danker had ten shopkeepers along Main Street paying him protection before Courtwright called him on it. He had four café owners, three Chinese laundries, two bootmakers, and a clothing store on his string, and he was rolling in money, living high on the hog, sweeping in more money than he had ever earned in his life. And all the shopkeepers were terrified of him—or so he thought.

There was one burr under his saddle—he couldn't convince Cassie to accept money from him, and stop working. She had gotten a job waiting tables at one of the restaurants paying protection to him. With his turn of mind Bud could not see the irony in this.

It really scalded his ass that she refused to stop working or accept a single penny from him. The stupid, ungrateful girl! She did condescend to have supper with him at his hotel once a week, and that was because, Cassie said, "You're my brother, and I have to respect that, even if I don't respect what you're doing. You should be ashamed of yourself, Bud Danker, making poor Theodore pay you money for nothing, when he sometimes hardly makes enough to pay his rent."

He smirked. "But he's protected, ain't he? Nobody has bothered him since he started paying me protection."

"But nobody had bothered him before either."

How could a man argue against such stupid female reasoning? Well, to hell with it! If she wanted nothing from him, she'd get nothing!

Then somebody snitched to Courtwright. He summoned Bud into his office one crisp, mid-October day. Frowning slightly, he looked at Bud levelly. "Mr. Danker, I have received some disquieting news about you."

Bud felt a tug of alarm. "What is it, sir? Something I've done?"

Courtwright didn't answer directly. He made a steeple of his fingers, leaning on his desk on his elbows. "I have been happy with your work. You have brought most of the saloonkeepers into line, except for Luke Short—"

Bud broke in. "He's a tough nut to crack, Mr. Courtwright. But I'm working on it, and I'll bring him into line soon, if that's what's bothering you."

Courtwright made a dismissive gesture. "No, that's not it. I know how difficult that little bastard can be. I'll probably have to settle his hash myself, sooner or later. No, what I'm unhappy about goes back to a talk we had some time ago. You wanted to sell protection to the merchants along Main, and I said no. Now I've learned that you have ignored my orders and branched out on your own. Is this true?"

"Who told you? One of those damned slanty-eyed laundrymen?"

"That, Mr. Danker, is not the question I asked." Courtwright slapped the desk with a sound like a pistol shot. "Is it true?"

Bud muttered sullenly, "Yes, sir, but I look upon it as a sort of sideline. I figured you just didn't want to get involved directly."

"You work for me, Mr. Danker. Anything you do is in my name and involves me."

Bud improvised a lie. "Sir, I didn't use your name." He could only hope that whoever had informed on him had not said otherwise.

"It doesn't matter whether my name came into it, everybody in Hell's Half Acre knows you work for me. Tell me." He leaned forward. "Don't you consider yourself well paid, Mr. Danker?"

"Oh, yes, sir," Bud said with a sickly smile. "But a few extra dollars never hurt anyone."

Courtwright was shaking his head. "What did I tell you once? Greed destroys people. Be content with what you have, so long as you are making out all right."

"That's easy enough for you to say," Bud said, surprised at his own daring. "I've been dirt poor all my life, until recently, scratching for a dollar, like a chicken in the front yard of the poorhouse."

"It's true that I've never really been poor, and I can understand your thinking." Courtwright steepled his hands again, staring at Bud thoughtfully. "And for that reason I'm not firing you, that plus the fact that you've done a good job for me. I've always been too softhearted for my own good," he said piously. "I'll take another chance on you, in exchange for your word." He rapped the desk with his knuckles. "You will stop all this side business at once, and you'll not do anything I don't tell you to do from this day forward. Is that quite clear, Mr. Danker?"

Weak with relief at the reprieve, Bud bobbed his head. "Clear, Mr. Courtwright."

"Your word, sir?"

"My word on it."

"Good, Mr. Danker. But if you break your word, I'll

run you out of Fort Worth, and see that your name is shit
not only in Fort Worth but in all the state of Texas!''

Bud escaped the office grateful for the second chance.
He well knew that he was making more money than he
possibly could anywhere else—he did not have the reputation to command big money as a hired gunfighter. But he
also left the office with rancor against Jim Courtwright
growing in him.

How did it hurt Courtwright if he, Bud, had a little
sideline going for him? Courtwright was living soft and
easy, hardly having to lift a finger nowadays, on the money
Bud brought in. All the risk was Bud's, and if anybody's
ass got burned, it would be his, not Courtwright's. Bud
had seen the man playing cards in various saloons— never
Luke Short's, of course—and he probably lost more money in an afternoon's poker game than Bud's weekly salary
came to. Also, Courtwright was something of a womanizer—
there was even a rumor that the bad blood between
Courtwright and Luke Short came about because Courtwright
had romanced Short's wife on the sly.

Puffing on a stogie, boot heels making an angry tattoo
on the wooden sidewalk, Bud strode along without too
much attention as to where he was going, until his anger
began to subside.

Finally he paused, getting his bearings. He had walked
quite a distance from Courtwright's office. He noticed a
man tacking a poster to an empty store front across the street.
As the man finished, Bud strolled over to study the poster.
He still couldn't write, but he had learned to read well
enough to decipher what was on the poster: "Coming to
Fort Worth, for one week, Oct. 20–26: The Holliday
Traveling Players . . .''

There were more words on the poster, along with
pictures of two of the players, but Bud's attention wandered
as an idea sprouted in his mind. Although he had never
seen a Toby show, nor did he have much interest in seeing
this one, he had heard a bit about the Holliday show. It had
a reputation in Texas, and word was that tickets were hard
to come by when it showed in a particular town. It almost
always played to a full tent.

What could be more vulnerable than a tent show? The threat of fire alone should scare the living daylight out of them, and even the threat of several rowdies disrupting a performance should spook them. They would be a prime target for protection insurance. And what was best of all, they were here one week and gone the next, so they would never go crying to Jim Courtwright, or anyone else. If the show owner had any sense, he would be happy to pay and get the hell out of town in one piece.

Bud drew on his cigar, grinning unpleasantly.

It didn't matter whether or not he got much money—it would be a way to thumb his nose at Courtwright. Even if Courtwright learned of it, it wouldn't matter, not really. Bud knew now that his days with Courtwright were numbered. He had learned well under the man's tutelage. Why not pick another town away from Fort Worth—San Antonio, Austin, maybe even out of the state—and start his own protection agency? He would be top dog, and the money would line his own pockets, not Courtwright's.

Excited by the idea, he strode on, his thoughts racing.

Bud was wrong in his guess as to who had gone to Courtwright. It hadn't been one of the Chinamen, or any of the merchants—it had been his own sister. Cassie was furious when she learned that Theodore Laker, her new boss, was paying protection to Bud. She liked Theodore— a big, easygoing man with a generous nature, and nice to work for. When Bud had, in a boasting moment, let slip that he was milking Theodore for protection money, Cassie knew that Bud had finally gone too far. This was the proverbial last straw, and she began to actively hate her brother.

She brooded about it for several days, then made up her mind—she went to Jim Courtwright. She knew that Theodore Laker wouldn't do anything on his own, and she was too ashamed to admit to him that the man he knew as Brad Dalton was her brother.

She was surprised at Courtwright. He was a handsome individual, and looked nothing like the violent, corrupted man she had expected. Not only did he welcome her warmly, he treated her with old-world courtesy, bowing her into his office and escorting her to a chair.

"I'll stand, if you don't mind, sir, while I speak my piece."

Courtwright said amusedly, "As you wish, ma'am. What exactly is your . . . er, piece?"

"I wait tables at the Laker Café."

"An honorable profession, I would say, although I should think that a lady as pretty as yourself could do much better."

A bit flustered by his flattery, she kept her voice steady. "A man named Brad Dalton works for you, I believe?"

His face became guarded. "That is correct, ma'am."

"Well, he is forcing Mr. Laker to pay him ten dollars a week protection money."

Courtwright's eyes turned cold and hard. "That is not on my orders, ma'am. My word on that, and I will put an immediate stop to it." He dipped his head. "And you have my thanks for bringing it to my attention."

Still Cassie hesitated. "There is one other thing . . . I would rather that Mr. Dalton didn't know I came to you."

"I would never violate the trust of a lady. You may rest easy on that, ma'am."

"I thank you, Mr. Courtwright."

Courtwright moved quickly around in front of her and opened the door, with a gallant little bow. "I have never eaten at Mr. Laker's establishment. I must make amends for that. Perhaps . . ." He hesitated, his eyes suddenly bold, as if he had just taken note of her beauty. "Perhaps you would honor me by taking supper with me one evening?"

She shook her head. "I work the supper hour at the café, except for one evening a week."

"Then would you do me the honor of dining with me on your free evening?"

"I am always engaged that evening."

"Oh?" Courtwright sighed theatrically. "This fellow, whoever he is, is a very lucky man."

Cassie stared directly into his eyes. "I have supper on that evening with my brother."

"Your brother?"

"Yes, Mr. Courtwright. My brother is the man you know as Brad Dalton. I am Cassie Danker."

She was rewarded by a look of utter astonishment on his face, as she gathered up her skirts and swept out. Maybe it had been a rash remark, but then she was sure that Courtwright already knew who Bud was. If he didn't, he *should* know. And if Bud had to suffer for it, she really didn't care all that much.

Cassie didn't see one of the posters heralding the appearance of the Holliday Traveling Players in Fort Worth until the day before they were to arrive.

She scanned the poster with a sense of pleasure, already determined to go. It would be difficult to get the time off, since she did work the supper hour, but maybe she could change shifts with the day girl. Cassie read the poster again, this time looking at the pictures—a man and a woman. There was something naggingly familiar about the woman. Doc and Lena Holliday . . . Lena!

Cassie gasped, peering closely at the picture. It was, it was Michael's sister! She didn't spare any thought as to how Lena Moraghan had become Lena Holliday, or how Lena had become the star of a tent show. All Cassie could think of was the horrifying fact that a Moraghan should be here, in Fort Worth. If Bud found out! Dear God!

She forced herself to relax. The likelihood was small. Cassie knew that Bud ordinarily had little time for such amusements. Even if he did by chance attend the show, he probably wouldn't recognize Lena. To the best of Cassie's knowledge, Bud had only seen Lena that one time—at the burying of Nora Moraghan.

Slightly reassured, she went on her way. Then another thought popped into her mind. If his sister was appearing here, would that mean Michael would also be in Fort Worth? Nacogdoches wasn't all that far away. Sighing, Cassie relinquished all thought of attending the show.

Lena vividly recalled her other time in Fort Worth. In fact, the show was setting up on the same vacant lot the medicine show had occupied. But the wagons came in from the north, from Jacksboro, where they had played last week, with a cool autumn breeze behind them, carrying away the stink of the stockyards and the packing plants. Doc led them several streets out of the way, carefully avoiding Hell's Half Acre.

As soon as the wagons were all on the lot, Lena said, "I'm going to wash up, Doc, and change into fresh clothes, then go uptown to the hotel where Mother wrote me that she and the others would be staying. I told them to wait there for me, since we never know the exact time we arrive."

"All right, honey. When you're ready to leave, give me a hail, and I'll have one of the roustabouts drive you in in the buggy. This is a rough town, no place for a woman alone."

"All right, worry wart." She kissed him lightly.

Doc stood for a moment, looking after her affectionately, until she climbed into the back of their sleeping wagon. For the hundredth time he marveled at his good fortune in meeting her, in marrying her. God, how she had changed his life!

And to think that it had all begun right here, on this very lot!

He gave his head a shake and turned his attention to the placement of the wagons for unloading. From among the inevitable crowd that had gathered, he selected a half-dozen strong young men to help set up, in exchange for show passes.

He became so preoccupied that he scarcely noticed when Lena left the lot in the buggy they'd bought this year, a roustabout at the reins. Doc gave her an absent wave and turned his attention back to supervising the unloading of the huge canvas tent, and the laying out of the three sections.

Everything proceeded smoothly. Soon, the canvas sections were in position, spread out flat on the ground, the three long center poles in the grommets, ready to rise into the air, and men were placing side poles at regular intervals, while others drove stakes into the ground for the guy ropes.

Content with the progress so far, Doc decided to take a

break. Leaning against one of the wagons, he lit a cigarette and drew on it.

A voice spoke at his elbow. "From what I overheard, I guess you're the man in charge here?"

Doc swiveled his head to look at the man beside him. He was slim, dressed all in black except for a white Stetson. His face was narrow, expressionless, his eyes as opaque as marbles. He was smoking a cigar.

Doc went tense inside, all antenna extended and quivering. There was an air of menace about the man. Doc drawled, "Yeah, that's me. I own the show. Doc Holliday." He didn't offer his hand.

"And I'm Brad Dalton."

"What can I do for you, Mr. Dalton?"

The man smiled, a slight baring of his teeth. "It's more a matter of what *I* can do for you." He glanced around elaborately, then swung one arm out so that his coat fell open, revealing a gun on his hip.

"I'm afraid I don't get your meaning, mister."

Without replying, Dalton drew deeply on his cigar until it had a long ash, then took two steps, and tapped the cigar with his forefinger. Burning ash fell on the ground mere inches from the canvas.

"What the hell!" Doc roared. "You could set that tent on fire that way."

Dalton grinned at him. "Just what I was thinking. Something like that happen, your whole show would go up in smoke, wouldn't it?"

Doc felt his gut tighten. He knew what was coming. It had happened to him before, both with the medicine show and the Toby show.

"Or even some drunks getting rambunctious during one of your performances could ruin a whole evening for you. Ain't that right, Mr. Holliday?"

"How much do you want, Dalton?"

Dalton blinked in surprise, then began to smile again. "Quick, ain't you? No beating about the bush. I like that, it means we should be able to do business together."

"How much?"

"Oh, I'm not a greedy man." Dalton waved his cigar.

"Fifty dollars for the week should do it. That way, you won't have to worry about fire, things like that. I'll see to it that you're protected all the way down the line."

Doc stared at him unblinkingly, keeping his temper under control with difficulty. Another time, other circumstances, he would have told this slicker to go to hell, to take his best shot. But this was the last week of the season, Fort Worth was a rowdy town, and he very much doubted that he could get any help from the police. Although it galled him to the core, there was no sense in borrowing trouble.

Even so, he couldn't help stalling. "That's a little steep, ain't it?"

Dalton got a mean scowl. "That's my going price, take it or leave it. But you'll be sorry if you don't take it."

Doc nodded resignedly. "All right, wait here. I'll be back shortly."

He strode over to the office wagon, unlocked it and went inside. He opened the safe and took out fifty dollars. He squatted on his heels for a few moments, eyeing the gunbelt and pistol hanging from a hook on the wall. He was sorely tempted. Yet he had never been too good with guns, thinking wryly of all the times he had stood on the medicine-show stage, firing blanks over the heads of the audience. That was about the extent of his marksmanship.

And even if by some remote miracle he should kill this gunfighter—he knew instinctively that Brad Dalton was a professional gun—he would still be in trouble. He would almost certainly be placed under arrest, at least until he could prove that Dalton was trying to squeeze him for protection money, *if* he could prove it. If not, he could even be tried for murder.

And if he was arrested, it wasn't likely that they would be able to show this week at all.

Sighing, he got to his feet and left the wagon with the money.

Monday night was Cassie's evening off, and that was the night she usually had supper with Bud. She had made up her mind that this would be the last time—she was going to tell him so tonight.

They always ate in the dining room of Bud's hotel. It was too fancy for Cassie's liking, yet she knew that Bud loved to show her off. It had slowly dawned on her that he had never introduced her as his sister. Also, she had never seen him with a girl, even back home he had never had much to do with girls.

On this particular night Bud was in an expansive mood, keeping up a constant chatter, drinking heavily. Each time the waitress came with a menu, he waved her off and ordered another drink. Cassie hardly ever drank anything at all, but to keep him company she had a couple of glasses of wine. She knew that Bud was subject to occasional drinking bouts, either when he was exhilarated about something or in a mean mood. She had seen him do that often enough back in Nacogdoches, and those times she was usually fearful of him, since he was usually in the grip of a black depression.

She suddenly tensed as she heard what he was saying. "Somebody went to Courtwright about me. Probably one of those damned slant-eyes. Whoever it was told him about the money I was collecting, and he got on his high horse. I had to promise to stop it. But I no longer give a damn. I'm going to leave Mr. High and Mighty Jim Courtwright and strike out on my own. I can do better on my own anyway." He emptied his glass with a toss of his head and ordered another.

Cassie said cautiously, "You mean here in Fort Worth?" She decided to postpone telling him this was to be their last supper together—she wanted to keep him talking.

"Naw. I want to go some place where I'll be top dog, rake in all that money myself." His eyes had a blurry look as he peered at her. "You can go with me, little sister. We'll be hip-deep in high grass, and you won't have to lift a little finger, ever again. That I promise."

"We'll see, Bud," she said, not wishing to say anything to change his mood.

Bud chuckled coarsely. "I'm running a slick past Mr.

Jim Courtwright. You know about this tent show in town, opening tonight?''

Cassie nodded, not daring to speak.

''Well, I had a little gabfest with the owner, fellow named Doc Holliday. He's paying me fifty dollars to see to it that his tent don't catch fire, or that toughs don't cause a fuss, while he's here. He paid me without a whimper. Ain't that something?''

''What if this Mr. Courtwright finds out?''

Bud shrugged, taking a drink. ''Let him. Like I told you, I'm quitting him anyway. So what can he do? And that reminds me, Cassie, I can get into the show free any time I want. I never cared much for that sort of foolishness, but I thought I'd go at least once.'' He chuckled again. ''Just to let him know that I'm earning my money, keeping an eye on things. The thing is, I can take you with me. How about it, Cassie?''

Cassie had gone cold all over. What if Michael *was* there, and Bud saw him? She knew better than to try to dissuade Bud from going, he would only get suspicious.

''Cassie, did you hear me?''

She had to force the words out. ''I have to work tomorrow night, Bud, you know that.''

''Aw, hell, sis!'' He sliced the air with his hand. ''You and that damned job! You can get off if you want, you know you can.'' He was getting drunk now—his words were slurred, his eyes out of focus.

''I just don't want to go. You can go without me.''

He thrust his face at her belligerently. ''But I want you to go with me, dammit!'' The waitress had come up quietly, and said something inaudible under the sound of his voice. He whipped around at her. ''What is it?''

The girl said timidly, ''I thought you might like to order now, sir.''

''I'll tell you when we're ready to order. Right now, you can bring me another drink.''

The waitress glanced at Cassie in silent appeal. Cassie nodded at her to obey. It was suddenly clear to her what course she was going to follow. It was the only thing she

could think of to do at the moment, and even that might
not help matters in the end.

They never did get around to eating supper. Cassie kept
urging Bud on to tell her of his future plans, and ordered
another drink for him every time his glass was empty,
ignoring the disapproving looks of the waitress. Cassie
even drank two more glasses of wine herself.

She was feeling dizzy and a little faint, when, much to
her relief, Bud suddenly made a retching sound. With a
look of surprise, he muttered, "I think I'm drunk, sis."

He tried to get to his feet, lurched, and caught at the
edge of the table to retain his balance. Cassie sprang up
and hurried around the table to take his arm.

"It's all right, Bud. I'll help you up to your room." She
felt like the worst kind of hypocrite and tried to avoid the
accusing eyes of the waitress as she helped Bud from the
dining room. She probably believes that I'm one of these
women who encourage a man to get drunk, Cassie thought,
and then steal his purse.

But it wasn't Bud's purse that she was after.

Bud had a thundering hangover when he awoke the next
morning—a thumping head, an upset stomach, and a poor
memory of last night's events. Lying in bed, he tried to
think back. The last thing he could remember was asking
Cassie to go to the Toby show with him, and her refusal.
Had they ever eaten supper? He couldn't remember. His
temper stirred. Why had Cassie allowed him to drink like
that?

In his own defense, Bud could claim that he very
seldom drank that much. The last time he could remember
was the night Jim Courtwright had hired him—he had
gotten roaring drunk and woke up the next morning in a
crib out back of one of the saloons, a smelly, blubbery
whore snoring next to him. At least he hadn't done that
this time.

He grinned painfully. Perhaps it was fitting that he
should have gotten drunk last night, this time to celebrate
his *leaving* Courtwright. Yet he did hate for Cassie to have
seen him like that.

He inched gingerly off the bed and moved to the washbasin in the corner, grateful that it held enough water to splash his face and neck. He was fully clothed except for his boots. Cassie must have helped him to bed . . .

His gunbelt! Where was it? Usually the first thing he did on awakening was to reach for the Colt to assure himself that it was still in his possession. He was reassured when he saw the gunbelt hanging from the bedpost at the foot of the bed. Then he blinked, trying to focus his blurred gaze. The Colt, his daddy's old Colt, wasn't there!

Frantically he began to search. He tore the bed apart, he looked under the bed, he searched every inch of the room. It simply was not there! Maybe it had fallen out of the holster when he had been helped upstairs.

He pulled on his boots and hastened downstairs. The clerk at the desk swore that the Colt hadn't been turned in. Bud insisted that everyone in the hotel be questioned. In the end the only thing he learned was that the woman with him in the dining room last night had helped him to his room.

By this time Bud was beside himself with rage and panic, certain that someone had stolen it from him, someone in the hotel. Cassie would certainly have no reason to take it. She was scared to death of guns, and she hated weapons of any sort.

He finally gave up and stormed out of the hotel, headed for Mrs. Bennett's boarding house. It was barely possible that Cassie might know what had happened to it. At the boarding house he was informed that Cassie wasn't in, and Mrs. Bennett did not know where she was. Although it was still far short of the time for Cassie to be at work, Bud hurried to the Laker Café. She wasn't there, either, and Theodore Laker informed him coldly that Cassie had been in, very early, but only to arrange for the day girl to work her shift that evening.

Now thoroughly baffled, Bud trudged along Main Street, the empty holster banging against his side with every step, reminding him of his loss. There had not been a day since Daddy was killed that Bud had not had that Colt at hand, or at least knew where it was. He felt lost and helpless without it, frightened inside, panic nibbling at the edges of his mind.

He finally went into a gunsmith's shop and bought another Colt. It was a newer model, it weighed the same on his hip, and it was no doubt as efficient as the old one, if not more so. But it wasn't the same. It had an alien feel to it, which Bud dimly recognized as being fanciful, but he couldn't help feeling the way he did. What if he was suddenly in need of a weapon? He had never killed a man with anything but Daddy's Colt.

He wandered the streets until dark, looking vainly for Cassie. He made three more visits to the boarding house, with no better results. The third time Mrs. Bennett angrily slammed the door in his face when she saw who it was.

Shortly before eight o'clock he found himself a part of the throng approaching the show tent. He really didn't know what he was doing there, except for the lack of anything better to do. By now he was almost convinced that Cassie *had* taken his Colt. But why? What reason could she possibly have? It didn't by God make any kind of sense!

The ticket taker had been alerted, and he waved Bud inside when Bud said, "I'm Brad Dalton."

The tent was already nearly full, and Bud had to take a seat in the middle of the next to last row, but that suited him all right. He would probably slip out long before the show was over, and this would make it easier.

There wasn't an empty seat left by the time the curtain went up, and a few people were even standing along the sidewalls. Bud found it all mystifying. Why would people pay good money to see players act out some tomfoolery on the stage? It wasn't real, not any of it. The money would be better spent for something you could put in your belly, or on your back.

Yet, before the play had progressed very far, Bud found himself caught up in it. He couldn't quite understand the reason, but there was something vaguely familiar about the play. It had to do with two feuding families, the Dentons and the Martins, on neighboring farms somewhere in the south. Neither family was too well off, and both had to struggle to survive. But the Denton family seemed to spend more time causing trouble for the Martins than they did working their farm. The Toby character—Bud eventually realized that he was portrayed by Doc Holliday, the owner of the show—came onto the scene in time to discover the father of the Martin family dead under mysterious circumstances. The Martins naturally accused the Dentons of killing him.

This was the real beginning of the feud, with bitter fighting raging between both factions. Toby flitted back and forth between the two families, trying to resolve the feud, without any success throughout most of the play. To Bud's surprise, and the surprise of most of the audience, he gathered, the play was far more serious than he had expected. The only comic relief was provided by Toby's bumblings. However, the audience remained in their seats, as did Bud, much to his bafflement. He had wit enough to realize that it was because the theme of the play had to do with a feud between two families. But on the other hand, it was not at all like the Danker-Moraghan feud.

Bud stayed to the end, and even remained in his seat afterward, mulling over the ending. Toby had finally resolved the situation by proving that the death was an accident, not murder, and making the unmistakable point that all feuds of such nature were pointless, farcical. Bud felt a prod of anger as this sunk in. It certainly didn't apply to the ancient feud between the Moraghans and the Dankers. There was a good reason for it, and all the blame belonged to the Moraghans.

The actors took their bows to repeated applause. Bud didn't join in the applause, but sat on in his seat, watching the Toby character with a malevolent glower. He felt like smashing his gun repeatedly against the head of that man in the silly costume—orange wig, bulbous red nose, breeches several sizes too large, and enormous, floppy shoes.

Then Holliday stepped to the edge of the stage, holding up his hands for quiet. When he got it, he said, "Ladies and gentlemen, we all thank you from our hearts for your kind attention and applause. Ordinarily, we would offer an olio performance at this time, but since our appearance in

Fort Worth is in the nature of a command performance, we don't think it would be quite fitting. Thank you all again, folks, and good night."

Two women who had been sitting next to Bud got up, but they had to wait for the aisle to clear before they could get out.

Bud overheard one of the women say, "I heard some place that this play was based on fact, about some old feud over in East Texas. I wonder if there's any truth in it?"

Bud sat very still, all senses alert, straining to hear as the other woman said, "It sure is true. It's based on the Moraghan-Danker feud over to Nacogdoches. Don't you know that the girl who played Myrtle, Farmer Martin's daughter, used to be Lena Moraghan? She wrote the play we just saw . . ."

Bud sat frozen as the tent slowly emptied. The words he'd heard had stunned him. Was it possible that the girl up there was a Moraghan, and that she had written a play about his family, poking fun at the Dankers? Even worse, had they somehow known that he would be watching and had put on the play to mock him? That fellow, Holliday, might have somehow recognized him.

Bud opened his mouth to bellow out his rage, but only an inarticulate snarl came from him. He got to his feet with an effort. His knees almost gave way, and he had to catch at the back of the folding chair in front of him to keep from falling. He looked around the tent, which was about empty now, with a few people still in the bleachers, and a clot of people at the entrance waiting to get out. But the front of the tent was empty, the stage curtain down.

Then he was in motion, knocking over chairs in his haste. He barked his shins and barely felt the pain. Gaining the unobstructed aisle, he began to hurry, almost running.

At the stage wagon he hesitated, then lifted up the curtain to peer under it. The stage was dark and empty. Where were the performers? He moved down the side of the wagon to his left. There was a strip of canvas hanging between the end of the wagon and the tent wall. Hearing voices on the other side, he shoved it aside, and came out

into a small area behind the wagon, and there they were—
all the performers.

Toby stood talking to the girl who had played the
farmer's daughter. They stood somewhat apart from the
others. Bud drew his gun, forgetting that it wasn't his
daddy's Colt, and advanced on the pair.

The girl saw him first. Her eyes widened, and she
clutched at her husband's arm.

Doc glanced around. "Dalton, what are you doing back
here? And why the gun? Is somebody causing trouble?"

The girl said in a carrying whisper, "That's Bud Danker,
Doc!"

Doc frowned. "Bud Danker? But he told me—"

"I can't help what he told you, that's Bud Danker!"

"Yes, I'm Bud Danker," Bud said in a snarling voice.
"And you're a Moraghan whelp. That play I just saw, you
were mocking me and my family. I'm going to kill you,
like I would any Moraghan, woman or not." He brought
the gun up.

Doc stepped in front of Lena. "Now wait, Dalton,
Danker, whoever you are. Put down that gun before
somebody gets hurt here." He started to advance toward
Bud.

"Get out of the way or I'll kill you, too! You're a
Moraghan in my eyes, you're married to one."

Cassie had arrived at the show tent early that evening,
bought a ticket in the bleachers, and climbed high up, the
second row from the top. She was bone-weary, having
walked the streets of Fort Worth all day, so Bud wouldn't
find her. The Colt she had taken from him was in her
pocketbook, and the added weight had been a burden. She
had never realized how heavy a gun that size could be.

She didn't really know what she was doing here, or
what she could *do*, if anything, yet she knew she had to be
here.

When the tent began to fill up, and Bud didn't show up,
hope started to rise in her. Maybe he had changed his
mind. She was seated where she could watch the tent
entrance, and her gaze never left it.

And then, only a few minutes before the show was due to start, she saw him. He came in, stopped a moment to look around, finally turning to scan the bleacher seats. Cassie tried to make herself as small as possible, turning her face away. When she looked again, she saw him making his way along the next to last row of seats on the ground, having to take the only vacant chair near the center of the row.

When the curtain went up, she alternated her attention between Bud and the play. The play was barely underway before she recognized what it was about, and dread filled her. Would he realize that it was based, loosely, on the Danker-Moraghan feud? And if so, how would he react?

The play was almost halfway through the last act before she saw him lean forward, his back and shoulders tense, and she knew that he was finally aware. Cassie never took her gaze off him from that moment on. She saw that he remained seated even after others were standing, waiting to get out. Then, as two women alongside him left, Bud stood up, swayed slightly, and caught at the seat in front of him. Then he looked slowly around the tent. It was almost empty now, but just as his gaze swept over the bleachers, two people directly in front of Cassie stood up to leave, screening her.

After the couple moved on, Cassie saw Bud hurrying down the aisle toward the stage. She didn't move yet, afraid that he might look around and see her. He lifted the stage curtain to peer under, then went to his left and disappeared around the end of the wagon. Only then did she get up and hasten after him. Just as she discovered the canvas at the end of the wagon, she heard a gunshot on the other side.

She pushed the canvas aside, fumbling in her pocketbook for the Colt, then dropping the pocketbook onto the ground. She halted just beyond the curtain, numb with horror at what she saw. The man in the Toby costume was sprawled on the ground, and Lena was on her knees beside him.

Tears running down her face, Lena glanced up at Bud. "He's dead! You've killed him!"

"And now I'm going to kill you, you Moraghan bitch," he said.

Holding the heavy Colt in both hands, Cassie leveled it. In a high voice she said, "Don't do it, Bud! Turn around!"

Bud went rigid. "Cassie?"

"Turn around!"

Bud turned slowly. His gaze went to the Colt. "Then you did take Daddy's Colt. Why, Cassie?"

"Drop your gun, Bud, or I'll shoot."

He tried to smile. "You wouldn't shoot your own brother, sis. You couldn't do that."

"I will! I swear to God I will. There's been enough killing, it has to stop. I don't want to shoot, but I will if you don't drop your gun."

Something in her face must have convinced him of her determination, for he slowly lowered his gun until it was pointing at the ground. Then several things happened at once. Two men rushed at Bud from behind. One knocked the gun from his hand, and then they held him immobile by both arms. Lena came to her feet, her face contorted, and rushed at Bud, her hands extended like claws.

"You murdered Doc, you bastard! I'll tear your eyes out!"

Michael was suddenly there, stepping in front of her. "No, Lena. The law will take care of him now, not only for killing Doc, but for Daddy as well." Still barring her way, he turned his head to look at Cassie.

Bud was also staring at her, his eyes filling with tears. "This wouldn't have happened if you hadn't stole Daddy's Colt. How could you do something like that, Cassie?"

Cassie had almost forgotten she was holding the Colt. She looked down at it in revulsion, then threw it from her, and wiped her hands on her skirt.

Michael was striding toward her. For just a moment she thought of running, but she stood still, her gaze on his face.

He took her hands in his, said gently, "You can't know how glad I am to see you, dear Cassie. I was afraid that I might never see you again."

# 17

Lena spent the winter months on Moraghan. She couldn't face living alone, with Doc dead. She refused to think about getting the show into shape to go on the road in the spring. She wasn't even sure that she would ever go out with it again. The thought of selling the show crossed her mind, but she and Doc had been the stars, it had little value without them. The mules, wagons, and tent would fetch very little.

For the first few weeks after that awful moment in Fort Worth, Lena had existed in a world of gray despair. However illogical it might seem, she blamed herself for Doc's death. That play . . . if she hadn't written that play, based on the Danker-Moraghan feud, Bud Danker might not have tried to kill her, might not even have learned who she was. No matter what happened to the show eventually, that particular play would never be performed again. She had destroyed every copy. The bitter irony of it was, Doc had been opposed to ever performing it. From the moment he had read it, he had been against it. It was far too serious, he'd said repeatedly, not Toby-show material at all, but in the end she'd had her way, with disastrous results.

It was a wet, dismal winter, but in spite of the miserable weather, Lena spent much of her time in the old cabin. The house of Moraghan was a happy house now, except for her. Michael and Cassie were married before Christmas. Being instrumental in saving Lena's life had somehow seemed to balance things in Cassie's mind, and she was no longer wracked with guilt over Bud killing Kevin. And the feud seemed to be finished now, for all time. Bud had been hanged back in January, and there were no

Dankers left in the Nacogdoches area, except Cassie, who claimed she was a Moraghan now, not a Danker. Even Kate and Bandy, although not married, were on good terms again. And Stony had decided to run for the state legislature, had been elected, and the Liebermans spent most of their time in Austin nowadays.

Lena felt that her presence in the main house inhibited the general happiness of the others. So, when she came to Moraghan after Doc's funeral, she went more and more often to the old cabin. As soon as her grief subsided somewhat, she found a kind of peace there. In the beginning it wasn't livable, of course, but she went to work, chinking the cracks, repairing the old fireplace, chopping wood for fires. She refused all offers of help. She found solace and forgetfulness in the physical labor. She took most of her meals at the main house, but she often spent the night in the old cabin.

One cold afternoon in February she made a startling discovery. Early on she had found one of the hearthstones before the fireplace loose, and intended to eventually repair it. On this particular afternoon, a fire roaring in the hearth, she inadvertently sat on the loose stone, loosening it even more. In annoyance, she inserted a flat stick between the cracks and pried. It came up easily. And there, underneath the stone, wrapped in an oilskin pouch, was a thick book.

She carefully removed the book and opened it. It was old, very old, the pages yellowed. A thrill went through her as she saw the lettering on the first page: The Journal of Sean Moraghan. The ink had faded badly, but the handwriting was still legible.

The first entry was dated August 18, 1835. Lena remembered being told that August of that year was when Sean and Nora Moraghan arrived in Texas from Tennessee. She experienced a stab of disappointment. It would have been interesting if her grandfather had started his journal earlier, when he was still a priest. But she recalled Kate telling her once that both Sean and Nora wanted to start clean in Texas, putting their past behind them.

The first entry concerned Sean's visit to an impresario

in Nacogdoches, about the land he had come to Texas to claim. At the end of the first entry Lena came across something of more immediate interest:

> We selected a name for our firstborn, Brian. Brian Patrick Moraghan.
> It has a strong, yet melodious ring to it.
> May the Lord God bless you for all your days, Brian Patrick Moraghan!

Piling more wood on the fire, Lena sat down to read on, avidly. She was confident that no other Moraghan knew of this journal, probably not even her grandmother had known. Grandfather Sean must have secreted it here, perhaps with the intent of showing it to someone someday, but had never gotten around to it.

How exciting it would be to show it to the others! To be fair, she supposed she shouldn't even read it until she could share it with her family. However, she couldn't bear to wait. She read on—about Sean Moraghan's service in the Army of Texas against Santa Anna, his gallantry at the Battle of San Jacinto, and his growing friendship with Sam Houston, and Grandfather's life together with Nora.

And then, near the end of the journal, she came across something that rose up off the pages like a blow, stunning her. She reread the passage, finding it hard to believe, but there it was in Grandfather Sean's own hand:

> Am I fearful of Nora's scorn if she learns that I once more turned on Kevin? He is not my son, God almighty knows, but he is Nora's!

Kevin Moraghan not Sean's son? How could that possibly be? Feverishly Lena thumbed through the journal, reading fast now, skimming through everything not referring to Kevin. Then she came across an even more startling entry, dated September 20, 1863, which she recalled was not long before her grandfather was gunned down by Sonny Danker. It was also written at a time when word had reached them that Brian had been killed in battle, a report later discovered to be erroneous, of course.

> Oh, Brian, my son, my son! How can I continue
> my life with the knowledge that my own issue, my
> own flesh and blood, is gone from this earth?
>
> Such thoughts do Kevin a grave injustice, I know.
> I have come, if not to love him as I would my own
> son, at least to respect and admire him. We have
> grown quite close, and I do sorely regret the doubts
> I had of him for all these years. Search as I may,
> I can find none of the Danker traits in him.
>
> Perhaps my Nora is right. Perhaps upbringing is of
> more importance than blood. If such be the fact, the
> responsibility for the admirable man he has become be-
> longs solely to Nora. God knows, I ignored him shame-
> fully for so very long. Worse, I scorned him. I found
> fault where it did not exist. Lord willing, I must en-
> deavor to make it up to him, in the time I have left on
> this earth.
>
> My estate is given into Brian's hands in my will.
> It was only fitting, not only because he was of my
> own flesh and blood, but also because he was the
> older. It has long been the custom that a man sees
> to it that his eldest inherits.
>
> Now that has all changed. Brian has gone from my
> bosom, and I must, in all conscience, consider Kevin
> as the rightful heir to Moraghan Acres.
>
> Soon, I must journey into Nacogdoches and consult
> with Stony about changing my will, making Kevin
> my heir. I do not feel adequate to the task at present.
> Certainly before Christmas and the New Year...

But Sean Moraghan did not live to see Christmas in
1863—he had been murdered by Sonny Danker.

But Kevin Moraghan, my own daddy, Lena thought, had
Danker blood in him? It must be true, it must be a dark
secret kept down through the years, with only Grandmother Nora knowing it. Thinking back to the stories she had
heard, of the suspicion that Nora had been raped by the
Danker brothers, Lena realized now that it must have all

been true, and one of them had impregnated Nora at the time.

She closed the journal and stared pensively into the flames. She knew that she could never, under any circumstances, show the journal, or even reveal its existence, to her mother, or Michael and Debra Lee, or even to Cassie. The revelation she had come across could conceivably rip apart the fabric of all their lives . . .

A knock on the door startled her. "Who is it?" Even as she spoke, Lena was hurriedly returning the journal to the oilskins and replacing it under the loose stone.

"It's Cassie, Lena! Let me in, it's freezing out here!"

Cassie's presence here, right on the heels of what she had just learned, almost sent Lena into a panic. "Just a minute, Cassie." She took several deep breaths, forcing composure on herself.

Quickly she toed a small throw rug over the loose stone and hurried to unlatch the door. Cassie stood in the doorway, shivering, a shawl wrapped tightly around her shoulders. Behind her a light snow fell like fine powder.

Lena gestured. "Come in, for heaven's sake! What are you doing out in that, anyway? There's nothing wrong at home, is there?"

"No, no, it's just something I wanted you to see." Cassie glanced around the cabin as Lena closed the door. "You've really fixed this old cabin up, Lena. It's nice and snug now."

"Cassie, you didn't come all the way over here just to look at the cabin. Now, what is it?"

Cassie's expression became serious. "Michael had to go into town for something, and he brought this back with him." She held out a folded newspaper.

Lena took the newspaper with a feeling of dread. It was a Fort Worth paper, dated February 9, 1887. Lena read the article that Cassie indicated:

At seven-thirty last evening, Jim Courtwright walked up to the White Elephant Saloon on Main Street, and called out Luke Short, owner of the saloon. Angry words were exchanged.

The verbal exchange led to death and violence when Courtwright drew his gun. Luke Short fired first. His bullet clipped off the tip of Courtwright's thumb as he was cocking his weapon. Before Courtwright could complete the "Mexican switch," tossing his pistol from his right hand to his left, Luke Short fired three more bullets, and Courtwright fell dead.

There is much speculation as to the cause of the gunfight . . .

Lena stopped reading, with an involuntary sigh.

Cassie said, "Brings it all back, doesn't it?"

Lena nodded, unable to speak for a moment, as the image of that tragic night in October sprang to her mind— Bud's Colt spitting flame, Doc staggering and falling to the ground. And as she had dropped to her knees beside him, he had tried desperately to speak to her, but then his eyes had rolled back, and he was gone.

Cassie was speaking. "I knew both of them, you see. Luke Short and Jim Courtwright. I met Short in his saloon the first day I was in Fort Worth. He seemed nice enough, but mean somehow, and cold." She shivered. "And Jim Courtwright also seemed nice enough, but he was a gambler, a crook, and a killer. Now he's dead. Bud was working for him, doing his dirty work. But then I guess you already know all that." She looked at Lena closely. "I don't really know why I wanted you to read that right away, but it somehow seems to put an end to all of it, doesn't it?"

Lena smiled suddenly, her depression lifting. "You know something, it does! Sort of like when I write 'finis' to the end of a play."

On a blustery March day some weeks later, Lena was in the old cabin again, doing a chore she had been postponing far too long. After the tragedy in Fort Worth and the show's closing, Lena had sent all of the show wagons to their New Orleans winter quarters, with one exception, placing Andy Jacks in charge there until he heard from her. The exception had been the office wagon, which she and Doc had also used as their living quarters. Michael had driven it back to Moraghan, and there it had sat closed up, like a coffin, until yesterday when she had had Bandy open it and haul the two large trunks holding all the costumes she and Doc had used over to the cabin.

Today, she was engaged in going through them. Her first inclination had been to postpone Doc's until last, but she had steeled herself to get the worst of it over with first. She was about halfway through it now, with his things stacked neatly on the floor beside her.

The sorrow she felt was poignant, but not quite as painful as she had anticipated. And she knew suddenly that she was taking the show out again in the spring. She stopped what she was doing and stared blindly at the wall. The show was her life now. What else could she do?

This sudden decision meant that she would have to set things in motion at once. It might already be too late to start the season on time. So they would have to settle for a short season, it would be better than not going on the road at all. In her mind she ticked off all the things she had to do. She would have to wire Charlie Dobbs, their advance man, to start on the posters. As soon as he had them in hand, he would have to hit the road, booking their show dates and hanging the posters in each town. She would have to wire Andy Jacks to check the wagons, tents, all of their equipment, and see to what repairs were necessary. And she had to get in touch with all the players and alert them. Thank heaven, there weren't many tent shows in existence yet, or the players would already be booked for the coming season.

The thorniest problem of all would be finding a new Toby. None of the present company could fill Doc's shoes. Andy Jacks was the only possibility, and he was not nearly good enough, in her opinion. Yet she might have to settle for him, if she couldn't discover anyone else . . .

Deep in thought, she hadn't been aware that the door had opened behind her. But now she felt a blast of the March wind, and knew it was open. She got to her feet all in one motion, whirling about.

Mark Moraghan stood in the doorway.

Her heart began to pound alarmingly. She made her face stern, and said tartly, "Well! Look who dropped in! You always were good at sneaking up on people, weren't you, Mark?"

"Hello, cousin," he said quietly, his eyes intent on hers. "I was afraid that if I announced myself, you wouldn't let me in."

"And I probably wouldn't have." It was on the tip of her tongue to tell him to turn around and leave. But she didn't. Why lie to herself? She didn't want him to go, she was glad to see him. She said dryly, "Where did you come from this time? What ship did you just step off of?"

He stared at her steadily. "I've been working down at your mother's place in the Valley. I'm sure you know that."

"But however did you manage to stay there all this time?" Lena knew that she was being unreasonable, yet she seemed impelled to hit out at him.

"I deserve that, I know."

He paused for a few moments, as though to collect his thoughts, and Lena took advantage to study him more closely. He had changed, she realized now. He was brown as a nut, and leaner and harder. Yet there was more than just a physical change in him. There was a sureness about him, as if an inner core of strength had coalesced and firmed up in him, and the cynical, self-mocking edges of his personality seemed softened, or at least blunted.

"I heard about your husband, and I want you to know how sorry I am."

"Thank you."

"Michael wrote me about it right after it happened. My first inclination was to come tearing up here, but I decided I'd better wait and give you some time to get over it."

"Something like that you never get over entirely. Doc was my husband, and he was killed right before my eyes."

"It must have been terrible for you," he said gently. He took a deep breath. "The reason I'm here . . . I've been doing a lot of thinking these past few months." He smiled wryly. "Being in one place that long, I've discovered, gives you a lot of time for thinking. I still love you, Lena, that will never change. But *I've* changed. I want you to marry me, if you'll have me, if you still want me.''

Her heart gave a great leap. She still wanted him, dear God, yes! But she wasn't ready to let him off the hook, not quite yet. ''Even if I'm your first cousin?''

''Even if.''

She looked at him for a long moment. ''There's something I want you to see.''

She went to the fireplace, pried up the stone, and took out the journal. ''This is something Grandfather Sean wrote, a personal journal. I want you to read a part of it.''

She found the page about Kevin, and showed it to Mark. He read it quickly, astonishment growing on his face. Finally he glanced up. ''Is this true, Sean Moraghan did not sire Uncle Kevin?''

''I don't think there's any doubt of it.''

''Does anybody else know about this?''

''No! And no one ever will. You must swear to me that you'll never tell. God knows what damage it could do.''

He nodded. ''I understand. It'll be our secret for all time.''

''In fact,'' she said, ''I'm going to make sure right now that no one else ever sees this.''

Taking the journal from him, she placed it open side down upon the flames. She felt a wrenching regret as she watched it begin to burn, a regret that history was being destroyed before her eyes.

Briskly she dusted her hands together, and turned to Mark. ''So now you no longer need to worry. We're still cousins, perhaps, but *distant* cousins.''

''Don't forget, I asked you before I knew that.''

''I know.'' Her eyes began to dance with mischief.

A tentative smile started on his face. ''Then you'll marry me?'' He moved to take her into his arms.

She evaded him. ''Whoa now. We have to strike a bargain first.''

He said warily, ''A bargain?''

''Remember I told you in New Orleans that I thought you'd make a good actor?''

''And I told you that I thought the idea ridiculous.''

"I don't think so at all."

She crossed over to the open trunk and began to sort through the items of Doc's various Toby costumes.

Mark ranged alongside her. "What are you up to now?"

"We need a new Toby for the coming season." She stood up with the orange wig, outrageously pink shirt, the enormous trousers, and the floppy shoes. "And you're going to be it. That's our bargain."

He backed away, his hands held up. "Lena, you've suddenly gone daft! There's no way you'll get me into that silly outfit!"

"If you want me, if you want to marry me, you'll do it."

"Do it or else?" His face set mulishly. "Those are your terms?"

"Yes . . . No, no, Mark, I didn't mean it quite like that. But I really do think you'd make a fine actor, a good Toby. I've interviewed a number of people since we've had the show, with Doc sitting in of course, and I've learned that I have a sort of sixth sense as to who will do well."

"But I've had no training, you know that, Lena."

"Neither had I. Neither have many of the people with the show. Doc didn't, yet he made a great Toby. It's the personality, the *projection* of the personality, that's important. You have that quality, in my opinion. Everything else, you can learn. A Toby show isn't Shakespearean theater, for heaven's sake! Darling, at least try the costume on," she said coaxingly, holding the garments out to him. "Please? If you love me?"

He stared at the clothes distrustfully, said in a grumbling voice, "You're not playing fair."

"Of course not," she said cheerfully. "To quote some sage, 'All's fair in love and war.' "

Almost as if they had a will of their own, his hands reached out to take the garments from her.

Lena said, "I'll turn my back while you change, so I won't compromise your modesty. Also, because I want to get the full effect all at once."

She turned and walked over to the fireplace, putting a fresh log on the fire, all the while with her ears attuned. At first she heard nothing. Then, to her relief, she heard the rustle of clothing as he changed.

Finally, in a small voice, Mark said, "You can look now."

She turned slowly. Even without makeup, the change in him was startling. The orange wig perched on his head like a small animal, the trousers billowed out from his narrow waist like a reversed hoop skirt in vogue before the war, and the enormous shoes projected out like snowshoes. But she was struck most of all by the expression on his face. He peered out at her from under the wig like a small boy seeking approval, fearful yet defiant. It was an appealing look that she knew would catch the audience, and his handsomeness would strike many female hearts. Already thinking ahead, she realized that it would be a mistake to use too much makeup. The costume alone would do it. With his dark good looks, he would be a different Toby from Doc, but it would work beautifully, she knew it would.

She was silent for so long that Mark's anxiety grew, and he took several steps toward her. Unaccustomed to the awkward shoes, he lost his balance and fell, coming down on his knees directly in front of her.

Lena began to laugh helplessly, and she dropped to her knees before him. Her laughter grew until it threatened to get out of control.

"You see?" he said indignantly. "I told you I would look ridiculous!"

Between gasps of laughter she said, "You don't seem to understand. People are *supposed* to laugh, you goose. That's what it's all about. It'll work out. Trust me, Mark."

He said slowly, "I don't know whether I believe you or not, but that's not the important thing right now. I asked you a question when I first came in. You never answered me."

"I made a bargain, I always hold to my bargains."

"Never mind the bargain. Do you still love me?"

All laughter left her. "I've never stopped loving you, darling, don't you know that?"

He sighed. "You can't know how wonderful that makes

me feel." A touch of the old self-mockery showed in his face. "Then you have your Toby, ridiculous or not."

"Right now, I don't want a Toby." She leaned forward and kissed him softly, and she felt his hands on her. Her pulse gave a great leap—his touch still had its old magic. Smiling, she said, "Right now, I want you, the man, not an actor on a stage. I want you, Mark."

## ABOUT THE AUTHOR

For CLAYTON MATTHEWS, author of more than 100 books, 50 short stories and innumerable magazine articles, writing is not only his profession but his hobby. Born in Waurika, Oklahoma in 1918, Matt (as he is known to his friends) worked as a surveyor, overland truck driver, gandy dancer, and taxi driver. In 1960 he became a full-time author with the publication of *Rage of Desire*. More recent books by Clayton Matthews include his highly successful book *The Power Seekers* (winner of the WEST COAST REVIEW OF BOOKS Bronze Medal for Best Novel in 1978), *The Harvesters*, *The Birthright*, and *The Disinherited*.